## THEY FOUGHT THE BATTLE OF
## CENTRAL PARK

"Pay attention. I'm heavily armed and an expert in guerilla warfare. I'm prepared to meet any kind of force. Central Park is mine and mine alone. I'm going to demonstrate my power, so listen up. The Twenty-second Precinct station house is on the 85th Street transverse in Central Park. I'm blowing it up at 2115. That's eighteen minutes from now. Anybody inside is grease. Got that?"

The detective was silent for a moment. Then he answered, respectfully, "Yes, sir."

"I'm aware that all calls to this office are tape recorded, so in case you can't remember, have it played back after I hang up."

He hung up, grabbed the bag and went around the north end of the boathouse to the thick bushes and rock outcroppings above the Lake. He got down on his knees and, with his hands, scooped away the dirt and leaves from the base of one of the bushes.

Concealed underneath the network of roots was a plastic garbage bag containing an AK-47 automatic rifle . . .

## THE PARK IS MINE

# The Park
# Is
# Mine

## STEPHEN PETERS

**WARNER BOOKS**

A Warner Communications Company

WARNER BOOKS EDITION

Copyright © 1981 by Stephen Peters
All rights reserved.

This Warner Books Edition is published by arrangement with Doubleday & Company, Inc., 1245 Park Avenue, New York, N.Y. 10017.

*Cover design by Gene Light*
*Cover art by Don Ivan Punchatz*

Warner Books, Inc.,
75 Rockefeller Plaza,
New York, N.Y. 10019

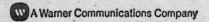 A Warner Communications Company

Printed in the United States of America

First Printing: July, 1982

10 9 8 7 6 5 4 3 2 1

To my mother and father

# ACKNOWLEDGMENTS

The author would like to thank several people for their assistance: Lt. Paul Glanzman of the New York City Police Department; Stanley Goldstein, NYC Department of Water Resources; Sheldon Levy, Richard Gottfried and Thomas C. Mulvey of Action Movie News, Inc.; Harry Ryttenberg, Julian Guzzo Mauritzen, Warren Lusteg and John Henry of Broadcast News Service, Inc.; Dr. Marty Wasserman; Charles Houk.

# NOTE

There are a few deliberate inaccuracies in this story. Some of them were requested by agencies of the City of New York.

# Central Park

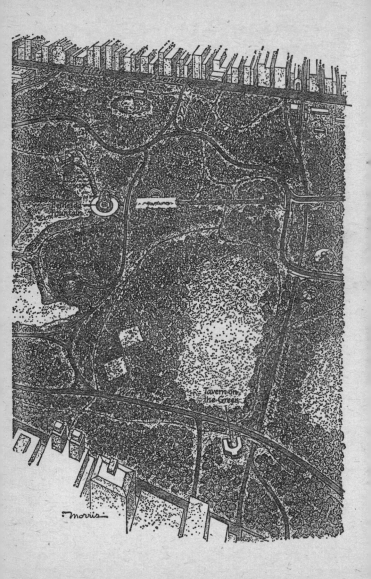

Tavern on the Green

Morris

# I

# Harris

He got off the IRT Broadway local at Columbus Circle and hurried to the exit stairs. The bag on his shoulder was heavy; he stopped to adjust the weight. Foul, humid air lingered on the platform. Arcs of light flashed in the tunnels and he could hear the scream of metal and machines. The express roared by behind him and he watched the train speed past, the dark forms of the passengers looming in the windows. A hot wind blew in his face and he ran up the stairs to the street.

He crossed Eighth Avenue and Broadway, walked past derelicts sitting on the steps of the *Maine* monument and went through the entrance to Central Park. He followed the West Drive until he came to the 65th Street transverse road and then crossed the roadway and the bridle path to the vast open space of the Sheep Meadow. Softball games were still in progress, overlapping with the soccer players, cyclists and joggers. He kept on going, past the vendors, past a man with black, swollen hands picking through a trash barrel, and stopped under trees near the concession stand at the north end of the Sheep Meadow.

He put down the bag and stuck his hand under his shirt, wiping away a film of sweat. He looked across at the skyscrapers on the West Side and on Central Park South. The sun was going down over New Jersey and the sky was red and hazy over the buildings. The huge digital time/temperature clock on top of the MONY building on 57th Street said 85°. The numbers went off, then reappeared. 8:23.

He put the bag back on his shoulder and started uptown, crossing the 72nd Street road and following a tree-lined walk toward the Fountain. Men selling drugs stood under the trees and spoke to him.

"Good smoke."

"Hey. Got that herb."

"Ludes and poppers, bro."

Strollers on the walk were heading back to the entrance to the Park at 72nd Street and Central Park West. Others guided dogs up the hill along the bridle path. The dogs sniffed at overturned garbage cans and piles of animal droppings. It was getting dark and people were returning to the apartment houses and brownstones on the West Side of Manhattan.

He approached the Terrace, an old stone structure made of yellow sandstone and granite, and stopped at the railing that overlooked the Fountain and the Lake. A small crowd remained near the Fountain, listening to cassette players, mingling with drug pushers and drunks. A three-card-monte game was breaking up and the crowd went with it, coming up the stairs to the Mall or disappearing on pathways bordering the Lake.

The shoreline was surrounded by tall, lush trees. In the distance, a few rowboats floated near the dock of the boathouse; attendants were pulling them from the water and stacking them along a fence. He checked his watch. It was 8:40. There were pay phones outside the boathouse and he wanted to be ready to make a call by 8:55. He jogged down the stairs and followed the edge of the Lake until a paved walk led through the trees to the Trefoil arch.

The arch passed under the East Drive and he hid in the darkness of the tunnel, watching the walk leading to the boathouse. The park lamps were beginning to shine in the fading light, but no one was there to enjoy the quiet, deserted walkways. He heard the sound of a car starting and a Parks Department car pulled away from the boathouse. He waited another minute to be certain the boathouse staff was gone; then he came out of the arch and walked over to the phones. He set down the bag and double-checked the parking lot north of the refreshment area. Taxi drivers would sometimes pull into the lot for a rest or to visit with other drivers. He didn't think anybody would be stupid enough to do it at night, and he was right—the lot was empty.

He went back to the phones, put in a dime and punched in a number. A man answered.

"City Hall, Detective Bellis."

He held his watch up to the light.

"Listen carefully. I have a message for the city. In five minutes it will be 2100 hours. From that time on Central Park is mine. Anybody inside the Park after 2100 hours is risking his life."

The detective interrupted him. He sounded annoyed and rude. "Who do you want to talk to? You want the Parks Department? Call them back tomorrow at nine A.M." The detective hung up.

"Goddamnit." He cursed out loud, put in another dime and punched in the number.

"City Hall, Detective Bellis."

"Did I just talk to you about Central Park?"

"Didn't I refer you to the Parks Department?"

"Pay attention. I'm heavily armed and an expert in guerrilla warfare. I'm prepared to meet any kind of force. Central Park is mine and mine alone. I'm going to demonstrate my power, so listen up. The Twenty-second Precinct station house is on the 85th Street transverse in Central Park. I'm blowing it up at 2115. That's eighteen minutes from now. Anybody inside is grease. Got that?"

The detective was silent for a moment. Then he answered, respectfully. "Yes, sir."

"I'm aware that all calls to this office are tape recorded,

so in case you can't remember, have it played back after I hang up."

He hung up, grabbed the bag and went around the north end of the boathouse to the thick bushes and rock outcroppings above the Lake. He got down on his knees and with his hands scooped away the dirt and leaves from the base of one of the bushes.

Concealed underneath the network of roots was a plastic garbage bag containing an AK-47 automatic rifle, a combat helmet and combat fatigues made from camouflaged material for use in the jungle. He put the shoulder bag on the ground and opened it. It was packed with banana clips—ammunition loads for an automatic rifle. He removed one and snapped it into place.

He took off his clothes, sealed them in the garbage bag, returned the bag to the hole and buried it. The combat fatigues were in good condition and fit comfortably, even though he began to sweat through them immediately. He double-checked the ground, hoisted the ammo bag and AK-47 and put on the helmet. Red letters scrawled on the front of the helmet said: PLAN B.

He moved quickly off the rock outcroppings and onto a walk, heading west around the Lake. Something sewn on the front of the fatigues caught his eye and he stopped under a lamp. A name tag was still in place over his right front pocket.

He laughed. He remembered that several years ago he'd removed the tag from his standard olive-drab shirt and stitched it on the camouflage shirt. He'd worn it casually, to parties and football games. That was in the mid-Seventies, when combat fashion had become suddenly chic.

He shook his head and read the name out loud.

"Harris."

He rolled the piece of material into a ball and shoved the tag into a hole in the hollow lamppost.

"Good-bye, Harris," he said.

He ran into the trees, holding the rifle in front of his

body. He paralleled the walk, moving quietly and expertly, invisible in the dark.

Weaver and Richie were speeding uptown on Amsterdam Avenue in a station wagon. The lights were synchronized for vehicles traveling thirty miles an hour, but Weaver was making all of them, because she wasn't stopping for red ones. This didn't always bother Richie, an ex-tow-truck driver, but lately Weaver wasn't even slowing down for lights that had been red from a block back. He knew from experience that a driver could keep pushing his luck and it might pay off for a while, but sooner or later you'd have a wreck. That was your employer's tough break, or whoever insured the truck, but Weaver had fifty thousand dollars' worth of video equipment in the back of the wagon. She wrecked that and nobody was behind her to bail her out. Her news service would go right down the toilet.

Weaver swerved the wagon around a bus and turned right, onto 96th Street. "Did you hear that, Richie? A ten seventy-five."

They were listening to the citywide fire frequency on one of the several radios inside the station wagon. With the radios, and particularly the Bearcat 250 programmable scanner, Weaver and Richie could monitor every important emergency transmission in the New York City area: fire, police by precinct and division, citywide EMS (Emergency Medical Service), transit police, SOD (Special Operations Division), Newark fire—and Weaver's competition, the three other independent news services in Manhattan.

Weaver knew that a ten seventy-five call indicated that units on the scene of the fire at 134th Street were requesting a full assignment, which meant additional trucks and a rescue company. It was certain to be an occupied building and therefore newsworthy.

Weaver could "read" the radio, weeding out from the

noisy mess of transmissions the important calls, the ones that were potentially bloody or exciting, where she and Richie could make dramatic videotape. Managing editors at the local TV stations liked that type of footage, and paid for it. You had to stay right on top of the city, especially at night, when the stations' union crews were not working, and that meant riding the radios. Richie had done something similar when he drove a tow truck, and he was getting better at recognizing subtle things, like the urgency in a dispatcher's voice. But Richie would have to admit that Weaver was incredible; she could read the radio in her sleep. In fact, fifteen mintues earlier, they'd heard a call that an EMS unit was responding to a jumper on the Manhattan Bridge. Jumpers were sometimes sensational, when they jumped, and Weaver had had the station wagon in the middle of the bridge when her attention was diverted by the original call for the fire on 134th Street. It was nothing special—a first alarm—but Weaver had a feeling. Forget the jumper.

They were on Central Park West, flying past 108th Street, two blocks from the edge of Harlem, when they heard another ten seventy-five and a second alarm go out over citywide fire.

"I told you this was gonna be a working fire. I hope there's something left by the time we get there." Weaver jerked the wheel to miss a pothole and took her eye off the road.

"Watch this guy!" Richie spotted a man, hidden by a bus, who was getting out of a taxi on the traffic side of the cab, which was a mistake. Weaver took the station wagon within a half inch of the man's face.

"I saw him!"

"Bullshit."

Weaver had originally hired Richie as a driver and camera assistant when she'd started her service three months ago, but he'd decided to concentrate on learning television production. Richie was twenty-two and tired of driving a tow truck or anything else. TV had more class. So Weaver had resumed driving. But a subtle competition remained between them. They were both kids from Brooklyn, but Richie was a little in awe of Weaver. She was older, twenty-five, and had been to college. But Richie was intimidated mostly by Weaver's looks. Her body was what he called "ripe," and depending on the circumstances, her movements drifted between the gracefully feminine and the abruptly masculine. The effect was confusing and attractive. Her face possessed a natural beauty, uncluttered by makeup except for a light blush, her concession to the New Yorker's lack of a suntan. Her brown hair was long and wavy. Her dark eyes were always unsettled and challenging. Above the eyes was Weaver's most prominent feature: bushy black eyebrows that tufted and curled, sometimes forming a malevolent, satanic mask and other times the mischievous frown of a child. A person might spot Weaver's figure in a crowd and pass over her as just another sexy girl; but if that person saw her move, and then caught a glimpse of her face, with those unusual, changing eyebrows, he would discover what Richie had had ample time to realize while spending ten hours a night in a car with Weaver: she was one of the most beautiful girls he had ever seen.

Of course, Richie never told this to Weaver. He accepted a role not unlike being her younger brother—which meant he tried to get a little edge on her whenever he could. He didn't attempt to understand her. He kept his eyes on the road and permitted himself only the smallest and most fleeting of sexual fantasies. In their line of work there wasn't much time for anything else.

Weaver appreciated Richie's reliability and she'd learned a few things from him about driving in city traffic. Richie drove occasionally when Weaver got tired, but she was faster. Her recklessness had been getting them to the breaking news stories faster than the competition in the last week or two. That was all that mattered. She was getting so good at it that sometimes they arrived at crime scenes before the police.

Weaver and Richie could see smoke as soon as they turned onto Lenox Avenue off 110th Street. They heard sirens and saw an EMS ambulance coming behind them. Weaver outraced it to 134th and turned into the block. It was jammed with emergency vehicles and she jerked the station wagon over the curb and onto the sidewalk. The car smashed into a parking sign and screeched to a stop. A headlight tinkled to the pavement. Weaver made sure the press card was in the window.

Weaver and Richie jumped out and went to the rear of the station wagon. Weaver noticed that she'd scraped away part of the "NonstopNews" logo painted on the driver's side. Richie opened the rear door and Weaver tucked in her shirt. She liked to wear baggy clothes on the job so she didn't call attention to her body, but it was so hot outside tonight that she'd worn a tight T-shirt and resigned herself to the leers and comments.

They put on their battery belts. Weaver lifted the Ikegami HL-79 color camera to her shoulder and Richie connected the BNC cable from the camera to the Sony BVU-50 VTR. He slipped a cassette into the tape machine. He put the strap from the VTR over his shoulder and lifted it with a grunt. That was another reason Weaver liked Richie. He could handle the heavy tape deck in tight circumstances.

Weaver turned on the camera and looked at the tiny TV image in the eyepiece. Black smoke was pouring out of a five-story tenement building in the middle of the block. Weaver had to shout over the radio transmissions and sirens coming from the fire trucks and EMS ambulances.

"I can name that smell in two notes!"

"That's easy! This here is your low-income housin' bein' renovated!"

"How many DOAs, Richie? Five? No, wait!" Weaver sniffed the air. "Six. One more in the closet."

"In the bathroom!" Richie laughed. "The skells. That's where they hide—in the shower."

"That's what I'd do. Get in the tub and turn the water on."

"And fuckin' pray!"

They crossed the street. Hoses crisscrossed the pavement and streams of water followed the curbline. Crowds of people, some of them residents of the burning building, were scuffling with the police. Weaver and Richie pushed through a group of onlookers and around a ladder company truck parked near the front of the building. Their eyes started to tear in the heavy smoke.

"It's beautiful, Richie!" Flames were coming from every window. Weaver was happy. The sky was darkening and, with a good background, the burning facade would look tremendous in color. She moved to her right along the sidewalk to get an angle. A window exploded overhead, showering them with glass fragments. Weaver zoomed tight to the doorway and set the focus.

"Light it and roll!"

Richie punched the record feature on the deck and switched on the sun gun. Bright light illuminated the facade, smoothing out shadows and sharpening details. He positioned the shotgun microphone attached to the tape deck to pick up wild sound.

"Speed."

Weaver began to tape the scene, panning up and getting a shot of orange flame against night-blue sky. A ladder company was moving into position over the roof of the tenement. She held her angle and got a nice shot of the huge jets of water pouring down into the yellow and black smoke. She panned slowly back down the front of the building and held on the doorway. She was going to stop tape when Richie spotted something. Besides operating the deck, holding the light and watching the sound level,

Richie had to be Weaver's eyes. She could only see what was on camera, and in an action situation, Richie had the responsibility to guide her to events as they happened.

"Pan left, Weav!"

A man stumbled out of a ground-floor window and fell on his back into a pile of garbage cans. He was clutching a large color television set. He was choking and gasping, but he held onto the TV set and crawled to the sidewalk. Weaver kept the camera on him. He stood up and put the TV at his feet.

"Damn! That shit is bad!" He started rubbing wildly at his eyes. Weaver zoomed to a close-up. The man seemed to snap out of shock for a moment. He grabbed his head.

"Oh God! My kids! My kids are in there!" He jumped from Weaver's close-up and tried to run up the stairs into the front entrance. Weaver stayed on him as two firemen grabbed him and restrained him from going inside. A cop assisted them and they pushed the man back to the curb-line. One of the firemen went to the sidewalk and returned the TV set to the man.

"Stop tape!" Richie punched the tape deck on Weaver's command. "Good one, Richie!" A team of firemen dragged hoses up to the sidewalk in front of Weaver's location. A young man in a denim jacket emblazoned with the word "Monsters" on the back came out of the crowd and approached Weaver.

"Hey! You Eyewitness News? Hey. I seen it, I seen the whole thing. Put me on TV!"

Weaver motioned to Richie and they moved out of the firemen's way to the right of the building's entrance. The young man followed behind. There was a commotion and loud yells in the doorway. Two firemen burst out the door with axes.

"Roll!"

"Speed."

Weaver took a wide shot of the walkup and the two firemen running down the stairs. One of them was overcome by smoke and he dropped to his knees a few feet in front of Weaver. Richie flooded him with light and Weaver moved close. A police officer stepped up behind Weaver.

"Come on. You know better than that. Let's go. Back up behind the hoses there."

"Stop tape." Weaver nodded at the officer and she and Richie walked away from the fallen fireman and into the street. They stopped between a pumper and an EMS ambulance while Richie checked the cassette. The young man was still with them.

"I told you, man, I know what happened. Yo! Come on."

Screams erupted from the side of the building and several gawkers tripped over the hoses on their way around the trucks. Weaver and Richie pushed in behind the crowd.

"Is that the rescue? Shit! Stay with me, Richie!" Weaver circled a group of people on the sidewalk and reached the side of the tenement. A rescue company was trying to reach some residents trapped on the fourth floor of the building. Weaver couldn't get the angle she wanted. She pulled Richie around a truck and bumped into another camera crew running up from a van parked in the street. The cameraman was Marty Gold. He and his assistant, Tom, were known as the top spec team in the city and Marty's company, Action TV News, was the first independent service to be successful. He had a fleet of vans, several crews, a central office with twenty-four-hour assignment desks and sophisticated radio hookups, and a wall of VTRs and cameras. He had expanded to Washington, D.C., and Chicago and was rumored to be a millionaire. He covered fires like the one on 134th Street for fun.

"Hello, Weaver! Nobody punched you out yet?"

"Just getting here, Marty?"

"Feel good now, Weaver. Being here first is not the whole thing. You oughta know that by now."

"Ten bucks we sell more tape tonight than you do," Weaver responded.

Marty turned to Tom and hooked his camera into a VTR. He smiled. "Maybe. But mine will be in focus." Tom laughed and winked at Weaver.

They were cut off by loud screams from the crowd. Richie steered Weaver toward the corner of the building and they stood tight against the wall. People in the crowd were exhorting the rescue team to hurry. Several residents on the fourth floor leaned out the windows, flames and smoke pouring out behind them. A man held a mattress out the window and looked ready to jump. The rescue company was not quite in position. The firemen yelled at the man to hold on one more minute. The ladder was within feet of the fourth-story windows. A fireman was crawling toward the top and a net was being readied below.

Weaver had her shot lined up. "Roll it."

"Speed."

A woman and child appeared in one of the windows. Flames licked out behind the woman and she climbed halfway out the window.

The rescue ladder moved very close to the windows. Weaver slowly zoomed in on the action. Suddenly the man with the mattress either jumped or slipped, his clothes ignited, and he fell four floors to the pavement. There was a thud and a shriek from the crowd. Weaver panned smoothly down with the fall and was perfectly framed when the man hit.

"Pan back up!" Weaver widened her shot and panned back to the windows. The fireman on the ladder plucked the woman and child from the flames and struggled to get them safely in the grip of rescue personnel coming up from below. A large section of overhanging roof began to break away. Weaver brushed some cinders out of her hair as chunks from the building started coming down around them. She heard shouts from somewhere to her right. Richie pulled Weaver back as more debris crashed down, bouncing off the wall of the structure. Weaver was able to tape the last fifty feet of the plunge, but the camera wasn't as steady as she wanted it to be. She told Richie to stop tape. There was a crunching sound and they jerked their heads up to see a concrete cornice snap free from the roof. They ran for the sidewalk and the cornice slammed down.

They retreated beyond the rescue vehicles and into the middle of the street. Their clothes were covered with a black film of ashes. They stared at each other, eyes wide, breathing hard. Weaver was exhilarated.

"Four stars, Richie! That puts the adrenaline in you, doesn't it?"

Richie fumbled with the tape deck. He pretended to be horrified. "I think I was on pause."

Weaver almost fainted. "What? Goddamnit, no!"

"Just kidding, Weaver." She leaned back against a police car and tried to catch her breath. Richie turned away so she wouldn't see him laughing. On one of their first jobs together, a jumper on the bridge into Grand Central Station, Weaver had told him to set the record function and then put the deck on pause. If the guy jumped suddenly she could record immediately without waiting for the tape to gain speed. They waited about twenty tense minutes and then the guy jumped. Richie got so excited he forgot what to do, punched pause, and thought that was wrong and punched it again. Weaver got a sensational shot of the guy falling to 42nd Street, but when they screened the tape there was no picture. Weaver took Richie's press credential and threw it into the toilet of the ladies' room at WCBS. Richie had figured that that finished his TV career and assumed it was back to the tow trucks, but Weaver had relented and things had gone fine since.

Weaver adjusted the weight of the camera and wiped sweat from under the shoulder attachment. "How we doing on the tape?"

Richie checked the cassette and decided to flip it over. The young man in the "Monsters" jacket strolled over from under an awning behind the police car.

"I got the story right here, girl. Put that camera on me."

Weaver ignored the kid. There were always people at every scene who claimed to have witnessed a crime or to have been conveniently present when the events transpired. They'd say anything to get their faces on television. She supposed that they sometimes convinced the affiliates' reporters and managed to get themselves interviewed. It didn't matter to Weaver. The stations didn't want interviews from her. They wanted tape that their on-camera talent could get excited about in the studio.

The kid said something else to Weaver, but he was drowned out by the siren of an EMS ambulance that was trying to back through the crowd in front of the building. Police officers were shouting at the gawkers to clear the way. Weaver and Richie hurried back across the street.

Two firemen were carrying an unconscious child out the entrance to the walkup. The little girl was limp and turning blue, and one of the firemen was attempting to revive her mouth-to-mouth. A woman ran out of the crowd, sobbing hysterically, and tried to embrace the little girl. Two police officers held her back, but she started screaming and clawing at them.

Weaver and Richie made their way to the rear of the ambulance. The paramedics took the child from the firemen and a mask service unit readied the resuscitation equipment.

"Have light and roll." Weaver took a wide shot and then went close.

The sobbing woman leaned into the picture and Weaver zoomed out to include her. The woman was pulled away into the street by what appeared to be her neighbors dressed in pajamas. Weaver followed her.

"Light her, Richie. Come on!" The woman collapsed and Weaver taped her for several more seconds. "Okay, stop tape." Richie turned off the sun gun and they turned back to the ambulance. A gray-haired man, naked from the waist up, grabbed Weaver's arm and jerked her around.

"What you doin', man! Suppose that was your mother? Who the hell you think you are? Don't you be doin' that shit, you hear me?"

Weaver was startled. The man stared at her. She tried to pull away, but he wouldn't let go. She didn't know what to say.

"I'm sorry. We're just doing our job."

"Job! Shit. Ain't nothin' escape the fuckin' tube."

Richie tried to step between them, but his hands were full and the VTR was in the way. The man attempted to grab Weaver's camera, and she took the opportunity to twist away. A fireman watching the altercation got in front of Weaver, but the man threw his arm out and tried to punch the lens. A cop restrained the man and pushed him back into the crowd. The fireman held Weaver's gaze.

"Better do your job elsewhere until things cool down."

She wanted to say something to him, but he started to cough. Black mucus dribbled from his nose and he hawked it up on the street. He turned away and started back to the burning tenement.

Weaver and Richie crossed the street toward the station wagon. Weaver heard a familiar voice behind her.

"Hey! Where you goin', girl? Let me run it down for you. Put me on, okay?"

Weaver didn't bother to turn around. She checked her watch and it was almost 9:00 P.M. "Richie, let's head downtown. We have plenty of time to hit Channel Five and PIX for the ten o'clocks."

"Okay. We got some great shit here, Weav. I know Five's gonna eat it up, specially that weeping woman stuff."

"Was Marty rolling when that guy jumped?" Weaver hoped like hell she had an exclusive on that.

"I don't know. I didn't see him. Things was fallin' on my head. Remember?"

They unlocked the wagon and piled the equipment in the back.

Richie removed the cassette and slipped it into a vinyl case. The kid leaned over Richie's shoulder and a hurt look came over his face.

"Don't do that! Man, I know what happened. Just put my ass on TV! I'm tellin' you, I seen who started the fire."

Weaver was halfway into the driver's seat when she heard this, but she got back out of the car. She spotted a police officer talking with some rescue personnel and shouted at him.

"Sergeant! We have a concerned citizen here." The sergeant didn't respond. "He says he saw who started the fire."

The sergeant turned around and his attention focused immediately on the kid. "Yeah? Who was it?" The kid lost the hurt look on his face. He began to edge away into the shadows of the tenement buildings. His feet scraped on broken glass, but the sound was lost in the ubiquitous radio noise. Flashes of red light played over his body. His eyes became hard and lines formed on his neck where his jaw was shut tight. He stared at Weaver.

"Shit. What you askin' me for? I didn't see nothin'."

He disappeared into the darkness and the sergeant wandered back to the crowd. Weaver and Richie smiled at each other and got into the station wagon. She switched on the scanner and the radios and drove the car off the sidewalk onto 134th Street.

One thing intrigued Harris about Central Park, and that was how quickly the character of the Park changed once the sun was down. He was certain that few places on the planet changed so dramatically between day and night. During the day, people filled the Park, lured in by the inviting natural environment. At night, Central Park was transformed into a dark, menacing presence, a no-man's-land replete with muggers, deviates, wild hordes of rapists and killers—all of it either real or imagined.

It was true that normal activities did take place at night: occasional rock shows at the Wollman Rink, lawn concerts with the Philharmonic in the Sheep Meadow, plays at the Delacorte Theater. These were attended by thousands of people, but as soon as the program was over they headed directly for the streets. To almost all New Yorkers, nighttime in Central Park remained a sinister and evil mystery. This aspect was vital to Harris' plans.

Harris appreciated Central Park for other reasons, too. He'd learned a lot about it. The design developed in 1858 by Frederick Law Olmsted and Calvert Vaux still existed today, and it was a wonderfully diverse environment. The landscape integrated natural rock mounds with man-made lakes and ponds, meadows, even waterfalls; trees and shrubs, carefully selected for appearance and function, lined the hundreds of walkways, creating quiet arbors and small, dense forests. Over the years, additions to the basic plan had provided ball fields, playgrounds and two zoos. A person could row a boat on the Lake, take a spin on the Carousel, sail a model boat, play tennis, or ride a horse on the four-and-a-half-mile-long bridle path. There were the simpler pleasures, too—a game of chess, a picnic in the grass, a peaceful stroll along the reservoir.

Central Park was an attractive fantasy world, full of little discoveries, where people escaped the city. Harris was certain that Olmsted and Vaux had intended it that way. Once, while standing sixty stories up on the roof of the Burlington House, with the Park stretched out below him like a big green map, Harris had been struck by the notion that Central Park was a small, incongruous country, its borders and entrances defined by short walls and green trees, the uniqueness of its beauty the only defense against the irrepressible march of monstrous steel towers.

Harris liked the image, because it reminded him of another small country, where everything, including himself, had been incongruous—and because the more he studied Central Park, the more suitable it became for his needs.

Harris had a fantasy.

He began to act it out on a cold, rainy night in the middle of November. By that time, Harris was tired of waiting.

Alone in Lower Manhattan on that early morning, Harris inspected and reviewed an enormous arsenal that covered the floors and walls of his apartment. With a cold, tactical analysis he selected priority weapons and supplies, those that he considered components of his first strike. Harris wanted to stock Central Park according to the chronology of his plan because it would help him to coordinate not only locations, but timings and events. Later, he would worry about the more complicated logistics: resupply and storage.

Harris jammed about a hundred and fifty pounds of materials into a canvas bag and watched the rain. He had made some preliminary reconnaissance patrols through the park in prior weeks to double-check on any possible late-night activity, so he wasn't really disappointed that the weather was lousy. It would further minimize the chances of encountering anyone.

At 2:00 A.M. the rain was hard. Harris took a taxi uptown, though he didn't want to. There was always the chance that the driver might remember him months later when it became significant—but it was too far to walk with the heavy bag and there were too many transit police on the subway.

Harris had the driver let him off in front of an apartment building on West 76th Street. He went into the entryway, waited until the taxi was gone, and then went back outside and over to the Park. Nobody was on the street and he was conspicuous lugging the bag. He went up Central Park West across from the Museum of Natural History and approached the Hunter's Gate entrance to the Park.

Harris was surprised at how nervous he felt. He reminded himself that all he had to do was get inside the Park without a policeman seeing him and he could roam around all night at will. When he was about a hundred yards from 81st, he could see the headlights of several cars waiting at the traffic signal. It was raining so hard that nobody was going to see him, but his nerves couldn't take it, so he hoisted himself up the wall between the sidewalk and the Park and jumped about ten feet down into the bushes and trees.

Harris was wet and cut up and the bag almost broke his back, but he was in. He got down out of the bushes and moved along a walk, back downtown toward the Lake. He moved in and out of the trees and didn't use the flashlight, but, of course, he saw no one. By the time he arrived at the Lake the rain had stopped. The smooth water reflected lights on the pathways circling the distant Fountain. Harris relaxed. He knew the next time would be easier. He knew that he could spend night after night working inside the Park without fear of detection. Later, when he did encounter people—gay men near 66th Street, an occasional bum, and the infrequent brave stroller—no one paid attention. If you were in Central Park at three in the morning, that was your business.

Harris worked in the Park through the fall, winter and spring. He buried his first-strike supplies before the ground became icy. He selected target locations, did more pre-strike reconnaissance and planned tactics. In the winter he went through countless rehearsals and timings. He spent hours exploring the sewer system and tunnels under the Park. He did as much innocuous research as possible, with charts and specifications available from municipal agencies. He went everywhere in disguise.

In the spring, Harris rechecked supply points and moved in the trickier antipersonnel weapons. He had to conceal more than a ton of equipment, ammunition and tools, and make sure no one stumbled on them in the ensuing months. Harris had to be very careful, and that took time: stopping, starting, being absolutely sure that no one saw a thing.

It was hard work. Everything had to be broken down into small loads which could be carried into the Park. The majority of the supplies had to be available and assembled within several hours on a single night. July 21 was the night.

After dark on July 21, as on any night, Central Park was an ominous black hole in the center of the city. Pedestrians moved along its edges, outside on the well-lit streets. The hotels and apartment houses and office buildings were walls of bright light on the surrounding avenues. Taxis cut across the Park on the transverses at 65th, 79th, 85th and 97th Streets. The 72nd Street road and the East and West drives were closed on weekends to permit their use by cyclists and joggers. On this night, there were no concerts, no plays—nothing. It was Sunday.

Harris was in the approximate center of Central Park, under heavy trees along the Lake. He was kneeling over a deep hole that had been concealed by a layer of dirt, leaves and plywood. On the ground next to him were the AK-47, a field harness and equipment bag, and a collapsible shovel. He stepped down into the hole and lifted out two crates. One contained an M-79 launcher; the other, 40-mm high-explosive grenades and incendiary devices that the M-79 fired.

Harris got out of the hole and unpacked the launcher. He pushed open the locking hatch on top of the weapon's face, pressed down the barrel and loaded in one of the incendiary devices. Both the M-79 and the 40-mm loads were a little damp, but still clean and working, despite having been in the hole since November. In fact, this was the first supply area Harris had stocked.

Harris slipped the plywood board back into place over the hole. It still looked good, but it didn't really matter now. He removed a notebook of charts from the equipment bag and put the flashlight on the top chart. It was a map detail of a section of the Park, showing the Lake, the Fountain and the West Drive. Harris' notations and symbols indicated burial sites, distances from landmarks and terrain features, and things to remember. Each chart page was decorated with these symbols. Harris made a new mark next to the symbol designating the first supply hole and smiled. He would never have believed it, but logistics could be interesting.

He strapped the AK-47 into place, picked up the equipment bag and filled it with grenades and extra banana clips. He secured the M-79 launcher in a customized holster around his waist and attached a pouch full of incendiary devices to his belt. He flipped down to the second chart and moved off along the edge of the Lake.

His combat boots sank into the mud and water. He went up a rise until the MONY digital clock was visible through the trees, blinking on and off, about a mile downtown. He was glad it wasn't raining on this night; he had no need for poor visibility and the navigational problems it created. The clock said 81°. It was still hot and people didn't react well in the heat.

Harris waited for the clock to change. It said 9:04. He checked it against his watch. He had eleven minutes until 2115 hours and his rendezvous at 85th Street with the 22nd Precinct station house.

Weaver remembered how her mother had been terrified by late-night telephone calls, or by the door buzzer going off after midnight. It didn't matter if it was a wrong number, or neighborhood kids fooling around in the apartment house lobby. Her mother would be too upset to go back to sleep, and she would stay up watching a movie or smoking. Weaver was then only five years old and, at first, her mother's behavior had confused her—until she saw a fireman's funeral on the news. On the screen was a long procession of men in uniform, a flag-draped coffin, a woman crying and a little boy dressed in a suit. It wasn't difficult for a bright little girl watching television, a little girl whose own father had completed training and become a New York City fireman two days before her fifth birthday, to figure out that phone calls and door buzzers in the middle of the night might mean that her daddy was lying in a hospital, all burned up. Or worse.

But Weaver's father always came home. Sometimes his hands were bandaged, or he coughed and had no voice. For the first few months he was in better shape than Weaver's mother, who was always tired, anxious, smoking two packs a day. Finally, on an off-duty Saturday, her father went out to an electronics store and returned with a radio equipped to receive police, fire and emergency frequencies. He slammed it down on the kitchen table and said to Weaver's mother, "Here, go ahead, you can stay up all night and listen to everything. You can hear the alarms, you can hear when my company goes out, you'll know how bad it is, you'll know when somebody gets it; and then you won't have to sit there in your cloud of smoke, scared shitless every time the phone rings. Okay?"

Weaver's mother never once touched the radio. She stuffed it in the closet and made some kind of emotional adjustment that allowed her to sleep like an ordinary person for the twenty years her husband served in the fire department.

When Weaver was eight she discovered the radio while rummaging through the closet. She took it to her room. Within two months she could understand every police code and all the salient emergency jargon that comprised the enormous volume of transmissions broadcast every day in the metropolitan area. She was fascinated by the arcane radio dialogues that created whole worlds of drama and melodrama, pain and suffering. There were worlds that sometimes began with a simple 10-13, officer needs assistance, and flourished into a four-hour nightmare of hostages, gunfire, corpses, arrests and bookings. Sometimes it was a world that came and went over the air in ten seconds: "Adam six, please respond to Broadway and Seven-oh. Man with a gun." "Central, be advised we are at that location, man is DOA. Adam six." Life and death. Weaver sat in her room imagining the faces and the guns and the burning buildings crumbling to the ground. When she heard her father's company respond to an alarm, she imagined him battling his way through flames and smoke to rescue a trapped child. After she started listening to the radio, she no longer wondered why her father would come home in the morning exhausted and beaten, but still too exhilarated to sleep.

For her ninth birthday Weaver's parents gave her a bicycle, with the hope that she would occasionally come out of her room to ride it. Weaver obliged them. She would come running out of her room and into the outside hallway, unlocking the bike and explaining that she would eat lunch later, after she checked out a two-alarm on Court Street or a bomb blast in Brooklyn Heights.

Weaver covered Brooklyn. She tried the subway, but it was too slow. She saved her allowance and indulged in secret taxi rides to fires and homicides outside the range of her bicycle.

But this freedom did not last long. A report from Weaver's fourth-grade teacher indicated that Weaver was restless and inattentive, and seemed unable to form peer-group associations. Weaver, the nine-year-old, didn't understand the analysis. To her it was a simple matter of the fourth grade being a big bore. How could she get excited listening to her friends talk about what they'd seen on TV, or hearing the teacher recount the dramatic events of history, when every night Weaver either listened to or witnessed the real thing, the awesome spectacles and the mysterious crimes. Finally, Weaver's mother cracked

**35**

down. The radio stayed off, except one night a week, and trips to crime scenes were prohibited (although many were still made clandestinely).

As Weaver's father said, though, these things have a way of taking care of themselves. He was right, temporarily. When Weaver hit thirteen and went to high school, she developed her looks and began to receive a lot of attention from boys. They found her so attractive that they overlooked her eccentric interests. Weaver never lost her fascination with the underworld of crime and violence, a world whose existence it was impossible for her to forget. But she liked boys, too, and high school produced other brief passions. Nevertheless, she occasionally convinced one of her dates that a jumper on the Brooklyn Bridge might make a more interesting evening than a drive-in movie on Long Island.

When Weaver graduated from high school, her grandparents gave her a car, in which she immediately installed a programmable scanner. Cars and scanners—they were tools that made the city's dramas even more accessible. Although Weaver wasn't sure what she wanted to do after high school, she knew that she wanted to be part of the action.

She needed something else—some other tool. She considered enrolling in the police academy, but, no matter what the recruiting publicity claimed, a female police officer could only get so far. Anyway, on the street, an officer was limited to his or her assignments. Her father was acquainted with cops and she'd often heard them complain about the routine and the boredom of long days in court.

Weaver decided to go to college in Queens. She spent the first two years trying to stay awake. Then she discovered a degree program in television production. She knew instinctively that somewhere in the technology of television were the tools that would not only find her a job, but would keep her on the streets of New York, tapped into the city's enormous energy and its capacity for thrills.

Weaver and Richie were in the station wagon, moving downtown on Central Park West, about 106th Street.

"Ten-four, rescue three."

"What's your status, one-three-one, K?"

"Twenty-four Charlie to central, K."

"What's your location, one-three-one, K?"

"EMS one-four-four, you have an unconscious at six one West Seven-three Street. Your cross is Columbus."

"What is your location, one-three-one, K?"

"Twenty-three ten, all first alarm units will receive one hour R&R upon their return to quarters."

"What is your status, one-three-one, K?"

"Twenty-three ten, ten-two."

"Do you have the status of one-three-one, K?"

"For Christ's sake," Weaver shouted, "he passed away!"

Weaver often wished she could talk back to the dispatchers. Thousands of humorous comments were possible. "He passed away." What else could you say about the driver of EMS one-three-one, who was sick and tired of looking at cardiacs, bleeders, and difficult breathings every night and was standing outside his ambulance on some dark corner, trying to revive his own brain.

Everybody that worked the streets needed laughs, and she and Richie indulged themselves whenever possible. Sometimes the transmissions they heard were so absurd that they wound up on the floor of the car, tears coming out of their eyes. Weaver's favorite experience was the time she and Richie were returning from a homicide in Brooklyn and passed a bad traffic accident that had just happened on the Brooklyn Bridge. Weaver used the car phone to call 911. This was when she became convinced that you could be a moron and still work for 911.

When the operator answered, Weaver reported that she

37

was with NonstopNews and they had spotted an accident on the Brooklyn Bridge, going into Brooklyn, by the first stanchion. The operater asked, "What's that location again?"

"The Brooklyn Bridge."

"Can you spell that?"

"Come on."

"Which direction was that?"

"Brooklyn bound."

"Where was that?"

"By the first stanchion."

"Which direction?"

"Brooklyn bound."

"From Queens?"

"Christ, from Manhattan."

"Where's the location again?"

"On the Brooklyn Bridge by the first stanchion."

"What's a stanchion?"

"Oh, God."

"The computer won't take Brooklyn Bridge. Where is it?"

Weaver liked this story. The commentators could talk about the city night after night for a year, and still they could never give a picture that had the clarity of one night listening to the radios.

She was laughing out loud at the recollection as she braked for a traffic signal at 100th Street and Central Park West. Richie made an exaggerated gesture of looking out the windshield.

"Congratulations. You stopped on a red."

Weaver looked over at the Park while she waited for the light. She thought she'd use 96th Street to cut across to the East Side and the Channel 5 studios. But there was no hurry. If they got the tap over to WNEW's editor by 9:30, he'd still have plenty of time to cut the story before the ten o'clock news.

The light turned green and she fell in behind traffic.

Richie got out the cassette of the Harlem fire and began to make notes on the label.

"What are you gonna write on there, Rich?"

"We had a jumper. Beaucoup flames."

"Hysterical victim. Cave-in. Write that down."

The car phone between the seats buzzed and Weaver picked it up.

"News. Hi, J.T." J.T. was a twenty-year-old Puerto Rican kid from the Bronx, the third of the three members of NonstopNews, Inc. He was calling from Weaver's apartment.

J.T. liked to refer to himself as an assignment editor, because the tasks he performed were analogous to that function. He sat in front of the same array of radios and telephones that was in the station wagon, plus two TVs, next to Weaver's bed. If he heard a transmission that sounded newsworthy, he called Weaver on the car phone to make sure she was aware of it. It was a good backup system. J.T. also screened all the evening newscasts, watching for videotape shot by NonstopNews. Weaver liked to know what made the air—not only for the personal satisfaction, but to verify what was used. She didn't like any discrepancies when it was time for the stations to settle the bills.

J.T. was calling Weaver now to see how she and Richie had made out at the fire on 134th Street.

"Did you do some good, Weav?"

Weaver slowed the station wagon and allowed a police car to roar past, heading downtown.

"Definitely, J.T. Gorgeous stuff."

"I need some beer, Weaver."

"Did you check my refrigerator?"

"You never keep nothin' but frost in that thing. I'm gonna step out for a minute. Okay?"

"Put it on your expenses." Weaver stopped the car for another light at 98th Street. "Hey, that reminds me, I got some bucks comin' from you guys in the DOA pool."

Richie smacked the dashboard. "You ain't countin' that guy that fell? He was still movin'."

"Come on, he was ready for the bag."

Weaver couldn't hear it, but J.T. was trying to find a piece of paper under Weaver's bed. He'd finally remembered to write down the DOA bets—money riding on which borough would yield the first dead person of the evening. He said, "Wait a minute, that was in Manhattan."

Weaver accelerated past 97th Street. "Right. I had Manhattan. And that's where the guy went off."

J.T. couldn't find the paper. "I had Manhattan."

"Bullshit. You had the Bronx. You always take the Bronx, you think it's so goddamn bad."

A car pulled away from an apartment building and Weaver had to brake fast to avoid a collision. She gave the horn a long push. "See that? Jersey plates. Christ, in Jersey, two hands, two feet, you get a license."

She stopped talking suddenly and listened to a radio transmission. J.T. had also heard the same call on his end.

"Did you hear that, Weav?"

"I heard it. Hold on a second." She turned to Richie. "Get the frequency list out of the glove box. I'm gonna punch in the precinct."

"The Twenty-second Precinct?" Richie asked. He referred to the list and read Weaver the digit code. Weaver programmed the scanner to read the transmissions from the Twenty-second Precinct, although the original call had come from the Detective Division, of which the bomb squad was a part. It had indicated some kind of bomb scare, and that sounded interesting.

"The Twenty-second Precinct is Central Park, right, Richie?"

"Yeah, but I heard that call as the bomb squad responding to the precinct house itself."

Weaver was skeptical. "No, can't be." She put the

phone back to her ear. "J.T., how did you copy that alleged bomb?"

J.T. was also punching a code into the scanner next to the bed. "I'm programmin' around, Weav, see what I hear, but Emergency Medical Service is sending units out of the station house in the park."

"No kidding. Wait a second." She and Richie listened to a transmission over the SOD radio.

"EMS one-two-one. Please respond to the two-two station house. You have a standby with the bomb squad. Do you know that location, K?"

"That's affirm, K."

"Okay, your time out is 2110, your ID number 927-642, operator 2251."

Weaver smelled a story. "I guess they're serious, Richie." She noted the street sign as the car went past an intersection. Ninety-fourth Street. "We're right near it."

"What about this tape?"

Weaver started to answer, but J.T. interrupted her.

"Weav, I got the competition's frequency on. They just got a call from WABC, I guess makin' sure they heard the bomb thing."

Weaver put the accelerator to the floor and swerved out into oncoming traffic, passing an entire line of cars stopped at the light on 92nd. She went through the light and ran a taxi into the curb.

"We're gonna check this out, J.T. Here's what you do. Call up that night assignment editor at Channel Five—what's-her-name. Lois. Tell her we made tape on that fire in Harlem. Your basic urban blight, but real action shit. Occupied building, we got a guy falling, the thud, everything. It's so good she can chroma-key it behind her opening. We'll bring it to her as soon as we do this. And don't sleep in my bed. I'm not paying you for that."

"This is gonna be a ten-ninety anyway," Richie said. "Who's gonna blow up a precinct house?"

"EMS one-two-one, be advised traffic is stopped east-bound on the eight-five transverse road."

Weaver heard sirens and looked in her rearview mirror. Spinning red lights were coming up fast behind them. "That would be one-two-one right there." She tried to get more speed, but she was already taking a block every five seconds. She let the ambulance go by. "I knew something crazy was going to happen tonight. I'm in the mood for it."

She ran the light at 88th Street, right behind EMS one-two-one, punched in a new frequency on the scanner, and rammed the car into a pothole. She flew out of her seat and a hubcap spun away, vaulting the curb and rolling into the dark bushes of Central Park. She yelled at Richie over the sirens.

"Remind me to call Avis and tell them the car is kinda tired!"

Harris was moving quickly along a walk near the Great Lawn. He veered off into the trees covering a hill that sloped down from the baseball diamonds to the West Drive. He stopped and noted the precise location on one of the charts. It was a supply point: Hill 250, 7/21, 2110. He was on time—about three hundred yards south and west of the police station on the 85th Street transverse.

Harris found the hole at the base of one of his landmark trees and removed field glasses, for use during night or day, a bottle of amphetamines and a .45 automatic with a holster and ammunition. He stuffed an ammo pouch into his fatigues, with clips for the sidearm, and hung the glasses around his neck. After verifying that the .45 was in working condition, he strapped the holster around his waist. He hoped that no close combat situations would develop, but he had to be prepared for any contingency.

He opened the pill bottle and sniffed the capsules. They seemed all right, so he stowed the bottle and ran up the hill toward the Great Lawn. People played baseball on the huge lawn in summer and touch football in the winter. During the season, Harris remembered seeing ambulances parked near the backstops during the football games, in anticipation of injuries.

Harris stopped on the edge of the grass and observed the terrain. The area was very dark and a halo of light hovered over the tops of the trees. He decided to cut directly across the playing fields and gain a few seconds. On a previous trip he had discovered a few kids playing basketball in the dark on courts across from the northern edge of the lawn. The playground was not far from the rear of the precinct house, and although Harris wasn't anticipating any immediate police reaction following the explosion, he wanted to make sure no kids were around to get caught in the line of fire.

Harris took off across the Great Lawn. All the equipment felt heavy, so he slipped the AK-47 from his shoulder into his hand. He looked downtown as he ran, watching the lights of the midtown skyline. It was the last time he would be able to expose himself in an open space, away from the cover of the trees and undergrowth. In a few moments, Harris would no longer be a vague threat, he'd be a target.

No one was on the basketball courts, so Harris moved immediately to a position about thirty yards from the rear of the station house. Car horns and loud voices drifted back into the Park from beyond the buildings. It was 9:12. Harris assumed that the bomb squad was searching the station. Given sixty minutes, they might locate the device he had planted at the back of the structure, but the time frame since the phone call to City Hall permitted evacuation and little else. When the explosion happened most of the debris would go

43

straight up and back toward the Great Lawn. Nothing lethal would fly out into the transverse. Or so Harris hoped. He really knew little about demolitions.

Harris brought the field glasses up to his eyes and scanned the area. A man in bomb squad gear was running along the side of the station house, continuing on out of sight. Another man was being pulled by a dog into some bushes next to the fence bordering the parking lot. The dog was about twenty yards from the bomb.

Harris lowered the glasses and did a supplies check: launcher, grenades, ammo; charts, light, pills. Everything was secure and he was ready to move. He looked up at the sky, at the glowing ring around the trees. He enjoyed being in the Park at night. It was really quite pleasant once you had nothing to fear. Harris pushed the change lever on the AK-47 from safety to full automatic.

When Weaver and Richie arrived at 86th Street, the transverse road leading eastbound into the Park was jammed with cars and taxis. The EMS ambulance, sirens blaring, turned into the westbound lane. Weaver tried to follow, but a uniformed cop standing next to a patrol car prevented her from taking the station wagon into the Park. She displayed her press credentials, but the car was a no-no, so they double-parked it on Central Park West. They started to unload the equipment from the back.

"You sure you wanna gear up for this, Weav? We're gonna have to shlep halfway across the park."

Weaver put the camera on her shoulder. "Hell, yes. Look at this mess. Cops and crowds—TV loves it. We can always get some crap tape for the file."

Richie got out the VTR and the sun gun. He was resigned to a fast night. He would have enjoyed a breather after that fire, but Weaver was all charged up and that meant they were going to do the town, up and down.

When the camera and tape were ready, they cleared the cop at the intersection and ran east on the roadway into the Park. The line of cars extended through the tunnel under the West Drive, past the Parks Department shop, to about fifty yards from the entrance to the station house. Most of the vehicles were taxis. Some of the drivers were standing in the street, arguing with police officers who were trying to get everyone back into their cars. The EMS ambulance was parked near several officers and two men in handcuffs who stood under the trees north of the transverse. Weaver guessed that the two men were probably muggers being held in the lockup before the building was evacuated.

She moved out from the trees and could see that the traffic on the opposite side of the station was backed up toward Fifth Avenue. Several patrol cars and a van roared out of the parking lot behind the one-story precinct house and moved along the roadway. It was becoming noisy. People were getting impatient in the heat and they started to honk their horns.

Weaver and Richie approached the front of the building and were stopped by an officer with a bullhorn. He was shouting at a taxi that had edged out of line. He was young and gave Weaver the once-over.

"You're gonna have to move back across the road, miss. By the trees."

Weaver nodded and she and Richie headed for the group of officers and the two muggers. Weaver didn't see the bomb squad truck, which was no surprise, since it usually was not brought to the scene unless a bomb was found. She loved to photograph it. The truck looked like a huge, orange iron lung. There were bomb squad personnel present, however, and she thought she might as well tape some of that.

"Richie, put the light on the entryway, let me see how that looks."

The cops were joking around, smoking cigarettes; nobody was taking the thing too seriously. They watched Weaver with amusement. One of them spoke to her, pointing at Richie.

"That's an awful big monkey you got there, miss. Is he gonna play somethin' for us?"

"Roll it."

"Stand by." Richie aimed the light. "Speed."

Weaver took a wide shot of the area, panning over the taxis and back to the crowd in the roadway. Some of the cops tried to edge into the picture. One of them waved at the camera.

"Hi, Mom."

Richie turned the light in his face and everybody blinked.

"Hey, get that light outta my eyes! Where's your manners?"

Weaver laughed behind the camera and stepped out into the street to get a shot looking east toward the trees and the lights above. The cop with the bullhorn yelled at her.

"Where you going? Stand back of the line there." A taxi driver wandered up to the cop.

"Officer, what is this, a bomb scare?"

"Nah, we're looking for cockroaches. Come on, get back in your car."

There was loud yelling from the front of the station house and Richie told Weaver to pan left to the action. Two bomb squad officers appeared in the brightly lit doorway of the building. One of them spoke into a walkie-talkie and in a few seconds two other officers ran out from the parking lot. One of the men had a sniffer dog on a leash and they moved across the roadway, passing nicely through Weaver's shot, and stood under the trees.

"Anything?" asked one of the men.

"Negative."

"What time is it?" One of the officers looked at his watch.

"Almost nine-fifteen. Five seconds."

"We'll give it two minutes, then call it a ten-ninety. We're not gonna confirm a device here."

46

"No kidding."

The man with the dog wanted to add something to the conversation, but the time on Harris' bomb was a little fast and the station house exploded three seconds ahead of schedule. The concussion blew the men off their feet and they fell to the pavement. The dog put his tail between his legs and took off for Fifth Avenue.

Harris was running east. He crossed over the East Drive and ducked into some trees behind the Metropolitan Museum of Art. He put the automatic rifle over his shoulder and took the M-79 launcher out of its holster. He heard sirens and ran around the edge of the building near the Drive until he had a view of the intersection of the transverse and Fifth Avenue, about fifty yards away.

The road divided a few yards from the avenue, one fork leading out of the Park onto Fifth Avenue and across to 84th; the other fork was one-way westbound, going into the Park for the traffic coming from the East Side. This westbound fork was backed up with cars from half a mile inside the Park, near the station house. Harris had counted on that. It meant that any emergency vehicles coming from the East Side would have to enter the eastbound fork to gain access to the Park, and would consequently pass close to his position.

Harris listened and observed pedestrians on the sidewalk as the sirens got louder. Many people were stopping to look in the direction of the explosion. He saw flashing lights as a fire engine approached the intersection. It was from Engine 22 on East 85th Street near Madison Avenue, the company closest to the 22nd Precinct station house, responding to the call just as Harris had expected. The fire engine slowed and swerved around traffic into the eastbound fork. Harris used the launcher to fire two smoke grenades into the roadway in front of the engine. They made a loud explosion and immediately obscured

47

the transverse with a wall of green smoke. The driver of the engine made a sudden stop and a police car following behind banged off the curb and crashed to a stop on a sidewalk next to the museum.

Harris moved forward so that he could see the engine in front of the clouds of smoke, with the Park and the jammed-up cars as a background. He didn't want any pedestrians in his line of sight. He aimed the AK-47 and hoped that he was still something of a marksman.

One of the firemen started to climb down from the cab of the engine and Harris opened up on the front of the vehicle. The headlights shattered and rounds pounded into the tires. The fireman dropped to the street and crawled back toward Fifth Avenue. Harris blew out the windshield and turned his fire on the wrecked patrol car just as the officers got out and crouched behind the doors. The AK-47 was a good weapon, an assault rifle. In seconds it ripped the front of the patrol car to pieces. Harris' fire was accurate and nobody, police or bystanders, was hit.

One of the officers reached into the car. Harris stopped shooting. He could hear the officer yelling into the radio.

"Ten Charlie to central! Ten-thirteen! Fifth Avenue and Eight-five! Ten thirteen!"

The officer's voice had a trace of panic. Harris was happy to hear it. He knew that the kinds of actions he was going to execute in the next half hour, in the next days perhaps, would be incongruous in an urban area, even one as sophisticated as New York. That incongruity would be terrifying and it would create panic, which was an important element in Harris' strategy. He watched now as the officers and pedestrians ran for cover. He loaded the launcher and lobbed another smoke grenade onto Fifth Avenue, causing an explosion followed by screams and blurred shapes darting through purple smoke. He grabbed the AK-47 and turned back into the Park. He was on a timetable and the intersection was in the condition he wanted: nonfunctional.

At 9:26 Harris crossed the East Drive and cut back toward the Great Lawn. Ahead and to his right he saw an orange glow and a cloud of black smoke rising into the darkness. He stopped in front of a lamppost surrounded by bushes and made a notation in his chart notebook. He was reaching into his pocket for a set of keys when a hand touched his shoulder.

Harris' heart did something it hadn't done for a long time, a funny little arrhythmic flutter. His mind comprehended in a second that bad luck was going to wash out the whole thing eleven minutes after it had gotten started.

He whirled around and faced a man. "Hi. Harry's the name and wine's my game."

Harry was filthy, smelled of dried urine and lurched a little to one side. He extended his palm and tried to focus on Harris. Harris didn't move. He waited for his heart to stop missing beats. Finally he cleared his throat and raised the AK-47 until the barrel was about two inches from the derelict's forehead. Harris smiled. "Hi, Harry. Get out of the park. It's not safe in here. Not for garbage."

Harry recognized a gun when he saw one and started to move back. He stumbled and ran backward, and when he was out of sight Harris could hear him yelling about locking up weirdos and cocksuckers.

Harris wiped sweat from under his helmet and stepped into the bushes around the lamppost. He removed keys from his pocket and unlocked a Yamaha XT 500-cc on/off road motorcycle that was chained to the pole. On Saturday night he had ridden the bike up Sixth Avenue and onto the East Drive with the rest of the traffic. When he got near the museum he pulled over to the curb and pretended to have mechanical problems. After the flow of cars thinned out, he pushed it onto a walk, drove it past the Great Lawn and chained it to the lamppost indicated on the charts. He assumed no one would pay much attention to it during twelve hours of daylight on Sunday. Harris was right.

He brushed some pigeon droppings off the seat and removed the heavy chain. He could hardly see the bike in the darkness. There were no shiny chrome handles or accessories. All surfaces were painted in flat black. He attached the large equipment sack to the luggage rack, got on and started the motor. The bike ran almost silently; a month ago he'd gone to Philadelphia in disguise and purchased special mufflers from a custom shop. The salesman had told him that the mufflers were effective, and they were. Harris revved the motor and it sounded no louder than a new refrigerator.

He secured the AK-47 on his shoulder and aimed the flashlight onto his watch. He'd lost a minute on the derelict. He put the bike in gear and rolled out of the bushes. After locating the orange cloud of smoke, he accelerated past the Obelisk onto a walk and past the Great Lawn, his fatigues flapping in the wind.

"Did you get it?" That was the first thing Richie shouted at Weaver in the seconds after the explosion. Weaver yelled yes, she had it, but she knew she had flinched. In fact, she had jerked back and nearly fallen over. On tape she probably had a loud blast and thirty seconds of the sky over New York. It didn't really matter. That alone was going to be sensational.

Weaver was still rolling, trying to get whatever she could from the chaos on the transverse road. Burning chunks of debris littered the street. The station house was a column of smoke and flame. The facade remained in place like a movie set, but the rest of the building had virtually disappeared. Weaver set up a low angle and shot vignettes of the flaming debris, panning up to the station house and the billowing smoke. She finished with a shot of a police car rolled over on the edge of the street.

She heard the screams of police officers trying to get the taxis and cars to make U-turns and head back out of the Park.

"Where am I, Richie?"

"Casualty comin'!" Richie put the light on a police officer dragging a colleague across the roadway. Blood ran down the man's face and onto his uniform. "Pan right, get the head."

Weaver swung the camera around in time for a close-up of the officer. She held the shot, letting him walk through the frame, and then focused on the background. Richie was right on top of the scene. He lit a group of officers and taxi drivers who were obviously in shock. They were pale and frozen, orange light flickering over their unblinking eyes. It was a great picture and Weaver zoomed closer until the image was composed only of faces.

"Stop tape." Richie punched the VTR and shut off the sun gun. Weaver took her eyes away from the camera and perused the area. A police car with its lights flashing slammed into a retaining wall under the bridge in an attempt to squeeze between the cars stopped eastbound and those trying to make U-turns and return west. The officer inside the patrol car was yelling and cursing over the loudspeaker.

"This is gold, Richie! Let's try and get closer to the building. It's gonna collapse and I want to get it before the Fire Department screws it up."

"Where the hell are they, Weav? They shoulda been here by now."

Weaver didn't know; she didn't care. "Come on. Don't step on any nails, this is a mess!"

They had started to jog east when an officer ran out from the trees and shouted at them.

"Yo! Can you shine that light over here?"

Weaver and Richie stopped and saw one of the bomb

**51**

squad officers lying on the ground in the darkness under the trees. An EMS medic was bent over him and had his hand in the man's mouth.

"Yes, sir." Richie went immediately to the trees and turned on the light. Weaver adjusted her lens and spoke into Richie's ear.

"Be ready to roll, just in case there's some bacon and eggs."

Richie nodded. Weaver was looking through the eyepiece when two smoke grenades exploded in the transverse road. Twenty people began yelling at once and everyone fell to the pavement. Many of the officers drew their revolvers. Weaver and Richie crouched as low as they could under the weight of the video equipment and edged along the road under the trees. Green smoke immediately obscured their view and Weaver found herself stumbling over the EMS medic. The officer who had accosted them accidentally stuck his gun in Weaver's face. Two more smoke bombs exploded in front of the cars and they could hear the screams of the passengers and drivers. Then the officer heard a sound that scared him, a sound he'd heard before. It was the firing of an automatic rifle. The bullets were ripping into the trees, fifteen feet over their heads.

Weaver couldn't see anything in the smoke, but she could hear the panic. A car crashed, glass broke and feet clattered over the pavement. Small-arms fire broke out, but it sounded like tiny pops compared to the steady snap of the automatic rifle. Richie crawled up to Weaver's side, breathing hard. The bullets made whistling noises and Weaver thought she saw a thin trail of light fly across the sky. She turned and banged Richie on the head with the camera lens.

"Fuckin' A!"

"Roll, Richie!"

"Stand by. Ah, Christ!" Richie fumbled with the deck. "Speed!"

52

Weaver panned along the roadway. She saw a clearing under a layer of smoke and they moved forward. She stopped and listened to the shooting sounds. Richie swore at her and pushed her ahead.

"Where's it coming from, Rich?" She searched for the sound with the live camera. "Where's it coming from?"

"A gun, Weaver! A goddamn gun!"

"Stop tape!" Another smoke bomb exploded and they ran for the underpass and the safety of Central Park West.

Two minutes after the action at the 22nd Precinct station house, Harris was moving south on the West Drive. He had the Yamaha at sixty miles an hour going downhill toward Transverse Road Number Two. When he was about a hundred yards from the entrance to the Park, he downshifted and vaulted the curb into the trees. He stopped behind the high wall on Central Park West and moved on foot to a position that gave him a clear view of the intersection at 81st Street and the Hunter's Gate.

The traffic light was green and vehicles were traveling eastbound into the Park. Harris loaded the launcher and waited for the signal to turn red. When the crosstown traffic stopped and cars started moving north and south on Central Park West, he fired four smoke bombs into the center of the intersection and secured the launcher in its holster. He snapped a new clip into the AK-47. He heard the sound of brakes and a collision, but he saw nothing except a cloud of smoke. He aimed the rifle in the direction of the trees that lined the walk next to the Museum of Natural History and expended the entire load, precipitating screams from unseen pedestrians.

The Yamaha was idling smoothly and Harris jumped back on, removed an AK banana clip from one of the equipment sacks and reloaded. He saved the used clip. The new one was painted yellow to indicate that it was a blank-firing device. He was holding the AK between his legs and revving the bike when he felt a throbbing under his feet. A sound penetrated through the noise of horns and sirens coming from the street. The sound got louder and Harris was confused. He gripped the rifle and the sound became a roar, closer and closer, shrieking in his ears. He twisted in his seat, sweat pouring into his eyes. The ground vibrated; his nerves went out of control and every impulse told him to bury himself in the dirt and wait for dreadful, pounding explosions. At the last second, he realized that the IND express was hurtling by beneath the Park, uptown to Harlem and the Bronx.

Harris listened to the train rumble and fade. He smiled and licked the dry corners of his mouth. He was really getting into it now. Sensations and feelings were overwhelming him, changing the space, creating territories distant and familiar.

He kicked the bike into gear and jerked away from the under-growth onto the West Drive. He could see several cars and taxis on the transverse road, heading west. They were slowing down, soon to be stopped by the developing chaos outside the Park at the intersection of 81st Street. Harris decelerated, waited for a gap in the traffic, and rolled closer until he had a view east on the roadway. No more cars approached, so he shot across the transverse. He passed close enough to the rear of a taxi to see the back of a woman's head in the passenger seat.

Harris continued south on the West Drive and took the right fork, which led up to the Women's Gate entrance to the Park at 72nd Street. He was going to come very close to the street, perhaps only fifty yards from the block-long facade of the Dakota apartments. It was certainly the chanciest of his early maneuvers, but he needed to hit this area, since it was a major entrance to the Park. There was no traffic, because the 72nd Street road was closed on Sunday, but there was something else. People congregated near the entrance at night, to sit on the benches and drink wine or to make pickups of drugs and lovers. Harris wanted to terrify these people and send them back into the streets with a message of fear.

He stopped the bike at the top of a rise and looked out on a row of benches. Two men were within twenty feet of his position, but they did not hear Harris' approach. He watched two gay men come up the walk from the street and disappear into the darkness. Harris wasn't too happy to see this, although he knew that gay men rendezvoused inside the Park on the West Side between 72nd and 66th Streets. He decided to smoke them out.

The M-79 launcher had a range of 400 meters and Harris was accurate to every meter. He stayed on the bike and lobbed two smoke grenades into the intersection and two high in the air over the Park wall. The men closest to him turned around at the sound of the launcher and Harris let the bike roll back a few feet into the bushes. The devices exploded and he pointed the AK-47 at the two men and pulled the trigger. The blanks cracked off with bright flashes. One of the men fainted and the other rolled off the bench and covered his head with his hands.

Harris released the clutch and took the cycle into the roadway, firing the AK-47 as he went past the benches. Many of the strollers on the sidewalk were frozen in horror, mouths hanging open at the incredible sight of an automatic rifle firing directly into their faces. Some didn't react at all. They assumed they were dead.

Harris continued down the hill toward the Drive and back into the shadows of the Park. He emptied the clip of blanks and looked over his shoulder. People were running hysterically into the wall of smoke and across Central Park West. Harris hoped they wouldn't be hit by oncoming traffic.

He slipped the rifle over his shoulder and passed very close to a bench next to the curb. A derelict shopping bag lady watched him go by. Harris slowed and circled back. He was still moving as he removed the .45 automatic and fired three shots into the ground near the bench. The woman stood up, lifted her huge, stuffed shopping bags and shouted at him.

"Up yours! You bastard!" She trudged up the hill toward the smoke.

Harris arrived at 65th Street and Transverse Road Number One. He stood on the overpass and blooped smoke grenades into the traffic. A taxi came through the smoke and onto the roadway. Harris jammed a clip into the rifle and shot out the tires and headlights. The taxi swerved and crashed into the underpass beneath him. He was leaning over to see the wreckage when something caught his eye.

Harris heard a popping sound and spotted two policemen crouched behind their patrol car. They were stopped behind the layer of smoke and he hadn't seen the flashing lights on top of the car. The officers were shooting at him. Harris dropped behind the stone railing. He asked himself why there was always this astonishment, a kind of bemused wonder, when you first were fired on. Only when you grasped the fact that someone was trying to kill you, and this took but a few seconds, did the sick feeling come over you and the adrenaline start to rush. He felt it now, and his body twitched as he peeked over the railing.

He didn't want to return fire because he couldn't see the car clearly or the street behind. Headlights came out of the smoke and another patrol car careened to a stop on the walk. This car Harris could see clearly. He waited for the officers to get out and then pounded a steady stream of fire into the rear of the car. The gas tank exploded and the officers retreated to the avenue.

Smoke was drifting back into the Park, so Harris abandoned his position on the bridge and scrambled down into the bushes. Branches banged his helmet and stung his face. He stopped and caught his breath. Through the haze he could see the twinkling lights of Tavern on the Green. The restaurant was across the transverse, about a hundred yards away. It was all glass and plants and shiny fixtures, and Harris had an impulse. He loaded a smoke grenade into the launcher and fired it high in the air over the restaurant. It exploded on the roof and dropped down into the dining area.

Harris got back on the Yamaha and checked the time. He could not allow his exhilaration to get him into anything else impulsive. He rolled forward and watched the transverse. A taxi slowed as it approached Tavern on the Green, trying to avoid diners who were running out into the parking lot. The sound of sirens was continuous in the background.

He accelerated and stayed in the shrubbery along the road. He crossed over the bridle path, sliding in the mud, and passed through a tunnel under a walkway. Harris was going about forty miles an hour through trees when he flew by the Carousel and jumped the curb of the Drive. He was beyond the center of the Park and coming up fast on Fifth Avenue and the East Side. The West Side was finished.

Traffic was going into the Park at 66th Street and Fifth Avenue, but nothing was coming out a block away at 65th. Nobody on the sidewalks or in the elegant apartment buildings was aware of this fact. They might have been cognizant of the increase in noise, except that few things had greater ubiquity in New York than sirens. There had been a loud explosion from somewhere uptown, but explosions were not unusual and if it was important they would eventually hear about it.

Nothing was out of the ordinary until a taxi's tires blew out on the way into the Park and it slammed into the wall bordering the trees. The driver and passenger got out and bullets tore into the windshield.

Within two minutes the intersection of 66th Street and Fifth Avenue was a blanket of smoke and disabled vehicles. Pedestrians and police officers cowered behind buildings and inside apartment house lobbies. No one moved, traffic came to a halt and drivers fled their cars in panic. People were yelling that a sniper was on the roof or that terrorists were attacking one of the hotels. The police officers didn't know what to think, but they recognized automatic weapons fire, and that was something they were not prepared to confront.

Police dispatchers were overwhelmed with calls for assistance, coupled with reports of weapons fire and explosions on the avenues and streets surrounding Central Park. Three minutes after a call went out for Radio Motor Patrol cars to respond in the vicinity of 66th Street and Fifth Avenue, another call reported an attack at the 79th Street entrance to the Park. Automatic weapons fire and smoke grenades stopped traffic; two vehicles exploded and burned. Pedestrians sought shelter in the lobby of the Stanhope Hotel and on the steps of the Metropolitan Museum of Art.

Following the attack on 79th Street, a captain who had been monitoring the situation at the 20th Precinct requested available units for the 96th Street entrances to the Park, east and west, on Transverse Road Number Four. Although the information he had was sketchy and slightly hysterical, it seemed that the attacks were aimed at the entry points to Central Park, and the 96th Street entrances were the only ones where a disturbance had not been reported. If these entrances were next, following some sort of pattern or timetable, he wanted officers there first, and maybe they could nail the perpetrators. At the least, the officers could stop traffic and reduce the danger to civilians. He hoped he had reacted in time.

The first RMP car to arrive at 96th Street and Fifth Avenue came downtown from 110th Street at the edge of Harlem. The officers found a traffic jam developing, with cars backing up from 86th. They learned from the radio that a Fire Department vehicle had been disabled and fired on while answering a call on an explosion in Central

Park. Nevertheless, traffic was still entering the Park on the 96th Street transverse. Fortunately, it was Sunday night and traffic was light going east and west.

The officers pulled the car up on the sidewalk and took positions on either side of the transverse roadway. Another RMP car arrived and halted traffic at the intersection. Two officers on foot ran across Fifth Avenue and moved past the street sign on a walk north of the transverse. They held flashlights and edged into the Park until they had a clear view of the roadway and the surrounding terrain. They saw no one until lights approached from the West Side and a patrol car drove slowly around the curve, shining a spotlight into the undergrowth. The officers in the bushes tried to radio their positions so the patrol car would not be surprised to see them. They had difficulty getting patched through, so one of the men ran out into the roadway to signal the car with his flashlight.

The officer heard something. It was a small sound like the click of a lock falling into place. Then he was blown forward by an explosion. The force of the blast rocked the patrol car and the windshield was shattered. The officers inside lost control of the car and it rolled to a stop against the retaining wall. They heard something cracking. A shadow loomed over them. They jumped out as a huge elm tree slowly fell toward the car. They tried to run out from under the line of fall, but the tree collapsed across the roadway and they were buried beneath the branches.

Fifth Avenue was showered with debris. One of the officers near the entrance to the Park ran into the street and dropped to his knees, blood running from his face. Drivers and pedestrians were sprawled on the pavement. Another officer came out of the Park, dragging his partner by the back of the neck. He sat him on a bench near the curb and was turning to go back into the Park when some debris falling from above narrowly missed his head. It hit the pavement with a loud clang. The officer looked down. It was a piece of metal, yellow, with numbers painted on it. It said: 96 Street.

Harris was standing on the shore of the Lake, under the thick trees of the Ramble, the most heavily wooded area of Central Park. He was listening for a particular sound, one that would rise above the drone of sirens and the soft clicks of the Yamaha's cooling engine. The cycle was parked behind him with the equipment bags and the AK-47 stacked against the rear wheel.

A fish broke the surface of the Lake and sent ripples toward the shore. Harris removed his helmet and wiped the sweat from his forehead. An explosion went off somewhere uptown. Harris smiled and looked at his watch. 9:43. Twenty-eight minutes had passed, from the initial detonation at the station house, to the actions at the transverse entrances, to the bomb under the tree at 96th Street. The operation was on schedule.

Harris decided to take a minute to rest and sat down on the soft ground a few feet from the water. He was more tired than he had anticipated. The last twenty-four hours had pushed his concentration and energy to the limit. Harris had been in the Park from Saturday night until dawn Sunday, rigging the two bombs and readying supply points for quick access. He had known that this would be rigorous. When he had returned to his apartment early Sunday morning he had been exhausted and had tried to sleep, but excitement and his mind's constant review of logistics had kept him awake and he was feeling it now. He removed an amphetamine from the bottle in the pocket of his shirt.

Harris swallowed the pill and put a flashlight on his notebook of charts. From his major supply locations he would proceed to specific deployment sites within his mission radius, which in this case was the entire rectangle of Central Park. Harris had what he considered a vague

60

frame of time to set up as much of his arsenal as possible; he had to be fast and organized. He no longer could depend on a schedule. From now on his actions would be retaliations to counterattacks by outside forces. It wasn't possible to have a timetable for this or to know what the immediate response would be. Harris could only stand ready, based on assumptions and contingency plans.

He turned to the bike, attached the notebook under the seat to a special flange that permitted quick access, and secured the rifle and equipment sacks. He got on, started the bike and skidded through the mud and water of the Lake, north across the Ramble. The air cooled his face and already he could feel the amphetamine making his heart pound. He hoped the counterforces would be confused and would take their time. The longer they waited, the longer he had to dig in.

The NonstopNews station wagon was a prisoner surrounded by a yellow wall of taxis. Richie was loading the equipment into the rear of the car and Weaver was in the middle of Central Park West, standing on the bumper of a cab, trying to get a view downtown. Through a light haze of smoke, she could see nothing but stalled traffic and flashing emergency lights. Nothing moved. Behind her patrol cars were parked across the intersection of 86th Street, blocking entry into the Park. Officers were pushing and shoving with spectators and irate motorists, trying to move them from the avenue onto the side streets or back into the apartment buildings. Mounted officers were attempting to extricate two Fire Department vehicles from the jam of cars.

Richie yelled at Weaver and she went back to the station wagon. He was inside listening to the radios.

"Weav, they ain't lettin' no fire department or emergency vehicles into the park. Some sniper unloaded on the engine company comin' in from the East Side. I heard it. These dispatchers are goin' apeshit."

Weaver stuck her head inside the door of the car and listened for a moment. It was difficult, even for her, to make any sense out of the jumble of calls and reports. In a minute and a half she heard at least twenty ten-thirteens. A ten-thirteen was always a priority call; the dispatchers were pulling units from other jobs and emergencies to handle the situation. This indicated a backlog, and when there was a backlog, you could be getting assassinated and no police units would come to help you. Weaver knew that something completely out of control was going on.

The car phone buzzed and Weaver grabbed it.

"News!"

"Weaver, this is J.T. Where are you?"

"Dead in the water."

"What location?"

"Central Park West and 86th."

"Are you guys okay?"

"We got shot at is all."

"No shit."

"It was amazing. Wait'll you see it. But listen, J.T., we can't move. It took us twenty-five minutes to get back to the goddamn car. I wanna get back in the action, but it looks like it's gonna be on foot, so we gotta know what's our number one choice."

"Well, I'd forget that, man. From what I can tell, things is stopped all the way around the park."

"What?" Sirens were continuous and loud and Weaver was unable to hear.

"Yeah, Weav. Some maniacs, man, throwin' bombs and shit, all over Central Park."

"No kidding. I can't hear you. Wait a second." Weaver got inside the station wagon and she and Richie rolled up the windows. Richie still had to raise his voice so Weaver could hear him.

"What's he sayin'?"

"He's saying there's more and we aren't getting it." She turned back to the phone. "J.T., can you hear me?"

"Yeah."

"We heard another explosion about five minutes ago."

"That must've been 96th Street. They sent a whole lot of cops over there."

"Anything since then?"

"I don't think so. I keep hearin' weird shit—half of it probably ain't real."

"Okay. I gotta go. Stay there. We'll be in touch. Bye."

She hung up and wiped sweat from her face with the sleeve of her T-shirt. A black smear stained the material. She looked out the window and saw bright lights moving on the sidewalk in front of Central Park. They were lights from sun guns carried by a camera crew and a reporter she recognized.

"WCBS, Rich." She watched the crew set up and start to interview a police officer and people in the crowd. Kids pressed up against the reporter and clowned for the camera, waving and gesturing, shouting expletives over the drone of sirens and police loudspeakers. Richie laughed.

"Man on the street. Ask the fuckin' skells, man, they always know everything."

"I wonder if that's live. It could be a bulletin. I wish we had a TV in the car, we got everything else."

"Call J.T. back and ask him."

"Screw it, there's not time." Weaver ran things over in her mind. She couldn't be sure, but it appeared that attacks had been made on entry points to Central Park. WCBS had sent a crew to 86th Street, but she was willing to bet the crew had been sent out after the station house exploded and just didn't make it anywhere close because of the traffic.

Weaver had been considering taking the camera on foot down Central Park West and taping whatever confusion appeared interesting. What would be the point now, if the affiliates were covering that? She didn't want to miss any more shooting, but it sounded like that had died down—and how could she get to it anyway, in this mess? Besides, she had tape in the deck right now that nobody else had and everybody wished they did. She turned to Richie.

"Here's what we're going to do. I'm taking the tape we made over to WABC. It's about ten minutes to ten, so we can forget the independent stations. I'll be lucky to get this around to everybody else in time for the eleven o'clocks. You stay here with the camera. Any break in the traffic, you move the car. Take it back to the apartment, but wherever, you let J.T. know. I'll find you. We just have to be mobile, that's all."

"Okay, Weav. Are you walkin' to 66th Street?"

Weaver thought about that for a moment. "No, it looks too crazy. I'm taking the subway." She collected the two cassettes from Richie and looked at herself in the mirror. "I look disgusting." Richie pointed at the street. The WCBS crew was interviewing a fireman and behind him a mounted officer was poised on his horse. The horse's tail was arched in the air and huge piles of dung were dropping to the pavement. Richie and Weaver glanced at each other.

"It's the best thing CBS will get all night." Weaver straightened her hair and jumped out of the car. Richie watched her run uptown toward 86th Street and the entrance to the IND subway. He moved over to the driver's seat. He thought he'd call up J.T. and tell him what it was like to hear bullets flying over your head.

Weaver was about to go down the stairs into the IND 86th Street station when the rumbling and screeching of a train came from below the steps. She ran down the stairs, cursing, certain that the downtown local was pulling out of the station and that it would be twenty minutes before another train made the stop. The tracks were empty, but she could still hear the roar receding in the tunnel. She bought a token and asked the man in the booth if she'd just missed the local. He hardly looked at her from behind the wall of Plexiglas as he spoke into the microphone.

"They just keep coming, lady. I don't have anything to do with it."

Weaver smiled sarcastically. "Next stop: oblivion. Right?" The man ignored her. She put her token into the turnstile and walked to the uptown end of the platform, where she could get on the rear of the train. There were only two or three people waiting on the platform, one of them a young man standing in front of a bench. Weaver spoke to him.

"I guess that wasn't the local, otherwise you wouldn't be standing here."

The young man seemed surprised that anyone would speak to him. When he turned to Weaver, dressed in an expensive suit, a leather attaché case at his feet, she knew right away that he was out of place in the subway. He was very good-looking and Weaver felt suddenly embarrassed at her appearance. The young man smiled at her, a nice smile, and loosened his tie.

"That was the express, I think. I hate the goddamn subway. It's like a ride through hell."

Weaver laughed. "I've thought that myself."

"It's unbelievable outside. I sat in a taxi for twenty minutes. I finally gave up."

"And now you've been down here for fifteen minutes."

The young man nodded. He pointed at Weaver's laminated press credential, hanging from a chain around her neck. "Are you a reporter?"

"Not exactly." Weaver looked down at the credential, at the cassettes. She could feel him watching her.

"Do you know what's going on?" he asked.

"I can't tell you too much right now. There've been some bombings, and a sniper. We have it on tape."

"Really? Who do you work for, one of the television stations?"

"No, I'm independent. We make spec tape."

"I've read about that. They call you guys the 'gore squad.' "

Weaver winced. "Yeah, that's what they call us." She could see that the young man regretted saying it.

"You don't like that name, do you?"

Weaver shook her head. Her company hadn't existed five years ago when a writer doing an article on the independent news services for *New York* magazine coined the term "gore squad," but it was a simplification. Her job was a lot more than ambulance chasing.

She heard rumbling sounds and used it as an excuse to step away and lean out over the platform for a view up the dark tunnel. The rails glowed in the distance and two headlights appeared between the tracks. She wanted to talk to this guy before the train arrived; she wanted to straighten him out.

She guessed it was because this was the second time tonight someone had made her feel defensive about her job. She was thinking about the man at the fire who had grabbed her and tried to wreck her camera. Weaver understood the guy's anger, but it was like she'd told him —she had a job to do. It reminded her of the gay demonstrations that she and Richie had covered in the Village a month ago. She knew that sticking her camera into the crowd was going to anger the demonstrators, that they would try to rough up any newspeople, which they did. Her camera got knocked around; there was an ugly scene and it looked great on tape. But that was her responsibility, to tell a story, to make it interesting. The news business depended on ugliness and tragedy. If she had had

66

the time to talk to the man at the fire, she would have explained to him the axiom: Tragedy sells.

Weaver stepped back from the edge of the platform. She glanced at the guy in the suit and he was still watching her. She didn't care what he thought of her work—she didn't care what any man thought. She had her own company; she didn't depend on anybody. The gore squad. Screw it. It was great. There was a lot of satisfaction in knowing that ten million people were watching something she shot on television. If it was gory, if it was irrational —so what? It was exciting, and that made news, and Weaver was involved with news.

She turned back to the guy, but the noise of the train was overwhelming. A hot, foul wind blew through her hair and the AA local roared into the station. The doors opened and the guy walked forward on the platform and went into another car. Weaver stepped into the car in front of her and a voice over the intercom told the passengers to "watch the closing doors."

When the doors closed, Weaver leaned against them. She shifted the cassettes in her hands. She shrugged. Maybe she'd run into the guy again. Maybe they could be friends. But she wasn't going to kid herself. She knew that in New York, even though he was in the next subway car, he might as well be in another country.

The train jerked forward and continued the trip downtown.

Weaver got off the AA local at Columbus Circle. She contemplated transferring to the IRT and riding uptown to 66th Street, but decided it would take too much time. She exited to the street. Central Park West was in bad shape, with police officers trying to reroute traffic onto Broadway and over to Ninth and Tenth Avenues. Weaver circled the Gulf & Western building and ran uptown on Broadway, all the way to 66th Street. The WABC studios were in the middle of the block, between Broadway and Central Park, and the street was blocked off at both ends by police cars.

Weaver went into the building. The security guard checked her credentials and she hurried downstairs to the newsroom. The activity on the floor was more hectic than on any of her previous visits. Assignment editors were shouting into telephones that rang incessantly. Production assistants were running between the desks and in and out of offices on the perimeter of the room. The eleven o'clock anchorman was at the rear of the newsroom, watching a color monitor tuned in to WABC and eating a sandwich. Weaver spotted an assignment editor she knew and went over to his desk. He was on the phone, but she spoke to him anyway.

"Is Roger Stein down here?"

The assignment editor looked up and recognized Weaver. He put his hand over the mouthpiece and stuck his nose close to her arm. "You smell funny. How you doin'?"

"Terrific. Is Stein down here?"

"Yeah, go on back." He returned to his phone conversation.

Weaver saw Stein come out of his office and she walked over. Stein was the managing editor of WABC Eyewitness News and when Weaver wanted to sell tape to the station, Stein was the man who made the decisions. He was young, Weaver thought about thirty-five, and he'd been a strong advocate of the independent news services. The unions didn't always appreciate this, but Stein wanted coverage, and he wanted sensational tape if it was available. The union crews couldn't always provide that coverage, particularly since they did not usually work at night, and overtime was ludicrously expensive. Weaver and her competitors received a flat one hundred dollars for any tape used in a story on the air, whether one second or fifteen minutes of tape was broadcast. Stein considered that a good deal for the station and he didn't care what the unions said. As long as the independent services were covering only breaking news stories, which was a gray area depending on the time before the top of the show, and were not receiving assignments from his editors, then nobody was in violation of union rules. Stein knew that his people cheated a little, in the late hours, and called the stringers out in the field to make sure that they didn't miss a potentially big story, but nobody was arguing with his methods. Channel 7 Eyewitness News was rated number one in an area with an audience of twenty million viewers.

Stein watched Weaver approach. Her eyes were darting all over the place and she looked like she was vibrating under her skin. These kids riding the streets, he thought, they were reckless and undisciplined, but that's what made them so effective.

"Good evening, Weaver." He leaned over and sniffed her. "What's that smell?"

"Smoke, guns, you name it. It is wild out there."

"That's what I hear. Tell me what's happening."

"I don't know, but it's rich. Picture this: I had to ditch the car and leave my camera assistant up on 86th Street. Did you know 66th is all closed off with cops?"

"Fuck it. I feel safer that way." An assignment editor yelled at Stein and he shouted back. "Tell him I can't talk to him right now." His attention went back to Weaver. "Okay. What have you got?"

"Pulitzer stuff." She handed him the cassettes and he read the notes on the labels.

"You got the bomb going off?"

"I jerked up a little, I admit it, but it's there."

"Shooting?"

"It was insane. Real John Wayne shit. We got about a minute or so."

"Shooting, that's great. What's this?"

"That fire in Harlem."

Stein read Richie's notes. "Jesus, you did fantastic, Weaver. I'll see what we can use."

"Can you make dubs real fast? I'd like to run this stuff over to CBS and NBC, if I can make it by the deadline."

"Fair enough." It was perfectly kosher for the services to sell the same footage to more than one station, since there was no copyright on news. Stein was pleased that she'd brought the tapes to him first, so he was happy to expedite the tape transfer and get Weaver on her way. He called to a production assistant.

"Bobby, I need immediate dubs." The tapes were hustled away and Stein went into his office, shutting the door in Weaver's face. She wasn't finished talking, so she pushed in behind him. A color monitor, tuned to WABC, was set up on a coffee table in front of a sofa. Weaver turned the volume down on a movie. Stein sat down at his desk and tried to ignore Weaver and his ringing telephone.

"Have you got crews out, Roger?"

Stein shrugged. "Anybody we could get our hands on in the last half hour. Tonight must be a stringer's dream."

"We'll do all right. Listen. Why don't you tell the guys on the desk to give us a shot once in a while? And don't tell me they're not supposed to."

Stein didn't want to talk about this, so he answered his phone. He spoke angrily to the person at the other end. "I can't now. We've got about sixty seconds to a news bulletin. Check the wire services." He hung up and looked at Weaver. "You still here?"

"Come on, Roger. One of your night editors called our competition on that bomb in the precinct house."

"Christ, you guys are wired into everything." He studied Weaver's face. Her wild eyebrows were twirled up and she looked quite sinister. Stein wanted to ask her out. "Remember, Weaver, you're still the new girl on the block. We've been doing business with the other services for a couple of years. Get a track record, then we'll know you better."

"If I don't go broke first."

"I know how tough it is working for yourself."

"Me and the bank."

"Don't worry, there's never a lack of breaking news in New York. And there is never going to be enough technology to keep our asses covered."

Stein opened a drawer in his desk and removed a release form for Weaver to sign.

"Okay, Roger. But believe me, it's going to be hard to beat what I brought you tonight. Marty or no Marty."

The movie on the monitor went to a commercial and then was followed by a graphic indicating a news bulletin. Stein waved at Weaver.

"Sign this. And turn the goddamn volume back up." She adjusted the television and listened to an announcer's voice over a picture of a podium with microphones.

". . . emergency press conference here in the muster room of the Twentieth Precinct. There will be a statement concerning the attacks within and around Central Park, just about an hour ago."

Weaver went over to Stein's desk. "Is that WABC cameras?"

"No. It's a pool. The Mayor's Office announced to us about ten o'clock."

On the television, a woman stepped up to the microphones. Weaver turned her back on the TV and tried to listen to the press conference, but something distracted her while she signed the release. Her signature seemed different, bigger, the letters long and slashing. Weaver stopped writing. She looked at her hand. Her fingers were shaking. She looked at Stein to see if he had noticed, but his attention was focused on the TV. He had a strange expression on his face. Weaver glanced at the set, then back to Stein.

"What did she say, Roger?"

He reached for his telephone. "Central Park is closed."

Harris was riding hard, zigzagging across the Park on perimeter surveillance, when he observed police vehicles sealing off the major intersections and the absence of traffic flow on the transverse roads. He was anticipating this, because then he could plan on relative freedom of movement for an unspecified amount of time. He returned directly to his major supply dump, near Transverse Road Number Two, in an abandoned aqueduct beneath the surface of Central Park.

Harris had discovered this old structure, in reality a six foot-high masonry pipe, along with a variety of abandoned four-and-five-foot-diameter pipes, diagrams of the old receiving reservoir, and existing and defunct water mains, while posing as a student and going over sewer plans at a city facility in Queens. Over a period of several autumn nights, Harris had tried to locate the aqueduct, digging down several feet into the ground until he was stopped by the top of the masonry wall. The stone had crumbled away easily and Harris was delighted to find a huge tunnel, in which he could stand erect, extending fifty yards in either direction. The ends were filled in with sand and the only access was his tiny, concealed opening from above. Later, Harris had conducted similar excavations and located old water mains and pipes, providing additional large underground areas for storage and, if necessary, hideouts. Interestingly, some of the sewer plans had been incorrect and he was unable to locate several conduits, but there had been a bonus as well. Harris found a long stretch of sixty-inch pipe where he could go through one tiny entrance and come out either of two exits, a hundred yards away. None of this pipe was indicated on the city sewer plans.

Now, on July 21, after Harris had observed the sealing-off of the Park, he could resume deploying some of the tons of weapons and supplies in the old aqueduct dump.

His first objective was the installation of antipersonnel devices for immediate defense and security against an attacking force: claymore mines, fragmentation mines, barbed wire and booby traps. All weapons and ammunition were segregated within the supply dump, but Harris had memorized and assiduously reviewed the precise spacings so that he could find anything, even in absolute darkness. Given the ability to move material with such alacrity, within minutes he was implanting claymore mines near the entrance of his underground storage area.

Harris liked the claymore mine. It looked like a curved, rectangular box, about ten inches long, resting on six-inch folding metal legs. The base was made from molded polystyrene and fiber glass. Seven hundred steel shards were imbedded in a plastic matrix at the front of the base. Behind the matrix was an explosive charge. When it was detonated, the shards dispersed in a single plane, in a 60-degree pattern one to five feet above the ground, to a lethal range of about 250 meters. The 3.2-pound mine was installed by unfolding the legs and positioning the device above the ground, aiming the horizontally convex face in the direction of potential enemy movement. The mine could be fired remotely by pulling a trip wire attached to the base, or the trip wire could be extended across a trail or road, where it could be disturbed, triggering the explosion. The claymore was particularly suited for security near a manned position or firebase, or an ambush position, because it could be precisely aimed and fired remotely. For Harris the claymore meant two things: he could set claymores up along the perimeter of the Park, near the walls, without the danger of fragments flying into the streets if an intruder triggered one of the devices. Secondly, when they were in place in the area around the supply dump, even if the worst happened in the next few hours and Harris had to retreat underground, he could defend the position and probably ambush and eliminate a large force; that is, once they were lured into the field of claymores.

It took Harris about an hour to complete work on the claymores, including work begun in the aftermath of the 96th Street explosion and interruptions for occasional surveillance trips. Harris noted the mine locations in his charts. He realized that he could have spent more time setting up additional devices, but he had to move on to other material. When committed to specific areas, these supplies would give Harris control of whole sections of terrain and permit certain tactics. This required the barbed wire, fragmentation mines and booby traps.

The idea wasn't complicated: using the concertina wire to block major walkways and open sections of ground, he could create "corridors" which any intruders would find it necessary to enter in order to execute a move of any distance or duration. It was analogous to a boxer "cutting the ring"—reducing his opponent's movement and forcing him to take punches.

The positioning of the wire was the first step in creating these deadly corridors. Harris had spent two eight-hour nights in June carting the big, flat bundles of wire into the Park in a rented van. He had to dig a special hole large enough to get the bundles down into one of the old water mains. Then, two nights ago, he had hauled them all back out and distributed them to various deployment sites. Finally he'd gotten sick of it and dumped some of the bundles in the bushes without covering them. If anybody found them, they'd assume the Parks Department was going to put them to some use.

From these sites, Harris began to unroll the wire into huge coils, adhering to the plans outlined in his charts. He concentrated on an area south of the 79th Street transverse, including the Lake and the Ramble, as well as the area east of the Sheep Meadow and the Mall. This sector, with its heavy undergrowth and variety of terrain, was the logical choice for engaging an initial probe by outside forces.

Harris used the motorcycle like a horse to extend the concertina wire in long lines through the trees and bushes. Unless someone was expecting it, sections of the wire were almost invisible in the darkness until the person was right on top of the coils. Harris tried to exploit this feature wherever possible, but the work was exhausting and in sixty minutes he had only about 80 percent of the concertina in position. Nevertheless, he was satisfied that the network of wire barriers gave him an adequate strategic advantage over ground-force movement in the sector.

Next Harris returned to various locations along the wire barriers where, during the preceding weeks, he had buried containers of M-16 A1 fragmentation mines. The 8-pound device was activated by a trip wire or by direct pressure, which resulted in a spring-loaded mine being thrown three feet into the air and exploding with an effective casualty radius of 33 yards.

Working as fast as possible, Harris removed the frag mines from their containers and concealed them in patterns tangent to the lines defined by the long coils of wire. He had to follow carefully a design worked out in advance on his charts, not only so that he wouldn't end up stepping on the mines himself, but because he didn't want to create a situation in which he could get trapped inside one of his own corridors. The pattern was relatively simple and keyed off visible landmarks, so that he could move quickly in a hot area without having to think about it.

Harris worked furiously on the frag mines for forty-five minutes, sacrificing safe handling for speed. He threw in a pair of claymores for good measure. When he was finished, the number of implanted devices still seemed pitifully small, but there wasn't anything he could do about it. He was getting nervous and decided to make a quick pass along the Park perimeter to see what was happening out in the street.

Harris hurried up the East Side and back down the West Side, bringing the Yamaha close to the Park wall, sometimes within twenty yards of the street. He observed that traffic on Fifth Avenue and on Central Park West was still moving slowly. Police activity seemed to be confined to expending traffic evacuation and keeping pedestrians away from the sidewalks bordering the Park, but the number of police vehicles was greater at the intersection of the 86th Street transverse and Central Park West. Harris lingered there. It appeared that police personnel were attempting to close off Central Park West from some point north. Still, nothing indicated an immediately threatening situation. Harris could see that the police were having difficulty clearing the perimeter streets and sorting out the confusion. Almost two hours had passed since the final explosion at 96th Street. Harris was glad as hell to have the time.

He returned to the 79th Street sector and began work on the booby traps. Many of the devices had been prepared in advance and were in various stages of readiness. They wouldn't demand much time to become operational. Harris traveled on the bike or on foot to the locations marked on his charts, where he exposed trip wires, embedded components and set release mechanisms. He ran a test on one device and found it to be deadly accurate.

Harris considered booby traps important for two reasons: once they were discovered, usually the hard way, they necessitated a casualty evacuation and precipitated slower enemy movement. The second reason was psychological. When a man witnessed the awful ripping and piercing of flesh from some silent and unseen "thing," he began to doubt the efficacy of his mission. It was simple. Booby traps terrified everybody.

Harris armed approximately fifteen devices. This phase of the operation took another forty minutes, including periodic checks of the Park perimeter, and left Harris kneeling on the ground, sweat dripping down from his face into a shallow pit dug parallel to a walk near the West Drive. The walk was intersected and blocked by a long roll of concertina wire angling into the bushes and up the tree-lined hill to Central Park West. Anyone approaching this position had three choices: retreat and find another avenue of approach; try to cut through the wire, which required tools and presented a target in open ground for long, crucial moments; abandon the walk and follow the path of the wire, right or left, into the undergrowth. This last choice was the one Harris had been anticipating when he dug the pit moments ago—but the equipment necessary to complete preparations was not in a secondary supply hole west of the walk in the trees. In fact, there wasn't even a hole.

Harris got up and ran to the cycle parked on the walk. He was angry with himself. Where was the goddamn hole? He yanked the notebook from under the seat and fumbled through the pages. More sweat dripped, smearing some of his notations. He stopped, set the charts on the seat and took a drink from a canteen attached to the belt around his waist. He thought he'd better stop and rest for a while; maybe resume perimeter surveillance for twenty minutes; at least pace himself, because stamina was soon going to be important. Right now he was exhausted and dehydrated.

Harris finished the rest of the canteen and reminded himself to refill at the water fountain near the bowling greens. He picked up the charts and tried to figure out where the missing hole was. Now he remembered. He was going to booby-trap both sides of the walk, so the hole was probably east, not west.

He didn't bother with the charts, but took the flashlight behind two tall trees twenty feet to the left of the walk. The supply hole was there, containing about fifty footlong bamboo stakes cut into sharp, pointed spikes. The stakes were stacked on top of a cloth sheet; Harris folded the ends together and moved the whole load to the shallow pit. He embedded the stakes in the ground, creating a tiny forest inside the pit, and in a similar hole on the opposite side of the walk. The holes were covered with a loose mat of foliage and twigs. Harris leaned back and admired them. There they were: your average punji-stick booby traps. *Let* somebody run into that wire barrier and decide to make a little detour.

Harris laughed to himself and stood up. His legs buckled from dizziness. That was it for the tactical setup in the 79th Street sector. He needed a quick rest. He couldn't count on any more time before a probe from the outside.

Harris cleaned up the area, storing a shovel and other tools in one of the supply holes, and drove the Yamaha south through a safe passage in one of the corridors. He stopped at the bowling greens next to the concession building and located one of his hidden C-ration packages. He drank some water and swallowed salt pills and vitamins, following them with a sandwich, which tasted lousy. He finished up and decided to go straight to 86th Street.

Harris drove around the Great Lawn and cruised past the smoldering remains of the 22nd Precinct station house. The transverse road was deserted, so Harris continued west, keeping just off the walkways, and crossed the Drive. He felt relaxed and a bit drowsy, but when he returned to the intersection of 86th Street and Central Park West he snapped back to attention. A torch beam aiming down from the Park wall flashed within two feet of his front wheel. He was forced to veer sharply into the trees, thudding over a rock outcropping and slicing into a row of bushes. The bike stopped on its own and Harris tumbled off.

He caught his breath, parked the bike and moved quickly south to Summit Rock—at 140.3 feet above sea level, the second highest point in the Park. The huge mound of stone afforded him a commanding view of the Mariner's

Gate, 85th and 86th Streets, and uptown on the avenue. The first person Harris saw through the field glasses was a man walking on the street, dressed in olive-drab combat dress, wearing a flak jacket, and carrying an M-16 automatic rifle. The street was empty; he could see police sawhorse barricades blocking the side streets perpendicular to the avenue. Then he scanned farther uptown and saw two large police vans and something he'd never seen before. It was a huge, shiny truck, like a mobile home, with several antennas on the roof and no windows. Letters on the side spelled NYPD. A group of about ten men in combat dress, holding automatic rifles, loitered around the truck. Some of the men were shining flashlights into the Park, the beams playing over the dark trees and poking through to the walks and roadway. Two police cars turned onto Central Park West and screeched to a stop in front of one of the tall apartment buildings. Officers held the doors open for two men in suits, who got out and went into the giant NYPD truck.

Harris climbed down from Summit Rock and crouched low in the bushes. He was breathing hard. He thought things over for a minute.

The police were going to make a move. They appeared to have made one smart decision already: they were coming in at 86th Street, the dead center of the Park. In the best of circumstances Harris had hoped for, the probe would have begun all the way at the top of Central Park, on 110th Street. He hadn't touched that half of the Park, except for the bomb on 96th. The police would have wasted two hours on what amounted to nothing more than a long approach march, just to get south of 86th, where all the action was going to take place. Somebody in the Police Department must have figured that out and assigned priority to the bottom half of Central Park. For Harris it meant that instead of having two extra hours to dig in, he would now have to hurry back to the supply dumps and get ready to beat the bushes.

Harris moved quietly back to the dirt bike. He could see a man in a flak jacket out on the street, not more than a few yards away. For safety's sake Harris didn't start the motor. He rolled the bike across the Drive, east toward the Great Lawn. He got on and raised the field glasses to his eyes. He panned across the lawn, south in the direction of the supply dumps. For now there would be no more installations of antipersonnel devices, no more digging around. The time had come to deploy the weapons he was going to use in person—weapons that were called "small arms." Harris found that term humorous. When they hit somebody, nothing seemed so goddamn small.

David Dix, the Deputy Mayor for Criminal Justice, was in a limousine moving up Amsterdam Avenue. Traffic was bad. In fact, it had taken ten minutes to get from the 20th Precinct on West 82nd Street to the corner of Amsterdam and West 85th Street, a distance of about five hundred yards. At this rate, Dix was going to arrive at his destination, 86th and Central Park West, in about an hour.

One of the three telephones in the rear of the limo buzzed and he answered. A very polite female police officer asked Dix if he could estimate the time of his arrival at 86th and Central Park West. Dix told her to hold on and tapped the partition in the middle of the car. The limo's driver slid back the Plexiglas window.

"Yes, sir."

"Say something to me, Bobby."

"The traffic is a bitch."

"Thank you." The driver returned the window to its place and Dix took the woman off hold.

"Officer, it'll probably be another fifteen minutes. Has the Commissioner arrived yet?"

"Affirmative."

Affirmative. Jesus Christ, Dix thought. "Tell the Commissioner I can walk over there in five minutes, if he'd like me to do that."

The woman put him on hold and then came back. Her voice was steady.

"The Commissioner said that you should stay in the car because of the unsafe condition on the streets, sir. He said to tell you that if anything happened to you the Mayor would be upset. Is that clear? Sir."

"Affirmative." Dix hung up. He and Robert Keller, the Police Commissioner of the City of New York, tolerated a relationship whose incipient adversary quality was rooted in the bureaucratic structure. The Deputy Mayor for Criminal Justice was the liaison between the Mayor's Office and the Police Department. When the Mayor wanted the cops to do something, Dix carried the message. Of course, the Mayor never "told" the Department to do anything. He suggested. It was Dix's responsibility to make the Mayor's demands sound like "suggestions." He was the classic man in the middle, the man taking the heat. But the position had prestige, particularly for someone thirty-four years old and on the way up.

Dix's job was really more than being a messenger. He participated in planning and strategy meetings, handled criticism and kept the Mayor informed on important police operations. Occasionally Dix performed these functions in public, as he had during the emergency press conference just completed in the 20th Precinct station house.

Ordinarily, Liz Mayberry, the Deputy Commissioner for Public Information, the DCPI, who was attached to the Department, conducted press conferences on police matters. But there had not been time, in the aftermath of the bombings and attacks, to adequately brief the DCPI on the entire situation. The explosion at the Central Park precinct house so astonished everyone, and led to so many confused reports, that the Mayor had asked Dix to sort things out before anybody went on the air and screwed things up.

The first thing Dix had done was call in the deputy chief in charge of the Intelligence Division. They had a

**81**

quick meeting in the back of the limo, the gist of which was that there hadn't been any recent activity from the known terrorist groups or militant political organizations. Dix reported this to the Mayor, who said it was too bad they didn't have anyone to blame the damn thing on; that Dix should use his discretion in handling any questions; that in particular he should avoid comment on a certain subject for which Dix had been given a folder containing a police report; and finally that it was the Mayor's advice to keep things vague and act calm. That was important: be very calm.

Dix thought that was a good idea, so he asked the driver to let the deputy chief off at Rockefeller Center. Dix waited until the chief was in a taxi and then ran around the corner to Charley O's and had a double martini. He felt nice and calm for the ride uptown.

They arrived at the 20th Precinct about two minutes before the scheduled opening of the press conference. Dix had no time to talk with Liz Mayberry, or to show her the contents of the folder. He tried to remain inconspicuous behind the podium at the front of the muster room, but it was difficult with all the cameras and lights. He liked to avoid public statements, because once the press zeroed in on any official, they never left the person alone. He'd found that out the hard way, while serving as an information officer in Vietnam.

Liz began the live broadcast by reading a prepared statement regarding the closing of Central Park and the traffic situation, with the usual plea for cooperation. She concluded with a reminder that there was no need to panic, no one had been killed or seriously injured, and all available manpower was working to apprehend the individuals responsible for the attacks. And so forth. The reporters immediately shouted out the obvious questions: Who was responsible for the attacks? No leads. Any terrorist group demands, any hostages? Liz glanced at Dix and he shook his head, almost imperceptibly. No, the Intelligence Division reported nothing. Very good, Liz. Next question.

Can you verify a report that Emergency Service attack squads are about to enter Central Park? Nobody had had a chance to tell Liz about that. She frowned in disgust.

Dix stepped to the microphones. "Mike, you know we can't talk about deployment."

"Doesn't the Department have rather complex scenarios for dealing with terrorists?"

"Right now we don't know if anyone's still inside the park."

"Then what are all those officers with automatic rifles doing on Central Park West?"

Dix remembered the double martini. "The Department has contingency plans. Had them for years. That's about all I can tell you, except that everyone should stay away from Central Park, and in one to two hours we'll be able to restore normal traffic flow. Thank you."

A pro in action; neat, clean, calm. Dix started to step away from the podium when another reporter shouted over the noise. Everyone fell silent. Dix recognized the voice, a feisty little AP guy who always seemed to single Dix out for punishment.

"Mr. Dix, one last question. There was a phoned-in bomb threat in advance of the station house bombing, isn't that correct?"

There it was. "I believe so."

"I have it from a source at City Hall that a lone man, a sort of self-styled guerrilla, is claiming sole responsibility for the attacks. Is that also correct?"

Dix fidgeted with the folder in his hands. He could feel Liz staring at his back. Maybe he should let her answer the question. No, that would be too unfair. He looked out at the cameras.

"I can't comment on that at this time."

And that's how the press conference had ended: one question too late. Dix didn't say a word to Liz Mayberry and ignored the crowd of reporters who followed him into the street.

Now that he was alone in the limo, he removed the folder from his briefcase and reread the police report inside. It was a transcript of the phone call made to City Hall at approximately 2100. The call was more than a bomb threat. There was something that disturbed Dix, something that gave the caller's warning a tingle of credibility.

The limo shot through a break in traffic and Dix was distracted from his thoughts. The car turned east onto 86th Street and crossed Columbus Avenue. Ahead, Dix could see patrol cars blocking off Central Park West. Uniformed Officers waved the limo through and the driver stopped the car on the west side of the avenue. A police van roared into the block and stopped behind the car. A chrome nameplate on the van's rear doors said: FLEETSTAR 2070A. The doors flew open and Dix watched five officers in combat dress jump out with M-16 rifles.

The driver held the limo door and Dix crossed the avenue. It was empty of cars and pedestrians, north and south for fifty blocks. A few newspeople were standing under an apartment building awning across the street from Mobile Command Post Truck 1. The city owned four of these huge trucks, each complete with sophisticated communications equipment, TV scanners, maps, radios, even living accommodations. Dix wondered if he could get a cocktail inside.

He was cleared by an officer, went up some steps, and entered the main communications area. Radio noise was loud. Technicians were busy testing the control console. Dix headed for a group of men conferring over a large, detailed map of Central Park. One of them was Commissioner Keller.

Keller looked like an actor with a Ph.D. He was an imposing man, intelligent, articulate. Dix respected him, as he did the other men in the room, although he was sure they didn't know it. At least two of them had, more than once, referred to Dix as a pain in the ass. He promised himself that tonight he would suppress his normal insouciance.

Keller greeted him and made room at the table.

"David, you know Chief Curran." Curran was Borough Commander for Manhattan North; another very sharp guy. Curran nodded.

"Chief Curran," Dix acknowledged.

"Do you know Julianno, captain of the two-two precinct?"

The ex-two-two precinct, Dix thought. "Sure. I'm glad you're all right."

"I wasn't near the building at the time."

The last man at the table was dressed in dark green combat clothes. He was Don Eubank, the assistant chief commanding Emergency Services. He was about forty-five, Dix thought. His body was hard and lean like a young athlete's, but the eyes, weary and brutal, betrayed his age and the ruinous stress of his occupation.

Whenever Eubank was on the scene, his command superseded everybody's—except, of course, the Commissioner's. In this case, even though Borough Commander Curran outranked Eubank, he would step back and let Eubank call the shots. Still, Central Park was Curran's backyard and he'd have something to say about strategy.

Eubank didn't always go into the field—it was called a "ride-out"—unless the Department anticipated a big operation. Tonight was big. Dix thought he'd seen at least three Emergency Service squads and assorted personnel otuside the command post. Emergency Service officers were specially trained and armed, and were experts in hostage situations and anti-terrorist operations. While the New York Police Department's special officers were not quite in the same league as Britain's Special Air Service commandos, or the United States' own Special Forces

Blue Light unit, many experts considered them extremely competent and the equal of any of the FBI's counter-terror personnel. In other U.S. cities, these special units were known as SWAT, an acronym that Eubank considered "some shithead TV name." Dix had allowed this name to slip from his mouth only once, but Eubank had regarded him warily ever since.

Eubank was a lifelong cop; his training and his contact with criminals, with violence, was based entirely on experiences in New York City. He'd survived because he was a smart, hard-core tactician—competent, aggressive, dangerous. He was never conservative when it came to experimenting with new police technology. He'd try anything once—chemicals, lasers, satellites—just so long as it gave the Department an edge.

Looking at Eubank, Dix was reminded of a story, possibly true, dating from about two years ago, when an ex-NYPD detective had gone berserk, held his wife and kids hostage in their house somewhere in Queens, and demanded a jet to fly him to East Germany. The man, armed with a shotgun, had kept two Emergency Service squads at bay for nine hours. He'd shot one of his kids and shoved the little boy out the door to prove he was serious. Finally Eubank was called to the scene, walked to the front of the house and stood on the lawn where the ex-detective could see him. Ten seconds later, the man threw the shotgun out a window and gave up.

Eubank acknowledged Dix. "How you doing, Dix? Bullshit anybody today?"

"I'm fine, Chief. Going hunting?"

Keller interjected, "Don, let's continue." Keller pointed at the map. "What about fire alarm headquarters on the seven-nine transverse?" He was referring to the Fire Department building inside the Park. It housed a computer system, complete with large electronic maps that indicated the status of fire personnel, equipment, and alarm boxes.

86

Several dispatchers and operators would have been in the building during the attacks.

Curran answered. "It's been shut down. Queens will be the covering borough. New York Tel and 911 have been notified."

"Aren't there water plant operators in the south gate house on the reservoir?"

"It's right across the street from the two-two house. We evacuated them when the station went down."

Eubank circled a detail on the map. "What's that?"

Julianno leaned over to see. "I don't know. Might be a rock outcropping."

Eubank snorted. "Look, maps are great, but I need accuracy when I'm in the field. What is this, about nine hundred acres?"

Curran asked Julianno, "Is your highway safety man on duty? He knows more about this park than anybody."

"I'll find out, sir. He may be in the two-oh after the house was blown up."

"Well, send a car for him and get his ass in here." Julianno moved to a telephone at the back of the room. Eubank pulled the map around so they all could see.

"Here it is. We're gonna make a grid search; three five-man squads. Actually a double grid, so we can back each other up. I'm taking squad three to a position about midway in the park." He circled an area south of the defunct station house, on the edge of the Great Lawn. "Squads one and two will take positions just off the eight-five transverse on the East and West drives. My squad will fan out and take the point; anybody on the Great Lawn is dead meat. That's obvious. We'll regroup at the Delacorte Theater. Then we sweep downtown, squads one and two alternating their box with three." Eubank showed on a diagram how the squads formed grids or boxes and intersected with each other during the move south. Squad three, Eubank's squad, would be in the middle of the

Park, in the leading or point position. "We'll be spread a little thin in an area this size, but I don't want to put a hundred officers in there. We'll be all over each other in the dark, and somebody will end up getting dinged. I'll be taking in my best men and we'll be able to move faster without the confusion." Eubank pointed out several locations on the four streets that formed the perimeter of the Park—Central Park West, Fifth Avenue, Central Park South and 110th Street. "It took a while, but they finally have the perimeter sealed off and clear of traffic. I've requested all available men in the two-two and two-oh and about a hundred ESS officers to man positions at intervals along the streets. If we pin down any suspects we can have fifty men inside the park on top of the location in five minutes. If our friends get nervous and try to slip out before we make contact, we'll nail them on the outside."

Curran frowned. Half the Park was not being discussed. "What about north of the eight-five transverse?"

Eubank replied, "Except for the bombs, everything was south of eight-five. Besides, it's practically half reservoir up there. We have a natural separation on the transverse road. From what I can tell, there's heavy cover around the ice-skating rink, about One-oh-eight Street." Curran looked skeptical. "Listen, Curran, I don't spend a lot of time in Central Park, but I know the proud third-worlders have a combat zone going on up there on a regular goddamn day. Know what I mean?"

"Okay," Curran asked, "but who's covering your ass on the transverse?"

"Additional Emergency Service units with RPM cars and uniform. If we don't find anybody south of eight-five we'll turn around and make the second sweep above the reservoir."

Dix knew that Curran wasn't happy leaving any uniformed officers inside the Park on the transverse road while Eubank was wandering around, but Curran didn't question it. Instead he asked, "What about gas?"

"I don't think it will be effective unless we corner suspects in a specific area. I don't want it drifting back into our positions. If we need gas, we'll call for it." Eubank turned to Keller.

The Commissioner looked up from the map. "I want this park open, Don. But this is not your standard operation. We're not storming an embassy or smoking out a psychopath. It's important that we contain the problem."

Eubank reacted quickly. "Commissioner, we've already spent two hours getting this thing set up. We can't take it any slower. If anybody's in there, next thing we know they'll have hostages and demands and our hands will get tied. I have carte blanche to take these people right out. Whammo. Correct?"

Keller didn't say anything, didn't even glance at Dix. He was smooth, Dix thought, so smooth. Keller knew from experience that the Mayor would have something to say about possible shootings, and he was going to let Dix ease into it without appearing to invite the intrusion. Dix thought he might as well dive in.

"Commissioner, I spoke with the Mayor on the way over here and it's his thinking that we should show some restraint. We've had destruction of property, but apparently no direct attempt on life."

Eubank rolled his eyes. "Guns and bombs, Dix. Christ, they kill people, you know."

Keller asked, "What is Hizzoner suggesting, David?"

"Well, suppose it is a militant group, say a bunch of Puerto Rican Nationalists. That's a very sensitive community. Maybe we can save some lives, avoid some aggravation. Same with the Black community. The Mayor has leaned heavily on them for support." Dix watched Keller suppress a sneer. Support, hell—the Blacks in New York had elected the Mayor.

"I know it's an election year, David."

Eubank was salivating. "Listen, this is an emergency. I can't wait for concurrences out there."

It was Curran's turn. "I'll tell you what we'll do, Dix. When we find somebody in there, we'll take a poll, ask 'em how they feel about getting their asses shot off."

Eubank again. "No, wait a second, here it is. We'll negotiate with the niggers, smoke a joint with the spics, and if it's Irish Catholics, we'll give them a hot plate and send them home. Will that make the Mayor happy? Christ, I have a job to do."

The Commissioner was satisfied. Dix's nose was bloody and Keller hadn't done a thing. "All right, gentlemen. We're all doing our job here." He turned to Dix. "Whatever that may be."

Dix brought out the folder.

"One more thing. I've been reading over the transcript of the bomb threat. The Mayor asked me not to say anything about it to the press, but there could be something here."

The response was predictable. Curran and Eubank looked at Dix like he was three years old.

Keller broke the silence. "The one-man guerrilla? I read that. It's pretty farfetched, David, in light of what's happened."

Dix pressed on. "Why would a terrorist group waste time with a phony message?"

Eubank stared right through Dix. Perhaps he was angry; perhaps he felt challenged. He said, "Try getting back to reality, Dix. We'll grind these people up. It doesn't matter who they are. We've got the goddamn power."

Eubank went quickly out the exit to the street.

Dix looked down at the folder. He turned to Keller. "It's the part about guerrilla warfare that bothers me."

Keller glanced at Curran. "I didn't think this was coming from the Mayor."

Dix closed the folder and stared at the map of Central Park, at the diverse and unusual terrain. A vague notion troubled him. Suddenly he was worried.

Images flashed across the map—distant, frightening images.

Harris was in the supply dump. The aqueduct was cool and damp; rust-colored water trickled down through the walls. Harris aimed a battery-operated torch over the long rows of crates and canvas bags. He had already moved the priority small arms and ammunition aboveground, but he'd returned below to consider an additional weapon. He walked farther into the tunnel and put the torch on a sealed crate.

Harris was thinking of the M-60 light machine gun. The M-60 was a 7.62-mm gas-operated weapon with an effective range of 900 meters. It ripped apart anything in its path. The M-60 weighed only 23 pounds and was easy to carry. If necessary, it could be fired from the hip. Still, Harris thought, it was easier to operate from the prone firing position. It might be awkward to maneuver on the cycle, and then there were the long ammo belts he'd have to string around his body. The gun had another disadvantage, too. It overheated quickly and was designed with a detachable barrel. During heavy firing, the barrel could get so hot that an asbestos glove had to be used to make the change. Harris had neither a glove nor a replacement barrel.

He decided to save the M-60 for other purposes. After extinguishing the flashlight, he climbed a ladder up to the surface. He took a manhole cover he'd lifted from a regular sewer drain and placed it over the entrance to the aqueduct. The motorcycle was parked nearby, with the AK-47 and the M-79 launcher leaning against the wheels. Harris put the launcher in the holster and the rifle over his shoulder. He tied a bandanna around his forehead, pressed his helmet down snug, made sure that the large equipment sack was secure in the luggage rack and got on. A row of fragmentation grenades was fastened to the handlebars; they vibrated slightly when he kicked on the motor.

Harris drove past the rear of the fire alarm station on the 79th Street transverse and was glad to see that it was dark and evacuated. He cut across the West Drive and followed the bridle path north to Summit Rock. He was very careful as he parked the bike and approached a reconnaissance position above 85th Street.

Activity was increasing on Central Park West. Harris watched uniformed police officers escort several gawkers and TV cameramen around the corner of 86th Street and out of sight. Two men came down out of the huge NYPD truck and ran up the avenue. Harris had to move closer to the street in order to keep the men in his line of vision. He raised the field glasses and focused on the entrance to the Park at the transverse road. His heart started pounding. At least a dozen men with M-16s disappeared east into the roadway. Harris lowered the glasses. He was no longer alone in Central Park.

Harris went silently to the bike. He pulled a flak jacket out from under the luggage rack and put it on. He fastened it tight around his chest. He removed from the equipment sack a bundle of AK-47 clips taped together in a long chain to facilitate fast loading. Harris unraveled the chain and wrapped it around his torso.

There was a small jar in his shirt pocket. He opened it and put two fingers inside. The jar contained Army-issue nightfighter cosmetic, which he smeared on his face until it became a black mask. After Harris blinked and covered his eyelids, he was practically invisible.

Harris put the jar away and referred to his charts. He decided to await the assault force near Hill 450, a position inside the Ramble.

He started the bike and went east and south, curving around the Delacorte Theater and Belvedere Castle. He came within sight of the calm, dark water of the Lake. Harris suddenly felt very alert. Details of light and sound and smell jumped at him from the night air, which floated like mist in the thick undergrowth. He studied the trees lining the far shore of the Lake. No fear—no enemy lurked there, hiding, planning, waiting for movement and battle. He knew, though, that soon this terrain would hold danger in every shadow and tree; that those who caused this danger would have to be found and engaged; that it was a struggle Harris thought to be necessary and endless. *Search and destroy*. He got excited just thinking about it.

Eubank's combat boots were clattering on the pavement as he followed the curve of the eight-five transverse down into Central Park. He was holding a walkie-talkie and carrying an M-16. A line of RMP cars was parked on the road, and uniformed officers leaned over the tops, aiming shotguns north and south. Eubank stopped near the bridge under the West Drive and observed the burned-out station house.

An Emergency Service sergeant, Manuel Beniquez, was on the other side of the bridge and Eubank yelled at him. Beniquez jogged over, fastening his flak jacket on the run, because Chief Eubank despised an open flak jacket. Beniquez was chewing gum and bouncing up and down on his feet.

"All set, Chief."

Eubank spoke into his walkie-talkie. "Squad three. Stand by. K."

A voice came back from the walkie-talkie. "Rog. Three."

Another voice: "Adam one, what's your location? K."

Eubank looked disgusted. He shouted into the radio. "Goddamnit! Who is that? Clear the band." Eubank hoped the dispatchers in the command post weren't going to screw things up. People might live or die in the next few hours based on proper communications.

He turned to Beniquez, who was young, very young, for an ESS sergeant, but tough and steady. Eubank only wished the sergeant didn't look so much like he was going out for a thrill-packed evening at Coney Island.

"Okay, Manny. As much as I hate the bullshit, Keller's right about one thing. This is terrain. We're not going to be able to secure a location. So stay sharp. Remember, if you make contact, force the perps toward me. If we start shooting, I want to keep it off the streets. The last thing I need is for some big shot to get his ass blasted up there in his living room."

"Right, Chief."

"And stay in touch. Watch the crossfire. Everybody got that?"

"Yes, sir."

"Let's move."

They ran back along the roadway and moved into the trees. They passed a small playground and came up on the West Drive, where Beniquez joined the four other ESS officers of squad two. A police truck with high-intensity lamps was parked in the road, its engine idling. Eubank nodded at the driver and the lamps were switched on. Long, bright beams illuminated the landscape, highlighting trees and bushes fifty yards in front of the vehicle. Eubank instructed the driver to keep the lights ahead of the squads and to stay in close radio contact. Eubank did not want the officers blinded or confused by the lights, and he did not want to expose their positions. For this reason he'd rejected an aerial search with spotlights and the accompanying machine noise. Eubank wished he was out in the hills somewhere, away from the mass of humanity, in some broad area with no hot sewer pipes and subway tunnels, so he could use the heat-seeking devices and noise detectors. Well, fuck it, he said to himself. It always comes down to one thing anyway. The power.

Eubank left squad two and continued on toward the top of the Great Lawn. The Park suddenly seemed very dark and very big, bigger than he remembered—but then he hadn't been in Central Park at night since he'd left the

Detective Division. He wasn't going to worry about it now. It was his hunch that whoever had blown up the precinct house and fired off the rifles and smoke bombs were long gone. Tomorrow, when he was sleepy from screwing around in the Park all night, he'd pick up the paper and read about radicals claiming responsibility for the attacks so they could publicize some worthless cause.

Eubank wasn't going to be careless, though. He was never, never careless. If they did find somebody, he just hoped they were a sampling of all races. Then there wouldn't be any moaning downtown.

Eubank found squad three sitting on Park benches on the walk circling the Great Lawn. The men looked a little out of place with their automatic rifles and flak vests. There were seven instead of the normal five because, at the last minute, Eubank had had an idea and requested additional men—two young Black ESS officers, Hardy and Daniels. They were smart and didn't take silly chances, but that wasn't why he'd wanted them. When Eubank had gone out to inspect the squads, he realized that everybody was white (or Hispanic). Why not have two Black guys as his point men? They'd be less visible in the dark than anyone else. It was logical as hell. He could hardly wait to break the news to Hardy and Daniels.

The officers stood up from the benches—alert, nervous, wiping sweat from their faces. Eubank spoke into the walkie-talkie.

"Squad one and two, are you in position?"

"Rog one."

"Ten-four. Two."

"Move." He turned to his squad. "Havermeyer and Davis with me. We'll circle the lawn on the west, everybody else around the other side. Rendezvous at the theater."

The men split up. Eubank and the two officers darted into the trees off the walk. To their right they could see the bright beams of the high-intensity lamps shining on trees near the West Drive as squad two began their search downtown. Eubank stopped Havermeyer and Davis near a clump of heavy bushes and rocks. He took a security position nearby and sent the two men into the brush. They emerged seconds later, shaking their heads.

The three men continued around the lawn until they reached the Delacorte Theater. They checked the entrance to the building and searched the small amphitheater and stage that jutted out over the small body of water known as the New Lake. Eubank heard crunching and splashing sounds as Hardy, Daniels, Dietrich and Warren approached from the east. Everyone crouched along the edge of the water.

Dietrich spoke quietly to Eubank. "Nothing, sir. It's spooky out there."

Eubank nodded. He unrolled a small map and Davis held a penlight on it. Eubank raised his walkie-talkie.

"Squad two. What's your position? K."

"On the seven-nine transverse, across from the museum." Eubank referred to the map. Beniquez was talking about the Museum of Natural History.

"Okay, two, we're right behind you. We'll go down into the road and around the fire alarm headquarters. Stay on the Drive until you see the Lake. Then hold. Got that?"

"Ten-four."

Eubank pulled Hardy and Daniels close to him. "From now on you have the point." Daniels rolled his eyes. Hardy farted and Eubank handed him another walkie-talkie. "Get up top there, on the Belvedere. Go down over the transverse. Wait for us when you hit the stream in front of all the trees. That's the Ramble. Got it?" Hardy stared at Eubank for a moment and then nodded. "Get going."

The two officers moved off, disappearing behind the theater. Eubank took the rest of his squad around the New Lake, a distance of about fifty yards, and descended a small stone staircase onto the pavement of the 79th

96

Street transverse. He looked east and saw the bright lamps from the truck preceding squad one as it moved on the East Drive, crossing the bridge over the transverse. He held the map under a streetlamp and radioed the officer commanding the squad, Sergeant Dell'olio.

"Squad one."

"One here, sir."

"Go down and check out the boathouse. Then double back and form your box. Follow the shoreline until you reach the walk directly across the water from the Fountain. We'll be crossing over you right there. K."

Eubank waited for a second. Dell'olio was probably referring to a map.

"Roger, one."

Eubank put away his map. So far, so good. They'd use the grid search on the heavy cover north of the Lake, as planned, then fan out to the avenues. The squads would be farthest apart when one and two made their moves on the strips of land between the drives and the Park perimeter. But in an emergency, either squad would be close enough to the street to call on uniformed and Emergency Service units for support, with the command post acting as a central dispatch. Eubank would try to stagger these perimeter searches so that his squad three wasn't left vulnerable in the center of the Park.

After the squads had circled the Lake, they'd pinch back along the 72nd Street road, three reforming a box behind one, two behind three and so on across the Sheep Meadow. All the angles were covered. Christ, Eubank thought, I should have been a general.

Hardy and Daniels mounted the long steps up to the Belvedere. It was a section of high ground, in fact the highest point in Central Park, atop a huge rock that overlooked the Great Lawn. They squatted against the stone railing and surveyed the landscape. Beyond the lawn were the dark trees surrounding the reservoir; east, the lights on

Fifth Avenue; directly below, the New Lake. The Belvedere Castle, a Disney-like structure with a tall tower and arched windows, loomed over them.

Daniels peeked over the railing down at the New Lake, which, as far as he was concerned, looked more like a big mud puddle with trash. He shifted his gaze to the castle. The tower made him feel very uneasy. It was so goddamn dark, he thought. He clicked the safety off his M-16.

"What you doin'?" asked Hardy.

"Shit. We could be in some joker's sight picture right now." Daniels imagined crosshairs centered on his head. "Eubank is into some crazy shit."

Hardy snorted. "That motherfucker went off years ago. Why does the man have to be here tonight? He never takes a ride-out no more."

"I hear you. That sucker be in an institution if it weren't for the Department."

They fell silent for a moment. Hardy motioned to Daniels. They might as well get it over with. They stayed low, following the railing to the side of the castle, and flattened themselves against the wall. Hardy removed a flashlight from his belt and ran it over the tower and roofline. Graffiti covered the old stone; the windows were smashed and empty. They came away from the wall and examined the entry door. It was chained and locked. Hardy turned off the light. He tried to peer through the darkness to the other side of the Belvedere. He could make out a chain-link fence with barbed wire running along the top.

"What's that?" Daniels asked him.

"Weather station. Some kinda equipment in there."

"Let's check it and get the hell off this thing."

They crossed quickly to the fence and put the light on the weather station. Not even the barbed wire had kept out the vandals. The instruments were twisted and bent and strewn around the grass; a pair of panties hung from an anemometer.

Hardy returned the light to his belt. In front of him and down through the thick undergrowth was nothing but the unknown. He thought that was kind of ironic. He'd grown up on 147th Street; he'd spent years fooling around in Central Park, playing ball, riding his bike, getting high. And at night, he didn't know any more about the place than Daniels did, who was from some diddy-ass town in Alabama. Wasn't that a bitch. He remembered what his mother used to tell him. "John, you listen, don't be messin' around in Central Park after dark." Dark, hell— he'd seen guys get their heads cracked in broad daylight in this fuckin' Park.

Hardy stared into the darkness and muttered to Daniels. "I knew I was gonna die in Central Park, man, since I was a kid. I knew it."

Daniels smiled, not a friendly smile. "Well, I'm so glad you're telling me that right now."

"Let's move."

Daniels took a breath. "I'm down."

They burst off the Belvedere into the trees. Only the slightest glint from the metal of an M-16 revealed their presence. Other than that, their blackness concealed them.

Beniquez had moved squad two south along the West Drive until they were approximately on a line with 78th Street. He was standing with Officer Weissman on a walk just north of the Bank Rock Bridge, which spanned the far northern tip of the Lake. He'd sent Walker, Michaels and Turner into the network of narrow walks and pathways that wound through the heavy trees and slightly hilly rock outcroppings, down to the shoreline. They'd been gone about two minutes.

Weissman was cracking gum, snapping it loudly in the humid air.

"Turn that gum off, Weissman."

Weissman stared at Beniquez and then smiled. 'Okay, Sergeant." He spit the gum out. "I hope Turner don't get trigger happy and blow some queers up by mistake. You know, this is where they hang out, starting here down to about 66th."

"I don't know as much about faggots as you do."

"I knew a guy in vice, man, told me about it. Christ, what's everybody so uptight about?"

Beniquez turned away. He was getting edgy. The truck with the lights was about fifty yards away on the West Drive. He'd used the lamps to search the small strip of land between the Drive and the Park wall along Central Park West. He had planned to aim the lamps behind the squad while they searched the area in front of the Lake, but the trees were too thick and the only thing the light did was get in their eyes.

Turner appeared out of the shadows, breathing hard.

"Sergeant. We found something. Just inside the treeline, down there."

Turner pointed south, toward the Lake. Beniquez told him to wait and moved back several yards on the walk until he could see the 79th Street transverse passing under the drive. The truck was maintaining a position on the overpass. He returned to Weissman and Turner.

"Okay, show me."

The three officers followed the walk as it curved down into the trees. Branches and low shrubs brushed against their arms, a pile of beer cans banged off someone's boot. They rounded a corner where the walk was intersected by two pathways. A flashlight beam hit Beniquez in the chest.

"Hold it, Sarge." It was Walker and Turner and Michaels. Walker put the light on the ground in front of him. "Do you fuckin' believe it, Sarge?"

Beniquez stepped forward. A huge roll of barbed wire crossed over the walk and disappeared into the bushes. Walker raised the light up so Beniquez could see the shiny strands of metal curling far into the trees toward the Bank Rock Bridge and the West Drive.

"Shut the light, Walker." The five men stood in the dark shuffling their feet, fidgeting with their rifles.

Walker spoke first. "Do you think the Parks Department put that in here for some reason?"

Weissman: "Tryin' to catch fags, man."

Beniquez thought for a moment. "No, that ain't no Parks thing. You could get fucked up on that. They wouldn't leave it in here, unless they told us about it."

Michaels pulled at a section of the wire. "This is the real stuff. Concertina. Like they use in the Army. We aren't gonna get through it. Not without some tools."

Beniquez leaned out close to the wire and looked right and left. "Hard to tell how long it is." He asked Turner, "Did you check that out?"

"Not yet. You want us to follow it? See how far the roll goes?"

Beniquez wiped sweat from his face. "No, wait a second." He brought out his walkie-talkie. "Truck two."

"Yes, sir, truck two."

Beniquez could hear the idling of the truck engine under the driver's voice. "Drive forward with your lights on the drive. Maybe a hundred yards. Take it slow. K."

"Roger."

Beniquez and his squad waited quietly for two minutes. Gnats swirled in front of their faces. A siren sounded somewhere outside the Park, then faded to a distant echo. A crackle of static came from the walkie-talkie.

"Sergeant, this is truck two. Be advised the drive is blocked off by what looks like barbed wire. What the hell's that in the road for?"

Beniquez answered, "What's your location?"

"About fifty yards north of the Seven-seven Street entrance, where it feeds into the drive."

"Can you take the truck off the road from there?"

"It's too steep. Part of the lake runs under the road here. There's a small footbridge west of my location. That's it."

"Can you see where the wire goes?"

There was a pause. "I got the lights on it. It runs west, up there toward the wall. I can't tell from here."

"Okay, maintain your position."

"Well, I'm not going anywhere."

Beniquez lowered the walkie-talkie and turned back to his men. Weissman was off the walk, poking around in the bushes several yards east along the wire.

"Weissman! Get your ass back here." They could hear Weissman's boots crunching through leaves and twigs. He stepped back on the walk and rejoined the squad.

Beniquez unfolded his map. He had to figure out what the hell they were going to do now. A gnat buzzed in his ear, startling him. He jerked and the barrel of his M-16 bumped Weissman in the stomach. Weissman gripped the barrel between two fingers and pushed it away.

Beniquez looked at his men. They were staring at him, waiting for a command. Perspiration dripped from their faces. He whispered to them.

"This is some serious shit."

Sergeant Dell'olio was standing outside the Trefoil arch, south of the 72nd Street boathouse, waiting for two of his officers to come back out of the dark passageway under the East Drive. Their boots echoed in the tunnel and they appeared in the light of a park lamp. Dell'olio waved them forward and the three men ran to the front of the one-story boathouse. Two other officers stood next to the pay phones. Dell'olio consulted his map.

He'd taken squad one to the far eastern tip of the Lake and searched the boathouse. Truck one was standing by in the parking lot north of their location. They would now circle back toward the center of the Park, moving in behind Eubank and squad three. Once they'd verified that the area north of the Lake was clear, they'd retrace their steps, go east out to the Conservatory Water and the Park wall, then continue downtown.

Dell'olio gave the command and the squad moved around the boathouse, then over rocks and bushes along a chain-link fence. They angled up and away from the water, losing sight of the Lake, and pushed through low shrubs covering a rock mound. They reached a paved walk which according to Dell'olio's map was one of a series of paths that cut through the trees and open spaces, eventually winding up in the Ramble. They went west for a few yards until Dell'olio realized that he'd passed two smashed-out park lamps. He ordered the squad to halt.

"Spread out. We'll take it on line. Jarvis on the point."

"Want light, Sergeant?"

"No. Wait till we're down on the main walk, so Eubank can see us."

Jarvis went ahead and resumed the search. The squad followed, single file. Dell'olio wondered why it all looked so unfamiliar. He was sure he'd been in this section of the Park only last weekend, playing with his two sons. Funny how he'd never paid attention to details of terrain; now every bush demanded his concentration. Central Park was beginning to feel very, very big.

Jarvis didn't see a thin wire that came out of the trees and stretched across the walk about a foot above the pavement. He stopped and looked to his left, catching a glimpse of lights reflecting off the surface of the Lake. He continued on.

His right leg pushed through the wire and he stumbled, almost falling over. He regained his balance and peered down through the darkness. He felt the ground with his hand and found the wire. He saw where it ran into the trees and he thought he saw a yellow pole sticking up into the low branches, but he didn't have time to verify that. Something exploded in his face.

Jarvis was thrown back into the officer coming behind him. The man screamed as fragments of metal tore into his neck. There was another explosion, and the third officer in line tumbled into the bushes on the opposite side of the walk.

Dell'olio froze for an instant when he heard the first explosion. He saw a flash, but the walk curved and he didn't have a view of the front of the line. He dove into the bushes just as the second explosion went off and the burst of light revealed a line of poles, about as tall as a man. God, they're bamboo, he thought, and that's grenades attached to the tops of the poles and they're going off one by one, here they come, right back to me, bang bang bang. He felt hot needles spinning inside his legs and arms.

He slumped to the ground. Pieces of leaves floated down on his face. He was dizzy, but he turned his head to look at the walk. The two officers who had been directly in front of him were sprawled on the pavement. One of them was moaning softly and sliding his legs around in a pool of blood. The other officer was on his face unmoving, his rifle tangled in the undergrowth.

Dell'olio laughed. What's the bush going to do with that gun? That's silly. Bushes don't hurt people. Stupid little thoughts ran through his mind. He reached for his walkie-talkie. His hand was red, and wet ... all wet. He raised the walkie-talkie to his lips.

"Hey, my hand. What the hell?"

A familiar voice came over the radio. "Say again. K."

"We're hit. God." Dell'olio tried to think of a number. Oh, yeah. "Ten-thirteen," he screamed. "Ten-thirteen!"

The voice again. "Squad one! What's your position? One, please respond."

Dell'olio thought of something funny. He said, "Squad one doesn't exist." He felt sick to his stomach. He looked down at his flak jacket. Oh, no. It wasn't fastened properly. He watched it slide open and saw a huge stain above his belt. He set down the walkie-talkie and threw up.

When squad three heard the explosion, they were moving west behind the fire alarm station, paralleling the 79th Street transverse. Everyone stopped immediately. Eubank tried to locate the sound; it seemed to come from the Fifth Avenue side of the Park. Odd, thudding explosions, he thought. Not gunfire—more like a small bomb. Grenades were like small bombs. The muscles tightened in his neck.

Incoherent babblings came over his walkie-talkie. He ordered the squad off the walk, slightly south, where there was some overhead cover. The men spread out, leaning against the trees, rifles ready. Eubank stood with Davis. They listened to the walkie-talkie.

"I can't make that out, Davis."

"I heard a ten-thirteen, sir."

Eubank tried Beniquez. "Squad two, what's your position?"

"North of the lake, east of the drive. What the hell was that?"

"I don't know." There was more static and a weak voice transmission. Something about a hand. Eubank looked down at Davis, who shrugged. "Manny, was that you?"

"Negative."

"All right. Abandon your position and go down to the lake. I want your squad underneath mine. We'll assist one. K."

After a second's pause, Beniquez answered. "Not possible, sir. We're blocked south by barbed wire."

"Barbed wire?"

"That's affirm. What you call it? Concertina."

Eubank flinched. "Jesus Christ." He looked quickly at his map. This was taking too long. He went back to the radio. "Manny, find a way over here. Fast. I don't care how."

"Roger. Two."

Eubank waited for the band to clear. "Command post, this is Eubank."

**105**

"Command. Go ahead. K."

"We'll assist squad one on that ten-thirteen. Move truck one down to the boathouse and tell him to put his lights in the trees."

Eubank checked the clip on his M-16. His men were still too close together. He wanted to sweep east, covering more ground.

"Spread out. Stay sharp."

The men began to move, lengthening the distance between one officer and the next to perhaps forty feet. Their steps were noisy, snapping through fallen branches, dodging trees and shrubs. Eubank fell in behind the officers. He hoped squad one had made contact with the perpetrators; they wouldn't get very far if they tried to leave the Park.

One of the men, it looked like Dietrich, tripped and Eubank saw an object swing down out of the trees. Dietrich jumped upright, as if standing at attention, and flew backward, flopping in the grass. A gurgling sound came from his throat and he grunted loudly. Eubank ran over to him.

A huge bamboo rake was imbedded in Dietrich's chest. He twitched for a few seconds and then was still. A rope ran across Dietrich's feet to a stump, then up into the trees and back down to the end of the booby trap.

Eubank was stunned. A flashlight beam illuminated Dietrich. His eyes were wide open and his lips were twisted in a death snarl. Eubank looked up and the light blinded him.

"Turn that out. Davis, help me get this thing off him." Eubank waited for his eyes to adjust to the dark again. He tried to lift the bamboo device, but he couldn't get enough leverage. All he wanted to do was get rid of the goddamn thing. "Davis!" He turned to look at his men. He could hardly see them—dark, frozen shadows, silent statues with guns. Warren, Havermeyer, Davis. They were standing

**106**

completely still, except that their heads turned up and down, side to side, like nervous deer. Their concentration was absolute, more intense than it had ever been in their young lives; they studied each foot of ground, each branch overhead. They saw that "thing" on Dietrich, and they were paralyzed with fear.

Davis cleared his throat. "Yes, sir. I'll work my way over." What he wanted to say was, "Fuck you, Chief, I ain't takin' one step."

Beniquez shoved the map into his pants pocket. Fuck the map. He knew what to do. They were just going to have to take some chances. That's what they paid them for.

"This is it," he told his men. "We leave the walk and follow the wire. If it cuts us off, we backtrack toward 79th Street. We'll go down into the transverse if we have to."

Everybody nodded. They were getting anxious standing in one place. They formed a line, keeping ten feet apart, and stepped into the brush. They had traveled east for approximately one minute when Turner, closest to the wire, sank up to his knee in some kind of hole. His mouth opened in surprise. Then he screamed. The other officers hit the ground, curling their fingers around the triggers of the M-16s. Turner dropped his rifle and clutched his leg.

"Help me. Shit!"

Beniquez crawled to him. A mat of leaves and foliage had collapsed around the hole. Turner's leg was impaled in a nest of sharp bamboo stakes. Blood oozed over the top of his boot.

"God damn!" Beniquez yelled at the others and they hurried over. They stared in shock. Turner twisted his leg involuntarily and let out a pitiful cry of pain. Beniquez motioned to Michaels. They handed their rifles to Walker and got a grip on Turner's calf. His pants were slippery with blood. "Ready?" Michaels nodded. They jerked up

on the leg and Turner screamed so loudly that Michaels'
right ear went dead. The leg didn't move. Beniquez very
carefully put his hand into the nest of stakes and felt
around.

"Walker, give me light." With the flashlight on the hole,
Beniquez could see that the stakes not only pointed up,
but several were in the side walls, facing downward to
create a fishhook effect. That scared him. A quick trace
of pain flickered through his mind.

Weissman saw it, too. "How the fuck are you going to
get his leg out of there? It'll get ripped to shreds."

Turner was drifting into shock. His head rolled back
on his neck. Beniquez worked several of the stakes free by
pushing them back and forth and cleared a few inches
around the foot. He was able to flatten two of the downward stakes against the wall of the hole.

That was as far as he got. Automatic rifle fire ripped
into the trees over their heads. The men rolled in the dirt.
The firing continued, close, from somewhere south.

Beniquez yelled over the loud cracking. "Weissman,
Walker, return fire!"

"Where?" The officers were confused.

Beniquez made a sweeping gesture toward the Lake.
"Lay it down!"

Walker and Weissman aimed their M-16s and opened
up, pouring out rounds through and over the barbed wire.
Walker was so nervous he was only on semi-automatic;
he tugged at the trigger, trying to make bullets come out
faster.

Beniquez inched his way to Turner, who had collapsed
backward, jamming his leg farther into the stakes. Beniquez heard the trees being torn apart by the weapons fire,
which was making whizzing sounds right above his head.
He punched Michaels.

"Fuck it! Grab the leg!" They wrapped their arms tight
around the thigh and yanked the leg free. Turner's eyes
bulged and he groaned from way inside his body. Beni-

quez tried not to look at the mess as they rolled Turner into the grass.

Walker's rifle made a steady pop-pop-pop, but there were no other shooting sounds. Weissman slammed a fresh clip into his weapon.

"Hold your fire!" Walker kept on shooting. Beniquez crawled to him and shrieked into his ear. "Hold your fuckin' fire!" Walker removed his hand from the trigger. It was suddenly quiet; only rasping noises were coming from the men, their chests heaving, air rushing in and out of wide-open mouths. Static crackled over Beniquez's walkie-talkie and he lunged for it.

"Squad two to command! Ten-thirteen! West Drive, cross is Seven-seven Street!"

A transmission came back, but he couldn't hear it. Weapons fire raked through the trees again, then lower, tearing through the tops of the bushes. The officers squeezed into the ground. Beniquez listened to the steady, terrifying snap of an automatic weapon and a round ball of fear clogged his throat.

The fire was circling them, south to east to north. Jesus in Heaven, we're going to get chewed up like garbage.

Walker squirmed across the grass and pushed his face very close to Beniquez. Walker's voice was high, like a little boy's. "God, what is it? It's everywhere, man, we gotta get away!"

Beniquez watched sweat pour into Walker's imploring eyes. Get away. Yeah, that was it. Get the hell *away*.

Beniquez twisted around in the leaves and faced Michaels. "Give me some cover fire. Me and Weissman will take Turner. Head for the drive."

Michaels and Walker edged across the walk and began firing their M-16s into the bushes, south and east. Beniquez and Weissman crawled to Turner, who was semiconscious, muttering face down into the grass. They lifted him by the armpits and dragged him back along the walk. Beniquez spotted a gap in the bushes and they veered off

**109**

the walk, pulling Turner between trees and down an incline. Behind them the sound of rifles stopped.

A jumble of radio transmissions poured out of Beniquez's walkie-talkie, penetrating the sudden stillness. He heard Eubank and the command post, but he ignored them and squelched the sound. He was already enough of a target.

The Drive came into view. Beniquez could see a section of road and the truck parked in front of the wire. The lamps were still on, blazing over the top of the concertina. He motioned Weissman to stop and they crouched down, leaning Turner against a tree. Beniquez called the driver on his walkie-talkie, careful to keep the volume low.

"Truck two, this is Beniquez. K."

"Jesus Christ—"

"Shut up and listen. Put the lights out. Back the truck up and turn it around. *Vaya*."

The lamps dimmed and then went out. The roadway returned to darkness. Beniquez watched the truck move in reverse and make a U-turn, facing north. When it rolled forward in line with their position, he spoke again to the driver. "Hold it right there. Open the passenger door. Then get out and take cover on the other side."

"Ten-four."

The driver did as instructed. Beniquez listened to the silence and studied the open truck door, only a short run away down the dark incline.

"Weissman. When we get to the truck shove Turner inside and shut the door. We'll get behind the other side and wait for Michaels and Walker. Then we'll drive the hell out of here."

Weissman got a grip on Turner. Beniquez stowed his walkie-talkie and hooked his arm around Turner's shoulder. He gave Weissman a sign.

The front of the truck exploded. A thousand tiny sparks arched away into the night, like fireworks, showering the pavement with a spray of metal fragments. Beniquez and

Weissman jerked back, dropping Turner with a thud. Beniquez saw red lights through the trees and two patrol cars roared down the 77th Street ramp, tires burning rubber as they stopped fast on the other side of the wire. The headlight beams shone through the concertina wire and illuminated the roadway near the truck.

Another explosion went off, right on top of the wire, and Beniquez could hear the bright, twirling fragments punch into the cars, shattering the windows. The headlights went out. There was loud yelling and automatic rifle fire strafed across the truck. Weissman rolled over to Beniquez.

"Did you fuckin' see that?" Weissman said.

Beniquez ignored him. More rifle fire came from his left. Small pops mixed in and he saw muzzle flashes beyond the roll of wire. The officers in the patrol cars were returning fire. But at what?

"Do you see anybody, Weissman?"

"What a fuckin' trip!"

Somebody ran out into the Drive, heading north. Bullets ricocheted off the pavement behind him and he tumbled off the street, disappearing down the tree-lined slope.

Weissman whooped. "Kill the fags! Kill 'em!"

*Dios mío,* thought Beniquez, this guy's completely gone. He grabbed Weissman's shirt and jerked his face around. "Carry Turner out of here. Go straight for the wall. I'll cover you. Move it!"

Weissman handed his rifle to Beniquez and smiled. He lifted Turner onto his shoulders and stumbled down the incline, past the truck and into the trees on the opposite side of the Drive.

Beniquez crawled to his left and tried to find cover behind a row of low shrubs. There was a low thudding burst several yards on the other side of the bushes and chunks of dirt pelted down on his back. An automatic rifle fired very close, the loud crack practically in Beniquez's ear.

He edged forward and two men plowed through the undergrowth, firing on the run. They were Michaels and Walker, each sending a steady stream of rounds down into the barbed wire on the Drive.

There was something wrong about that. Beniquez saw it in an instant. They were shooting at fellow officers.

A rush of fright shot through Beniquez. His mind raced. *Maybe that's all we've been doing, shooting at each other; maybe there isn't anyone else, maybe we've been tricked.* He felt suddenly sick. *I've ordered officers to fire on their own men. What if squad three is right behind me and we've cut them down? Mother of God, what if they cut us down?*

Beniquez screamed at Michaels and Walker, but they kept firing and darted out of sight. He found a whistle in his shirt pocket and blew on it until his teeth almost broke on the metal. The rifle fire stopped, but the small pops of service revolvers continued from the direction of the Drive.

Beniquez cursed; anger permeated his fear. *Everybody's* trying to kill me—God, every fuckin' body. He jumped up, expecting a hole to burn in his flesh, and ran low into the trees. He found Walker and Michaels lying in the grass next to a walk. They turned their guns on him and he froze. Their faces were milk-white; their lips quivered; they were out of control.

Beniquez dropped down on the walk and Michaels started babbling.

"What are we gonna do? There's no way out!"

"Shut up. Those are cops down there." Michaels blinked. "That's right, cops. We gotta use 'em, understand?"

The shooting stopped. Beniquez forced his breathing to slow down and raised his walkie-talkie. "Squad two to command. K."

"Go ahead, two."

"Tell the officers in the RMP cars on the West Drive to hold their fire. We will be crossing approximately fifty yards north of their location. Be advised there is a casualty comin' out on Central Park West near Seven-seven Street."

"Roger, squad two. This is Chief Curran. Report your status. Who the hell's shooting in there?"

Beniquez heard a faint noise and immediately squelched the walkie-talkie. A series of dull, thumping explosions began, north, then closer, coming toward them, one by one. Michaels panicked and ran through a clump of bushes. There was a scream. Beniquez and Walker crawled south on the walk, the pavement scraping away the skin on their knees and elbows. Dirt and debris sailed up to the trees. Beniquez felt something warm slice through his ankle and rolled off the walk into the grass. He jammed his fingers under the top of his boot, and then held his hand in front of his eyes. The fingers were shiny with blood.

Automatic weapons fire resumed, the bullets whizzing over his head. Beniquez's heart pounded and he couldn't think. He staggered forward and tripped over Walker. Michaels was right in front of them, tangled in barbed wire. He was writhing in the sharp coils, cutting his hands and face in an attempt to get free.

Walker crawled to Michaels and yanked him out of the wire. Beniquez stood up and moved forward along the concertina, ordering the two officers to follow. He saw that Michaels' rifle had slipped from his bleeding hands, but it wouldn't make any difference. Who were they going to shoot at?

Beniquez hobbled through the undergrowth, the two officers following behind, down to Bank Rock Bridge and the edge of the Lake. The wire roll ended. Walker started to run up on the short wooden bridge, but Beniquez held him back. That route would only lead over to the Drive and probably behind the wire blocking the roadway. They had to get south of that wire and evacuate with the RMP cars.

"Into the water! Let's go."

The three men ran around the bridge and stepped into the Lake, half swimming, half walking through the shallow water and muck.

When they emerged on the other side, the shooting had stopped. They hurried across a thin strip of land and approached a narrow finger of the Lake that ran under the West Drive. Beniquez didn't hesitate to wade in. He led the men through a dark tunnel until they were west of the road. A small wooden foot-bridge crossed over the water. Beniquez told Walker and Michaels to wait, climbed up the embankment and squatted on the bridge.

Pain throbbed in his ankle and he went down on one knee. He looked to his right and spotted the patrol cars, outlined in the shadows. Two ESS officers were hiding behind the vehicles and a third was stretched out on the pavement. The wire was to Beniquez's left. They'd finally gotten past it.

He shouted at the officers and identified himself. Walker and Michaels climbed up on the bridge and they ran for the Drive. Beniquez collapsed against one of the patrol cars. The officers were in bad shape, and the one on the street was probably a DOA.

A uniformed sergeant crawled around the rear of the car. He was older than Beniquez and of equal rank, but an ESS sergeant gave the orders in an emergency situation. He was waiting for Beniquez to give him instructions.

Beniquez grimaced. "Does the car start?"

The sergeant didn't bother to answer; he slid his arm up to the steering wheel and turned the ignition. The car started.

Beniquez moved away from the door. "We're gonna get in and drive out."

114

The sergeant narrowed his eyes. "Evacuate?"

"Ain't you seen enough?"

"We can't all fit in this car."

"Load the wounded in the trunk. Fuck it. We're finished."

The sergeant and the two ESS officers placed the DOA in the trunk. One of the men was moaning, a dark streak glistening on the side of his face. Walker and Michaels helped Beniquez into the rear of the car. The seat was covered with slivers of glass; the windows all the way around were blown out and strands of shattered safety glass spilled to the floor. Walker leaned close to Beniquez's ear and his face had a strange intensity, as if he was coming to a terrible realization. His voice was a hoarse whisper.

"Grenades."

That was all he said.

The three other officers climbed into the front seat and the sergeant swung the car around, moving it slowly along the Drive and turning right onto the 77th Street ramp. Beniquez could see the lights on Central Park West and he felt like he was waking up from a nightmare. Michaels jabbed him in the ribs.

"Hey, look down there." He was pointing at the dark ground below the ramp. There was a man walking on the bridle path.

"Stop the car."

Beniquez ordered the sergeant and Walker to get out. They crouched behind the car and everyone inside sagged down in the seats. The man veered off the bridle path and headed straight for the car. Walker aimed the M-16; he was shaking, ready to kill anything. The man was within twenty yards when the sergeant ordered him to halt. Beniquez recognized the man. He was the driver of truck two. Beniquez yelled from inside the car.

"Hold your fire, Walker." Walker started to pull the

trigger and the sergeant pushed the M-16 into the ground.

Beniquez leaned out the window. "It's okay, he's a cop."

The driver moved closer, one step, another; then he seemed to come down on something and a loud boom threw him into the air, spinning him like a stuffed toy. Pebbles and fragments sprayed over the car and everyone ducked. Walker yelled and bolted up the ramp for the street. The men heard no other sound. Eyes wide with horror, they peered out at the dark ground. The body had landed ten feet from the explosion, lying in a horrible, twisted pose. The sergeant stood up, in a daze, and moved away from the car. Michaels moaned and Beniquez turned to him. Chunks of flesh and clothing stuck to his shirt, slick little dots of blood reflecting in the light from the avenue.

The sergeant stepped off the ramp as if he intended to go down and help the driver. Beniquez snapped out of shock.

"Don't go down there, Sergeant! Don't do it."

The sergeant turned back and stared at Beniquez. His service revolver dangled from his hand. "My God, do you know what that was?"

A last twinge of fear chilled Beniquez. He didn't know. He didn't want to.

Ten minutes had been required for Eubank and squad three to move east a distance of twenty-five yards from the spot where Dietrich had been killed by the booby trap. To Eubank those minutes had seemed dangerously long; he'd been forced to slow his men down, to tread carefully forward using the flashlights to search every foot of ground. Exposed to fire, afraid of every step, unable to react quickly and according to procedure, unable even to retreat with reasonable safety—Eubank perceived all these horrors within seconds of Dietrich's death. When they'd pulled the bamboo device from Dietrich's chest, everyone gagging as a jet of blood shot up from a two-inch hole in the flesh, Eubank had perceived something else: Somebody wanted it that way. Somebody had planted that booby trap knowing exactly the strategic and psychological results.

Eubank had then been seized by a nightmare vision of a swarming, alien enemy, something from a war he'd never experienced. *Vietnam.* Eubank's mind threatened to run away from him, swept along by a terrifying rush of adrenaline. What was he thinking about? He was in *Central Park* and he was a cop and maniacs were loose. He grabbed reality, the policeman's only world, and was awed by the tricks of the mind. He'd felt that surge of adrenaline before, but somehow different, and he knew that it had always come from anticipation, from knowing he had the power. Suddenly the situation had been reversed and he was helpless, pinned down like the criminals he'd so often surrounded with an overwhelming force.

Who was doing this to him? Who had the power? And the most frightening question for a policeman: Did we find them, or were they waiting for us? An intimation of danger settled permanently inside his mind.

Despite these horrors, Eubank had steadied himself and made some fast decisions. He knew that squad one had been assaulted. Shooting was coming from squad two's last reported location. In the confusion, neither squad one nor two had responded to calls from the command post. This disturbed him, but he had heard squad two's ten-thirteen and knew that mobile command had sent RMP cars to assist. He had radioed the command post that he would continue with his plan to assist squad one. Curran wanted to send in Emergency Service units from the East Side to back up squad three. Eubank overruled him.

He didn't want any more officers in vulnerable positions. Eubank was no fool and he knew that the situation had drastically changed. There were individuals, armed and definitely organized, who had fired on officers. But based on what he'd seen and heard so far, sooner or later he'd get a crack at them. All he wanted now was to be in a position to bring down on the perpetrators the forces he had at his disposal. His first priority was to move his squad someplace where it could function.

With that in mind, he had decided to leave Dietrich's body where it had fallen. Under the circumstances, the body could not be carried out. After arrests were made, EMS personnel could return for it. There was no other choice.

Finally, after two minutes of conversation, he'd pulled Havermeyer, Warren and Davis into a tighter circle and convinced them that with caution they could work their way east toward squad one and the Drive.

Ten minutes and twenty-five yards later, Eubank and his men were moving forward, drenched in sweat, tentative, disoriented, laboring under the constant and contagious intimation of danger.

A branch snapped under someone's foot and the officers froze.

Four flashlight beams focused on the ground in front of Havermeyer, but there was nothing. They heard a distant explosion and a last burst of gunfire, then silence and the sounds of their breathing. The four men stared at each other, carefully shuffling their feet. Each man felt impotent, isolated, wondering what was happening to his fellow officers. Eubank thought they'd better find out.

"Lights out for a minute." He waited until the beams clicked off and then called the command post. "Squad three to command. What is the status of squad two? K."

A dispatcher answered. "Squad two reports officers shot at Seven-seven Street." There was a pause. "Stand by, three." The Commissioner's voice came back and it had an edge that worried Eubank. "Don, two's back on the street. There were casualties. It looks bad; these guys are a mess. You'd better pull back to a secure area. Assist squad one and get the hell out of there."

Eubank didn't like that idea, but he wanted a quick end to the conversation. "Roger." He had another thought. "Command, have EMS ambulances standing by at the cross of Seven-two Street and the East Drive."

"Roger, command."

Eubank looked at his men, searching for signs of panic. He was sorry they'd heard the Commissioner. Damn, Eubank thought, we're not through yet. He returned the walkie-talkie to his lips.

"Squad three to Hardy. K." Nothing. He tried again. After several seconds, a short burst of static came back. Eubank knew what it meant; that Hardy was probably listening at a very low volume and had opened his channel for only a second to indicate that he'd copied Eubank's transmission. Eubank assumed that Hardy was attempting to maintain silence, so that he and Daniels did not endanger their position. Maybe they were onto something. Eubank decided to force them to respond anyway; he needed them now.

"Three to Hardy. Respond. This is priority. K."

A garbled transmission filtered through the static and Eubank couldn't make it out. Something about a motherfucker.

A loud bang startled Eubank and he jerked his head up. The sky exploded into a strange and eerie sun, covering the trees, the men, the ground in the unearthly glow of a phosphorus grenade. For long, terrifying seconds the men gasped upward, immobilized by the peculiar concentration of shock. What was happening was so alien, so completely out of their realm of experience, that not even their instincts or their training permitted them to react. They stared stupidly into space and listened to a whooshing sound cut through the air, faint, then louder, closing in.

Boom. The trees ripped apart; a downpour of leaves, branches and earth slammed into the officers. They rolled to the ground, trying to bury themselves in the dirt. The

**119**

awful whooshing began again. Boom. Havermeyer screamed and flung his arm out. The phosphorous glow faded, but in the last flickering light Eubank saw Havermeyer's shaking hand, a finger gone, bones jutting through red flesh.

Boom. The sound pounded into their ears, triggering one more surge of adrenaline, stealing their reason, destroying the last vestiges of their composure. Eubank shouted at his men to move. Davis and Warren crept forward, hugging the ground. Eubank grabbed Havermeyer and shoved him ahead. The booms stopped and Eubank rose to his feet, ordering his men to follow. A burst of automatic rifle fire crashed through the trees, forcing them down again. Eubank darted out of the trees onto a walk, his men crouched low behind him. He turned his M-16 in the direction of the shooting and emptied his clip into the bushes. He signaled Warren and Davis to lay down fire, and they opened up across the walk. Havermeyer gripped his rifle in one hand, shooting wildly, bullets spraying into the trees. Eubank reloaded. The pattern of sound changed.

"Hold your fire!"

Silence. Havermeyer wheezed. A crinkling of leaves, not close. They cocked their heads, listening for the sound. Nothing.

Warren was shaking. Davis rubbed sweat from his eyes. Eubank had an odd thought. Why aren't we dead?

He didn't think about the answer. He positioned the men behind him and they took off east on the walk, bent over, boots scraping on the pavement. They rounded a corner at the intersection of two walks and a dark form blocked their path, lurking in the shadows several yards ahead.

Eubank waved the officers to stop fast and everyone got down low, edging into the border of shrubs. They stared intently at the unmoving form, each man's fingers curled snugly against a trigger. The black shape became a murderer, a monster, an animal, a rock and, finally, when Eubank aimed a flashlight down the walk, a body.

Davis groaned. "Oh, shit, that's Mike."

"What?"

"Mike Levinson."

They'd found squad one.

Eubank turned off the light. All four men ran quickly to the fallen ESS officers. They checked the bodies, one by one, nausea welling up in their throats. The wounds were devastating; the faces cold, blue death masks; the eyes locked open in surprise. Havermeyer seemed to go into shock when he saw the mangled corpses. He sat down in the grass and lowered his head.

Eubank found Dell'olio stretched out in the bushes, static still coming from the walkie-talkie next to his hand. Dell'olio was alive. Eubank immediately stretched him out on the walk and listened to his breathing. Little bubbles of blood sputtered on his lips.

Warren and Davis stumbled over. Warren turned white. "I'm gonna puke," he said.

"Shut up. Listen, this is what you do. Get Havermeyer on his feet. Then you guys lift up Dell'olio here and walk out to the East Drive. There'll be ambulances."

Warren and Davis looked blank. They turned and stared at the bodies of the dead officers, then into the bushes and trees. Davis aimed his flashlight into the dark undergrowth and he saw bamboo poles, the ends burned and splintered. Eubank knocked the light from his hands and it went out.

"Shit. Move it." Warren was trembling again. Eubank relented. "Listen to me. These guys got this far before anything hit them. Retrace their steps till you see the boathouse. You'll be okay. I'll cover your back."

Eubank went to Havermeyer and helped him up. Davis put his arms under Dell'olio's shoulders and Warren grabbed the feet. Eubank made sure their rifles were secure on their backs.

He remembered Curran's offer of assistance, changed his mind, and decided to get help.

"I'll wait here. Davis, when you get to the drive, I'll have units there to assist you and the EMS. Get a couple of officers and come back here. We're gonna drag these bodies out. Understood?"

Davis nodded. Eubank watched them move off down the dark walk, struggling with Dell'olio's heavy frame. Havermeyer followed unsteadily, his damaged hand in his pocket, as if it were something that didn't belong to him, some object he'd found on a stroll through Central Park.

Eubank stepped off the walk and squatted in the matted-down foliage where he'd found Dell'olio. He leaned on his hand for support and felt something wet. Blood. He wiped it on his pants and reached for his walkie-talkie. He spoke as quietly as possible.

"Squad three to command. K." He smiled ironically. What squad?

"Go ahead, Don." It was the Commissioner again.

"Are those ambulances in position?"

"Affirmative."

"Tell them to move north to the boathouse. I have two officers shot, coming out that location."

"Roger."

"Send units to assist Officer Davis. I have three DOA's in here. You tell them this is a ten-thirteen, officers are down, they better be ready. K."

The Commissioner didn't respond for several seconds. Finally there was only a short burst of static. Eubank thought he heard the word "command."

Eubank settled back, safety off the M-16, selector on full automatic. In some sort of paradox, he felt power return to him, despite the fact that he was alone and definitely outmanned. He hoped the perpetrators had observed the evacuation of Davis and the others. He hoped they would make a mistake, presenting him with an opportunity to blow their brains out. He couldn't believe that whoever was doing this was so infallible, so organized, that they wouldn't screw up. In his experience, criminals, radicals, no matter who it was, they always screwed up. This was too perfect.

He shifted his legs and caught a glimpse of the bamboo poles. Grenades. He thought he'd heard grenades, but he'd hoped it was just his bad imagination. Now he was willing to bet that grenades had killed those officers lying on the walk. And those whooshing sounds. Mortars? A nerve tingled in his neck. Vietnam. Why was he thinking about that again? His mind raced through images of soldiers and jungles. Christ. What did he know about that? The closest he'd come to Vietnam was on Fifth Avenue when he'd banged his nightstick into an antiwar demonstrator ten years ago. Or was it a prowar demonstrator?

His eyes focused on the bodies of the dead ESS officers. What the hell was happening? A conspiracy? He knew that the Department had discussed this sort of thing before; detectives, off duty, over beers, running down scenarios for emergencies. How did it go? What if a bunch of asshole radicals stockpiled a load of weapons, because it was so easy to get the stuff, you could buy a tank if you had the money, and what if these lunatics decided to take something, like a nuclear power plant or City Hall or the Iranian embassy? Or Central Park.

Eubank knew the answer. Policemen would die.

Boots scraped over pavement, east; then a rustling of leaves, not close enough for him to measure. The sounds stopped and Eubank listened for movement. He ground his teeth together. Come on, psychos, one time—stick your heads out so I can destroy you.

A voice popped out of his walkie-talkie, surprising him, and he almost pulled the trigger on his M-16. It was Davis.

"Chief, that's us comin', east your location. Didn't want you to drop on us."

Smart boy, Davis. "Roger, let's go."

He watched several dark shapes approach on the walk, preceded by a flashlight beam. Eubank stepped out of the bushes so that the officers would see him. The light ran quickly over his face and was turned off. Davis moved close, keeping low, followed by six uniformed patrolmen in flak jackets, guns drawn. Eubank thought he recognized one of the men. He spoke quietly to him.

"Is that you, Sergeant Giamone?"

"Yes, sir."

"We've got some bad shit here." Eubank pointed at the bodies. "They're DOA, three of them."

"Oh, no."

"Don't look at them. Take your men, carry the bodies out to the drive. If anything happens, don't stop. We'll cover you."

The six patrolmen holstered their guns and lifted the corpses. Eubank and Davis squeezed into the bushes, making room for the officers to start back along the walk. The men struggled under the weight, trying to crouch down and move as fast as possible. Eubank let them get several yards ahead, waiting until their backs were just visible in the darkness. He felt Davis's breath on his neck.

"Let's go."

Bang. A smoke bomb flashed in the bushes on the opposite side of the walk. Eubank and Davis dropped to the pavement. A green cloud spilled over their backs, enclosing them in a dark fog. Eubank saw flashes through the smoke and two more devices exploded somewhere up ahead. He heard shouts. He rolled to his right, off the walk, and into the undergrowth. Davis followed, banging into his legs, unable to see. The haze seemed to get bright, reflecting light from beyond the wall of smoke. The high-intensity lamps on truck one, Eubank thought.

There was a thump inside the cloud and Eubank's forty-five-year-old reflexes twitched like a teenager's. He grabbed Davis in a headlock, rolling, crawling, scratching as fast and far into the bushes as possible before the grenade exploded, sending out a deadly rain of metal.

Davis groaned and twisted in the tangle of arms and legs, but neither man was hit. Boom, and they heard the trees tear apart. Another boom, this time farther away, east. Eubank swiveled his head around. East? No, he wasn't sure. He'd lost his direction in the smoke. Boom. Closer—dirt pelted their faces. They had to move or die.

Eubank shouted at Davis. "Grab my belt." Eubank jumped to his feet running low, blindly searching in the fog, banging into trees. Davis clutched a fistful of cloth, desperately trying to keep from becoming separated.

Suddenly they were out of the smoke. Davis let go of the shirt and they both fell to the ground, exhausted, choking for air—and lucky. Lucky, because they were kneeling two feet from a shiny roll of barbed wire.

Davis tried to say something, but the words wouldn't come out of his throat. Eubank stared at the wire. It curled off around the trees, angling down a rise until it disappeared in the heavy growth of the Ramble. Beyond was the Lake, a few lights reflecting on the surace, most of them shining from across the water in the direction of the Terrace and Bethesda Fountain. Eubank could barely make out the huge circular fountain and the tall winged statute in its center, Angel of the Waters. But now he knew where he was—on a small peninsula of land, facing south. The boathouse, the East Drive, the ambulances— help was far to his left. He cursed the wire, feeling a paranoid chill. Somebody was really fucking him over. There was no way to get down to the water. He and Davis either had to go back the way they had come, back into the smoke, probably to get themselves blown to pieces, or they could follow the wire, which would take them west, deeper into the Ramble and farther from possible safety and assistance.

"Fuck it." He'd said it out loud.

"What, sir?" Davis' voice was a rasping gag.

Four explosions echoed behind them, far enough away that neither man reacted with more than a turn of the head. Sirens began over the explosions, louder, followed by squealing tires and the distant burst of an automatic rifle. Eubank heard a barrage of small pops and recognized the sound of service revolvers returning fire. He knew what was happening. The perpetrators had circled their position and were now attacking the ESS, uniformed and medical personnel on the East Drive. Jesus, how many of them were there?

Eubank held the walkie-talkie to his mouth, but lowered it without speaking. He had an idea. Maybe he and Davis could double back toward the seven-nine transverse and come down on top of the attackers. One last chance to nail somebody. He thought it over quickly. From the sound of things, it was certain that mobile command wanted to pull back all units as fast as possible. Eubank knew he should be on the scene to give the final command to evacuate. As long as he and Davis were still somewhere inside the Park, a few officers would have to remain behind for security. Those officers would be in a dangerous position. Would the delay caused by his little detour be worth the risk?

Eubank couldn't remember the terrain near the transverse—whether there was any cover available where he and Davis could secure a location.

He raised the walkie-talkie back to his lips. "Eubank to command. K."

There was a long pause, probably because of the mess on the East Drive. Finally Curran answered. "Chief, what's your location? We've got problems. K."

No kidding. Eubank almost laughed. "We're cut off in here. Now listen, is that highway safety man there?"

"Roger."

"Is there a tunnel, or bridge, just south of the seven-nine transverse, the cross in the East Drive?"

The response was immediate. "Negative."

"Stand by." Eubank lowered the walkie-talkie. Curran tried to say something through the static and Eubank squelched the sound. He turned to Davis. "We need cover."

"We need the fuckin' marines." Davis didn't look away from Eubank's hard stare.

Eubank took ten seconds to think out loud and explain the options to Davis. The smoke was dissipating, but any straight approach to the East Drive would still be obscured. They might also get caught in their own officers' line of fire. That was a problem they didn't need.

Eubank made the decision. "We'll detour west about fifty yards, paralleling the wire here, and then cut north till we get to the road. If we don't find anyone we can come down to the boathouse and assist the RMP cars." Davis coughed. Eubank added, "And get the hell out of here."

The shooting seemed to subside; a few isolated pops continued and finally stopped. The drone of sirens persisted. Eubank jumped up and darted into the dense forest of willows and elms. Davis followed. They kept the long roll of wire on their left, using it as a guide through the undergrowth. The air was humid and cool, smelling of sap and leaves. As they pushed farther into the Ramble, the landscape became dark and impenetrable. They were forced to slow down, switching the flashlight on and off, always watching the ground in front of them, unable to forget a sudden and indelible image, a mental photograph of flying yellow spears and Dietrich's gurgling death rattle.

They passed within yards of the Lake, where it curved along the peninsula, and Eubank turned north.

A shot snapped through the quiet air. Davis cried out, collapsing to the ground. A jolt of adrenaline pounded

**127**

Eubank's heart for the tenth time in the last half hour and he dropped down in the blackness, falling next to Davis' prone form. He waited for the explosions, the whistling bullets, the chunk of metal that would finally slam into his head, murdering him, but nothing came.

The only sound was Davis' groaning. Eubank groped for the flashlight, keeping the beam tight to the grass, and watched Davis writhe around. He was doubled over, clutching his leg, a bloody hole in the top of his boot. Eubank moved the beam down Davis' leg until the circle of light rested on a small dugout section of ground. Inside, a bullet casing pointed up from a sleeve of bamboo, the bottom of the cartridge pressing down on the tip of a nail. The bullet, of course, was gone. Eubank marveled at this simple booby trap. What a cheap way to hurt somebody. He muttered, "I'll be damned."

Davis emitted a hiss of profanity. "Help me, Chief."

Eubank returned the light to Davis' leg. The bullet had shot clean through boot and foot. Davis was just now starting to bleed.

Eubank had no choice now but to retreat to the East Drive. There was no sense delaying evacuation and risking anyone else's life.

He helped Davis stand up, taking Davis' M-16 and slipping it over his shoulder with his own. Davis tried to put weight on his foot, but his leg buckled and he wiped tears from his eyes. Eubank whispered to him.

"Lean against this tree, Davis. Put your arm out."

Davis balanced himself and Eubank got down on his knees and switched on the flashlight. He checked the ground around their feet, brushing away patches of leaves and twigs. Perhaps twenty cartridge booby traps were implanted within the reach of Eubank's arms, fanning out from the barbed wire in random directions.

"Jesus Christ, Davis, don't move."

"I'm feeling faint, Chief."

Eubank moved the light and found far too much blood under Davis' dangling leg.

"What the hell?" Eubank was confused and ran the light up Davis' leg. Blood flowed heavily from the crotch of Davis' pants. Eubank stared at the wet red stain and realized what had happened: the bullet had blasted up through the boot and torn into Davis' groin. Eubank flinched: *That was the idea.*

"Oh God, Chief. What is that?" The voice was a whimper.

Eubank jerked up. Davis' face was white. His eyes were fixed on the terrible wound, his mind tumbling through discovery, curiosity, surprise and, finally, the first awful rush of pain. Eubank stood quickly, turning the light away, and caught Davis as he sagged down from the tree. He slapped Davis' face and said soothing words into his ears. Davis went into shock, mumbling incoherently, but Eubank managed to get him upright, slipping one of Davis' arms around his shoulder. Eubank held the light in his free hand and with great caution danced the two of them between the booby traps, retracing their steps east along the wire.

The Lake came into view and Eubank stopped on the small arm of land that jutted out into the water. Breathing heavily from the effort of dragging Davis through the undergrowth, he backed against a tree, using the trunk to support some of Davis' weight. Davis seemed to drift out of shock and he squeezed Eubank's arm.

"I'm hurting, Chief. What's happening?"

"We're on our way out. Be quiet."

The sirens had faded; the only sounds were their breathing and Davis' low moans each time a wave of pain rolled through his abdomen. Eubank peered into the darkness. Several yards ahead, wisps of smoke still lingered in the bushes and trees; blurred flashes of red light from the emergency vehicles shone through the haze like the distant beacons of a lighthouse. Eubank turned back to Davis, whose eyes were rolled back in his head.

"Davis, look at me." Eubank grabbed Davis' chin and wiggled his head. "We're gonna move fast now. Put your arm around me. We'll be out of here in two minutes. Stay with it."

Davis reached out for support and they moved away from the trees. Davis groaned in pain, clutching Eubank, and hopped clumsily with the last vestiges of his strength. Eubank struggled onto a walkway that angled north and followed it, hoping to circle the smoke and find a clear path to the East Drive. They traveled ten feet and were blocked by another roll of concertina.

Leaves crunched and a black shape seemed to pass in the shadows on the other side of the wire. Eubank froze, unable to discern anything in the darkness. He heard a sound like a soft motor, to his left, behind him, circling. The ground yielded unfathomable signals: branches snapped, bushes rustled, the noises beating like hammers in his ears. The sounds stopped. There was a metallic click, perhaps a gear falling into place.

Davis moaned. His eyes rolled back in his head. Eubank squeezed him tightly and turned slowly around, feeling helpless under the officer's weight, unable at this critical second to reach for his M-16 and rake the black trees with fire.

Click. Eubank tensed. He knew it was the sound of an ammunition clip being locked into an automatic rifle. He stood absolutely still. There was breathing; not his, not Davis', but very close, only feet beyond the wire. Eubank tried to see, wanted to see the men who would be his killers. Shapes and forms appeared and disappeared, floating like specters in the dark, murky air. Eubank thought he saw a wheel, an arm, the barrel of a gun. In an instant of sudden clarity, not unlike the moment of death, he understood what was happening. One by one, officers were being driven from the Park; somehow, someone knew he

**130**

was still there. He stared across the wire. His mouth fell open. *They've come back to get me.*

For the first time, Eubank was afraid. A warm flash of panic tingled in his neck. He lunged away from the wire, pulling Davis into the clouds of smoke. The haze swirled around them and they were covered in a green shroud. They stumbled blindly through invisible bushes and trees, Eubank flailing his arm against the fog, until their legs tangled and they fell hard on the pavement.

Eubank gasped for air and scraped the ground with his fingers. They were on a walk, but leading where? He rolled Davis off his back. He was lost, trapped—and then he saw the blurred outlines of flashing lights, closer now, a short run through the smoke. He rose to his knees. A breeze touched his neck.

A soft motor hummed in his ear and something crossed the walk behind him. It slithered into the smoke, brushing through long, whipping branches. It stopped and the motor idled. Davis screamed. Someone revved the engine and hot exhaust, a killer's deadly breath, blew into Eubank's face.

He jumped up, grabbed Davis' shirt collar and dragged him like a dead fish, moving with a speed made possible only by fear. He ran hard for the flashing lights and lunged free of the swirling smoke.

The thumping of his feet, the hysteria of his flight, made Eubank's vision unsteady and incoherent. Angels and abstractions flew into his eyes; dull black corners, light glinting from shiny surfaces, a building, cars, spinning red balls and crouching men with guns. Eubank pounded forward and collapsed on the East Drive.

There were shouts and two medics hurried out from behind EMS 141. They placed Davis on a stretcher and loaded him into the ambulance. Two uniformed officers helped Eubank up from the roadway and they moved into cover behind a line of patrol cars parked in front of the boathouse.

Eubank was hyperventilating. He rubbed sweat from his face and forced his breathing to slow down. Sergeant Giamone leaned over him and took Davis' M-16. Eubank turned around, sliding his own rifle into his hands, and faced the boathouse and the dark landscape beyond.

There were eight or nine RMP cars and EMS vehicles along the Drive, with maybe fifteen officers maintaining positions behind the cars. Truck one was parked on the Drive above the Trefoil arch, the short tunnel that passed under the roadway. Eubank looked up at the truck and spoke to Giamone. His voice was a little shaky.

"Is everybody out of the park, Sergeant?"

Giamone was confused. They were standing in Central Park. He studied Eubank. The man didn't look good, but it wasn't the time to go into that. Giamone replied, "I think everybody's out, sir. It was a little hairy for a while."

"I know. Let's get back on Fifth Avenue." Eubank closed his eyes, trying to make his mind work. "Tell the truck up there to turn those lamps on and we'll follow him out on Seven-two Street."

"Yes, sir."

Eubank reached for the walkie-talkie in his belt, but it was missing. He yelled at Giamone, who was heading back to an RMP car on the drive.

"Sergeant, call mobile command and tell them we're on our way in."

Giamone acknowledged with a wave.

A blast of automatic rifle fire ripped into the line of cars. Glass shattered and tinkled to the pavement. An officer fell, clutching his legs. Bullets sprayed over the area and tore into the boathouse and the pay phones that stood in front of the building. Several officers began to return fire.

Eubank slid down behind an RMP car. The snapping of the guns cleared his head and he raised his M-16. He fired the entire clip into the wall of darkness beyond the trees, shooting at everyone, at no one, at a relentless and invisible enemy.

An explosion went off above Eubank's head and truck one erupted in smoke and glass. Fragments of metal ricocheted off the pavement and were deflected by Eubank's flak jacket. He rolled to the ground and looked up at the Trefoil arch. The driver tumbled out of the truck and crawled out of sight on the Drive.

Eubank edged forward, reached into the RMP car and found the loudspeaker on the radio. His voice resounded over the shooting. He ordered the officers to start the cars and evacuate, then dropped the mike and jammed a fresh clip into his M-16. He returned to the rear of the car and continued firing west into the trees. An ESS officer scrambled up to the side of the car and shouted at Eubank.

"Are you coming sir?"

Eubank lowered the M-16. "No, I'll cover you. Get moving."

Eubank ran to the front of the car and shouted down the line to hold fire. The shooting stopped. Several officers jumped into their vehicles and started the engines. A smoke bomb exploded in front of the boathouse, then another and another, in a series of bright flashes back along the roadway. The entire area was immediately swallowed by the billowing, multicolored clouds.

Eubank heard squealing tires and saw headlight beams poke through the smoke, heading south on the Drive toward 72nd Street. Someone shouted a command and there were two gunshots: service revolvers.

Boom. Eubank jumped. He knew what was coming. Metal, dirt, asphalt rained down through the smoke. There were screams. Eubank hoped they were only cries of terror as he rolled back under the Drive and into the damp, dark tunnel of the Trefoil arch.

The smoke interfaced at the entrance to the arch, like

**133**

some science fiction portal, and Eubank banked away, farther into the tunnel. Automatic rifle fire resumed. Someone appeared under the arch, vanished, then darted inside. It was an ESS officer, eyes bulging, out of control. He ran through the tunnel, oblivious to Eubank, and out the other end. Eubank watched him and saw a faint light on the stairs at the east end of the arch. He squeezed his M-16, hesitated, resigned himself to the hopelessness of his position, and followed the officer out into the Park.

Eubank ran a short distance along a walk and the lights of Fifth Avenue appeared through the trees. He slowed, exhausted, listening to the weapons fire subside and finally stop. He kept going, moving over a small rise, and approached the Conservatory Water. Even in the darkness he could make out the shape of the beautifully sculptured pool, and behind it the Krebs Memorial Model Boat House, perhaps twenty yards from the avenue. He was struck by how suddenly Fifth Avenue represented safety and refuge; how the Park had become something frightening and impenetrable. A memory of himself in uniform, watching kids sail boats in the small boat pond, lingered briefly in his thoughts, only to be instantly replaced by the brutal sound of a whooshing projectile.

A thundering blast shook the ground. It was followed by another explosion and debris showered down over him. Eubank fell and curled into a ball. There were no more explosions, but a steady crack of weapons fire opened up somewhere behind him on the East Drive. Eubank raised his head. He felt dizzy, but he was aware of blurred shapes moving through trees and pathways. He stood up, wobbling, and saw officers fleeing toward the avenue, bright bursts of light going off around them like flashbulbs as they fired blindly into the darkness. Many of the men pulled wounded colleagues behind them, struggling forward, their single desperate purpose to escape death at the edge of Central Park.

Eubank got up and took off toward the avenue. Bullets

seemed to change direction, slashing into the leaves above his head. He darted to his left and zigzagged along the edge of the small boat pond. A huge man loomed over him and he ducked under the Hans Christian Anderson statue. He circled the pool, stumbled momentarily and regained his balance, his legs stretching out for the last yards to the Park wall and the avenue. He laughed, triumphant, death cheated again. He saw the street and the sidewalk and lights and cars and buildings and a yellow forest of bamboo stakes rising inevitably toward his face, propelled by his own foot sinking down on the trigger-end of a deadly fulcrum, a teeter, totter punji stick trip board. Leaping up from the ground, this strange messenger of pain and death overwhelmed Eubank's senses and precipitated one final hallucination. An apparition lingered briefly before him of desolate incinerated jungles— of soldiers, anonymous and condemned. And in the nightmare, he screamed as tortured reflexes moved his arms slowly, so slowly, to deflect the sharp stakes slamming into his throat.

Chief Don Eubank, commander of Emergency Services, did not quite escape his invisible enemy. He passed out two feet short of the exact perimeter of Central Park.


"Stop tape."

Weaver waited for Richie, who was standing next to her, to indicate that they were no longer rolling. She turned her head from the eyepiece, holding the camera steady, and glanced at him. He was transfixed by the chaos on Fifth Avenue.

"Richie! Turn us off."

He reached and punched the tape deck.

"Sorry, Weav."

"Kill the light."

He shut off the bright sun gun.

Two loud pops went off across the avenue, inside Central Park. Weaver and Richie ducked instinctively. Someone shouted and several police officers ran out from behind the jam of ambulances and police cars parked in the middle of the street. A siren shrieked on East 75th Street and an NYPD van stopped in the intersection. A squad of ESS officers jumped out and lined up on the sidewalk a few yards from Weaver and Richie. Weaver tugged at Richie's arm and stepped off the curb onto Fifth Avenue, winding their way through the mess of vehicles. After several yards Richie stopped suddenly in front of her and Weaver bumped into him. She adjusted the camera on her shoulder and saw that they were standing behind a patrol car parked along the curb on the west side of the avenue. Nothing was between them and the sidewalk. They had an unobstructed view of the Park.

A thin haze drifted over the Park wall, reflecting the yellow beams of the tall streetlamps. Dark shapes moved inside the haze, indistinct figures floating in an illusory light, gaining substance and form as they crawled inexorably closer. Weaver's heart beat faster. Arms reached out over the pavement and a figure stumbled into the hard light at the edge of the curb. A wounded police officer rose to his knees, waved a gun at the sky and collapsed in the street.

Reflexes moved Weaver's hand to the camera lens and made her voice tell Richie to roll tape. She took a tight shot of the fallen officer, then went wide. Officers appeared out of the dark background of Central Park, came closer through the haze, hoisted themselves over the stone wall and tumbled to the sidewalk. Some of the men scrambled to the street, guns down, wild looks on their faces. EMS personnel rushed into the picture and assisted a wounded officer who had been carried out of the Park. A flash of gunfire erupted in the darkness beyond the wall, forcing Weaver down; she maintained a level image and taped the medics dragging the officer forward to the avenue. She panned back to the wall. A hand curled over the top and a stream of bright bursts went off behind it. An ESS officer stood up, threw a rifle on the sidewalk and lifted up another officer whose head rolled limply on his shoulders. He struggled to get the man over the wall until an EMS medic crawled into the scene to assist him. Weaver stayed with the action until the men moved beyond the curb.

She shouted at Richie to stop tape. "How we doing on time?"

Richie raised the VTR and checked the cassette. "About ten minutes more." He was gasping for air.

So was Weaver. She leaned over the hood of the patrol car and noticed that a uniformed sergeant and a plainclothes officer were right next to Richie, kneeling on the street, their revolvers pointed at Central Park. She realized that it had become very quiet; there was only an isolated shout, a fading siren, an ambulance door slamming behind her. She stood up more and looked north on the avenue. All along the curbline, officers in flak vests crouched behind patrol cars, trees, unmarked vehicles, every man aiming a revolver or a rifle into the blackness on the other side of the wall. They looked as if they were waiting for a command to fire into the landscape—as if they could somehow shoot down that dangerous and implacable suspect, Central Park.

What a great picture! Weaver put her eye to the camera. A commotion broke out up the sidewalk and several officers ran to the wall, spoiling the shot. Weaver swore and stepped away from the car. Richie followed closely and they ran up the avenue.

Weaver squeezed between the line of cars, next to the crowd of officers and medics gathering in front of the Park wall. She tried to push her camera close enough for a possible shot, but a plainclothesman shoved her out of the way. He was serious.

"Get the fuck back!" he shouted.

A film crew that Weaver didn't recognize moved in and

turned on their lights. They received the same treatment. There was a lot of shoving and some harsh words. Weaver motioned to Richie to stand on the curb. She positioned herself next to him and waited.

A stretcher appeared out of the crowd, pushed by EMS personnel. An Emergency Service officer was lying on top. His face and neck were red. There seemed to be a hole in his throat, and blood spurted out, covering his flak jacket. Weaver heard some of the officers mumbling; she thought she heard the name "Eubank."

An ambulance backed up to the curb. The film crew turned on their lights again, illuminating the area. They were jostled by the officers, but the lights stayed on. The policemen cleared a path to the rear of the ambulance. No one seemed to notice Weaver.

She whispered to Richie, "Plenty of light. Got it?" Richie nodded. "Roll."

Richie whispered back, "Speed."

Weaver taped the stretcher as it rolled to the curb. When it bumped down into the street, the man on the stretcher regained consciousness. He grabbed one of the medics' hands and the stretcher stopped. The man sat up; blood spilled into his lap. The medics gently tried to get him to lie down, but he wouldn't. He turned slowly around, wincing in pain, and looked in the direction of the Park.

Weaver slipped away from the curb so that she could get an angle on the man's face. She zoomed tighter. The man stared into Central Park. His eyes opened very wide; he seemed to see something in the darkness of the trees. He raised a shaking arm and pointed; he tried to speak, but his voice was nothing but a choking sound. He pointed again and turned to the officers. They watched him blankly, sweat pouring from their faces.

The man lowered his hand. He looked back at the Park again, narrowed his eyes and sagged down on the stretcher.

Weaver taped the medics as they lifted the stretcher

into the ambulance and shut the doors. She panned up and framed the flashing lights as EMS 131 wound its way through the cars and sped south on the avenue.

Weaver stopped tape. An officer walked up to one of the men and handed him a walkie-talkie.

"Lieutenant. The P.C. wants to talk to you."

The lieutenant had a brief conversation over the radio and then spoke to the crowd of officers.

"That's it. Let's get set up and clear the street." He started to walk away, then turned back. "Wait a second. Stay away from the wall there. I have orders that no one is to go inside that park. Not even three feet. Understood?"

The officers glanced warily into the bushes. They holstered their guns and dispersed. Weaver and Richie crossed to the other side of the avenue and watched the patrol cars and emergency vehicles drive away from the Park, heading downtown or east, into the side streets. Several uniformed and ESS officers remained, setting up police barricades on the sidewalk. A few patrol cars were positioned at the intersection of 72nd Street and the Park. No other traffic moved on Fifth Avenue. In a matter of minutes the darkness absorbed fifty men and Weaver and Richie were alone in front of an apartment building.

Richie moved ahead, and as they stepped off the curb behind a sawhorse barricade at 77th Street, a voice hissed at them from a dark alcove at the side of one of the buildings. An officer with a rifle leaned out and told them to get the hell off the street. Weaver peered into the block and up and down Fifth Avenue. She realized that officers were hiding in the shadows of every stairway and service entrance. Unmarked cars were parked on the corners of each block.

The odyssey of John Hardy and Dewayne Daniels, south from the Belvedere, across the Ramble, and to the narrow shore of the Lake, had been the single most frightening experience in their five years as police officers.

"Things," as Hardy would say later, "—bad things was out there the whole time."

It had started as they'd made their first tentative steps into the trees bordering the Ramble, feeling lost, feeling certain that something ugly was going to happen. Their fears were justified when the nervous silence was shattered by five dull booms—not firecrackers or guns, but something bigger.

Hardy had pulled Daniels close, down into the bushes, and whispered, "I told you we was gon' get fucked."

In the ensuing hours, their entire trip through the Ramble was spent face down in the black, impenetrable undergrowth, crawling forward, inch by inch, while a storm of lethal projectiles sailed over their heads. It seemed that every time a lull developed in the barrage and they attempted to gain a few yards, another explosion pounded down, sending sheets of fragments tearing through the trees. This was always followed by the crack of automatic weapons and a deadly crossfire of bullets streaming close above the ground. They had no choice but to squeeze into the leaves and dirt, trembling, unable to return fire or to defend their position. Their sense of reality was distorted, then crushed, by the persistent, incongruous firestorm.

They had remained motionless in one spot for thirty minutes, listening to the guns and explosions, the screams, and a confused jumble of transmissions from the walkie-talkie. Finally, when the weapons fire had stopped, they shut off the walkie-talkie and waited out another fifteen minutes of sweaty silence. Strange sounds drifted out of the darkness; clicks, snaps, the crunching of branches, a soft whir passing within feet of their position. They held their breath and heard the sound of something being fired out of a tube; the sound came again and again, followed by a long line of distant booms.

140

They'd jumped up, seized by an overpowering and simultaneous panic, and fled into the bushes, expecting to be cut down at any second by the bursts of rifle fire that opened up from every direction. They stumbled over the huge rocks into the Gill, a small stream running off the Lake, and splashed across, plunging deeper into the Ramble. Walkways appeared before them and they followed these circuitous paths into the trees and a labyrinth of barbed wire. Daniels had become tangled in the sharp coils, slashing his arms and back; Hardy tripped over him and fired his rifle into the ground, detonating a device that exploded out and away from them, spewing forth a hideous shower of fragments that cut a small willow tree in half.

Exhausted, lost, chased by the ubiquitous gunfire, they'd somehow discovered a way through the wire and down to the shore of the Lake. There they waited, listening while the sounds of shooting and sirens receded in the distance, until they were certain of their isolation—positive that in the confusion they had been abandoned to the mercy of some maniacal killers.

Hardy tried to spit into the Lake. He whispered into his walkie-talkie. "Hardy to squad three. K."

No response.

"Squad three. Goddamnit, do you copy?"

There was no reply. Hardy fiddled with the walkie-talkie and angrily threw it into the mud at the edge of the water. He slammed his rifle butt into the metal casing.

"Shit."

Daniels smiled, a sudden flash of white teeth. "Ain't nobody listenin', blood. They all dead and gone."

Hardy wiped sweat from his forehead and looked across the calm water of the Lake. A light mist was rising from the surface. He and Daniels were hiding in the thick brush that bordered the narrowest channel of water. Only fifty yards separated them from the opposite shore. To his right, Hardy could make out a bridge spanning this channel. It was the Bow Bridge, a beautiful cast-iron structure that connected the Ramble with a rolling meadow known as Cherry Hill. The bridge didn't look particularly beautiful to Hardy. It looked like a way out.

He moved closer to Daniels. "How you feelin'? You bleedin' or what?"

Daniels' shirt was stuck to his back. He pulled it away from his skin. "It hurts is all. It ain't bad."

"Man, we got to get to the street."

"Fuck you."

"Come on. It's a miracle nobody seen us yet."

"You think so." Daniels eyed the menacing terrain. "How come we ain't seen nobody? Where are they John?"

"How the fuck should I know?"

"I'll tell you. They jus' waitin' out there for us to do some chump number and then they gonna pick us off."

Hardy was disturbed by Daniels' logic; but he wasn't going to sit in the dark, scared shitless, until daylight. "Are you comin' with me or not?"

"I ain't movin'. That is some real shit out there."

"You see that bridge, Dewayne? All we gotta do is cross over and Seven-two Street is right there." Well, almost, Hardy admitted to himself.

"You sure?" asked Daniels.

"Hell, yeah. I used to sell weed down there all the time."

"How long ago was that? Ten years?"

"What you sayin', Dewayne? Shit, this motherfucker don't change. Seventy-second Street gonna be right where it always been, till the day you die."

"We're dead already."

"Stop that."

Daniels thought it over. He got up on one knee and put his M-16 on full automatic. "Okay. But don't be on my ass, 'cause I'm gonna blast anything that don't look right."

"I hear you."

Hardy moved ahead several yards, poking the ground in front of him with his rifle. Daniels came up behind him and they stopped.

"Ready, Dewayne?"

Daniels nodded. A bush rustled behind a rock outcropping in the trees. They froze. A grenade thumped in the mud and rolled up to their feet. They both stared at it for an eternal second. Daniels screamed and dove into the bushes. Hardy swayed back, farther, blue circles forming behind his eyes, bright yellow balls danced in the circles, and gravity tugged at his shoulders. He fainted.

The cool, damp mud smacked Hardy's cheek and he woke up one second later. His windpipe was closed; his breath caught in his throat. He tried to move, heard a whimper in his mind that was a baby calling for its mama, and watched the grenade crack open, thousands of sharp razors spinning out into his body.

But there was no explosion; he shook his head, clearing away the dream of death. He leaned forward and peered at the ground. A minute passed. Nothing happened. He crawled closer to the grenade. It rested in the mud, unchanged, exactly as it had landed. He found the flashlight in his belt and aimed it at the grenade. The pin was still in place. He went closer; something didn't look right. He scooped the grenade out of the mud; a white piece of paper was attached to it with a rubber band.

A high-pitched voice came out of the bushes. Daniels. "For God's sake, what are you doin'?"

Hardy removed the paper. His hand was shaking violently. "There's a note on the grenade."

"What?"

"A note."

"Don't be fuckin' with me."

"God, you know what it say? It say: 'You got ten seconds to get out of the park.'"

Daniels moaned. Hardy set down the grenade carefully.

He looked all around the landscape; the park throbbed and breathed. The trees were teeming with unseen enemies.

A shape tore out of the bushes; Daniels careened into the water, holding his rifle in front of him, and made a dash for the Bow Bridge. Hardy hesitated for only an instant and then followed his partner over the bridge, down to 72nd Street and across to the East Side, where they were almost gunned down by officers stationed on Fifth Avenue.

During their wild run for safety, Hardy, compelled by the curiosity of mortal fear, looked back over his shoulder and had a vision of a man on a black motorcycle. But Hardy didn't believe it. It was all part of the nightmare, and the image was supplanted by another; one that months later would continue to plague his dreams, waking Hardy with a violent jerk, frightening his girl. And he would lie there in his bed, in his apartment two blocks from Central Park, grinding his teeth and shivering in his own sweat.

The dream was simple.

A grenade.

Harris sat on the Yamaha at the south end of the Mall. He looked north along the entire length of the tree-lined promenade. Tall branches became buildings on a dark and deserted avenue, extending before him like a parade route in a city that waited to celebrate the victors.

Harris accelerated and moved slowly forward. A leaf fell on his shoulder and he accepted the silent cheers of an imaginary and vindicating crowd. He laughed and drove faster, his flak jacket flapping in the breeze. He raced by the bandshell and heard the ephemeral notes of some patriotic anthem.

The bike vaulted the curb at 72nd Street. Harris continued on over the wide Terrace and bounced down the stone steps to the Fountain. He brought the bike to a spinning, twirling stop and faced the Lake.

He yelled. His body vibrated. He raised his arms in triumph to the glowing night sky.

No one yelled back. The silence electrified his senses.

Harris lowered his arms. He was in control and out of control and he loved it. He had longed for this internal ride, missed it, savored its recollection. He'd suffered patiently the years when, in isolated moments, dreams and memories suddenly grasped for shape and form, always falling short, always lingering on the edge of reality. Now, here, the waiting was over. It didn't matter that this ecstasy was brief—that days, even hours later, he would be left empty, searching again for an elusive satisfaction, for a surge of fear and power.

That's what it had always been, a need—sometimes latent and subdued, sometimes pervasive and overpowering. Harris had lived with it since the day when a whirling machine hovered over a burning forest and he'd jumped down out of the known world.

Harris pounded the handlebars and jumped up and down on the seat. He rolled the bike to the edge of the huge, circular Fountain, removed his helmet and plunged it into the pool of water. He splashed his face, letting the cool streams trickle down his chest under the sweat-soaked fatigues. He scrubbed away the black smears of nightfighter cosmetic. Exhaustion lurked behind his excitement, but he could not let it overtake his concentration. Even though his heart was beating a mile a minute, Harris took another amphetamine.

He drained his canteen and checked the time; three hours until daylight. There were things he should be doing. He turned off the bike and retrieved his notebook from under the seat. He sat on a stone bench under a lamp, with his back to the Lake. His knees and hands were shaking. It took fifteen minutes before he could sit still and think. Finally, Harris was able to study his charts.

He hadn't expended much of his arsenal in defeating the assault force. Nevertheless, he'd made only a skeletal

**145**

deployment of the bulk of his weapons. None of the stuff was doing him any good sitting underground in the supply dumps. The entire perimeter of the Park was vulnerable. Now that he didn't have ground forces to contend with, he'd better spend the next three hours committing anti-personnel devices, like the claymores, to areas where they could be effective and provide security. There was also the task of constructing his firebase.

Harris rubbed his eyes. The speed tickled his head. He slammed the notebook shut and got back on the bike. Just for kicks he zoomed around the Fountain, keeping his eyes on the giant angel in the middle of the pool and the four cherubs beneath her. He remembered from his research that the cherubs represented Temperance, Purity, Health and Peace.

Harris spun away from the Fountain and hopped the cycle up the stone steps to the Terrace, onto a walk that led through the trees to the Bow Bridge. He was heading for the supply dump, but first he wanted to survey the scene of combat.

He went over the bridge and drove through the mud on the shore of the Lake. A rock mound jutted out of the trees and he slowed, shining his flashlight over the soft ground, until he found an unexploded fragmentation grenade near the water's edge. He shoved the grenade in one of his equipment sacks and angled up from the Lake into the Ramble.

Harris spent the next thirty minutes winding slowly through the walkways and heavy undergrowth, checking the status of the barbed wire and booby traps. He observed the signs of intense weapons fire, the debris, the chewed-up ground, even several small craters. His corridors appeared intact; one claymore had been detonated near the Lake and he found a punji pit that had claimed a victim. He reset the bloody stakes and covered the hole with a mat of leaves.

146

He went west on foot toward the Bank Rock Bridge and the Drive and made a quick search of the area. The long roll of concertina wire still extended across the roadway and the disabled truck and patrol car remained where they had been abandoned. Harris decided against crossing the Drive until later, when it would be necessary to come close to the street and set up the claymores. He turned back into the Ramble and, on his way to the bike, discovered an M-16 lying in the bushes.

He stood there and looked at it for several seconds. It had been a long time since he'd held one in his hands. He was almost afraid to touch it, afraid of the memories that might come flooding back. He realized that the way it was resting there, with a little blood on the handle, was an old dream and the memories were coming anyway. An explosion shook the ground and the gun dropped from someone's hand. Who was that yelling? No, he didn't want that to happen now, and he reached down quickly and grabbed the rifle, squeezing it hard. The touch of the cold metal and plastic jolted Harris and he came back from the dream.

The weapon was real, solid and tangible; he held it and caught his breath. He'd forgotten how light the M-16 was compared to the AK-47. It was like a toy, but very effective in the jungle. For a moment, he regretted not having any magazines for an M-16. He might have considered using it.

He put the M-16 over his shoulder next to the AK and retraced his steps to the dirt bike. He drove east through the Ramble, in the direction of the fire alarm station on the 79th Street transverse. The air was cool and damp, and a dew was settling on the leaves and bushes. Wet branches scraped across his face as he moved out of the thick growth and saw a rope dangling from one of the tall trees.

He was so startled by what appeared in front of the

147

bike that he braked too quickly, stalled and nearly tumbled over the handlebars. He jumped off and the bike fell on its side.

A body was stretched out in the grass. One of the booby traps, the rake-like "Malayan gate," was on the ground next to the dead man.

"Oh, no." Harris said it out loud. His voice was weak. He put his hands over his eyes. He couldn't look at the body. He started walking in a circle, his feet kicking through the wet leaves. He talked to himself.

Oh, shit, why did they have to leave him here?

They've got to come back and get him.

No, they can't do that.

Oh, shit.

Harris stopped; the dead man was stretched out at his feet. He took one quick, nauseating glance at the body. Every ounce of exhilaration and excitement drained away from Harris.

The dead man did not have the right face.

Harris gasped when he was eighteen and watched his arm fly out in a reflective attempt to break a fall from his motorcycle. The pain was slight, but he gasped again later in the doctor's office when the doctor told him he had a non-displaced radial head fracture of his right arm. No cast was necessary, but Harris was not supposed to move his arm for ten days, and it would be a month before the arm had full strength. The doctor assured Harris that the injury wasn't serious and that there would be no permanent damage.

"Serious?" Harris laughed bitterly. "This is a death sentence."

The doctor had been taking care of Harris and his brothers since they were born, so he did not need an explanation for Harris' dramatic assessment of a minor fracture. He knew what such an injury could mean to a high school outfielder batting .426 with 12 home runs, apparently destined for the first time to be all-league, and only a month into his final season.

Baseball was what Harris termed a "priority game." It had been important to him since he was seven and began playing t-ball in one of the leagues organized in the suburban communities north of Detroit. But baseball did not deter Harris' participation in other games. In fact, he and his two older brothers had a reputation among the mothers in the neighborhood for introducing everybody's children to a variety of sprained ankles, black eyes and deep cuts. There seemed to be an endless need to compete, to devise more sophisticated ways to play, and Harris and his brothers were the inventors. But the Harris family was well liked and the boys were nice kids. They always wore expressions of sincere remorse when appearing on a doorstep with a wounded friend who'd been scraped raw during the wild climax of Bike Tag, stating regretfully, "Gee, Mrs. Snyder, we're sorry about Terry's bike."

Bicycles, skateboards, BB guns and, finally, when Harris was fifteen, motorcycles. Mrs. Harris had tolerated every horror and potential tragedy that her boys flirted with from the time they were five years old, but motorcycles tested the limits of her nerves. No amount of reasoning could discourage the boys, once their father had given tacit approval. If they saved the money they earned from mowing lawns, he said, it was their decision what they wanted to spend it on. Harris watched his older brothers with envy for two years; watched them race away into the night with Marcia Peterson or Claudia Detweiler clinging to their backs, the girls' long, jean-wrapped legs wound around pulsing Hondas.

Harris purchased his first small Yamaha on his fifteenth birthday (with help from his father). Harris knew that his mother was going to worry about him; she always worried most about him, because he was the youngest. So, before he took the cycle out for his first ride, he sat down with his mother and said, "Mom, I'll be okay. Really. I gotta have some way to get to practice all summer, so you won't have to drive me all the time. This is priority, Mom. I'll be careful. Really."

Marcia Peterson's sister Carrie suffered a minor concussion in a fall from Harris' cycle two days later. Harris was unhurt, much to the relief of the man who coached Harris' Babe Ruth League team that summer. The coach thought Harris had potential as a baseball player, if he could get Harris to concentrate on the game instead of Carrie, Linda, Patti and motorcycles. He was the first coach to try to warn Harris about how certain activities could jeopardize an athelete's future. "Girls are in my future, right?" Harris had replied. "And they like my bike." Harris pitched two no-hitters that summer, despite three crashes on his well-traveled Yamaha.

All the warnings about potential injuries were replayed in Harris' mind on the day he left the doctor's office and went home and explained to his parents that his senior season had been washed out, and just when he was going to have a good year. His mother didn't say I told you so, nor did his coach, later. Everyone was sympathetic. Harris wanted to cry, but he didn't. His father bought a six-pack of beer and took Harris for a ride, and they talked. His father reminded him that his arm was going to be okay, and that there was always Legion ball in the summer. And he said that maybe the injury wasn't such a bad thing. Instead of rushing blindly toward graduation, caught in the excitement of the team and practices and playoffs, Harris would now have a chance to think about what he was going to do after high school. He would have a chance to make some decisions.

Harris took his father's advice. Sort of. He spent the last month and a half of high school thinking about Diane Stevens; about the terrific summer they would be spending together, and about how hard it would be to say good-bye to her in the fall when Harris went away to college.

Harris was a good student, and he'd been accepted by

the University of Michigan, where it was planned that he would follow his two brothers and probably end up pledging the same fraternity. But Harris wasn't sure that's what he wanted to do. Two things were making him hesitate. One was Diane, and the unpleasant possibility of saying good-bye. The other was the draft. The future of student deferments was up in the air and there was talk of a draft lottery later in the year. The last thing Harris wanted to do was go reluctantly to college and then get yanked out for military service midway in his freshman year.

By late summer Harris had made up his mind. He didn't want to go to the university in the fall. He decided to enlist. Nobody but Harris liked this idea, but he had his reasons. An enlistment would remove the uncertainty of the draft, and his induction would not take place until December. He'd have time to spend with Diane, and also Carrie Peterson, who'd lately been attending his ball games. It was simple: Harris was going to have a great time, driving with Diane up to Ann Arbor for parties, picking Carrie up from Michigan State on weekends, working, saving money, getting a new bike. And after two years in the service, he'd have a clean, paid-for, uninterrupted run through college.

Harris' mother watched the newscasts and listened to the death toll of American soldiers in Vietnam. When Harris left for the induction center in December, she did not cry when they said good-bye. She listened to Harris tell her, "It's okay, Mom. Really. Nothing's going to happen. They won't even send me over there. I'll fall down or something and get another radial head fracture. Don't worry. I'll be careful. Really." He was inducted into the Army in December of 1969.

Harris was discharged from military service in 1972. In July 1978, he was on vacation, standing on the IRT subway platform at Columbus Circle. It was 3:00 A.M., and Harris wasn't concentrating. He was at the end of the platform, the most dangerous place to be late at night.

There were few people; the last cars of the train would be empty. Everybody had told him that, but Harris was tired; he was drunk; he was a tourist.

He heard a low rumbling in the distance. Someone was standing behind him. He turned around. Two kids, teenagers, were a few feet away on the platform. They were looking over their shoulders, checking out the station. One of the kids stepped forward and pushed a knife against Harris' throat. Harris felt sweat drip into his eye. He blinked. The other kid was moving behind Harris' back. Harris grabbed the knife, felt it slice his palm, and then his head snapped and a white flash covered his eyes.

Harris was kneeling on the platform, watching blood puddle up in his hand. The rumbling sound was becoming louder. Somebody's hand was in his pocket. Harris was dizzy and sat down. The noise was very loud. He shifted his weight. There was a scream of metal, a roar, and the air was buffeted. A small man stood over him, holding his wallet. Another man was leaning over the edge of the platform, swiveling his head back and forth. Harris' heart pounded. The two men were dressed in dark, loose clothes. They carried AK-47 assault rifles, and their eyes were tiny, probing slits.

Harris' chest exploded with adrenaline. A huge machine flashed through his vision and he heard the small men yell; he heard their voices choked away and the dull thud of bodies being hit.

Harris stood on the quiet platform in front of the exit stairs. His trousers were ripped. His fists were shaking, but he held his hand up so the blood wouldn't drip on his sportcoat. At the end of the platform Harris could see two dark shapes lying on the pavement, writhing in the filth. One of the shapes pointed at him and cursed in Spanish.

A Black man came down the stairs and stepped onto the platform. He saw Harris' hand and frowned. The Broadway local screeched into the station and stopped.

The Black man got on the train. The doors started to close. The man held the doors open and waved at Harris to get on. Harris shook his head.

"No, man, thanks. I'm waiting for a medic."

After that night in 1978, the dark, slit-eyed faces began to confront Harris: stalking him, accompanying him, appearing and fading in an odd conversation of voices. They were dreams without sleep, images so sharp and gripping that vision and hearing gave way to smell and taste. At first, Harris was confused and frightened; he resisted, dreading the cold sweat, the dry mouth, the insane clarity of fear. And then he *adjusted*. A little twist of the mind. Something he'd done before, to keep from going crazy five thousand miles from home.

Harris began to welcome the trips in and out of his parallel world.

Harris flipped over the Malayan gate with his foot. The bamboo stakes attached to the crossbeam were dark and stained. Harris closed his eyes again. He wished he could throw up all the amphetamines, slow himself down and drift into a heavy sleep.

But he forced himself to go through the motions of re-rigging the booby trap, avoiding any glance at the body. It took fifteen minutes to get the proper tension on the trip wire, and then he got on the bike and went across the 79th Street transverse to the old aqueduct. He went down into the supply dump and removed some rope and a large opaque sheet of plastic that had been protecting some ordnance crates. Then he drove back to the Ramble and did the most difficult thing he'd ever done in his life.

Harris formed a bag with the plastic and covered the body, binding it tight with the rope. It took all the concentration he could muster not to see the dead man's face. When he was finished, Harris moved away from the bag and discovered another M-16 nearby, which he pushed under the ropes encircling the plastic. He dragged the body to the motorcycle and draped it across the seat, like a dead cowboy on a horse.

He drove slowly out of the trees, following a walk that led to the boathouse, and went north on the East Drive, behind the Metropolitan Museum, past the 79th and 85th Street transverse roads.

The Drive curved around the reservoir and came close to Fifth Avenue. Harris accelerated faster on a short straightaway; he passed within yards of the street and could see the apartment buildings, the traffic lights, a police car parked at the curb. When he saw the round facade of the Guggenheim Museum, he slowed and pulled the bike into the bushes next to the four-foot-high stone wall separating the Park from the avenue.

Harris rolled the body to the ground. He walked to the wall, crouched down and leaned his head out for a look.

No traffic moved on Fifth Avenue. Two blocks uptown, three police officers sat in a car across from the small entrance to the Park at 90th Street. Downtown, there were only empty sidewalks and dark windows.

Harris went back into the bushes and dragged the heavy plastic bag to the wall. He removed a ball-point pen and a piece of paper from his pocket and wrote a short note, which he slipped under the rope. He peeked at the street one more time, lifted the bag with a grunt and dumped it over the wall. It thumped on the sidewalk.

Harris hurried back to the bike. He heard a car door slam. He kicked the starter. Nothing. Again. It wouldn't start. Christ, he thought, it's run out of gas. Not possible. Feet pounded on the pavement. He tried again. The bike started. He raced the engine; a low whine passed through the special mufflers. He heard voices. Harris spun the wheels in the dirt and disappeared into Central Park.

The three officers in the patrol car parked opposite the Engineer's Gate at 90th Street were drinking their tenth cup of coffee when a dark object floated over the Park wall and fell onto the sidewalk. The events of the last six hours, the rumors of what had happened, had made the officers extremely nervous, and they yanked out their revolvers while still inside the car, shattering a thermos and spilling the hot coffee on their uniforms.

They lunged out of the car and were joined by plainclothesmen and ESS officers who materialized from dark doorways and side streets. Several RMP cars and unmarked vehicles roared in from all directions, a blaze of headlights illuminating Fifth Avenue. Everyone converged on the object. They approached cautiously, keeping their guns aimed. When they were close enough to see what it was, they stood frozen on the curb.

They saw the M-16 jammed under the ropes and all had the same sinking feeling. They knew that a dead person was wrapped inside the plastic and that the person was probably a cop.

Several officers moved down the sidewalk and leaned over the wall, trying to see through the dark bushes. A plainclothesman warned them to stay away from the Park.

One of the men found the note. He showed it to the others and no one spoke. They stared at the plastic mummy.

The note said: "DON'T COME BACK."

The mobile command post was still parked on Central Park West. Inside, the control room was quiet. Two dispatchers monitored radio calls at a low volume and a uniformed officer with a shotgun stood near the entrance.

David Dix and a plainclothes officer, Charlie Meyers, were sitting at a table littered with coffee cups and diagrams of Central Park. Meyers, a middle-aged man, looked beat to hell. He wasn't used to being on duty so late. It was 3:30 A.M.

A telephone rang and one of the dispatchers answered. The Mayor wanted to talk to Dix. He excused himself to Meyers and picked up a wall phone extension.

"Yes, sir."

The Mayor's voice was hoarse. "Why are you still there?"

"I don't know, sir. I don't know what else to do."

"I hope we don't have to say that in public."

"Don't worry."

"Is anybody else there, David?"

"No. The P.C. and the Borough Commander have gone to the hospital."

"Which one—do you know?"

"Mount Sinai. That's where they took Don Eubank."

"All right, I'm going over there, too."

"Do you want me there, sir?"

"No. Save it for tomorrow. Go home. There's nothing we can do before Monday morning."

"It is Monday morning."

The Mayor hung up. Dix slumped down in a chair across from Meyers. A sheet of paper that Dix had avoided looking at was in front of him on the table. It was a police report on the officers who had been killed or wounded in the line of duty on July 21 and 22.

Dix read the numbers and stared blankly at Meyers. "Six killed, ten wounded. That's more officers killed in one night than in an entire year in New York."

Meyers started to say something, then stopped. Dix could see that the man was suppressing a strong emotion.

"You okay, Meyers?"

Meyers shifted in his chair and sat up straight. "I'll tell ya somethin', Mr. Dix. I been the highway safety man in the two-two precinct for eleven years. I mean we've had our muggers in this park, and the bike thieves, and the fags and the gangs and the dope dealin'. I've seen it all. But tonight. I ain't ever heard of somethin' like this. Not in my worst nightmares."

Dix knew how the guy must feel. After all, Meyers' own station house had been blown out from underneath him. "Believe me, Meyers, this thing was planned for a

156

long time. There's nothing anybody could have done about it."

"You think so?" Meyers mulled that over. "If that's true, then they done it right under the precinct's nose. That bothers me."

"Don't blame yourself. The guys on the beat have enough to do. They can't be on top of plots and conspiracies and God knows what else."

Meyers was getting edgy. "All that conspiracy shit—excuse me, Mr. Dix—that's somethin' for the Intelligence Division, so they can play with themselves. The guys in the two-two, we've handled the criminal element in this park before. We'll clean 'em out again."

Dix shook his head. "No. This is something else, Meyers. We're going to have a hard time getting this park back." Dix was sorry as soon as he said it.

Meyers stood up. He was angry. "I can't buy that, Mr. Dix. I'll never buy that. Nobody's gonna take this park away."

Meyers slammed his briefcase on the table. He took a deep breath and gathered the diagrams of Central Park. He folded them very carefully and put them in the briefcase. He went to a wallboard behind the table. Several photographs of the Park's terrain were pinned to the board; they were nice pictures, many in color. Meyers lingered over one of the photos for a long time. It was an aerial shot of Central Park, showing a long, green rectangle of trees, with sunlight reflecting from the Lake and the reservoir. The Park looked beautiful and serene—the way Meyers wanted it to look, the way he'd worked hard for eleven years to maintain it.

Finally he stepped back from the photographs. He ignored Dix and went out the exit without speaking.

Dix watched him leave and listened to the dull static from the radios. He played with the stubble on his chin and looked down again at the police report. He reread the list of names. Some he recognized: Dell'olio, Dietrich,

157

Beniquez. These guys were all so young, he thought. What could they possibly know about unconventional jungle warfare? None of them had been in Vietnam. Everything they knew about guns and violence, they'd learned in training or from watching television. Sure, many of them had been involved in shootings and in tough police operations. They were brave. They were experts in anti-terrorism and the urban assault, but tonight they had been in strange territory.

Somebody had depended on that.

Dix leaned back in his chair. "This is something else." Isn't that what he'd told Meyers? The possibilities had nagged at Dix's mind since he'd first read the transcript of the phone call. He remembered trying to express his concerns to Keller and Curran. And Eubank. But he'd been too vague. He couldn't have foreseen the night's events. Even so, he'd suspected that the Department was dealing with something they just were not prepared to handle.

Dix thought back over the past three agonizing hours. He'd been there in the command post, listening with Keller and Curran to the hysterical reports of the officers in the field; officers who, in the confusion, were unable to adhere to any basic procedure; who were prevented by the unfamiliar circumstances from informing each other of specific locations and movements of personnel. When the reports of the wounded filtered in with the wild stories about grenades and booby traps, Dix reread the language in the transcript of the phone call and his suspicions became a cold, hard fear. The weapons, the tactics—it was all too familiar.

As the situation had deteriorated, Dix had tried to get Keller's attention to urge him to order the Emergency Service squads out of the Park. He explained to Keller that guerrilla fighters possessed power and strategic advantages way out of proportion to their numbers; that this had been the obvious lesson of Vietnam.

158

Vietnam. It was the wrong thing to say. Right then Keller had closed the door on Dix. He didn't want to hear about Vietnam. He didn't want to hear about Dix's experiences in the war. This was the 1980s; this was a matter for the Police Department of the City of New York, and Dix had better not interfere with a bunch of crazy bullshit.

Ten minutes later, a wounded officer, Beniquez, was carried from the Park and demanded to speak with the Commissioner. Beniquez was bleeding badly, but he wasn't in shock when he told Keller that some kind of mine had killed the driver of truck two. Keller was incredulous, so he ordered a team of officers and medics to go down into the Park and find the body; he wanted to see for himself. Two minutes after Keller saw the mangled corpse, the operation was called back and all personnel were instructed to evacuate the Park.

Dix had seen the body, too, and he had had a brief conversation with Beniquez before he was taken away in an ambulance. Beniquez described what had happened to the driver: the explosion, the rain of metal. One word had popped into Dix's mind.

Claymore.

Dix turned around in his chair and studied Meyers' photographs of Central Park. In a certain sense, one could say that the Park looked like a miniature jungle, complete with forests and rivers and hills. Dix was startled by the thought. He remembered, earlier, standing over the large map of Central Park and being struck by the same concept. A brief flurry of old images and fears had run through his mind. It still disturbed him, because there was an amorphous danger inherent in such a concept. Guerrilla warfare . . .

There it was. Someone else, with a particular background, observing Central Park, must have been struck by a similar concept. Dix stood up and faced the photos. He began to form a theory.

Vietnam was a school for violence. Whoever was in the Park was almost certainly an extraordinary graduate of this school. Perhaps it was possible that one man, armed with the skills, the weapons, the expertise that the caller claimed to possess, operating in a conceived environment, and driven by strange and dangerous emotional forces, could indeed take over Central Park.

The miniature jungle.

Dix almost believed it. He wanted to believe it because, if there was such a man, Dix's analysis might prove useful. But how? How could he prove his theory? He knew the Department would never understand the complexities of the situation, in particular the Vietnam angle. They were like Meyers; it was beyond the realm of their experience. Theories were worthless. Reality counted.

Dix felt discouraged. His only hope was that the Department, especially the brass, had learned something from the reality of what had already happened. Maybe they wouldn't blunder ahead with any more bad decisions and the subsequent needless casualties. But Dix remembered another kind of brass, another command, who'd taken their time learning the lessons of combat, and consequently a lot of people had gone down the drain.

Dix rubbed his eyes and shivered. No sense thinking about that; just a bunch of old animosities that he thought had been locked away for good. He moved away from the photographs. He couldn't think anymore. He found his suit coat, said goodnight to the officer with the shotgun and went out the command post exit.

Central Park West was an empty asphalt strip. ESS and uniformed officers in patrol cars were stationed around the command post; they smoked cigarettes and talked in low voices. Litter was piled up over the curb in front of the apartment buildings; probably thrown there by a crowd of reporters, Dix thought.

He walked over to the wall in front of Central Park. He leaned over and looked up the wooded slope that led to a small playground and the West Drive. He squinted, trying to see the dark ground, and wondered what lethal device might be buried there. Dix laughed at the irony. People were always complaining about how dangerous Central Park had become. After tonight, nobody would be able to take a walk, even in the daytime.

Well, he thought, somebody could.

An officer approached Dix and asked him if he'd mind stepping back from the Park. Dix nodded and walked over to 86th Street where the limousine was parked. The driver was asleep in the front seat. Dix woke him and they drove over to the East Side, to Dix's apartment on East 65th Street.

During the ride Dix had an idea. When the car arrived in front of his building, he ran inside without saying good-night to the driver. The night security guard tried to complain about reporters hanging around the entrance, but Dix ignored him and hurried into the elevator and up to his apartment. He went immediately to his bedroom, sat on his bed in the dark and made a phone call to Mount Sinai Hospital.

After five minutes of conversation with several operators and nurses it was verified that the Mayor was still in the building. Finally he came on the line.

"Yes, David."

"I'm glad I caught you. How's Don Eubank?"

"Not good. He was critical. Now they're saying serious but stable."

"What about the family?"

"His wife is here." The Mayor was distracted by someone and Dix could hear him cover the mouthpiece. "Sorry, David. I've got to go. What's up?"

"I've been going over in my mind everything that's happened, which I won't go into now, but what I'd like, sir, is your permission to handle any further communications from inside the park. I want to have a chance to talk to this person."

The Mayor hesitated. "Or persons."

"I don't think we can rule out the possibility that it is a lone man. That's my thinking now. There are certain things at work here . . ."

The Mayor cut him off. "I follow your thinking, David."

Dix respected the Mayor's ability to make fast decisions; he never required much hand-holding or useless exposition. "Then you know what I'm driving at. If this man calls again, I might be able to get through to him. My background could be helpful. At least I can narrow down the possibilities."

The Mayor responded quickly. "Go ahead. But let's not narrow anything down when we're talking to the press."

"I'll make arrangements for a phone hookup or a call transfer. Whatever's necessary."

"Try going to sleep. We have a staff meeting in three hours."

"That's my advice to you, too, sir."

"You're right, David. At about 9:30. I'll be facing the burning question of where my son's going to jog this morning now that Central Park is closed."

Dix laughed. "Tell him to try Riverside Park.

"No good. He got mugged there the last time he tried it. Good-night."

Dix set the phone down. He rubbed his eyes. He stood up from the bed and switched on a lamp next to the dresser. He looked at himself in the mirror, but his attention was diverted by several framed photographs on the wall. The pictures had assumed the inconspicuousness of familiar furniture. Dix was noticing them for the first time in years.

He pulled the lamp closer to the dusty frames. The photos were souvenir shots of Dix during his military service in Vietnam: in uniform posing with other officers in front of the U.S. embassy; at a press conference, surrounded by microphones; standing with General Abrams at MACV headquarters in Saigon; in combat gear, jumping out of a helicopter somewhere in Tay Ninh province.

Dix turned to the mirror and compared his face to the way he looked in the pictures from 1967 or 1968. His hair was longer now; he had wrinkles around the eyes and mouth. But Christ, Dix thought, he looked better at thirty-five than he had when he was twenty-three. The kid in the pictures bristled with tension; the eyes were narrow and tight; the face wore an expression of perpetual urgency, with lips curled around hard, strident speech. Dix sighed. What a world.

Dix pulled the photo of the helicopter off the wall and sat on the bed. He liked this picture better. He couldn't see himself clearly—just a figure in flak jacket and helmet, holding an M-16. A real dynamic action shot: gung ho and combat crazy. It was around mid-1967, when he'd gotten fed up sitting around MACV headquarters manipulating war zone stats and press releases; when he'd grown tired of being the golden boy of the command staff, the young and very smooth spokesman for the official "view"; and, most of all, when he'd become disgusted with the perverse symbiotic relationship between the staff and the press corps and the embassy. He'd insisted on being attached to the 173rd Airborne Brigade so he could "experience the war," the real war, not the sick nightmare that drifted in and out of Saigon. He knew that the guys who'd been out there in the combat zone for months and years thought he was a real half-ass. He knew it when he flew in by helicopter and joined a battalion of paratroopers who'd jumped into a full-scale engagement. They'd watched him cross the lz in his clean, unmarked fatigues, and they'd looked away, and no one had spoken to him for two days.

But Dix had stayed with it. After one month in the bush, he was ordered back to Saigon, because he was too valuable to the MACV staff. When he returned to Saigon, he was even more disenchanted with the war, with the strategies and politics and abuses. On occasion, he indulged in public criticism. After that his so-called career with the command staff was all downhill. He stayed drunk and kept his mouth shut just enough to slide out of the military with good credentials and a reasonable reputation.

Dix set the photo on the dresser and sagged back on the bed, resting his head on a pillow. One month. It was laughable; they'd made contact with the enemy maybe twice. The experience had been valuable anyway, because Dix brought back something else from that month in the bush besides a bad attitude. He'd learned about the stress of combat; how it could distort the mind and change a person irrevocably. True, this was not so much from his own experiences under fire (which had terrified him), but from his observations of the men in the battalion. Observations, that's what it came down to: Dix the observer. But at least he'd been there, as one soldier called it, "hanging out with the mighty death monster," watching it work over these young guys, scaring them, thrilling them, downright beating the hell out of them, until, in the end, they became some other kind of human beings.

Dix had forgotten a lot of things about his four years in Vietnam, but he'd never forgotten the faces of those men. He hadn't thought about them for a long time—not until tonight. Now he couldn't stop remembering.

He rolled over and fell asleep in his clothes. His thoughts were on an anonymous man—a man, Dix guessed, who also could not stop remembering.


"Here, kitty."

A cat came out of the dark undergrowth and sniffed at Harris, who was sitting next to an old stone arch called the Glen Span. Behind him was the Loch, a wide stream that ran between the Pool at 102nd Street and the Harlem Meer, the large body of water at the northeast tip of Central Park. A few yards downstream from the Glen

Span was one of several small waterfalls called cascades. Harris was eating Vienna pork sausages from a can and listening to the sound of the water pouring over large boulders and down into the Pool.

He held out a piece of sausage to the cat, a dark tabby wearing a collar, which meant somebody owned it.

"Here, kitty."

The cat was suspicious; it sniffed all around and then rubbed its head on the bridge, against a stone defaced by graffiti that said Jose 102. Harris stuck his arm out farther and the cat sat down and wouldn't move. Maybe it doesn't like the looks of this AK-47, Harris thought. The rifle was over his shoulder, so he removed it and leaned it against the Yamaha parked in the short tunnel under the Glen Span.

He went back to the cat and tried again. "Come on." Harris tasted the sausage. "Ummm. Yeah, real good. Come on."

The cat couldn't resist and stuck its nose up to Harris's hand, sniffed one more time and took the piece of meat away into the bushes. Harris lost sight of it in the dark, but he called out softly, "Careful, kitty. Don't step on any mines."

Harris finished the rest of the can, then walked down the ravine and climbed the rocks above the cascade emptying into the Pool. Empty ordnance crates were stacked on the rocks and he threw the can into one of them, along with several beer bottles he'd found near the Loch. He unzipped his pants and peed over the waterfall. Cool air drifted in and it felt good on his sweat-soaked crotch. He looked at his watch and up at the sky. There was about an hour until daylight. He'd spent the last two hours setting up claymore mines on the perimeter of the Park, along 59th Street, up Central Park West and Fifth Avenue, and finishing on 110th Street. In between he'd put some mines in a zigzag pattern in the open areas of the Sheep Meadow and the Great Lawn. The number of devices in place was still thin, but the process had been time-consuming. Reasonably careful handling was required and accurate locations, duly noted in the charts, were mandatory if Harris wasn't going to end up blowing himself to pieces. He'd also been slowed down because the work made it necessary for him to move close to the street, often within sight of the sidewalk. Renewed police activity had begun some time around 4:30 A.M.; Harris had installed several claymores within earshot of policemen's voices. All this had left him with an hour of darkness and a lot of work still ahead. His firebase, which would be his staging area for the duration of his stay in Central Park, had not been constructed, and Harris knew he'd be working on that right through the dawn.

He watched the waterfall for another minute and then carried the empty ordnance crates to a deep hole dug in the bank at the west end. He didn't bother to cover the hole, but returned to the cycle and made a notation in his charts. He saw that he'd marked the wrong page. Fuck it, he thought. He was going through the motions now. It wasn't fatigue. Harris was depressed.

He started the bike and drove south, winding along the edge of the West Drive, past 96th Street and the tennis courts, and stopped next to the chain-link fence around the vast, calm reservoir. In the darkness he could barely see the south gate house on the distant opposite shore. A cloud of gnats floated over the water and buzzed in Harris' ear.

He tried to shake himself from his depression. He tried to ride the last residues of adrenaline and amphetamine. Harris punched the fence. The whole thing was going bad. He'd lived for this one night. He'd thought he'd created the perfect construction, but it wasn't perfect. Something was lacking. Something was wrong and it kept dragging him down, spoiling the fantasy.

A dead man in a plastic bag.

Harris squeezed the fence until it cut his hand.

He could not stop seeing that face in the grass. It was the worst possible intrusion into Harris' parallel world—a world that he accepted, that he'd been operating in, pursuing an awesome reality. It was a world with no rules, with an incredible power to alter reality, creating shape and form, that rose up and truly existed; and on this night Harris had found them, had recognized their faces, saw them with their AK-47s, creeping in the night, swarming over the walls, mysterious purveyors of terror and death. There was no mistake.

The discovery of the body destroyed the illusion. There was no way to deny it: It had the wrong face.

No! Harris grabbed his head; blood ran into his eyes. He wanted to scream. He needed to face the unknown, to maintain that ephemeral world. He needed to confront the inevitable, crushing fear. Because fear could make you do a lot of things. Amazing things.

Harris screamed and his voice echoed over the reservoir. He waited for someone to retaliate. When no voice returned except his own, he knew that the dead man in the plastic bag was his failure to maintain the dream, to understand the need.

Harris felt sick and bile rose in his throat. He sagged against the fence, dangling from the wire. He fell back on the bike, accelerated quickly and circled the reservoir, crashing through the trees and bushes. He continued south and drove hard. His emotions receded with the speeding landscape.

He passed 85th. The cool air relieved his nausea and he felt empty and dull.

He crossed the Park near the Delacorte Theater, hit the East Drive and raced toward the Lake. He was resigned to failure. He rationalized the attempt.

He crossed 72nd and his resolve returned. He wasn't going to quit.

He shot past the Rumsey playground and the Mall. The Park was his. The potential was still there. The faces—

the right faces—would return, and he would always find them. It was a priority game.

He crossed the transverse.

He was a soldier and he was standing ready....

Harris turned the bike off the Drive just past the 65th Street transverse. He followed a walk through the Green Gap arch, another dark, stone tunnel under the Drive, and stopped at the rear entrance to the zoo. He got off and filled his canteen from a water fountain on the hill that overlooked the elephant cages.

The Central Park Zoo occupied several acres between 65th and 62nd Streets. The main entrance was on Fifth Avenue, in front of an old building called the Arsenal, which housed the headquarters of the Department of Parks and Recreation. At one time Harris had considered blowing it up instead of the 22nd Precinct house, but the police station was far more strategic, and the entire zoo was in the southeast corner of the Park, where he expected little action.

Harris took a long drink from his canteen and walked to the tall gate at the bottom of the hill. He had walked through the zoo several times, but he hadn't really thought too much about it. The entire area was enclosed. Surveillance from the outside was easy. Harris wondered if there were any security guards or animal keepers on duty at night. He hadn't checked on that. He assumed that if anybody had been inside, they were probably evacuated when all the shooting started.

Harris knew he should be setting up his firebase, but he went to the bike and removed a flashlight from an equipment sack. He put a new clip in the AK-47 and scaled the fence next to the gate. He moved quickly around the elephant cages and past the picnic tables in front of the snack bar. There he had a view of the central plaza that most of the zoo surrounded. It was very dark, except for the old park lamps that were scattered around the seal pool and the walkways in front of the cages. Harris couldn't see any animals; they were locked up in the interior cages inside the buildings on the perimeter of the plaza. He crossed to the building on his right. The door and lock were not difficult and Harris broke in easily.

The space was pitch black, but he felt the presence of the animals right away. He smelled them. He heard a gentle rustling, a pawing and scratching. He moved farther into the room. He knew from a previous visit that he was standing in a long, narrow corridor with cages on either side. He could hear breathing, or perhaps sniffing; big sniffs, from large noses.

Harris clicked on the flashlight. He aimed it at one of the cages. Two red, glowing eyes appeared in the beam. They stared at Harris, hypnotizing him, the liquid surfaces shimmering and unfathomable. He shifted the beam and a leopard stood frozen in the light. It lowered its head and began to pace silently around the cage, repeating the same rectangle over and over. A low growl came from another cage, behind Harris's back. He turned and ran the flashlight over the row of cages. He saw a black puma, a cheetah, llamas, zebras. The animals watched him, eyes reflecting the light. They were nervous and they wandered in their cages; they sniped at each other. There was a loud clawing, a whine, then a roar. They were voices speaking from another place, calling forth images of another world. Harris felt sweat trickle down his neck. He switched off the light. The animals shouted from their black prison. The sounds echoed and reverberated like the sounds of the jungle.

The noise increased: chirping, howling, roaring. Harris felt dizzy. He heard rain pour down. A monkey cried out. What monkey? He dropped the flashlight and it broke. The monkey screamed and Harris heard another sound pierce the air. A rifle snapped; it poured out rounds and rounds and he could hear someone yelling and a helicopter pounded over his head, weakening his knees, forcing him to the ground. The sounds overwhelmed him, devoured him, and Harris, the anonymous soldier, collapsed to the floor and curled into a ball and listened to the shooting and the explosions and the jets and the screams of death.

# II

# Weaver

The appearance of the dead man in the plastic bag confirmed that someone was still inside the Park and sent another shudder of fear through the already demoralized Police Department.

Fast decisions were made. Commissioner Keller, the Mayor and other high-ranking officials held a meeting in the early hours of the morning in a conference room at Mount Sinai Hospital on Fifth Avenue. A plan was immediately approved to evacuate every apartment, hotel room and hospital room that faced Central Park on one of the four perimeter streets. If your windows looked out on the Park, whether you were rich or poor, you were out. Many of the residents moved in with neighbors in the same building; others, like the guests in the hotels, found accommodations elsewhere. Access to these buildings was permitted only through service entrances on side streets. The evacuation began with few difficulties, except in the tenement buildings lining 110th Street in Harlem. Some residents did not have alternative accommodations in the already crowded buildings, so the Mayor authorized housing for several families in hotels, at the City's expense. Many of the apartments facing the Park on 110th Street were not cleared until 6:00 A.M.

Strategy was the primary topic at the meeting. One of

**173**

the first proposals suggested a call to the Governor for the assistance of the National Guard. This had a tinge of panic associated with it and was set aside for later consideration if things got worse, particularly if the shootings and explosions spilled out into the streets. The prevailing opinion was that if the perpetrators were still in the Park by daylight, then a terrorist group would probably be making demands, with a negotiation process beginning sometime during the day. At any rate, their movements would be severely restricted in the daytime, presenting the department with a number of strategic options. It was agreed that the worst thing that could happen would be for the perpetrators to escape before dawn and get away with it.

The resulting plan called for every available officer and Emergency Service squad to maintain positions on the four perimeter streets. The Commissioner did not want one foot of this perimeter to be without surveillance. He canceled the leaves of all off-duty officers, to replace the men in the field who were occupied with the Park operation, and ordered twelve-hour shifts to handle what was surely the largest backlog of all time. He was also anticipating rush-hour traffic problems and he wanted everybody on the job. He didn't care how many hundreds of thousands of dollars in overtime it was going to cost the City. The Mayor let that one go by.

At 4:30 A.M. the Park was encircled by police personnel, joining officers who were already in concealed positions. Nothing happened.

By seven o'clock a bright sun was out and the Park looked like it always did on a nice summer day, except deserted. All the binoculars, all the eyes saw nothing unusual, nothing threatening. The thought crossed everyone's mind that maybe no one was in there; that maybe the perpetrators, whoever *they* were, had managed to slip out, perhaps through the subway system or sewer tunnels.

Commissioner Keller had considered that possibility, but there had not been enough time or personnel to do anything about it.

Another hour dragged by. Around eight, people started piling into Manhattan from Long Island, the Bronx and New Jersey. The Monday morning traffic became an unmovable mess, because two major avenues were closed for a distance of fifty blocks, and six crosstown arteries (the transverses, Central Park South and 110th) were interrupted by the big, green barricade of Central Park. Manhattan, particularly in midtown, looked as if it were reeling from another transit strike.

The Mayor and the Commissioner had to make a decision. Two things were known: no attempts had been made to harm any property or life outside the Park, and absolutely no one had been observed inside the Park during or after the attacks, night or day. Whoever was responsible was either gone or in hiding. The Mayor and the Commissioner decided to take a chance.

At 9:00 A.M. Central Park South and 110th Street were reopened. Police personnel and RMP cars were positioned at intermittent points along the streets, and most heavily at the entrances and exits of the Drives. Pedestrian traffic was permitted on sidewalks on the opposite side of the street from the Park. Residents of the evacuated apartments and hotel rooms were allowed to return, although some guests discovered that they preferred the St. Regis and the Barclay to the Plaza and the Park Lane. Nevertheless, the hotel managers were relieved; July and August were big months for tourism in New York. But they filed away in their minds the fact that the Mayor had made life miserable for them.

Commissioner Keller kept a close watch on the situation from the command post, but there were no incidents and the crosstown traffic problem improved immediately. Thirty minutes later, Fifth Avenue and Central Park West were reopened, with a similar deployment of uniformed

**175**

officers and Emergency Service squads at various locations. Some traffic lanes and key side streets were turned into routes open only to emergency vehicles, including a section of the northbound lane on Central Park West, where the command post was parked. Traffic Department personnel manned all major intersections. Repeated warnings were broadcast to stay away from the Park because of the possibility that explosive devices remained inside, abandoned by the individuals responsible for the terrorist attacks. Still, crowds lingered on the street corners, gawking at the Park, feeling some vague thrill of danger.

By early afternoon the traffic calmed down, although the fact that all four transverse roads remained closed continued to foul up the crosstown flow. Cab drivers, recalling the transit strike, agreed that the traffic was bad, but that it could be worse. Pedestrians stayed on their side of the street, with a few exceptions. The news media had a field day. Everyone else made adjustments and went to work with something interesting to talk about while the Mayor and the Police Department decided what to do next.

Richie was sitting on the hood of the station wagon on West 68th Street at the corner of Central Park West. He was drinking a cup of coffee and watching Central Park. Barricades with the inscription "Police Line Do Not Cross" were on the sidewalk in front of the Park, and extended north and south as far as Richie could see. An hour ago he'd thought the avenue looked like it was ready for Macy's Thanksgiving Day Parade, until it was reopened to traffic about 9:30. The traffic was still light, but getting heavier. An endless stream of joggers ran past the station wagon and a group of police officers stationed near the Park wall and 67th shouted encouragement to the female runners in their tight gym suits. A man with binoculars stood a few feet away, under an apartment house awning, and scanned the bright green landscape of Central Park. The man had been there, staring into the binoculars, for forty-five minutes.

Richie looked downtown at the digital clock on the roof of the MONY building. It was 9:46 and 72°. It was going to be hot again. He turned to look at Weaver, who was asleep in the car, slumped over the steering wheel. Somebody whistled and Richie saw J.T. coming toward the car on 68th. J.T. waved and then stopped to look at his reflection in a glass door. Richie laughed. J.T. was good-looking and "looking good."

J.T. never showed signs of fatigue, although he worked hard for Weaver, staying in her apartment monitoring radio transmissions almost every night from 8:00 P.M. to 6:00 A.M. In three months on the job, knowing nothing about television and with only a rudimentary understanding of the police and fire departments (based on two arrests for drug possession and one juvenile conviction for turning in false alarms) J.T. had become proficient at reading the radios and communicating with television personnel. His approach to the work, to everything, had a Latin enthusiasm. He was a sharp kid, a hustler, and his childhood in the South Bronx had taught him the value of a job. A job was an escape.

J.T. peered in at Weaver and came around to the front of the car. He was carrying a rolled-up newspaper. He was bouncing up and down, wide awake.

"Hey, Rich."

"Hey, J.T."

"You oughta get Weav to come back to her apartment some time, man. I spend more time at that place than she does."

Richie nodded. "She don't leave that car for nothin'. She lives in that car."

J.T. went to the curb and looked up and down the avenue. "Things calm down a little?"

Richie slid off the hood and joined him. "I hope so. I need to change my underwear. I think I shit in my pants three times last night."

"Don't tell me, man. I wished I coulda been there."

J.T. unrolled the newspaper and showed it to Richie. It was the *Daily News*. A huge headline said. GUER-RILLA: "THE PARK IS MINE." "Did you see this?"

Richie said, "I seen it already."

"Do you fuckin' believe it?"

"I don't know. I don't care. All I know is that nothin's been happenin' for a while. We've just been cruising or sitting on our ass. I could be home sleeping."

"Come on, you love it."

"I ain't the one who loves it."

Richie sipped his coffee and J.T. went back to the car. He climbed up on the hood and pressed his lips to the windshield. He tapped lightly on the glass.

Inside the car, the Bearcat scanner was on low volume, sending out transmissions. Weaver was breathing heavily, her shoulder jammed against the door. She heard the tapping and woke up. She saw J.T.'s lips pressed against the glass and honked the horn suddenly. J.T. jumped in surprise. He rolled off the hood and slipped the *Daily News* under the windshield wiper so Weaver could read the headline. She waved him away and he walked back to the avenue.

Weaver tried to sit up. Her back ached. She leaned forward and studied the front page. Under the headline was a nice photograph of a wounded police officer on Fifth Avenue. She looked at herself in the rearview mirror. Her eyes were very puffy. She smelled her armpits and winced. The T-shirt was dirty and stained. The front seat was littered with burger wrappings and cups. She shoved them on the floor, sliding over in front of the glove compartment. She opened it and a load of cosmetics, picnic supplies and tampons fell on her feet. She found a T-shirt in the back of the compartment and surveyed the street. No one was watching, so she quickly changed shirts. Her breasts jutted out and she tugged at the material to give them some room. She crammed everything back in the glove compartment, including the tampons, although she felt silly carrying them around. She hadn't had a period in four months, and she wasn't pregnant. She hadn't slept with anyone for a long time. Her doctor told her that her menstrual cycle was screwed up because of stress.

Weaver laughed to herself. Stress. Bring it on. She didn't care if she never had another period.

She got out of the car, locked it and walked over to Richie and J.T. The sunlight made her squint. J.T. smiled at her.

"All right. The vampire comes out of her coffin."

"Right, J.T." Weaver grabbed a drink of Richie's coffee. "Okay, tell me."

"Are you ready for this?"

"Come on, J.T."

"We made every affiliate last night and the networks replayed this morning. The fuckin' 'Today' show! They had your bomb shit and the cops on Fifth Avenue. Everything."

Weaver was ecstatic. She clapped her hands.

J.T. went on. "That ain't it complete. We had the fire on all three locals and two webs. We can expect another replay maybe tonight."

Weaver shook her head. "Unbelievable."

Richie and J.T. slapped hands. Richie said, "I gotta hand it to you, Weaver. I never thought this stringing shit was gonna pay off."

Weaver asked J.T., "Were we exclusive?"

"Nah. They cut in some of Marty's stuff, I think. And the other service, unless it was a union crew. UPI had film on."

"We get paid the same anyway. I just like to beat their ass."

**179**

J.T. punched her arm playfully. "Don't worry, Weav. You scored. Thing is, how we gonna follow that?"

Richie cut in. "Hey, I wouldn't mind a coupla relaxing homicides or a booking. I don't need the bullets flyin' every night."

"Richie, we'd be lucky to get something like this again," Weaver said, hoping it wasn't true, praying it wasn't true. She had a sudden feeling that last night was a one-in-a-million shot.

She curled her toes over the curb and stared into Central Park. A jogger stopped in front of her and bent over, trying to catch his breath. A man with a poodle on a leash crossed the avenue toward the Park. Weaver turned away. The thrill was starting to wear off; she felt restless and a little dejected, but she wasn't going to let her partners see it.

"Listen, we're gonna stay on top on this story," she said.

Richie disagreed. "What's left? They'll open the park in two days and that'll be it. You don't think it's one guy in there, do you?"

"I don't know. I hope somebody's still in there."

"They're just trying to sell more papers, that's why they're playing it up. If you ask me, there ain't nobody in the goddamn park. You wait, it'll be like that La-Guardia bombing. Nobody'll ever know who did it."

Weaver shrugged. It didn't make any difference to her who did it or how many were responsible. The story was the biggest in the country and ripe with possibilities. Anything with national interest could mean getting her tape used by the networks, and that was crucial for her reputation.

J.T. pointed at the Park. "After we eat breakfast we could get some tape of these cops and the barricades."

Weaver looked down the avenue at the group of police officers near 67th Street. "It's nothing pictorially. These cops, it's just a bunch of sandwich talk."

180

J.T. said, "I can perk 'em up. You just gotta step out here—" He moved off the curb and shouted, "He's got a gun!"

Two of the cops jerked around and glared at J.T. Weaver smacked him and told him to be quiet. He laughed. "Works every time, Weav."

She waited for the traffic to clear and crossed the avenue. J.T. and Richie followed her and they stood in front of the sawhorse barricades, about twenty feet from the Park wall. Weaver could see through the trees, past a playground and all the way to the bridle path. A light breeze blew down from the tall apartment houses and the Park appeared quiet and peaceful. The man with the poodle came up behind them. The dog was whining and barking, struggling against the leash. His tiny feet clawed at the curb and he sniffed in the direction of the Park. The man scolded the dog. "Tiny! Damnit. Come on, baby."

Weaver asked him, "What's the matter?"

The poodle continued whining. "He's got his spot. In the park. He just won't doo-doo unless he goes in this one place, but it's way in there by the bridle path and we can't go in."

"I don't think you'd want to be in there today."

The man yanked at the leash. "Yeah, isn't that something? One guy shutting down the whole park. At least that's what they're saying. I hear the cops really got wiped out."

Weaver didn't like this guy. "Yeah, they're saying that too."

The poodle jerked away and the man followed him up Central Park West. All along the avenue were other dog walkers, many in the same predicament. J.T. watched the dogs and shook his head in disgust.

"You know what my brother says? He says they're nothing but assholes on leashes."

Weaver turned away from the view. "Yeah, but which end of the leash?"

They were starting to cross back to the west side of the avenue when the air thumped above their heads. The sound grew louder, finally becoming so overwhelming that they were forced to cover their ears. Weaver raised her hand to shield the light and saw four helicopters come out of the sun and roar down over Central Park. They flew within feet of the treetops. She whirled around to follow the flight path and read the identification markings painted on the sides. Large letters said: NYPD.

"Oh, Jesus. What happened?"

Harris woke up on the floor of the zoo. He was wet with sweat and the AK-47 and M-16 were digging into his back. He sat up, feeling weak and light-headed. Long rays of sunlight fell on the cages. He sensed someone and turned around. A zebra was watching him and chewing on some hay. It walked away, farther into the cage, and dropped a pile of dung on the floor.

Harris stumbled to his feet and almost fainted. He found his way out of the cage room and moved quickly to the rear of the zoo. He went over the fence and ran through the trees until he located the motorcycle.

He went north, staying in the trees and pathways west of the Drive, and stopped on the shore of the Lake near the heart of the Ramble. He relaxed in the sun for a while, listening to birds and the buzzing of insects. Fish jumped in the water. The first splash startled Harris and, for a moment, he thought someone was shooting at him, but eventually the soft morning air and the gentle lapping sounds of the Lake steadied his nerves. He stripped off his fatigues and went for a swim.

When he was dressed again, Harris started the bike and checked the gas. There was about half a tank. He put it in gear and prepared to go up the hill into the trees, then stopped and got off. He walked to the water's edge and heaved the M-16 into the middle of the Lake.

182

*   *   *

Three hours later, about 10:00 A.M., after a lot of hard work, Harris sat in the middle of his firebase, not far from the 79th Street transverse. He was eating a canned fruit cocktail. Scattered around him on the ground were food cartons, a pick, a shovel, bamboo poles, tools, a stack of fragmentation grenades, empty ordnance crates, the M-79 launcher and a box of magazines for the AK-47. The entire area was shaded by a very heavy cover of trees.

Harris' firebase was a scaled-down version of the standard fire support base used to back up infantry operations or search-and-destroy missions. He had even followed the standard drill used for construction. He tied a rope to a stake positioned at the center of the site, extended it in a circle to mark the bunker line, and built one nine-foot bunker from pierced-steel planking and sandbags. (Ordinarily there would have been several bunkers at fifteen-foot intervals.) Next, he extended the rope farther and, using bamboo stakes, marked out the wire perimeter beyond the bunker line. He then surrounded the firebase with triple-dannert barbed wire (three coils in a pyramid structure). There was a small entry and exit point on the perimeter, which Harris booby-trapped. He set up camouflaged claymore mines between the bunker and the wire and at several other points along the perimeter. He could fire the mines remotely from inside the bunker. Instead of the prefabricated twenty-foot observation tower that was ordinarily used, Harris substituted a wooden platform placed in the branches of a tall oak tree just outside the entry point. He nailed steps onto the tree trunk, leading up to the observation post. In addition, Harris placed several M-16 A1 mines in the ground outside the firebase, but not within a radius of forty yards.

The final feature of the firebase would not have been found in the standard version. Harris's bunker was located next to a manhole and he had punched through the side of a masonry wall that formed the entry into a large

**183**

conduit. In an emergency, Harris could get into the manhole, crawl through the pipe for a distance of a hundred yards and come out aboveground, only a short run from the entrance to his old aqueduct supply dump.

By Harris' own estimation, his firebase was a real tight little bitch.

Harris finished the fruit cocktail and tossed the can into a garbage pit near the wire. He rummaged through a carton of rations and found three containers of vitamins. He took heavy doses of everything. He felt well, although his muscles ached and his hands were cut up. He was mentally tired, but there were always the amphetamines to keep him alert. He was hoping for a quiet day, or at least an easy morning.

He thought he'd better clean the AK-47. The rifle was functioning perfectly, but there was no sense taking a chance. The AK-47 did not jam as frequently as the M-16, but he'd put it through some hard use in the past thirteen hours.

Harris was looking for a tool kit in one of the boxes when he heard a sound that sent a chill right up to his brain.

Helicopters.

Just for a second, Harris had a thought that the helicopters were coming to drop supplies, which would have been a normal occurrence during the construction of a fire support base—but he knew better. He grabbed the AK and shoved in a fresh magazine. The unmistakable sound of buffeting air drew closer. Harris found his binoculars and carefully ran through the gap in the wire perimeter. A helicopter roared by overhead. He couldn't see it through the thick trees and it circled away in the distance. He could hear another helicopter somewhere downtown; then another, from the West Side. He started to sweat as he climbed the forty feet up to his observation post. He squatted on the platform and put the binoculars to his eyes. Through the branches and leaves, he had a view of the entire Park. He panned over to the East Side and the glare of the sun reflected in the glasses. Two helicopters hovered over the Lake and the Ramble; two more were farther south, over the Fountain and the Mall.

Harris shifted his view to the West Side and a movement caught his eye. He focused the lenses. A man with a rifle was walking on the roof of an apartment house on Central Park West. Harris panned along the entire row of tall buildings. Men with rifles were moving into positions on every roof.

The air thumped behind him. He flattened himself against the platform as a helicopter thundered by, ten feet over his head. The branches shook until Harris was nearly tossed over the edge.

Harris knew the pilot could not see him, but he raised his middle finger to the sky anyway.

The limousine let Dix off on East 100th Street, near the entrance to Mount Sinai Hospital. He told the driver to keep the car handy because he wouldn't be long. Dix was certain that Don Eubank didn't care if he visited him or not, but it was a courtesy, and Dix always observed the formalities.

He went in the emergency entrance and bought a cup of coffee from a machine. He took a minute to wake up. He'd been a little fuzzy during the staff meeting at Gracie Mansion. Apparently the Mayor had decided to let him sleep through a pre-dawn strategy meeting at the hospital, which was fine with Dix. Anything he could have contributed would no doubt have been met with hostility anyway. Come to think of it, Dix thought, that's probably why the Mayor let him sleep.

Dix spotted a WPIX reporter walking through the waiting room, so he ducked into the snack bar and tried to blend into the machines. The reporter stopped at the admitting desk and Dix made a sneaky move to the elevators. He went up to the top floor and at the nurses' station was directed to Eubank's room. A uniformed officer allowed him inside.

The room was dark. The drapes were pulled and only a small lamp was on over the bed. There was a low wheezing sound. Dix waited for his eyes to adjust and went over to the bed. Eubank was on his back and the bed was tilted forward. He was very pale. White bandages covered part of his neck and face. The skin around his throat was purple and he was breathing through a tube running out his throat to a respirator.

Dix coughed. "How you doing, Chief?"

Eubank raised his hands and shrugged.

Dix felt like an idiot. The guy can't talk, stupid. He noticed a pencil and a pad of paper on the nightstand. "Just let me do the talking, Don."

Eubank managed a sarcastic smile.

"Yankees-Red Sox tomorrow night. Gonna be big."

Eubank tried to laugh and rubbed his eyes.

"Look, Don, I don't know what to say. I'm glad you're okay. Keller's got half the Department on overtime. They'll get whoever's responsible. You know that."

Eubank stopped smiling and made no other acknowledgment.

A nurse stuck her head in the door. "Excuse me. Are you Mr. Dix?"

"Yes, ma'am."

"There's a phone call for you. Do you want to take it in here?"

Eubank waved at Dix that it was all right. Dix was a little surprised, but he assumed that the Chief probably wanted to feel like he was still close to the situation. Dix obliged him. "Thank you. Send it in here."

In a moment the phone on the nightstand rang and Dix went around the bed to answer it.

"Yes."

"Who's this?"

"This is David Dix from the Mayor's Office. Who's this?"

"Cut the shit. What's all the messing around with the phones? Are you trying to trace this? Everybody knows where I am by now."

Dix felt his throat tighten. He'd arranged for his calls to follow him wherever he went all day long, but somebody should have warned him that this particular call was coming.

Dix turned his back to Eubank. He could hear a man breathing at the other end of the line. He tried to think quickly. He said, "There's no trace. I asked them to patch you through directly to me. I want to talk to you."

"Try listening first. You better calm the police down. You'd think after last night they'd want to lighten up."

A loud noise came back over the phone—some kind of machine. Dix asked, "What was that?"

"Helicopters. That's what I'm talking about. I said this park was mine and that's it, top to bottom."

Dix reached behind an air-conditioning unit and opened the drapes. Bright light poured into the room through a large window that overlooked Fifth Avenue and Central Park. Twenty stories below, the Park gleamed in the morning sun; a light haze lingered over the buildings on the West Side. Dix could see the Harlem Meer and the reservoir, and the East Drive winding through the trees.

Dix leaned close to the window and looked downtown. He saw four helicopters circling in a search pattern below the 79th Street transverse. Dix said, "I can see them out there." He winced. Christ, that was a lame thing to say. "What do you want me to do?" he asked.

"Tell them to stop flying around. I especially wouldn't want them to try some gung-ho shit and land one of those things."

"Why not?"

"I got the park mined, that's why."

Dix decided to get aggressive. "Are you alone in there?"

"What do you think?"

"I don't think you could do it by yourself."

"Listen, I can make some believers out there."

Dix looked down into the Park. He tried to imagine the man's face. His heart beat faster. He knew that now was the time to take a chance. He said, "I say you called in your react last night when things got hairy."

The man started to respond, then hesitated. "Say that again."

Dix swallowed. "How many fire teams you got there backing you up?"

There was no reply. Dix went on. "Nobody goes on a fire mission like this without security."

Again there was no response. Dix closed his eyes. He started to have doubts; he waited through a minute of silence.

The man's voice came back, less firm, reluctantly. "There's no react. I'm out here . . . I'm out here by myself."

Dix pursued him. "Then I think you shot your wad. Those choppers got you worried."

"I'm going to shoot one down."

"With what? Have you got LAWs in there?"

"Good-bye."

Dix jumped. "Wait. Don't hang up. I believe you. I'll get them to call off the choppers. Don't bring anything down."

The man didn't say anything, but he didn't hang up. Dix inhaled and took one more shot. "We can talk to each other. People out here, you know what they're like. They don't understand how dinky dau it can get."

There was a long pause. Dix heard the man sigh, a tired breath of resignation.

The man said, "Yeah. Dinky dau. If you know, then tell them. Incoming or outgoing, I like it either way."

He hung up.

Dix held the receiver in his hand. His heart was still pounding. But he was satisfied. His hunch had been right.

He turned around to hang up the phone. Eubank had a strange expression on his face. Dix set the phone down and followed Eubank's gaze. He was staring out the window, his eyes locked on Central Park. Sweat dripped from Eubank's temples and his breathing was labored.

"Don. Are you all right?"

Eubank didn't move. Dix closed the drapes and the room was dark again. Eubank wheezed and wiped his forehead. Dix circled the bed and stood close to him.

"Chief, that was him. The guy in the park." Eubank dropped his eyes and wouldn't look up. Dix continued. "I know everybody in the brass is looking for some political thing, some crazy radicals. That's not it. This is a Vietnam veteran. No politics involved. I don't know what he wants, but if I can talk to him again, maybe I can find out. These war experiences, they're ... see, it's there somewhere, you just have to say the right things and it comes out."

Eubank refused to acknowledge anything that was being said. Dix put his hands on the bed and leaned over, trying to look into Eubank's face. Dix knew he was pushing hard, taking liberties with a man who was badly hurt.

"I'm asking for your support. If I can sit on the Department for a little while, just get them to consider the possibilities, then maybe we can avoid another horror show like last night."

Eubank flinched. Dix said, "Don, I have to tell you this. You were there. There was shooting, there was an assault, but you never saw anybody. Why? Because that's the way it works. Believe me, this guy exists. I've seen what guys like him can do."

Eubank looked up. His face was wet with perspiration. Dix watched him closely. There was no resistance in the eyes. There was something else—something Dix was not used to seeing in Don Eubank. Fear.

189

Dix nodded. "You know, don't you?"

Eubank lowered his head. Dix turned to go and felt Eubank's hand grab his coat. He turned back. Eubank picked up the pad and pencil from the nightstand and scribbled a note. He handed it to Dix.

The note said, "What does dinky dow mean?"

Dix put the notepad on the bed. "It's Vietnamese. It means totally crazed."

Dix left the room.

Harris hated the sound of helicopters. Most people never got close enough to one to know what a terrifying and disorienting sound they emitted. Even when a helicopter was there to help you, to rescue you, to pluck you from some burning nightmare, like an angel of mercy, the blast of air and noise still scared you half to death.

It was as much a desire to get rid of that sound as any possible threat that caused Harris to hide in the trees near the Delacorte Theater with two 66-mm LAW/M-72 A1 portable one-shot rocket launchers. Each launcher weighed 2.2 pounds, consisted mostly of fiber glass, and was completely disposable after use. The LAW fired an armor-piercing projectile to an effective range of 375 yards.

A helicopter dropped down over the New Lake. The water flattened out and created a sheet of ripples. Harris moved closer to the theater building and circled to his right, staying in the shadows of the trees. He stopped near the stage, within a few yards of the shoreline. The helicopter rose up, hovered and then swung around behind the Belvedere Castle. Harris removed the AK-47 from his shoulder and set it down. He was in full combat gear, wearing his helmet and flak vest, with the M-79 in its holster and grenades in an equipment bag on his back. He checked the treeline to make sure his rear was covered. He didn't want one of those snipers on the rooftops to get in a lucky shot.

Harris sat down. The helicopter came back, heading

right for him. He armed one of the launchers by pulling off the caps at each end of the tube. He hadn't fired one in a long time and he was pretty sure that he wouldn't come close to hitting a moving target. Even if he missed, though, it might scare the shit out of the pilot and convince the police to recall the helicopters.

Harris raised the sight on the LAW and watched NYPD 020 glide over the New Lake and dangle in front of him like a duck on a pond.


Dix arrived at the mobile command post fifteen minutes after ending his visit with Don Eubank. He'd talked to the Mayor during the ride and the Mayor had given him the green light, but Dix was not looking forward to facing Keller.

The command post was busy. Radio operators were communicating with Aviation units. Charlie Meyers was supervising several officers who were marking locations on huge wall maps of Central Park. Keller and Curran were sitting at a table with a lab technician that Dix recognized. Curran was examining a plastic bag that contained metal fragments. The Commissioner was on the phone. Dix waited until he got off and then approached the table.

Dix said, "We've got to call off the helicopters."

Keller and Curran gritted their teeth. The lab technician excused himself from the table.

Dix continued. "The Mayor doesn't want to take any chances with Department personnel."

Curran tried to speak calmly. "Dix, we have an emergency situation here. Chains of command are out the window."

"I talked to the perpetrator." Both men tensed. Dix said, "The guy's gonna put one of those choppers right in the ground if we don't back off."

Keller reacted immediately. "What guy? David, we're facing a terrorist group of some goddamn persuasion, re-

**191**

gardless of what the media says, or the Mayor, or some nut in Central Park."

Dix was not surprised. He studied Keller's face—a poker player's face. Dix knew that Keller was probably thinking a lot of things; perhaps even about unconventional warfare and the obvious Vietnam connection. The basic problem was that the Commissioner did not want to admit that one man could have carved up the elite of New York City's Police Department.

Dix sat down at the table. "Sir. We have no M.O. for terrorists. No hostages, no demands." Dix picked up the plastic bag containing the fragments. "What about the weapons that were employed in last night's attacks? Surely, by now, you've come to a realization about that. Did you know that the park is mined?"

Curran interrupted. "Who told you that? We haven't seen one lousy person in there, and neither has anyone else."

Keller gestured at Curran to quiet down. "If there are explosive devices remaining in the park, which I'm not going to dispute, then they're going to be used as leverage in negotiations, when we do get some demands."

Dix was feeling frustrated. "Commissioner, I've made contact with the man. I might be able to cool him out, and maybe nobody else will get hurt."

Curran got angry. "How can you swallow that shit? That's what they want you to think."

Dix ignored him. "Sir, I'm convinced it's one man. I'm asking for time."

Keller tapped his fingers on the table. He did a rare thing: he lost his temper. "David, you don't have to tell me that there may be some very dangerous people in that park. I'm going to stay right on top of them with everything we've got. Goddamnit, I'd like to call in the marines. I'd like to have the Green Berets and the commandos. Unfortunately, we have a constitution in this country, and a *posse comitatis* act that prohibits me from using the armed forces for domestic problems. Sometimes I'd like to piss on the Constitution." Keller lowered his voice. "For now, this department is going with what it's got, with caution. And that's how we're going to play it in public. Understand?"

Dix slumped back in his chair. An officer called to Keller and he and Curran went to the radio console. Everyone was asked to be quiet and the operator turned up the volume. Dix swung around and listened to an exchange between the pilots of the helicopters.

"Aviation one northbound on the castle."

"Roger, one, keep circling that location."

There was a pause, then another transmission.

"Aviation two, I have movement near the theater. Do you see that? K."

"Two, that's affirm on the downtown side."

The pilots stopped talking, but apparently a channel was left open. Dix could hear the rotor noise. It seemed to roar suddenly. A scream penetrated the speaker and startled everyone in the command post. There was a bang, followed by hysterical voices and static. Dix ran for the exit and jumped out onto the avenue. Keller and Curran appeared behind him. They held their hands up to block the sun and spotted a helicopter, wobbling, trailing smoke. It slowly dropped down out of the sky and disappeared beyond the trees somewhere downtown on Central Park West.

Jimmie Robinson had a gun. Angel "Dust" Manero wanted to see it.

"Show me that thing."

"Are you high?" asked Jimmie. "I don't want you doin' this with me if you're high."

"I wanna see it."

Jimmie looked down 110th Street. Heat waves undulated over the hoods of cars. The sun beat down on the roofs of the long row of Harlem tenements on the north

**193**

side of the block. The brown buildings all looked the same to Jimmie. Same height, same dirt, same roaches. Jimmie looked across the street at tall green trees. Cops were standing in front of patrol cars near Lenox Avenue, where the East Drive came out of Central Park. Farther west, at Seventh Avenue and the Warrior's Gate entrance to the Park, more cops were sitting on sawhorse barricades. They were talking and fooling around with the winos and the residents of the tenements, who'd been driven outside by the heat.

An unmarked car drove slowly past. Jimmie knew the two officers inside and he smiled and gave a sarcastic wave. The officers observed him with hard, narrow eyes and a calculated disinterest. The car continued on toward Fifth Avenue.

Jimmie turned his back to the street. Sweat glistened on his black chest. He was wearing a sleeveless denim vest with an insignia on the back that said: JR, Stone Killers 121.

He removed a wine bottle from a paper sack, checked over his shoulder one more time, and let Angel look inside. A .38 Special was at the bottom of the bag.

"Is it loaded?"

"You know, Angel, sometimes you are a dumb motherfucker." Jimmie drained the wine bottle and dropped it on the curb under a parked car. He wrapped the gun in the bag and shoved it into his back pocket. "Ready for a little walk in the park?"

Angel cracked his knuckles and smiled. "Yeah. Let's nail this sucker, man. Guerrilla, my ass."

Jimmie held out his palm and Angel slowly smacked hands. They crossed 110th near Lenox. They stood in the road in front of the barricades and acted casual. No one paid any attention to them. They walked west until they were midway between the two entrances to the Park. Jimmie watched the cops for a moment, then he ducked under the sawhorses on the sidewalk. Angel followed and they jumped over the short stone wall and ran into Central Park.

They moved past a line of trees and onto a walk. They were still only a short distance from the street when Jimmie heard someone yell at them to halt. He looked over his shoulder and saw cops running on the other side of the Park wall. He turned back into the trees. Angel veered off the walk and ran across the Drive into open ground. He laughed and waved at Jimmie to follow. Jimmie knew the fool was high and he wanted to kick him in the ass and tell him to slow down, but there was an explosion and Angel twirled in midair as a bloody cloud arced out from his chest. His body landed against a tree and the branches tore apart over his head. Angel rolled to the ground, tried to sit up and collapsed. He stared at the sky.

Jimmie didn't even think. He spun around and ran for the street. He came through the trees and saw the Park wall. Police officers were kneeling on the sidewalk. They were aiming revolvers and shotguns straight at Jimmie.

He froze. He raised his arms. He felt a tugging at his sneakers. He looked down and thought he saw a wire running over the grass into the bushes. His eyes watered and he felt dizzy. He thought he saw wires crisscrossing everywhere, winding around his feet, clutching at his ankles.

His right knee started to buck back and forth and he couldn't stop it. Jimmie looked out at the cops and whimpered.

"Help me."

Weaver was bored. It was about 6:00 P.M.; she and Richie were sitting in the station wagon on a street in Kew Gardens, watching a Queen Anne burn to the ground.

"Ten-four. Fire was throughout."

"That's correct, two-three. Be advised, as far as we know the building was unoccupied, but there are still firefighters in the structure. One seven five three."

"EMS one two two, there is no phone booth on Forty-third and Broadway."

"Roger, we couldn't get anybody on land lines."

Weaver turned down the volume on the radios and rolled up the window. Smoke was drifting into the car. "What a drag."

Richie shifted around in the seat. "It was a two-alarm. We had to check it out."

"Screw it. It's nothing but a rubbish fire."

Weaver watched an odd-looking woman being comforted by a friend. They came around one of the fire engines and passed close to the car. The woman was very tall and heavily made up. Tears streaked with eyeliner ran down her cheeks.

Richie asked, "It that a he-she?"

"It looks like one. God, don't tell me that was a house full of transvestites. Maybe we should have taped it."

They stopped talking and heard a transmission for a shooting in Queens. It was followed by several more transmissions that indicated a homicide and a body at the scene.

Weaver asked Richie, "Where was that?"

"118-23 30th Avenue in Astoria. Are we goin'?"

"I guess so." Weaver started the car and pulled away from the burning house. "I'm getting tired of these homicides. The guy's a stiff. He just lies there."

"Weav, you been spoiled."

She drove the station wagon over to Queens Boulevard and headed for Astoria. She didn't talk the rest of the way. She thought that Richie was probably right. Three months ago, to chase down a body—to careen through traffic and arrive at a crime scene before the corpse was loaded on the morgue wagon—was a real thrill. After last night, she didn't have the same sense of excitement. All afternoon she had felt a vague frustration, or longing. She couldn't get rid of it.

The helicopter crash earlier in the day had been interesting, though it wasn't really much of a crash. The rear rotor had been damaged, but the pilot had managed to maneuver the helicopter over Columbus Circle and hover for several minutes. It fell only a short distance to the street and the pilot walked away. Weaver hadn't actually witnessed the crash, and by the time she and Richie got there and were ready to tape, the helicopter was burning. She made some nice pictures, but a union crew had beaten them there anyway and within minutes five more film and tape units were on the scene. The same thing had happened later in the day when two members of an East Harlem gang attempted to enter the Park Boom, and the newspeople stampeded 110th Street.

Since then, Weaver had been keeping a close ear on the radios, hoping for further developments around the Park, but nothing had happened. The rest of the day had been uneventful. It began to take on the smell of something Weaver hated: routine.

"Turn here, Weav."

The address on Thirtieth Avenue was in the middle of the block. An ambulance and police cars were parked in front of the house. Weaver stopped across the street. She spotted the Action TV News van parked among the police vehicles and groaned.

"I should have driven faster. I can't believe Marty was out here in Queens."

"He's one of those psychics."

"I hope not," Weaver lamented. "Let's get this over with."

They hooked up the equipment and crossed the street. The body was in the driveway, lying in a small pool of blood. It was covered completely with a plastic sheet. Weaver cursed. A visible person lying in a twisted death pose was always more interesting than a lump under

**197**

plastic—but once the body was covered, the cops would never pull off the sheet for the cameras.

Weaver taped the scene anyway, including the house and some detectives moving round the yard. She stopped tape and a voice called to her.

"Just meat going to market, Weaver."

It was Marty. He and Tom were leaning on a police car, smoking cigarettes. Marty's camera was resting on the trunk. Weaver walked over while Richie turned off the sun gun and wound the cable.

Marty blew out a smoke ring. "You got here a couple minutes too late. The guy's eyes were open, Weaver. Wide open. Fuckin' great. Shot DOA right in the driveway."

Weaver acted unimpressed. She could feel Tom staring at the front of her T-shirt. "Who was it?"

"Perry Como. I don't know."

Tom interjected, "Family dispute. They got the brother-in-law over at the precinct."

Weaver lifted the camera from her shoulder and held it at her side. "Watch any tube lately?"

Marty dropped his cigarette and stepped on it. "I been too busy with my broker. But I heard, Weaver. I'm happy for ya. I mean that sincerely. I love any kind of Cinderella shit. But here it is Monday, right?"

Weaver was ready with a retort, but Marty's beeper activated. He and Tom turned away as if Weaver and the conversation had never existed. They were immediately to their van. She returned to the station wagon, where Richie was standing in the open driver's door listening to the scanner.

"Did you hear anything on the radio, Richie?"

"Nope."

"I should get one of those beepers."

"Then what? You gotta have an assignment editor around the clock, so he can call you like a dog."

"That's true. I can't afford either one."

Weaver put the camera in the rear and they drove out to the precinct for the booking of the suspect in the shooting. They waited forty-five minutes for the walkout and the detectives obliged the camera by jerking the suspect's head up before shoving him in a police car. Weaver taped the scene and the cops hammed it up for the newspeople in a minor scuffle with the suspect's girl friend. Weaver ran into a detective she knew and thanked him for the performance. She asked Richie to drive back to Manhattan and on the way they stopped to cover a gruesome car-truck accident on the Grand Central Parkway near LaGuardia. Traffic grew heavy and it was another hour before they pulled off the FDR Drive at East 96th Street.

They drove into midtown and circled Central Park. It was about 7:00 P.M.; traffic was thin and the streets around the Park were quiet, almost normal, except for the presence of policemen and barricades. Richie was turning the station wagon onto Columbus Circle when Weaver told him to stop.

A crowd of people were milling around the burned-out helicopter that had been dragged up on the wide circular walk in the front of the *Maine* monument. Kids were playing inside the helicopter's plastic bubble and bums were passed out on the steps under the statue. A group of teenagers were leaning on a police car, listening to a cassette player and passing a joint. Cops mingled with the crowd and stood near the sawhorses, chatting with pedestrians and the proprietor of a newsstand.

Weaver heard a train rumble by under the street. Several people came up out of the subway exit near the Park wall. She told Richie to wait in the car and wandered into the crowd. A wild-looking Puerto Rican kid wearing a headband jumped over one of the barricades and Weaver watched him dance up and down on a walk just inside the entrance to the Park. Beer spilled from a can inside a paper sack he was holding over his head. A

**199**

cop stepped over the sawhorse and shooed the kid away, threatening him with a nightstick. The kid darted back into the street and was cheered by the crowd. The cop wiped his forehead with a hankie and did not bother to pursue.

Weaver walked past a group of vendors who were doing a healthy business and bought an ice cream bar. She went around to Central Park South and discovered why the bulk of the crowd was gathered on the corner. A WNBC reporter and a mini-cam crew were taping man-on-the-street interviews. People were whistling and waving, trying to jam their faces into the camera's angle. Weaver pushed closer and watched the reporter move the microphone from person to person. He asked a middle-aged woman, "How do you feel about the park being closed?"

The woman answered without hesitating. "I think it's terrible. We use the park all the time. My husband jogs there. What's happening to New York anyway? There's so many scum. I'm gonna move to California."

The reporter shifted the mike to an elderly man with a yarmulke on his head.

"What does the park's closing mean to you, sir?"

"Me? It don't mean a thing. The place ain't safe anyway. They shoulda closed it years ago. What a *shtarker*, this guy who took it over. He cleaned the dump and don't know it."

A young kid forced his way into the picture and the reporter gave him a chance. "Go ahead."

"This is wild, man. Do you believe it? Man, he can keep the park forever. It's dynamite. They ain't never gonna take him off."

The crowd yelled and the reporter was jostled from behind. He held his ground and asked a woman with a briefcase, "The guerrilla seems to have supporters. How do you feel about that?"

The woman was stiff and unsmiling. "I think it's disgusting. Policemen have been killed. How do you think their families feel?"

The reporter was excited. The crowd was getting raucous. He asked a pretty teenage girl, "What do you think the police should be doing?"

The girl's eyes flitted back and forth as she spoke. "What can they do? I heard they tried everything. I don't know, but I'm never going back in as long as he's in there."

The reporter turned around and held the mike out without looking. "And you, sir?"

The man was dirty and disheveled. He staggered and Weaver could see that he was probably drunk or stoned. The man tried to focus and put his hand on the mike to steady himself. He said, "You know, you gots to be cool and everything. Man wants to take a vacation in the park by himself, I can dig that, you jus' stay out and stop all this foolin' aroun'. You know he be gettin' tired of holdin' that park real soon. 'Less he got some pussy in there." The man jerked his head up. "Oh, hey, sorry, was I on TV?"

The reporter pulled the mike away and said, "Stop tape."

Weaver moved away from the crowd. She shook her head. What a job, she thought. She'd never envied the reporters, despite the glamour and the salaries. What a waste of time, trying to look pretty all day so you could ask a lot of questions. News wasn't questions. News was events.

Weaver finished her ice cream bar and walked east on Central Park South. She stood in front of the barricades and looked into the Park. It was getting dark and long shadows fell from the buildings and hotels. Two squirrels were chasing each other through the trees on the other side of the Park wall. She thought about the interviews and she laughed. She knew that it was only a matter of time before whoever was in the Park became a celebrity; that the press would play it up, build an image, create a

**201**

myth. She didn't think there was anything wrong with manipulating the news. God knows the stations altered her tapes all the time. They'd make up anything; a burning, vacant building was suddenly occupied; a wife beater who gave up, sobbing, on his knees at nine-thirty turned into a psycho with a shotgun by eleven. The public swallowed it. What bothered her was that the public absorbed everything, little stories and big stories. The stimulus had to be constant or even the most dramatic events got lost in the overwhelming flow of information.

Weaver shrugged and threw her hands in the air. She had to remind herself, "A maniac closed Central Park." But she knew that in two days the enormity of the event would be mitigated and trivialized by the great adaptability of New Yorkers. She did not want that to happen, but she understood New Yorkers. She was one of them.

She tossed her ice cream stick into the Park and returned to the station wagon. The reporter and minicam crew were gone and the crowd was breaking up. A derelict was sitting in the helicopter, settling down for the night. Weaver made notes on the day's cassette while Richie drove the car up Central Park West and parked near 66th. He stayed with the radios while Weaver carried the cassette over to WABC.

The newsroom was moderately busy as the staff prepared for the eleven o'clock. Weaver found Roger Stein in his office. His feet were up on his desk and he was eating a sandwich. She sat on the sofa and poured a cup of coffee from a dripmaker.

"Help yourself, Weaver."

She put the cassette on the desk next to the sandwich. Stein ignored it and continued to eat. When he was done he asked, "Something wrong, Weaver?"

"Why?"

"You don't look like a speed freak tonight. You almost look tired."

"I am tired."

"Good. I'm going to pay you a compliment. I just want you to know a compliment is coming, in case you're slowed down enough to recognize it."

"Do you want that pickle?"

"No."

She reached across the desk and lifted up a pickle from the deli wrappings.

Stein continued, "That stuff you brought us last night was beautiful. That close-up of the cop, Eubank. Sensational. It was worth a million bucks."

Weaver chewed the pickle. "Thank you, Roger."

Stein started reading the notes on the cassette. "This is just a lot of street stuff. The burned-out helicopter, okay, but we have that three times. How many cops and barricades can we run?"

"Why don't you screen it?"

"What else is on it? What's this here, it says 'scoop'?"

"That's a guy that got spattered a hundred feet along the parkway. They were scooping him up with styrofoam trays."

"I might run that. Anything else?"

"Some freeze-dried blood maybe. A homicide in Queens."

"I know about that."

"We were a little late getting there. They had him in the bag. Basic crime scene."

"Why didn't you go after that murder in Brooklyn?"

Weaver moaned. "I don't know. I wanted to stay close to this park thing."

"We've had nothing on that since noon. Keep on top of the spot news, Weaver."

"I don't want this thing to die down, Roger. It's too big."

Stein put the cassette down. "Let me tell you a quick story," he said. "There was this guy, had a service like yours a couple years ago. I think he was out in Staten Island. Anyway, you remember that Ku Klux Klan shit they had in Brooklyn? When some crosses were burned on a few lawns out there? It was played up real big. Hell, we must have run tape on that story for six nights running. Those flaming crosses at night, they looked great. Well, this guy from Staten Island was having a hard time, nothing was breaking, no plane crashes, nothing. It was dead as hell. So he makes up about five crosses from two-by-fours and keeps them in his van. He showed them to me. He told me when it got so dull he couldn't stand it anymore, he was gonna stick one in somebody's yard, ignite it, drive around the block until the cops came and he'd be right there to tape it. Fucking crazy guy."

Weaver was thinking about something while Stein was talking. She wasn't aware that he'd finished. "Are you listening, Weaver?"

She put down her coffee. "Yeah. I was wondering where I could get some two-by-fours."

"Jesus Christ. The guy was just kidding."

Weaver laughed. "So was I, Roger."

Stein took his feet off his desk and leaned forward. "What I'm trying to tell you is that everybody's gonna have to wait for something to happen. The cops are in a bind right now. They took a hell of a beating, and not just physically. It's their move. Until then the station's gonna try and jack things up a little more. We're doing some stuff with a military expert at eleven, batting around the guerrilla angle. A shrink is supposed to be on also."

"What the hell's he gonna say?"

"That the guy took over the park as a stunt. Like when that kid climbed the World Trade Center. Remember? Or that woman who swam around Manhattan? The shrink's idea is that there's no more adventure left, like climbing mountains is old hat. He says the city is the last adventure. In fact, that's our lead-in."

Weaver slumped back on the sofa and rolled her eyes. What a lot of crap. Things happened. That was all there was. Practically nobody cared why. They could screw the analysis.

Stein answered his phone. Weaver started thinking again and when Stein put the phone down, she jumped up, startling him.

"Don't move so fast, will you, Weaver?"

She tapped her foot. She could feel her energy returning. "How about something exclusive?"

"Like what?"

"Would that be worth more to you? I mean, could we negotiate on the standard fee?"

"Possibly. Have you got a fish on the line?"

Weaver smiled. "What if I can get something on the park? Nobody else will have it. I can bring it in tomorrow. You can tease it all day for the six o'clock."

Stein looked out at the newsroom. "I'll tell you what. You bring me the tape and we'll see." Weaver nodded. Stein didn't like the way her body was suddenly tense again; the way she was grinding her teeth. As she turned for the door he stopped her and said, "Wait a second. I don't give any guarantees. I don't want you to think I'm encouraging you to take any chances. Understood?"

Weaver studied Stein's face. "We understand each other, Roger."


Harris watched the sun go down while he walked in the cover of trees on the West Drive. It was dark by the time he stopped in front of the Civil War monument near West 69th Street. He read the inscription underneath the statue of an old-time foot soldier leaning on a long musket. The words were carved in the stone and said: IN HONOR OF THE MEMBERS OF THE SEVENTH REGIMENT, N.G.S.N.Y., FIFTY-EIGHT IN NUMBER, WHO GAVE THEIR LIVES IN DEFENCE OF THE UNION 1861–1865.

Harris leaned against the statue and looked up through

**205**

the trees to the apartment buildings on Central Park West. Heat rose from the pavement of the Drive and the monument's stone was still warm. Harris was naked from the waist up, except for his flak jacket, and the weight of the AK-47 and equipment sack over his shoulder was making him sweat. He was holding an M-21 7.62-mm sniper rifle.

Harris didn't see anyone on the rooftops of the apartment buildings—it was too dark and far away—but he was certain they were still there. He set down the equipment sack and removed an AN/PVS-3 electro-optical night sight, known as the Starlight Scope, and attached it to the rifle. The scope amplified existing ambient light so that a marksman could see targets at night. It was so sensitive that a target could be pulled into the sight picture from a pitch-black landscape using no other light but that of the stars—hence the name.

Harris put the scope to his eyes and made adjustments until he could focus on the distant buildings. He panned along the roofline and a man appeared in the strange image created by the scope. The man leaned against a railing, pointing a rifle down at Central Park. Harris could see that the man also had his eye to a Starlight Scope.

Harris lowered his rifle. He wondered if someone had his head lined up at that very moment. He felt a little twinge of fear and backed up behind the statue. So, he thought, it's paranoia time. He was going to have to move very carefully, night and day. But wasn't that the way it should be?

He picked up his equipment sack and walked parallel to the Drive, changing his path to keep in the cover of the trees and hills. He found a bench on the edge of the Sheep Meadow and sat down near the beautifully manicured lawns of the bowling greens. He remembered watching the old men roll balls on the short grass, adhering to some arcane set of rules. He'd been impressed by the silence of the game, by the calm and peaceful atmosphere it created.

Harris took a drink from his canteen. He made a mental note to get a refill from the water fountain and concession stand that were right behind him. He rubbed his neck. He didn't feel that tired. He'd spent most of the day resting in the firebase. He'd set up a few more mines and booby traps, but he was almost out of mines, and it had been too hot to do much work. Enough mines were in position anyway; enough to provide adequate security. All that he really wanted to add to certain sections of terrain were rolls of concertina and several small bunkers. He didn't need much else. His normal mission radius was obviously limited. Most of his time, particularly at night, would be spent on reconnaissance.

He thought he might as well do the barbed wire before midnight and started to stand up, but sagged back on the bench. He didn't feel motivated; he didn't have that burst of energy. Since he'd shot down the chopper, he'd felt like he was biding his time. Maybe he needed the emotional respite—a kind of R&R. Things couldn't be dinky dau all the time.

Dinky dau. Harris closed his eyes. He heard a voice on a telephone. The voice relaxed him; the vocabulary soothed him and recalled the companionship of old conversations. Words and faces talked to Harris and he felt comfortable, surrounded by friends in the midst of the danger and fear. The voices were familiar; they reassured him that a world existed beyond the night and the jungle. Hearing those voices made him want to step back into that world.

Harris opened his eyes. Sweat dripped from under his helmet. Across the Sheep Meadow, the digital clock was blinking in the darkness. It was 10:58 P.M. He'd been asleep almost two hours. He stood up and ran his arm over his face. He picked up the sniper rifle and went to the water fountain. After drinking and filling up the canteen, he walked past the concession stand and down a hill to 72nd Street. He studied the sky and the treeline and made a run for the other side of the road. He ducked into the trees around Cherry Hill and went over to the Bow Bridge. Harris stopped in the middle, sat on the cast-iron railing, and let the cool air rising from the Lake dry his face. He raised his rifle and looked through the Starlight Scope. He shifted his seat until there was a view through the trees. The scope found a marksman on a roof and the crosshairs centered on his head. Harris pulled the trigger. There was a click.

Harris said, "Bang."

He slid off the railing and walked to the other side of the bridge. Cartridges for the sniper rifle were in an ammo pouch in his pants and he snapped one into the chamber.

Following the shoreline of the Lake, Harris forgot his dream; he always forgot the good dreams. As he continued through the Ramble, past a roll of barbed wire, he knew only that something was going to happen, that he wanted something to happen—but he didn't like waiting for it. Maybe he would have to force a change in his situation. After all, he thought, that's why he was there.

He decided to rest, to think, while man-made eyes searched for him in the dark. He moved out of the Ramble, toward his firebase, toward sleep.


Radio transmissions were coming from Weaver's bedroom, but she couldn't hear them. She was in her living room, having an argument with Richie and J.T., and their voices were getting loud.

Richie shouted her down. "I ain't gonna do it, Weav."

J.T.: "I'm with him, man. You'd have to be crazy to go in that park."

Weaver was exasperated. She stood up and circled her color TV, which was on, with the audio tuned out. "Wait a second. Think about it. There's nothing to it. We're sneaking in at night. We'll hide out in one spot until morning, when there's enough light. We just walk across to the West Side, making tape, and walk right out. Exclusive

208

shots inside Central Park—deserted, empty sidewalks, the whole thing. Fabulous pictures. We'll get a huge bonus."

Richie snorted. "I can spend it from my wheelchair after I step on some fuckin' mine or somethin'."

J.T. went into the kitchen for a beer. Weaver kept after Richie. "Listen. We're going in on the transverse roadway. We'll stay right on the drive, nowhere near the open ground. Now I don't know what a mine looks like, but hell, I can see one on the pavement. I don't have to step on it."

J.T. was back with his beer. "Right, Weaver. What happens when this guy in there sees you and drops a grenade on your dumb head?"

"It's a big park, J.T. We'd have to be awful unlucky to run into him on a fifteen-minute walk-through. He might not even be in there by now."

"Sure," J.T. said, "that helicopter just got tired and fell down."

"That was twelve hours ago."

Richie got out of his chair near the window that overlooked East 78th Street. "You can stop, Weav. I'm not doing it. You can fire me."

"I'm not gonna fire you, Richie."

"Good. Call me when you're ready to ride the car." He was angry. He slammed the door on his way out of the apartment.

Weaver cursed loudly. She went into her bedroom and sat on her bed, listening to the Bearcat scanner on a table next to her pillows. Her camera and VTR were on the floor. She checked the lens cap and made sure the BNC cable was wrapped tightly. J.T. was standing in the doorway, sipping beer and watching her.

"What are you doing, Weav?"

"I'll go myself. It might even be better."

"Shit. You gotta relax, Weaver. This job ain't everything. You can't be a twenty-four-hour guy."

Weaver almost snapped at him, but she controlled her

temper. J.T. had a lot of feelings, and he didn't conceal them. He had a lot of girl friends, too. If he'd been older and she'd met him under different circumstances, Weaver knew she might have been very attracted to him.

She turned her eyes away from the doorway. "Are you gonna help me get ready?"

J.T. finished his beer and came into the bedroom. He leaned over the bed and started to massage Weaver's shoulders. "Let's go out, eat somethin', have some drinks. Come back here and smoke a joint. Okay? Forget about all this shit. I'll stick around for a while. I practically live here anyway."

Weaver didn't like the sound of that. "Not with me you don't." She twisted away from under his hands.

"Man, I ain't talkin' nothin' serious. Just a little contact."

Weaver was getting nervous. She stood up and lifted the camera to her shoulder. She adjusted the harness and tried to ignore J.T. He looked disgusted.

"You are hard core, Weaver. What are you afraid of, somebody find out you ain't a brick?"

Weaver's breathing accelerated. She didn't want to listen. She fiddled with the zoom lens. J.T. backed away from her.

"Man, that's all you ever do, hold on to that camera. Don't you ever touch nobody?"

Weaver lowered the camera and stared at him. Neither spoke and finally J.T. turned away, heading for the door. Weaver called after him, "Are you gonna help me?"

J.T. yelled back as he left the apartment. "I'll get the car. That's it. You can fuck with this if you want to, but not me."

Weaver didn't move for several seconds. She felt bad. J.T. was only concerned for her safety. But she was mad at him. He'd had a rough childhood, in a rough neighborhood. She'd assumed he would understand her ambition and the pressure on her to succeed. He probably did. But he still didn't know how ugly it could get on the job; how she had to keep her distance; how the camera protected her. She was always looking at the hard side of life in a tiny TV image. She liked that little distance between her and the world. It was the only way.

Weaver put the camera on the floor and fell back on her bed. She covered her face with her hair. Maybe she should let J.T. come on to her; let *someone* come on to her. Her mother was always complaining that Weaver's social life had never been normal; that nothing had changed since high school. She was still up all night, lingering over murders, accidents, suicides; hanging around cops. Her mother said that Weaver never got involved with anyone, never once followed through and learned anything about the people she photographed for her so-called news stories.

Weaver knew that ordinary people didn't understand her participation in the ugliness and tragedy. She was always getting asked, "How can you look at that stuff all day long?" "How can you stand it?" The people who asked those questions didn't know about the little girl with a radio in her bedroom and a fast bicycle; about the tiny TV image that made the ugliness so much easier to take. Weaver was accustomed to that ignorance. But she'd never told her mother or anyone else how afraid she was of her own unrelenting drive for excitement. That's what scared her; made her feel like she was different. Everyone longed for excitement, but Weaver was worried that people would not understand how this longing could become something else; a need. A need that dominated everything.

Weaver cringed inside. She wasn't a brick, goddamnit. She'd like to get involved with people. She often hoped, during the course of her job, when her path crossed someone interesting or attractive or sympathetic, that she'd have time to look for him again, to find out what hap-

**211**

pened to him later. But there never was a "later." There was only the city and the news and the endless speed of the action.

Weaver jerked up from the bed. She grabbed the VTR and slipped the strap over her shoulder. She picked up the camera. The weight of the two units was tremendous, but she didn't care. She stopped in the doorway and looked around her bedroom. The walls were covered with dramatic photographs of accidents, Mafia assassinations, fires. Two black-and-white televisions were at the foot of the bed. The scanner was still on, searching through the frequencies. She didn't shut it down. J.T. would be coming back for the night. She turned off the light and left the apartment. She had a job to do.

Weaver parked the station wagon on the east side of Fifth Avenue, near 78th Street. She put the press card in the window and got out. Light traffic moved downtown. It was about 11:00 P.M. She walked north for a block until she had a clear view of the intersection of 79th and Fifth. The ubiquitous barricades blocked 79th where it entered Central Park and became a transverse road. Three police officers stood on the sidewalk near the southern end of the Metropolitan Museum of Art. They were far enough from the actual entry point on the transverse roadway that Weaver had difficulty seeing them in the dark. Perfect, she thought.

She turned around to walk back downtown and discovered a problem. Another cop was on the opposite side of the intersection, the south side of 79th Street. He was sitting on a sawhorse in front of a wide walk that was one of the pedestrian entrances to the Park. His position was only yards away from the transverse road.

Weaver stopped and leaned back against the wall of an apartment building. A woman came out the entrance and flagged down a taxi. Weaver saw a phone booth on the other side of the street, midway between 79th and 78th.

She stepped to the curb and watched the cop for a moment. She looked back at the phone booth. She waited for the traffic to clear and crossed the street. She knew that no pedestrians were allowed on the west side of the avenue, so she tried to be inconspicuous and moved quickly to the front of the booth. She looked inside, read the phone number and ran back across to the apartment house. The cop had not seen her.

She locked the station wagon and found another pay phone on 79th near Madison Avenue. She called her apartment. J.T. answered.

"News."

"J.T., this is Weaver."

"What happened?"

"Nothing yet. I want you to do something for me."

"I told you, man . . ."

"Come on, J.T. Just this one thing. I want you to call this number. Ready?"

"Shit."

"362-2408. Got that?"

"Right."

"After I hang up give it about two minutes, then call. Let it keep ringing. When someone answers, hang up. Okay?"

"Weav, are you gonna be cool now?"

"Don't worry. Tell Richie the car's on Fifth Avenue near Seventy-eighth Street. Don't sit there with the radios off while I'm gone, either. If this works out, we'll be able to get an office with a real assignment desk. Won't that be nice?"

"Don't stroke me, man . . ."

"Bye. Call that number."

Weaver hung up. She returned to the station wagon and unlocked the rear door. She put a fresh cassette into the VTR and shoved the BNC cable into her belt. She lifted her camera, put the VTR over her shoulder and put the battery belts around her wrist. She walked uptown and stopped just short of the traffic light at 79th Street. Across the avenue, the dark transverse road curved down into Central Park and disappeared. Weaver looked for the officers near the museum. Their backs were turned. She watched the cop directly across the avenue. A circle of light fell on him from a lamp in the tall bushes on the other side of the Park wall. He was chewing his fingernails. A New York *Times* truck went past and Weaver lost sight of him for a second. When the truck was gone, the phone in the booth was ringing.

The cop looked up at the phone, then went back to chewing his fingernails. The phone kept ringing. The cop stretched and lit a cigarette. He tried not to pay attention to the phone. He stood up, stared into the Park, took a drag on his cigarette. He looked back at the phone. He moved to the sidewalk and looked uptown toward the museum. Weaver followed his gaze. The officers were talking with a cabdriver. The phone continued to ring. Finally the cop couldn't stand it and he went for the booth. Weaver immediately started to cross the avenue. She watched the cop answer the phone as she ran to the transverse road and into Central Park.

She moved quickly down the roadway, staying as close to the trees as possible. She groaned under the weight of her equipment. After several yards, the trees gave way to an embankment and a high wall as the road angled down under a bridge. Weaver slowed down. It was very dark and she saw no one behind her. No one screamed at her to stop. She kept going, through a tunnel that passed under the East Drive, and approached a building on her left. It was the fire alarm station, so she knew she was midway between the east and west sides, in the center of the Park. She stopped in front of the building and looked for a place to hide. She did not want to be out in the open. She didn't think the police marksmen would be concentrating on the transverse roads, but she hoped that if they spotted her, they'd have enough sense to recognize what she was doing. That was something she hadn't bothered to discuss with J.T. and Richie. No sense making things more difficult.

The landscape behind the building was so black and scary that Weaver ran to the other side of the transverse and stood against the wall bordering the roadway. She could see the trees and foliage jutting out high overhead. She didn't want to get anywhere near grass or bushes, particularly at night. She decided to walk several yards farther west, to a tunnel, where the transverse passed under the Belvedere. There was a small stone staircase cut into the high wall before the tunnel. The steps led up to the Park. Weaver stopped and peered at the staircase. She put her nose right down to the steps and studied the stone. It looked all right. Weaver went up about three steps, rested her equipment on the stairs, and sat down. It was a good place to wait for first light. She was in a tight little niche, surrounded by concrete walls and the tall trees at the top of the staircase. She was under the Park and off the road.

The air was humid and warm. She was sweating and breathing heavily. She tried to relax. Her back ached from carrying the equipment. Someday somebody was going to reduce the weight of the VTR and camera to a one-person unit, and then she could really swing. She laughed out loud and startled herself. A firefly blinked at the bottom of the stairs and she jumped again. God, she thought, calm down. It's just seven more hours. That's all.

Weaver removed a candy bar from her jeans. It was soggy and melted. She ate it anyway. For her, eating was a tranquilizer. She looked up at the trees and wondered what part of the Park was at the top of the stairs, and if she could get a good shot of the landscape from that location. She wasn't all that familiar with Central Park. She wished she'd studied a map. She shrugged. Too late for that now.

She found three more candy bars that she'd stuffed in

her back pocket. She ate all three and listened to crickets and the dull hum of the traffic outside in the city. There was no breeze; nothing moved. Fireflies blinked around her, but this time she didn't jump.

Dix gave up trying to reach the security guard on the house phone. He wanted to know if any reporters were in front of his apartment building. He was almost certain there would be; he'd spotted a car with NYP license plates on the block when he'd come home earlier in the evening.

Dix turned out the lights, locked up and got on the elevator. Ordinarily he would have used the service elevator and avoided the front entrance, but he was going to need a taxi. He didn't have the limo; he'd thought he was going to stay home and sleep. Then he got restless and wanted to talk to somebody, so he'd called his ex-wife and she'd agreed to meet him for a late drink. Very late, since he was supposed to have been there at 10:30. It was after eleven.

When the elevator doors opened, Dix saw the security guard asleep in a maintenance closet off the lobby. He woke him up.

"Did you see any reporters outside?"

The guard glared at him and rubbed his eyes. "What do you think, Mr. Dix? They live here now."

"I don't suppose you'd like to go out and get me a taxi and bring it down to the service entrance?"

"Are you kidding? Ask me around Christmas. I do favors then."

Dix couldn't blame the guy. The reporters were a nuisance that made more work for the building staff. Dix turned away and resigned himself to facing the press. He'd already been interviewed three times since noon and the Mayor had insisted that he appear live on WNBC's six o'clock news to answer questions and sound optimistic, authoritative and dynamic. As always, the reviews had been good.

Dix pushed through the entrance doors and stood on the sidewalk with his eyes closed. He didn't hear anything except horns honking.

Could it possibly be? he thought. Nope. Feet ran toward him on the sidewalk. He opened his eyes. An AP reporter and a woman from WINS radio stood in front of him. The woman he knew by name.

"Hello, Ms. Rubin."

"I saw that, Mr. Dix. You can't close your eyes and make us go away."

Everybody laughed. Dix moved closer to the curb and tried to see if there were any empty taxis entering the block. Both reporters turned on cassette recorders and held up microphones. The smiles went away. Ms. Rubin asked the first question.

"How can the Police Department still maintain that the park's closing is the work of terrorists? Doesn't the public have a right to know the Department's progress?"

Dix saw a taxi and stuck his arm out. His mind reached into an old file and answered the question. "Ms. Rubin. You know we are not standing still. I cannot speak for the Police Department. But I know they feel they are close to gaining a strategic advantage."

The AP reporter practically choked. "Strategic advantage! We're no longer speaking of apprehending anyone and reopening the park?"

Dix stared blankly at the man. "The Department is seeking to apprehend the perpetrators and reopen the park, using any means available to it. That's all I can say."

The taxi pulled up to the curb. As Dix was climbing in, the AP reporter asked him, "Are you calling up the Guard?"

Dix yelled back, "That's up to the Governor."

The driver was not moving the cab. He was making a note on his trip sheet. Dix wanted to smack him in the head, but the plastic partition was in the way. Ms. Rubin pusher her microphone in the open window.

"Do you know the identity of the man in the park?"

The question caught Dix by surprise. For a moment, he considered answering—but he knew better, and rolled up the window in Ms. Rubin's face.

It was hot in the taxi as Dix rode over to the West Side. The driver took Fifth Avenue to Central Park South and they went around the southern half of Central Park. It was odd to see the empty sidewalks on the perimeter, but Dix had to admit that he was getting used to it. The Park had been closed more than twenty-four hours. He imagined what it would be like if the Park were closed permanently; a no-man's-land haunted by some legendary phantom.

The driver turned his head and said something through the partition. Dix said, "I didn't hear you."

"I said it's hotter than a bitch, isn't it?"

"Yeah."

"It was supposed to rain. They ain't predicting the weather any better than when I was a kid."

Dix leaned forward and looked at the driver's picture on the hack license under the dashboard. His name was Morris Levinson. He'd probably been driving a taxi for thirty years.

The driver continued. "You work for the city? I seen those reporters back there."

"I'm with the Mayor's Office."

"What are they gonna do with this park? Huh? Thirty minutes it takes to go crosstown."

"I really don't know."

"You know what I think? I think the city should surrender. That's right. Give up. This guy in the park, sign a treaty with him, give him a medal, everybody goes home happy. We'll name the park after him."

The driver stopped the taxi on West 63rd Street in

front of Dix's destination, a bar called O'Neal's Balloon. Dix got out and stooped over to look in the driver's window. "Hey, Morris. Are you available for my next press conference?" The driver laughed hard. Dix paid his fare and included a big tip. He went into O'Neal's and found his ex-wife sitting at a table in front of a window facing Columbus Avenue and Lincoln Center. She was looking great. Dix kissed her and sat down.

"I'm sorry I'm late, Marianne."

She pointed at the bar in the main room. "I was watching the TV in there. I figured if you weren't here you were on the tube."

Dix ordered a double martini. "God, I can't stand it. I even said the word 'perpetrators' twice today."

"That's what bureaucrats do." She smiled to soften the remark.

"Be nice to me, Marianne." He watched her run her hand through her blond hair. His drink arrived. He sipped it and tried to relax. "You know, I feel like I've been back in those press conferences during the war. I'd say one thing for the generals, how we were licking VC ass all over the place, when I sure as hell knew it was something else altogether. It's the same with the P.C. and the Mayor and the Department. I've got to juggle all these statements and policies, I've got reporters hanging all over me, and I'm giving them a big line of bullshit."

"Why? What's been happening?"

Dix told her about the phone call from the man in the Park. He said that the conversation had convinced him that a psychological solution might be possible, but the Department had damaged his chances of finding that solution when they'd forced the man to shoot down one of the helicopters.

Marianne finished her drink. "What is the Department going to do now?"

"I don't know. Keller is still saying that a terrorist group is responsible. We've been meeting all day, but they

**219**

don't have many options. They're going to have to let things ride for a while, see what develops. The lab identified some fragments as part of a claymore mine. I could have told them that. Now they've got the FBI investigating the weapons dealers and stolen arms caches. But, so what if they identify a suspect who might have had access to the right kinds of weapons? What are they going to do? Bring the suspect's mother down to the park and beg him to give up?"

Dix ordered another martini. Marianne let him keep rambling.

"They've got these marksmen all over the goddamn skyline, but I went up there and looked. It'd sure be a one in a million shot. One thing I know for sure, Marianne. The Department's not going to listen to me."

Marianne jumped on him. "Does that surprise you? They ignore whatever they feel like. Cops are like the military. They have one solution to violence. More violence."

Dix felt an old argument coming on: "It's not that simple."

"Really? Let's say you're right. You're dealing with a Vietnam veteran. Why don't you keep working on a peaceful solution? Bring it out in the open. Find a way to get this man to put down the guns and give up. Push for it."

"I'm with you. But I don't know if there's time for that now. Remember, I'm a public official. A kid got killed going into that park today. I have to consider the public's safety. The lives of police officers are on the line. I'm supposed to support the Department. I can only push so far. I don't like the bullshit, but that's the way it is."

"You don't have to p.r. me." Marianne was angry. "David, if you're so sick of getting paid to bullshit the public, why don't you quit?"

"I'm so good at it. That's how I went from a junior information officer to a deputy mayor."

Marianne stared at him. Dix could never hide from that stare. She said, "I know why you wanted to talk to me. You wanted me to help you rationalize what you have to do. When it comes down to it, you're going to go along with whatever will bring a conclusion to this problem. Even if it means somebody gets killed."

Dix tried not to look at her. "I don't know what to do. People have already been killed. We can't wait for this guy in the park to get bored and walk out. I'll keep trying , but it's not up to me. I need to communicate with the guy. I'll keep pleading my case to the Department as long as there's time." Dix knew that was weak.

"Quit, David."

"I can't."

"You won't. Because violence is something you understand."

Dix turned away. There it was. He'd been somewhere, learned something hard and ugly, learned a rationale that accommodated shifting circumstances. Dix had a private face and a public face. He alternately abhorred and supported violence. This dichotomy confused and angered Marianne. Her perspicacity never failed—she always nailed him for it. Maybe that's what he wanted from her; he needed to sort out these disparate feelings, but he was never able to shake his own confusion. It was one of the reasons he and Marianne weren't married anymore.

Dix felt her hand touch his arm. He looked at her and was very unhappy. She said, "David, I'm worried about you. If you keep rubbing shoulders with these kinds of people, you're going to end up like them. Cops, soldiers—you give them guns, they want to use them. That's their life. It always ends up the same. Somebody gets killed."

She left the table. He didn't try to stop her. He looked out the window and saw her walk to Columbus Avenue and hail a taxi. He sat for a long time, watching the traffic go by, past the water that flowed up through the colored lights on the fountains in Lincoln Center.

Dix went home to his apartment on East 65th Street. He went into his bedroom and got undressed. He stopped in front of the dresser and stared at the photograph of his Vietnam service. He looked at himself in the mirror. Then he removed every photograph from the wall and shoved them in a drawer.

He turned off the light and went to bed.

Weaver's elbow slipped off her knee and her head banged against the concrete wall of the staircase. She woke up.

"Oh, Christ."

Morning light filtered down through the trees. The sun glinted on the surface of the camera. Weaver looked at her watch. It was 7:45. She stood up and kicked a pile of candy wrappers away from her feet. She stretched and listened to the birds. There were a lot of birds singing and they seemed to be happy. No wonder, she thought. No cars or people to intrude on their space.

Weaver continued to listen for other sounds, but there was nothing ominous. She walked slowly up the steps until her head was above the ground level of the park. She could see a walk directly in front of her and the small pond called the New Lake, just beyond the walk. In the background was the wide-open Great Lawn and, to her left, high atop a rock mound, the Belvedere Castle. A light haze gave the view a soft focus. It was going to make a hell of a shot.

She went back down the steps and hooked up the camera, VTR and batteries. She was so excited that she didn't feel the excessive weight on her sore muscles. She made a test pan, watching the tiny TV image in the eyepiece, and was satisfied with the light balance. She adjusted the microphone on the VTR. She decided to tape a narration on the audio track of the cassette just for kicks, although she knew Stein would never use it.

Weaver went to the top of the stairs. She checked the

pavement on the walk very carefully, stepped away from the staircase and stood under the trees. She wasn't going to move one more inch. Just get the shot, go back down the stairs and walk out to the West Side in the middle of the transverse road, taping on the move.

Weaver rolled tape. She allowed five seconds for speed and began a broad pan over the landscape. In the eyepiece she saw the shimmering water of the New Lake. She began her narration.

"Central Park is strangely quiet without the bustle of people and cars." Weaver frowned and put the tape on pause. "Crap. Let me try that again." She hit the pause button and resumed her pan.

"Central Park is deserted, quiet. Here along 79th Street is what it looks like to the one man who now controls this vast green space in the middle of Manhattan."

She panned up to the Belvedere Castle and the distant skyline on Central Park West. She continued talking. "There, high above the park, on the rooftops, are the ever-present police marksmen waiting for the one false move that will end this siege."

She brought the view down and panned across the Delacorte Theater, the Great Lawn and the ball fields. She panned up above the treeline and saw the buildings on Fifth Avenue. As she circled the camera back to the bushes and the far edge of the New Lake, something appeared in the tiny TV image. It was blurred. She adjusted the focus. It was an army helmet. Words written above the brow said: PLAN B. Weaver panned down. A man in camouflage clothes was pointing a rifle at her.

Weaver's mouth fell open. She pulled her head away from the tiny TV image. She looked at the man and her eyes wouldn't blink. Suddenly, she lost all memory of who she was or what she was doing.

Harris looked quickly over his shoulder, up at the treeline, then back. He said, "Put that shit down and get on your knees."

Weaver didn't move. Harris circled her and checked out the staircase. He put the barrel of the rifle against the back of Weaver's head.

"This thing is pure information. Know what I mean? Hello. Good-bye."

Weaver set down the camera and VTR, unfastened the battery packs and dropped to her knees. She knew she was going to die and she raised her hands to her face. Harris jammed the rifle into her head, forcing it down.

"Put your hands on top of your head."

Weaver hesitated. Harris clicked off the safety and went on semi-automatic. Weaver heard the sound and put her hands on top of her head. Harris moved around her and pushed over the VTR. He fumbled with the eject lever and removed the cassette. After stomping it to pieces, he kicked in the front of the VTR. He stepped back and kept the rifle aimed at her.

"Stand up."

Weaver's knees were trembling, but she managed to get herself upright.

Harris said, "We're going through there." He pointed at the thick trees on the shore of the New Lake. "Do what I say or you might step on something unpleasant." They moved off the walk and Harris guided her through the bushes and undergrowth.

Weaver kept her hands on her head; she stumbled and her eyes wouldn't focus. After about fifty yards Harris stopped and cleared away some leaves over a manhole cover. He pushed the heavy disk to the side and exposed a dark opening leading underground. Weaver could smell damp, stale air.

Harris pointed the AK into the hole. "There's a ladder. You'll see it." She got to her knees again and felt for the ladder with her feet. She climbed down and Harris followed her, pulling the manhole cover into place and switching on a flashlight. He dropped down beside her and stepped back quickly. He gestured with the beam and

Weaver moved farther into the dark space. It was cold. Water leaked from cracks in a stone wall. She caught a glimpse of crates and sheets of plastic. She felt the rifle in her back and froze.

Harris moved a few feet away, to the opposite wall of the aqueduct supply dump. He set the flashlight on a stack of crates so that the beam illuminated Weaver. He held the AK out from his waist and rummaged through a box on the moist ground. Weaver saw him remove something.

Harris said, "Take off your clothes."

Weaver didn't think she had any fear left, but a chill tingled in her neck.

Harris looked her up and down. "Strip that thing."

Weaver tried to talk. She choked, tried again. "Please. Please don't do that."

"Let's see some skin. Right now." He poked her with the rifle, knocking her back. She winced in pain and touched her chest.

"Okay. You don't have to do that."

"Get started."

Weaver began to take off her shoes. Her hands shook as she set them down. She reached for her T-shirt and Harris raised the rifle. He had a sudden thought that she was a cop.

"Be slow. If you're hiding anything in there besides your tits, you're gonna get pacified. Most ricky-tick."

Weaver pulled her T-shirt over her head, exposing her breasts. She stepped out of her jeans. She was naked except for her panties. Harris studied her body. He told her, "Turn around." Weaver faced the wall. "Drop your panties." She lowered them to her knees. There was no gun hidden between the cheeks of her ass; Harris had seen that trick before. "Okay, turn back." She faced him. She was trembling badly.

She said, "Please. You do what you have to do, but don't hurt me."

Harris was confused. Then it hit him and he laughed. "You think I wanna mess with that skinny thing? Jesus." He held up his hand. He was holding a set of jungle fatigues. He threw them to her and she reacted too slowly. The clothes hit her in the chest and fell to the ground. Harris said, "Put those on. From a distance you'll look like me. Then maybe those sharpshooters will make a mistake and grease you instead."

Weaver's mind went completely blank again. Her hands moved; she pulled up her panties; she picked up the fatigues and put them on. She looked at him.

Harris's voice echoed in the dark aqueduct. "Not a bad fit."

Activity was light in the mobile command post on Central Park West. Dix could hear SOD transmissions in the background. He was sitting with Keller, Curran and Charlie Meyers. Meyers had been briefing Keller on the intricacies of Central Park's landscape and a lot of other information that Dix thought was a waste of time. As far as he was concerned, Keller and the brass were playing with themselves. Dix didn't know what the hell he was doing there, except that's what the Mayor wanted. Nobody had said two words to him in the last half hour.

Keller looked up from a map detail and said to Meyers, "I know enough about Central Park to run tours in there now."

Meyers nodded. "I only showed you the half of it, sir. I'll need to get a guy from the Department of Water Resources to come up here with the sewer specs. We could spend another two days on what's underground."

Curran shook his head. "God forbid any terrorists are down there wandering around."

Dix was feeling loose, with the courage of the depressed. "Terrorists?" he said sarcastically. "Militants under every bed, right?"

Curran smiled and hardly reacted. Dix was embarrassed. He realized that Curran was riding him.

"Dix, you're a little edgy, aren't you?" Dix looked at the floor. Curran said, "You were right about the helicopters. We'll give you that. But we're not ruling out anything. Any policeman will tell you that's just when you get a bad surprise. And I know the Mayor doesn't like surprises. You sit on your side of the fence and we'll sit on ours. One man or fifty in Central Park—frankly, I don't give a shit who's right."

Keller stayed out of it. He let the silence last for a minute and then told Meyers, "You get hold of that guy at Water Resources. Tell him to be ready with the necessary specs around the clock. And tell him to have someone backing him up on a twenty-four-hour standby."

"Yes, sir." Meyers left the table. The Commissioner excused himself. He had another meeting with the FBI. Dix was ready to get even with Curran when an officer in uniform interrupted.

"Mr. Dix, you have a priority call."

Probably the Mayor, Dix thought. He got up from the table and went to a phone at the console. He didn't see Curran conferring with the officer; he didn't know that an elaborate phone trace was going into effect at a switching station on the East Side; he didn't know that Curran was about to order five Emergency Services marksman teams into positions high above Central Park; he didn't know that the one person to whom he wanted to speak was on hold at the other end of the line.

Weaver couldn't remember much about the last thirty minutes. She probably never would. She had images: glimpses of barbed wire rolling through the bushes; holes dug into the soft earth along a lake; a strange gun on the hip of the man who was scaring the hell out of her. She saw herself crawling through undergrowth, running over a road. She saw leaves and branches; details of a terrain. Her senses were alert; in those thirty minutes, she tasted, smelled, touched Central Park.

They were standing now, near the rear entrance to the zoo. Harris was outside a phone booth with the receiver to his ear. He held the AK-47 loosely at his side. The sniper rifle was over his shoulder and the M-79 launcher was in its special holster. He wore his flack jacket and had a field harness on his back.

The booth was at the bottom of the short hill that curved down from the East Drive. The area was in the shade of heavy trees. Right behind Harris was the Green Gap arch, the large tunnel under the Drive. Weaver leaned against the phone booth; she was exhausted and dehydrated. Her hands were tied behind her back. She tried to shift her weight.

Harris looked at her suddenly. "Stand still. Don't try and run for it. If the snipers don't get you, something from me will."

He gripped the phone with his shoulder and removed a new banana clip from an ammo pouch. He snapped it into the rifle and put the old one back in the pouch. Weaver watched him warily. Harris looked up at the sky. They were not that far from Fifth Avenue, but no buildings were visible through the trees. Harris returned his attention to the phone. He was getting impatient listening to a variety of clicks. He wiped a ring of sweat away from his helmet.

A voice came on the line. "Dix here."

Harris took a breath. "I talked to you last time, right?"

There was a long pause. Harris thought the voice had hung up.

"Hello?"

"Right. It was me."

"I was hoping you had some juice, but I guess not. I had to pop one of those choppers. You want to try again?"

228

"Talk to me."

"I'm going to let somebody in the park."

There was another pause, then, "Who?"

"Some fool tried to get in the park at 110th Street yesterday. I found his body this morning before it got light. I moved it closer to the wall. It's only about three feet from the sidewalk. Somebody can pick it up. Need I say, that whoever it is, they shouldn't try to go one inch past that body."

"Okay. When?"

"Any time." Harris was keeping his eye on Weaver. She was staring at the ground. Harris continued. "One more thing. I was near the zoo this morning. I saw some people in there. I suppose they're keepers."

"I knew about that. There's nothing we could do. The animals have to be fed. The keepers volunteered. They won't try a damn thing."

"Well, I've already decided to let them continue. But I'll be checking them out, and if I see anything that doesn't look right, I'm gonna lob a frag in there. Goodbye."

"Don't hang up."

Harris turned around and surveyed the area. He put his hand on the booth and leaned against it. He tapped the AK on the glass door. Harris didn't want to hang up. He said, "I know you're tracing this. They fucked around again when I called."

"Hey, no. It takes time to get patched through to me."

"I'm gonna hang up."

"I promise there's no trace."

Harris started to hang up. He put the receiver halfway down. He listened to the hum of the traffic, the horns honking, an airplane passing overhead. He brought the phone back and said, "Okay. Last time we talked you said some things. You said you wanted to talk to me."

"Yeah, you know—the usual stuff, like where you from

soldier, we're all proud of you, we'll have you home soon."

Harris laughed. "Are you kidding? I remember that."

"I'll tell you something. I used to set that shit up for a general. One of those little trips in-country so he could mingle with the grunts, do the old hometown thing. Give out a meritorious unit citation and then sky out without getting his boots muddy."

"I hear you." Harris nodded. "Your boots ever get muddy."

There was a slight hesitation. "I know what you're thinking. I did bush time. Not very much. I had to ask for it."

"Ask for it?" Harris let out a long breath. "Ask for it. Talk about dinky dau."

"You really think so?"

Harris rubbed his temples. He started to say something and stopped. He stood silently; a cloud of gnats circled in front of his face.

Weaver was listening to the conversation. She turned slightly, leaning her shoulder against the booth. She watched Harris struggle for words.

Harris said, "Maybe that's not so crazy. Asking for it."

"That's what I'm saying. You're asking for it too."

Harris banged the AK against the booth. "You don't understand." Harris looked up at Weaver. Her eyes were locked on him. He turned away so she couldn't see his face. He looked down at himself, at the weapons, at the perspiration on his fatigues. "You can't possibly know," he said.

"I think I do. Maybe together we can talk this through, figure out what you want from this."

Weaver moved and the booth creaked. Harris turned quickly and stared at her.

"No, we've talked too long. They're gonna do some trace. They'll tape my voice."

"Don't hang up. There's no trace. I know you want to talk to me. That stuff about the zoo; that was bullshit. You know why you called."

Harris couldn't take his eyes off Weaver. "Well, I've been kind of out of it. I haven't talked to anybody for a long time."

The voice waited. There was only breathing. Finally the voice spoke. "I know where you came from."

"Do you?" Harris squeezed the AK-47. "I know some guys who would know. But they're dead. I don't think you can tell me that."

"Christ, I've heard that before. Listen, nobody chose the thing, did they? It just happened to you. We didn't do it the same way. Okay? There it is. But I'm the one out here who's listening to you."

"Yeah, I'll think about that," Harris said. "Maybe I'll call you again." He was going to slam the phone down, but changed his mind and hung up gently.

Weaver and Harris stood in the shade of the trees and watched each other. A small branch snapped and leaves floated down in front of the booth. Harris kicked idly at the leaves with the toe of his boot. He heard branches crack and more leaves dropped to the ground. Something whistled and thudded into the hillside. Harris felt like he was moving underwater as he shoved Weaver away from the booth and under the Green Gap arch. The whistling sounds increased; the trees ripped apart. Dirt kicked up and one of the booth's plastic panels shattered. Harris ran into the middle of the tunnel. Weaver stood, frozen, just inside the entrance and saw the phone booth explode. Harris ran back to her. He yanked her away as chunks of concrete blew away from the arch. Plastic, metal and pieces of the telephone spun out and bounced off the walls of the tunnel. There were no shooting sounds—only the whistling of the bullets. In thirty seconds the fusillade ended. Dust and leaves drifted around the opening to the arch. The booth had been reduced to a Swiss-cheese shell.

Harris reacted immediately. He switched the AK to his shoulder and readied the sniper rifle. He pushed Weaver ahead of him and they went out the other end of the Green Gap arch. They cut back over the Drive and moved across the 65th Street transverse, Harris exhorting Weaver to hurry. Harris knew they would be exposed on open ground for several yards, but he was taking a chance. He wanted to get close to Fifth Avenue before it was too late.

They went into the trees along the Drive and down a hill to another arch, named Willowdell. Weaver tripped and rolled up to the entrance. Harris nudged her with his boot and she crawled inside. She sat back against the wall, gulping for air. Harris could see that she was very pale, but her eyes darted and betrayed her alertness. He checked the rope binding her hands. Blood oozed from her wrists. He told her, "Don't fuck around. I'm going to do some shooting. Just to let them know they missed."

Harris ran out of the tunnel and followed a walk that led to a wooded area not far from the rear of the Children's Zoo. The high ground around the Denesmouth arch gave Harris a view of the buildings along Fifth Avenue. He set up and got into a firing position. He looked through the scope and saw that the avenue had been blocked off uptown near 72nd Street; there were no cars or pedestrians anywhere near his location. He saw police personnel coming out the entrance to one of the tall apartment houses. He panned up the facade of the building until he could see the roofline. A man was standing on the edge, in front of an ornate railing, watching Central Park through binoculars. Another man stood next to him. He held a rifle and a walkie-talkie.

Harris aimed and fired. He lowered the rifle and tried to see the roofline with his naked eye. The two men had disappeared. He looked through the scope again and focused on the target area. After a long thirty seconds, the two men stuck their heads up, farther down the railing. Harris fired, aiming again at the ornate stonework. This time he didn't wait to verify his accuracy. He rolled off the small hill and ran back along the walk.

Weaver was not under the Willowdell arch. Harris cursed. He put the sniper rifle over his shoulder and changed back to the AK-47. He hurried out the other end of the arch. Weaver was standing just to the right of the walk, in front of the bushes that covered the incline leading up to the Drive. Harris first saw her from the corner of his eye and he was startled. He turned the gun on her.

"What are you doing?"

Weaver shook her head.

"This whole place is booby-trapped. Try and get that. I'm the only one who know where it's safe to walk."

Weaver twisted her arms back and forth. "I can't feel my hands. Will you loosen the rope?"

Harris ignored her. He stood on his toes and looked up at the Drive. Sunlight glared off the asphalt.

"Will you loosen my hands?"

Harris unfastened his flak jacket.

"What are you going to do with me?" Weaver persisted.

Harris turned to her. He didn't want any more questions. He wanted to think. "Don't say anything else. Just stand there."

Harris stepped back into the shade under the arch. He thought about the phone call. The voice had lured him into a moment of reality, of hope. The moment had been crushed, suddenly, instantly. Harris sure as hell didn't need the rude goodbyes anymore. But what else was there, if he didn't have the voices? Harris was confused. He wanted the night and the fear. It was easier then.

He looked up at the sun. He wanted to move. Alone.

Harris guided Weaver back through dangerous terrain to the underground supply dump. She said nothing as she descended the ladder. Harris tied her feet, retied her hands. He left her in the dark hole and went out into the park and passed the day in a way that made time irrelevant.

On patrol.


"We missed."

This was Curran's assessment of the morning's shooting.

Dix was furious. He asked Curran to step over to a quiet area of the command post.

"You missed," Dix said. "That's all you're going to say?" Curran nodded. Dix continued. "You missed more than that. From now on I expect to be informed on Department strategy. The Mayor expects to be informed. And don't tell me this was an emergency. You used me, and that will never happen again."

Curran responded with a trace of boredom. "Dix, we couldn't tell you about the trace. It might have colored your conversation."

"Bullshit."

Curran snapped back. "Listen, we almost nailed whoever was on that phone. We're not passing up any opportunities to expedite this goddamn case. I'm sure the Mayor can appreciate that."

Dix was exasperated. "See if you can understand this. I might have been able to talk this guy out of the park. I had him. Christ, that was your opportunity to expedite this case. But not now."

Curran narrowed his eyes. "I'll pass that on to the officers in the hospital."

The hammer. Right in the head. Curran walked away and Dix stood alone, making judgments, shaming himself. He knew Curran was right. Dix was angry and feeling betrayed, only because he'd gotten what he wanted. He'd had his phone call, his chance, and now his little scheme had been taken away.

Dix left the command post and waited for the limousine

on Central Park West. He watched the traffic coming off 86th Street, the cars and taxis detouring as they hit the barricades, traveling north and south to make the trip around Central Park. The sun made him squint, and as his gaze fell on the cool, green Park, he felt his anger return. He thought about the officers in the hospital, thought about the dead men. He knew Curran was wrong. If the Department was permitted to find its own solution, fifty more men would end up in the hospital, or worse. Everything in Dix's experience told him that. A voice on the phone had removed any doubt.

A horn honked and Dix saw the limo pull to the curb in front of the command post. As he walked to the car, Dix considered going public with what he knew, getting some leverage against the brass—but he'd never liked that kind of ploy. It was too much like all the other things he'd learned: the public face, the cover-up, the bullshit. There was a better way. And on the ride downtown Dix decided to do the one thing he'd learned that few people, including Marianne, ever saw him do. Pay hardball.

When Dix arrived at City Hall, he went to his office and made several long-distance phone calls. He used the power of his position to lean on reluctant secretaries and base commanders. In thirty minutes he found the man he was looking for. The man agreed to catch the next commercial flight to New York. Dix hung up and told no one.

Weaver slept and dreamed she was entombed in a pyramid. She woke up sweating, her arms and legs aching and stiff. The absence of light and sound in the old aqueduct was disorienting. Time didn't move. The city punished her for her knowledge of its horrors; it condemned her to its subterranean bowels.

She slept again and woke up shivering. She tried to sit, but she felt dizzy and reclined on the damp ground. When she heard the manhole cover being lifted, she knew it was night, because no shaft of light fell through the round opening above the ladder. A flashlight beam moved toward her.

Harris put the light in her face and she turned her head away. At first, he thought she'd been crying; then he realized that the streaks on her face were trails of dried sweat.

Harris untied Weaver's hands and feet and they climbed up to the surface of the Park. It was dark, but a full moon and the city's glow provided a dull light. Weaver looked at her watch. It was covered with blood. She rubbed her wrists and winced. Harris put the manhole cover in place and stood with the AK pointed casually at the ground. Weaver heard a thousand sounds: the crickets, the hum, her heartbeat. She tried to see Harris in the fading light. His face was relaxed; his eyes were heavy-lidded and sleepy; dark curls spilled out of the combat helmet. He was almost smiling.

She asked him, "What time is it?"

"Be quiet. We'll follow that walk over there. See it? I'm going to say this one more time. Don't deviate with your feet. Got that?"

Weaver nodded. They stayed on the walk, moving past tall bushes, and turned off into a stand of heavy trees. They passed between two huge rolls of barbed wire. Harris directed Weaver to the far end of his firebase, and told her to sit down near the bunker. He stacked the AK-47, the sniper rifle and the launcher against a crate of fragmentation grenades and stripped to the waist. After strapping on his holster and .45 automatic, he toweled off and put on his flak jacket over his naked chest.

Without speaking, he spent fifteen minutes finding picnic supplies among the boxes and crates, and prepared something to eat on a camp stove. Harris set out two paper plates and a canteen. He pulled a crate up next to the stove and sat on the edge of the bunker, a few feet from Weaver.

They studied each other. Every few minutes Harris looked over his shoulder, scanned the treeline, checked his back. Weaver looked around, too—at the barbed wire, at the collection of weapons and supplies, at the empty ground inside the perimeter. On the way in, she'd been told to avoid that area. As she sat there now, the entire space became sinister and deadly. Weaver started to get worried all over again.

The food finished cooking and Harris dished it out. He broke the silence. "It's canned stew. I jazzed it with a high-protein powder. It's shit, but it works." He handed Weaver her plate. Her hands shook as she accepted it, and Harris noticed. "Are you gonna be able to hold on to that?"

Weaver looked at her plate. She tried to swallow and couldn't.

"Mouth dry?" Harris asked. Weaver nodded. "Fear," Harris said. "'It can last for a long time. My spit went out once for two weeks." Harris started to eat. Weaver sat still for a while and then reached for the canteen. Harris's eyes followed every movement. She drank and ate slowly. Harris talked in between mouthfuls.

"I'll give you this, though. You didn't panic when they opened up on that phone booth. I've seen guys pee in their pants on the first round whistling through the trees. And then get flat in the mud and pray to every god they could think of. I did that myself. Sometimes it feels good. When you go all the way."

Weaver ate only a little. She poked at her food. She listened to Harris, but said nothing. Harris finished eating and stuffed his plate in a plastic garbage sack. He took a drink from the canteen and leaned forward to see Weaver's face.

"Are you gonna say anything or what?"

Weaver cleared her throat. "My job."

Harris waited expectantly. "Yeah . . . your job."

Weaver knew she should force herself to speak. Cops

had always told her that in any hostage situation, the hostages should talk to the captors, keep them in conversation, lower the tension. She sat up straighter and said, "I've seen a lot of things on my job. Shooting sometimes. I guess that's why I didn't pee in my pants."

"You a correspondent?"

"Sort of. I run a news service. I get what the stations can't. Mostly at night. The rough stuff."

Harris stood up and removed an apple from the crate. He offered one to Weaver, but she shook her head. Harris remained standing. "I used to hate correspondents. Then I kind of respected them. They were definitely crazy. Wilder even than the grunts sometimes." Harris took a bite out of the apple.

Weaver was confused. "Grunts?"

"Right. The troops. The men in green." She was still frowning. Harris stepped closer. "How old are you?"

"Twenty-five."

"No wonder. You remember the Vietnam War, don't you?"

"I remember seeing it on TV."

Harris choked on the apple. He coughed hard and threw the core into the tree. "TV! Yeah, it was a real hit, a real long-running show."

Weaver was nervous. She stood up too quickly and was light-headed. She stumbled and brushed Harris's arm. He jumped back, grabbing the AK-47. He held it between them, the barrel an inch from her waist. "Don't ever come any closer than this."

Weaver touched her forehead and closed her eyes. "Okay. I won't. I do get scared when you point that at me."

Harris watched her. She looked like she was going to faint. He put down the AK. "Why don't you just sit."

"What's gonna be . . ." She couldn't finish. She was still dizzy, so she sat on the crate, in Harris's seat. She found her voice again. "What do you plan to do?"

Harris put her plate in the garbage sack. "I did it."

"What?"

"I took the park."

"But why?"

"I had two weeks' vacation. I might do this once a year."

Weaver didn't know what she was saying. She was running on instincts. "But people got killed."

Harris was fiddling with the stove, but he stopped and faced her. "They killed themselves. I warned them to stay out. I could've shot up a hundred people, but I didn't."

"It won't make any difference. They'll find a way to get you."

"You think so? I'm good at this. I found you so goddamn easy. You think anybody could do that?" Harris waved his hand at the dark trees of Central Park. "You get a real feel for it after a while, knowing when things aren't right. I can read a landscape like a book. And I didn't learn that off the television."

Harris walked away and stood over the bunker. He could hear her breathing.

Weaver asked him, "Is that what you were talking about on the phone? Vietnam?"

Harris went back and stood in front of the crate. "This guy I was talking to, his name is Dix. Do you know who he is?"

"He's a somebody in the Mayor's Office, I guess."

"He's a vet. But it just goes to show, you can't trust anybody."

"What was he saying to you?" There was no answer. Weaver looked up at him. She tried to remember what had been happening at the phone booth, when she was still in some sort of shock. She remembered his face. She thought she'd seen something; she thought she was seeing it now. She took a chance. "Dix knows something about you, doesn't he?"

Harris didn't move. A light breeze blew against the

239

moisture on his chest and he felt a chill. He turned away and paced around the ordnance crates. He picked up the M-79 launcher. He snapped it open and shut.

"Remember what I said about going all the way?"

Weaver didn't answer. Harris put the launcher in the special holster and placed several grenades in an equipment sack. He picked up the AK-47 and walked to the opposite end of the firebase, stopping near the steps nailed in the oak tree. He climbed up into his observation post, vanishing in the dark branches.

Weaver sat quietly. The black trees loomed over her. A voice came out of the leaves.

"It can be a real motherfucker."

Weaver watched the moon appear through gaps in the dense foliage. An hour passed. Weaver rested on her side, curled up, her head on her hands. The silence disturbed her. There were no familiar sounds, or lights, or actions. Her eyes closed and she was struck by the strange notion that New York City had disappeared.

Dix stood on Barrow Street in the West Village, not far from the Hudson River. The street was dark and quiet, one of the narrow, almost European streets that crisscrossed downtown west of Seventh Avenue. Many of the brownstones and smaller structures were over a hundred years old. Dix was leaning against an arched doorway that led into a mews inside one of the buildings. At the back of the mews, past several apartments, was a heavy wooden door with a small window at the top. Chumley's, a small restaurant and bar, was behind the door, but there were no signs or advertising on the entrance, or on the door around the corner on Bedford Street. Chumley's had been a speakeasy in the 1920s; the management had preserved the door with its tiny window, and the inconspicuousness of the establishment's location. It no longer had the ambience of an illegal club, but Dix liked the feeling of privacy and the food wasn't bad. He'd admit, though, that mostly he liked the unmarked entrances; you'd never know Chumley's was there, unless somebody told you.

A taxi came toward him on Barrow Street and Dix looked expectantly in the window as it passed. He was waiting for a man he hadn't seen in ten years. Dix wasn't sure that the man, Roy Maitland, would recognize him. The last time Maitland had seen him, Dix had been a kid in a uniform. Dix wondered if Maitland would be in uniform tonight. He'd forgotten to ask Maitland to wear civilian clothes; but then, Dix thought, maybe Roy didn't wear a uniform anymore. He wasn't exactly sure what Roy was doing, or what his rank was; maybe he was CIA now. Dix didn't have to know. All that mattered was what Maitland used to do, and Dix remembered that quite clearly. Dix was certain there were a lot of people, many of them dead, who remembered what Colonel Maitland of Special Forces used to do. If they could speak from their graves, they would recall the clandestine surveillance in the deep jungles, the behind-the-lines guerrilla force, the private armies and the private wars. Maitland existed, as did others like him, but not too many people knew who they were. They didn't talk about themselves; and if you knew them, you didn't talk about them either.

Dix walked to the corner and looked down Bedford Street. It was about 11:00 P.M., but Dix could see a lot of activity on Christopher Street at the end of the block. Some sections of the Village were just getting started. Dix fidgeted. He felt like going into Chumley's and phoning the St. Regis, where he'd reserved a room for Maitland, but he heard another taxi on Barrow Street. Roy Maitland got out in the middle of the block and walked toward him. Maitland wasn't in uniform, but Dix could tell he was in the military from a mile away. He had the clean look of the professional soldier.

Maitland walked up to Dix and stood a foot away from his face. Neither man spoke. They didn't shake hands. Dix knew that there were things that had to be said and he waited until they were seated in Chumley's, in a booth, with beers in front of them.

"Where was it, Roy?"

"It was Okinawa. You were on your way back to the World. I was going in the other direction."

Dix drank half his beer. "We kept bumping into each other. In bars. The odd couple."

"I remember." Maitland clicked his teeth together. He looked around the room, at the empty fireplace, at the walls decorated with the book jackets of 1920s novels. He made Dix wait and then he looked directly into his eyes. "You were pretty fed up then. Even in Saigon, those times when I used to see you over at Command. You had some rather critical things to say about the fighting men. I might have respected that had it come from a larger experience."

There it was, Dix thought. He looked down at his beer. One had to pay for one's mistakes. He wasn't surprised; so many mistakes had been made in Vietnam, and they always had a way of catching up.

Dix forced himself to look at Maitland. "Roy, I was tired of the whole mess. It just spilled over onto the men. That's all."

"It was easy to question the Forces, when you'd washed your hands of the war. It didn't make it any easier for the men who stayed behind. I wish you'd thought about that."

"I've thought about those men, Roy. Believe me. It took time to understand. A long time."

"I wish you'd thought about it when it counted."

"Some of these old resentments just won't go away, will they, Roy?"

Maitland was silent again. Then he said, "Dave, you were a kid then—and drunk all the time. That's why you got away with it. When I heard your voice on the phone this morning, all I could see was that kid, shooting his mouth off. It's as much curiosity as anything that got me to come here today. I guess all I wanted was a chance to kick your ass a little."

They stared at each other. Dix noticed the gray hair in Maitland's temples, the deep wrinkles around his mouth. Maitland saw the dark circles under Dix's eyes, and the unshaven beard. Maitland didn't smile, but he extended his hand. Dix took it and they shook over the beers.

Maitland said, "Are you a deputy mayor, or is that a bunch of bullshit?"

"I am. But I'm not doing so well. I've got a big problem and I need your advice."

Maitland nodded. His voice had a trace of sarcasm. "I've been watching the news. I couldn't avoid it."

Dix briefed him on the events of the past three days. He told him about Eubank, about the weapons, about his conversations with the man in the Park. Maitland didn't seem surprised.

"I bet it didn't take you too long to figure out the background of this guy in the park. I knew it had to be something like that. I knew it the first time I got word of the action."

"That's why I need your help, Roy. You spent years in the bush. You know as much as there is to know about guerrilla warfare. We're coming up on the fourth day the park's been closed. The Department's not any closer to a solution. I need to know how this guy's operating. How I can get at him."

"And you're going to ask me." It wasn't a question.

"Advice only."

"We might have a problem."

Dix had a suspicion, but he suppressed it. "This is an off-the-cuff thing, Roy. Nobody knows I'm consulting you. At some point the ranking officers and the Commissioner might know, but that's all."

"That's how I'd want it." Maitland didn't have to think it over. "I'm here. I'll tell you what I can."

They finished their beers. After the waiter brought another round, Maitland took over the conversation.

"You have a unique situation, Dave, but it's not without

its similarities to other insurgency operations, like Vietnam. You have only one insurgent, but he's creating the same problems. All guerrillas still operate under a set of old strategies. The first stage for the insurgent is defensive: he occupies a terrain and then holds off a larger force. Second is equilibrium. He gains strength and solidifies his hold. The third stage, counteroffensive. He uses his base as a staging area to occupy new territory and repeat the process."

"Counteroffensive?" Dix smiled and they both laughed.

Maitland said, " I don't think that applies in your case." He sipped his beer and went on. "Now, your response—counterinsurgency—is where the trouble starts, like the Nam. You can begin to occupy a small area, driving out the insurgents. But they will infiltrate again. In your case, let's say you cleared out and secured a quarter mile of park. The guerrilla could hide out; he could even leave the park and come back. This is the difficulty of defining a controlled area."

Dix laughed. "Sometimes I wouldn't define Central Park as a controlled area."

Maitland nodded. "Okay. Even if you get a large force into the park, they will suffer heavy casualties. This has already happened. You can't have a police officer on every square foot, so you still face the question of who is controlling the terrain and during what hours. The day belongs to the troops, the night to the guerrilla. It would take a long time, especially with a large, visible force."

"I don't have to tell you about time."

Maitland was silent for a minute. They ordered another round and Dix asked, "What do you think, Roy?"

"In the Nam we had airpower, which precludes position warfare. That's not going to work here. You're not concerned with supply routes. What you need is some kind of counterinsurgency force unique to the situation."

Dix had a thought. He cast a line in the water. "What

about that anti-terrorist force that they formed at the unconventional warfare center at Fort Bragg? The one they tried to use in Iran."

Maitland was startled by the question. It was only a slight hesitation, but Dix's suspicions were confirmed. He knew now what Maitland had been doing in the past few years. He also knew he should not ask Maitland to elucidate his connection with the anti-terror force.

Maitland offered a brief response. "You mean the one commanded by Colonel Beckwith?"

Dix nodded. Beckwith didn't do it all by himself, but that was another question to be left unasked.

Maitland said, "That force is under the armed services and can be used on foreign soil only. And you knew that."

Dix went to the men's room. While he was gone, Maitland had an idea. It was an ominous and spectacular idea that had begun forming that morning, fifteen hundred miles away at a base in Texas—an idea that intrigued and stimulated Maitland, shaking him from boredom and inactivity. It was the real reason he was sitting in a restaurant in New York, allowing himself to be pumped by an ex-information officer.

Dix came back from the men's room.

Maitland said, "Listen, I know some people. They might be available.

"Who?"

"I can't tell you that now. I'd call them mercenaries for lack of a better word." Dix squirmed a little in his seat. Maitland held up his hand. "These people are experts in jungle warfare. They know as much as I do. They could be the answer to your problem."

Dix frowned. "Mercenaries. I don't know about that."

Maitland sat back in the booth and let Dix think. He asked, "What does the Police Department have planned?"

"They've been working on something today," Dix said distractedly. "I haven't been briefed yet. I don't think it's

245

going into effect until tomorrow. But I don't believe it's going to work. They just don't comprehend what they're facing. They don't understand what's happened to them in the field. They think they're going to have one shoot-out and it will be over."

"Sounds familiar."

Dix looked up quickly. That was all he needed to hear. "Okay, Roy. I want you to approach these mercenaries. Right away. Can you spend some time on it?"

Maitland nodded. He sure as hell could. "I'll make arrangements to stay here for a couple of days. I don't think it will take any longer than that."

They finished their beers and Maitland started to get up. Dix held his arm. "One more thing, Roy. If you line up everything, and I get the Department to go along, I want your people to understand that this is not just a mission to terminate."

Maitland sat down. "Explain that."

"I want them, if there's any chance, to take the guy alive."

"That's ridiculous."

"It probably is. But tell them, terminate if necessary, only we're not sending them in as hired killers."

"Is that the Department's policy?"

"Fuck the Department."

Maitland was an officer and a lifer. He was indifferent to the vicissitudes of war. Personally, he didn't care what happened to the guy in Central Park. He said, "I better go back to my hotel and get on the phone."

Dix paid the check and they left Chumley's. They passed through the mews to Barrow Street and stopped a taxi on Seventh Avenue. Dix told Maitland to ride uptown alone.

"I'm going to walk around for a while."

As Maitland opened the car door, Dix stopped him. "I know how much you disliked me, Roy. I knew the years didn't make any difference."

246

Maitland turned and faced Dix. "I act without motives a lot of the time, Dave. I don't think you'll ever understand that. It's too straight."

Dix looked uptown, at the endless stream of traffic coming toward him. "I couldn't live with myself, Roy, if the Department went on making the same mistakes that . . ." Dix let the words hang.

Maitland was not afraid of words. "That the Forces made?" His jaw tightened. "Check this, Dave. We don't make those mistakes anymore."

Weaver was awake. She was lying on her back, looking up at the sunlight on the leaves. A blanket covered her; she could not remember falling asleep. She sat up. Her feet were tied to a network of strings that were attached to several empty food cans. The cans dangled over a small roll of barbed wire on the edge of the bunker. She could not stand or move her legs without making an alarm.

Harris was a few feet away in his sleeping bag. Weaver saw a black motorcycle parked near the stack of weapons. She sat up farther and looked at Harris. He was on his back, breathing heavily, but his eyes were open in a dull stare. Weaver fidgeted and coughed. He didn't pay any attention to her. She didn't want to wait for him to acknowledge her.

"Can I get up now? I have to go to the bathroom."

Harris didn't move.

"Are you listening?" Weaver asked. She stretched her neck and peered over the sleeping bag. Harris still stared at the trees. Weaver reached out and nudged the corner of the bag, forcing the cans to tinkle against the wire. Harris jerked up, rolled out of the bag and aimed a .45 automatic at Weaver's head. He almost pulled the trigger.

Weaver covered her head. Harris stood up and lowered the gun. "Don't ever do that. You could really get the hurt put on you doing that."

Weaver's voice was a little shaky. "Your eyes were open. I thought you were awake."

"Now you know."

Harris put the gun in his holster and untied the strings on her feet. He moved away and drank from his canteen. Weaver stood up and tried to focus.

"I have to go to the bathroom."

"There's a hole outside the wire. Wait a second." Harris turned away and set the canteen down. He found his flak jacket and put it on. When he looked up, Weaver was walking toward the entrance to the firebase.

"Stop." She kept going. She was halfway through the gap in the wire when she tripped. She saw something falling out of the trees. Her legs buckled and arms slammed her down. Harris tackled her against the barbed wire and a ten-foot log studded with metal spikes thudded into the ground a foot from their faces.

They didn't move for a moment. They could feel each other's breath. Harris removed his arms from her waist and stood up. Weaver got to her feet, being careful to avoid the sharp spikes. Her fatigues were snared in a strand of wire and Harris had to disentangle her. She straightened up and pulled a large fold of the camouflage material out of her crotch.

Harris said, "You better calm down."

"We walked right through here last night."

"That was last night."

Weaver looked at the log, then at Harris. "Right."

Harris pointed at some bushes just outside the firebase. "The hole is over there."

Weaver started to take a step and stopped. "I'm all right between here and there? Nothing's going to fall on me?"

Harris nodded. Weaver went to the bushes and found the hole. Flies buzzed over the ground and there was a bad smell. She saw another row of bushes several yards farther along the wire perimeter and asked, "Do you mind if I went over there?"

Harris stepped out and took a look. "I wouldn't mind." Weaver started for the bushes and Harris added, "But they say even a little piss will set off those fragmentation mines."

Weaver stopped. She asked Harris not to look. She waved away the flies and squatted over the hole.

They spent the next hour eating breakfast: canned fruit and peanut butter straight from the jar. Harris shaved his three-day beard and dressed in full combat gear. He gathered supplies in a large pack and armed himself with the AK-47 and the M-79 launcher. Weaver tried to wash off, but gave up on it and resigned herself to the smelly fatigues. Harris told her to tie her hair back and at 8:30 they left the firebase and stood in the trees on a walk behind the Belvedere Castle.

Harris consulted a chart in his notebook and returned it to the pack. He felt the sunlight on his arms. "Nice day." He smiled at Weaver. He was feeling good, and he didn't want to think about why. "Let's go."

"Wait." Weaver wanted to say something. She struggled with the words. "You saved my life this morning."

"I'm a hero."

"You know what's going to happen to you. You can't be here forever."

"What's gonna happen?"

Weaver looked at her feet. "I don't want you to get hurt."

Harris watched the sun reflecting on her hair. He put his fingers in his shirt pocket and brought out two amphetamines. He swallowed both of them. "I have to get a little wired. I haven't been sleeping too well lately."

"Look," Weaver said, "I'm saying that maybe you should think about giving up."

Harris checked the clip in the AK. "I'm not ready to leave yet."

"Leave?"

"I can walk out of here any time I want. Go over the

wall at night. Or through the sewer system. Nobody would know. If I put my street clothes on, I'd mix right in. The authorities wouldn't like that."

"They'll identify you. They'll catch you."

"Nope. It'll be too late. Only one person's seen my face."

Weaver's throat closed up. "Me."

"Yeah, I know," Harris said—he, too, startled momentarily by the realization. "That's going to be a problem." Then he looked at her and smiled. "Unless you're KIA."

"What's KIA?"

"Killed in action." He nudged her ahead on the walk. "Let's move."

"Wait." Weaver tried to stop. "Where are we going?"

Harris was exuberant. "This is a patrol! We're checking it out from five-niner to one-one-zero."

They hiked uptown, executing moves in the bushes and trees, patrolling along the West Drive. They came as close to the avenues and streets as possible, carrying out reconnaissance at the major entrances to the park. Harris set up a surveillance point near Summit Rock, and for forty minutes they observed the comings and goings around the mobile command post. By noon they were back beating the bushes, scouting Harris' booby traps and the barbed-wire barriers.

They stopped for a rest in a wooded area north of the 95th Street transverse road. They were out of breath from a fast run over the bridge that spanned the roadway. Harris drank from the canteen and offered it to Weaver. He checked a notation on one of his charts. He motioned to her and they plowed through the bushes and down the embankment from the Drive, moving forward to a vantage point on a narrow walk. They could see Central Park West through the trees. Harris crawled ahead and examined a thin wire stretching across the pavement. As he moved back, crouching low, he said, "Looking real good."

He waved Weaver a few yards north and they stopped. She could see an object hidden in the grass. Harris crept close, checked it, and then sat down next to her.

Weaver pointed at the object. "What's that thing?"

"A claymore mine." Harris took off his helmet and smoothed his long hair. "It's antipersonnel. Amazing shit. It can be aimed so the frags explode out into a specific target area. And know what? You could sit here and wait for somebody to walk into range and fire it by pulling that wire."

"Wonderful."

Harris laughed and slipped his helmet on. "Let's keep going."

"Let me have another drink." He gave her back the canteen. She poured water in her hand and splashed her face. She said, "Can I ask you a question?" She didn't wait for him to agree. She pointed at the claymore. "Where did you get all this stuff?"

Harris took the canteen from her. He mulled over her question. He shrugged. "I guess it doesn't make any difference if I tell you. Some of it I brought back with me, souvenirs at the time. Like this AK-47 rifle. It was the standard weapon for the NVA."

"The NVA?"

"North Vietnamese Army, the regular army, not the Viet Cong. A lot of guys brought back rifles. This thing here is a grenade launcher. The army abandoned thousands of these launchers, and a lot of other shit, too. A guy I knew in Nam stayed there until the thing was over, right up to the evacuation of Saigon, and he was a real dealer. He hung around with a lot of black market types and he smuggled loads of weapons back to this country. He sold most of them. We were pretty good buddies at one time, something that happened once in combat which he remembered me for, so he gave me the launcher as a gift."

"For Christmas?"

Harris smiled. Boy, she was a smart-ass, he thought. But he enjoyed talking to her. "All the mines, like those claymores—now that was weird how I got those. It was about six months after I was back in the States, killing time before school. I got a message from this same guy, through another friend, and from what I can tell he wanted me to do him this big favor, which was go to San Diego and claim this shipment. It was supposed to be marijuana. So I did it. It was a truckload of crates, and I had no trouble. The shipment came through the Navy down there and they didn't ask me one question. This guy in Nam had a lot of juice, I guess. Anyway, I delivered the stuff to a place in Los Angeles and I'm going to get paid, but they open the crates and they're full of claymores and frag mines. They didn't want them. It was actually supposed to be marijuana. So I was stuck and I didn't feel like fucking with it anymore, so I kept them. I rented a truck and drove home; I was living in Michigan at the time, and I held on to the crates for years. They were in my basement. Once in a while, when I got drunk, I'd show a claymore to a friend and they'd get a big kick out of it."

Harris looked over his shoulder and checked his watch. He wasn't in any hurry and the amphetamines were making him jabber. He continued. "Okay, about a year ago, when I . . . when I decided to do this park thing, I tracked down that guy from Nam. He wasn't pissed off at me. I don't think he really cared what happened. He's got a lot of money and he knows where to buy and sell weapons. So we worked it out. These guys in the weapons business don't ask a lot of questions. I sunk about nineteen thousand dollars I raised into arms and ammunition and other shit like the barbed wire. He let me trade in some of the mines for grenades and rocket launchers. Those goddamn mines are worth over a hundred dollars apiece. When one of them blows off I can't help seeing a hundred-dollar bill exploding into space."

Harris stood up. "Nineteen thousand dollars. It seems like a lot, but when your credit's good, there's nothing to it."

Weaver wiped her forehead and stood next to him. "I know what it's like to get money for something you're serious about."

Harris saw himself kicking her camera equipment and almost apologized. Instead, he said, "Let's go. I want to check on some more of those hundred-dollar bills."

They followed the West Drive toward 110th Street. They moved close to the perimeter and Harris verified that the body of the kid who'd been killed by the claymore was gone. Nothing looked suspicious, so they swung south. Harris used Weaver to help him position rolls of concertina in the undergrowth near the ice-skating rink at the western tip of the Harlem Meer. Near the Huddlestone Bridge, an old, arching structure made from huge stones, Harris constructed a bunker which gave him a strategic blocking position at the end of a barbed-wire corridor. He enlisted Weaver's help again, for digging and hauling dirt. Two sheets of pierced-steel planking were concealed in a supply point behind the skating rink and Weaver and Harris carried them to the site and secured them in the bunker. The work and the heat were tiring. When the bunker was finished, Harris led Weaver west, along the cool waters of the Loch.

The section of terrain that included the Loch, the Pool and Harlem Meer, with the cascades in between, was one of the most beautiful in Central Park. It was seldom seen by most New Yorkers, because of its proximity to Harlem and its reputation for criminal activity. As Weaver walked through the lush foliage, past the waterfalls and the trickling stream, she was astonished that such a place existed in the middle of Manhattan. When they stopped near one of the cascades, Weaver collapsed on the soft ground at the edge of the Loch, took off her boots and plunged her feet in the stream.

She shook her head. "I would never have believed it."

Harris set down his weapons and field harness and squatted next to her. Cool air drifted around the waterfall; the tumbling water had a relaxing effect. They rested and ate canned food. Rays of sunlight flickered through the tall trees and made Weaver drowsy. She napped. When she awoke, Harris was standing in the Loch, his fatigues rolled up, splashing water on his head with his combat helmet.

He saw that she was awake and said, "You know, Central Park is nice, without all the shitheads in here." He climbed out of the stream and sat on the bank, putting his boots on. Water dripped from the black curls of his hair. He stretched out in the thick grass with his hands behind his head. Weaver watched the muscles twitch in his arms and listened to him.

"We'd go away out on these patrols in the jungle," he said. "There'd be these birds with the most amazing calls. No Tarzan TV shit. This was the real thing. These birds could do operas. We'd listen to their songs for hours and watch the sunset. Really fine sunsets. Of course, all the dust and the napalm probably did that."

"Did it bother you," Weaver asked, "when it got destroyed?"

Harris smiled at her. "Want to know something? Destruction can be beautiful. At night, some real bitch of a battle way off in the distance. This black sky, totally black, like a giant movie screen. There'd be a first flash, then a few more. Rockets going off. There were these arcs of light, tracers flying all around, making these patterns. It would keep getting bigger and fill in. You'd just sit there in your hole with your mouth open."

Weaver imagined the Waldorf in flames. "I guess I'd have to see that."

"I'm telling you," Harris said, "this war was in color."

They sat on the bank of the Loch and watched the sun slip over to the West Side. Then they resumed their patrol, moving west briefly so Harris could bury ordnance crates that he'd left exposed on a previous night, when he'd been confused and alone.

They were circling east, on a line with 103rd Street, when Harris stopped suddenly and disappeared into the bushes. Weaver went ahead for several yards before she realized she was walking alone. She waited on a walk next to the bridle path, but Harris did not reappear. A wasp darted in and out around a tree trunk and came close to her face. She took a swipe at it. She listened for footsteps. Maybe he's peeing, she thought.

Weaver got tired of waiting and went back on an unpaved footpath surrounded by forsythia and elm trees. She didn't see Harris. When she was sure she'd backtracked too far, she turned around to retrace her steps. A pair of eyes were six inches from her nose. She jumped. Harris was standing in the bushes, right in front of her, and she hadn't seen him. He was standing absolutely still; his eyes were wide and unblinking. Weaver felt suddenly afraid. As she watched him in his camouflage, he seemed to undergo a metamorphosis: he was a lizard, a chameleon; he melted into the bushes and trees; his shape and form disappeared into the landscape. Still his eyes stared at her.

No lips moved, but a voice told her, "Stop breathing."

She tried to stand without motion; she became aware of her fingers and toes, of her heart beating and the blood moving; she thought she could hear the blood squirting in her arteries, and she cursed her noisy body. Then she heard another sound, a low rumble. It got louder. There was a throbbing under her feet. The sound came closer, faster, and became a roar, pounding the air, crushing the silence. She saw sweat drip into Harris' eyes and he moved his arms and the rifle appeared like some alien dagger. The ground shook. Harris twisted and fell, flashing the rifle in her face. She watched him squeeze into the dirt as metal shrieked and clattered. Weaver kept her eyes on the rifle and listened to a subway train speed by underneath Central Park.

The noise of the train faded quickly, receding in the tunnel under their feet. The AK-47 was pointed at Weaver's groin and she eased away from the barrel. Harris emerged from the dirt. He tried to lick his lips and his tongue made dry, cracking sounds. His face glistened with moisture. His head twitched. Weaver knelt down next to him.

She said, "That was the IRT express."

Harris looked at her. "Goddamn trains. Jesus. They scare the shit out of me every time."

Harris fiddled with the rifle. Weaver watched him try to move a small lever. He couldn't do it; his fingers were trembling. He pointed at the AK. "It's on full automatic. Would you mind putting it on safety? Just push the change lever down." Weaver put her hand out. She hesitated and they stared at each other. She pushed the lever down.

Their patrol took them south, curving around the eastern end of the reservoir, on the jogging trail that led to the front of the south gate house. They stopped on a short footbridge over the bridle path and observed the burned-out station house across the 85th Street transverse. After crossing the road, they climbed the fence at the back of the precinct parking lot and passed the basketball courts and the Great Lawn. They executed moves parallel to the East Drive, went past the boathouse and the Lake, over to the Conservatory Water, and west to the Mall and the Fountain. They watched a swarm of pigeons on the long promenade and Harris wondered aloud if the birds were getting hungry without the usual load of litter and garbage.

By the time Harris and Weaver had worked their way south of the 65th Street transverse, the sun was behind the buildings on the West Side. They stopped near the rear of the zoo and watched the sky turn purple and red. Harris moved under the Green Gap arch, unloaded his heavy pack and found his binoculars. He guided Weaver up the embankment at the side of the Drive, where there was a clear view of the zoo's buildings and open-air cages. Harris scanned the area, paying close attention to three men hosing down the elephant cage. The elephant was pacing nervously, scraping its trunk on the tall, wrought-iron enclosure.

Harris handed the binoculars to Weaver. "Those aren't keepers."

Weaver looked through the glasses. "How do you know?"

"They always use the same guys with an animal, so they'll get familiar. That elephant is ready to step on someone." Weaver returned the binoculars and Harris surveyed the surrounding terrain. "You know what I ought to do? Lob a frag in there, out on the snack bar, and watch the elephant trample those guys. Might do some good. I found out when I was doing some research on the park that the federal government condemned this zoo. It's lousy for the animals."

Harris and Weaver slid quietly down the embankment to the front of the arch. Their boots crunched on chunks of plastic, the remains of the shattered phone booth. Harris whispered, trying to point out a section of open ground and a walk leading down to the zoo.

"We're going to dig some holes in a line off that rise. We'll come back after dark and lay in some mines. Just in case."

Weaver was momentarily fascinated by the bullet-ridden booth. Harris finally had to tell her to follow him into the tunnel. She leaned against the concrete wall while Harris removed his notebook and a collapsible shovel from the equipment pack. He groaned softly and pinched his thigh. Weaver tried to stretch her neck. They were both dirty and wet, exhausted from the tension created by the need for total concentration.

As Weaver followed him out into the fading light, she began to feel something else besides fatigue. Fear. It crept up on her again, with the shadows, and she wanted it to stop. She waited until they were standing under tall Austrian pines, on a short hill above the zoo, and said, "That was a little freaky back there by the waterfall. When the train went by."

Harris closed his notebook and put it on the ground. "If you want to know, those trains sound like something else sometimes."

"Does that happen to you very often?"

Harris unfolded the shovel without answering.

"Does it?"

"It happens is all." He pulled at the pine needles. "Certain things, like a sound, a face maybe, it'll take me right back to the bush. It's like 'click' and I'm there. Sometimes it's okay, certain recollections. The nighttime is so strange. Sleeping with your eyes open. The body makes these weird adjustments." He turned away. "You don't want to hear this."

Weaver stepped in front of him. "Please."

Harris let out a breath; the tension seemed to fall away from him. "I was in the hospital once for a week, in Saigon."

"You were wounded?"

"No, nothing like that. I had some kind of intestinal virus. I remember this one night, I got real high with this medic and we shot three ccs of vodka into a vein. You wouldn't believe how drunk that can make you. About two in the morning I was wandering around and I let myself in the X-ray room. There was a fluoroscope in there, so I turned out the lights and positioned this mirror across the room so I could see myself and then I turned the fluoroscope on and stood behind it. I watched my bones move, these beautiful, delicate things, sliding around in their muscles. It was incredible. After that, when I got back to the battalion, I kept myself real tight. I never had my flak jacket unfastened. I always had working weapons; man, I never took one fucking chance. I was king paranoid. And then it just wore off and I did a complete about-face. I got so scared that I figured the only way to keep from getting destroyed was to out-destroy all the other motherfuckers. And you know what?" he asked. "It worked."

He started to turn away again.

Weaver did an instinctive thing—she reached out to touch his shoulder—but she hesitated. Harris saw her hand and his face changed.

"Forget that," he said.

"I want to hear about that stuff." Weaver remembered something. "Like what you were talking about on the phone."

Harris glanced in the direction of the crumpled booth. "Forget it."

Weaver didn't want to. She tried to smile. "Okay, I'll tell you something about me, then you tell me something about you."

"Don't tell me."

"My name's Weaver. Valerie Weaver. That's a secret, that part. I grew up in Brooklyn. My father was a fireman. I like doing TV. Where are you from?"

"The suburbs."

"You went to college, right?"

Harris almost laughed. "Is the next question, what did I major in?"

"Okay, tell me."

"Drug abuse."

"All right. If that's the way you want it." Weaver kicked the dirt and walked away from him. Harris cut her off.

"Okay, you want to know what happened?"

Weaver nodded. She wanted to know; she wanted to talk her way through the fear.

Harris said, "I came back home. One nine seven oh. Right off a three-day firefight, into a plane and down to San Francisco and the World. It was terrific. A-1. A girl sold me a flower at the airport, and know what she called me? A murdering pig. Nothing to it. I finished college, got a job, and here I fucking am."

"Wait a second. What about all that? I mean, between when you got back"—Weaver hesitated—"and when you did this? Were you in trouble?"

Harris frowned. "Trouble? Hey, I was a civil engineer. Great job. Standing around manholes, listening to a lot of crap from architects and contractors. Up at eight, home at seven. What home? Shit. Apartments. Sit around the pool and drink beer every weekend. High drama. Jim and Betty broke up; Betty won't come out of her apartment. Jim's stoned and he and Mike have a hard-on for some new girl. And two weeks later it snows and it's those real fulfilling days with Wide World of Football, getting psycho over the Stupid Bowl. It's seven again, got to get downtown and watch a contractor fuck up the new storm drain. Piss on it! The whole thing was boring as hell." Harris slammed the shovel into the ground and started to dig.

Weaver kept after him. "You could have found an exciting job. Anything that wasn't routine."

Harris continued digging. "That was all too complicated. This is simple. Like the Nam."

"How could killing and destroying be simple? I do some wild things, but I could never kill anybody."

Harris stopped digging and faced her. "That was just part of it." Words were coming, but he stopped them. Finally he spoke, forcing a casual voice. "I liked the Army. I stayed over there as long as I could."

"You wanted to stay there?"

"Shit, I even extended twice. Seems like we just got dug in when we started pulling out."

Weaver paced in front of him. It was too easy. He wasn't telling her everything. She stopped and watched him take the AK-47 off his shoulder. She asked, "Not everybody that was in Vietnam felt that way, did they?"

"Don't kid yourself. A lot of guys didn't want to leave Nam. It was relevant right to the goddamn minute."

"You can get something like that off the street."

Harris dropped the shovel. He moved closer to her face, almost nose to nose. "No, that's wrong. If you wanted it, you had to stay in Nam or go back. But guys couldn't do that anymore." He stared into her. "It's not a problem for me."

Her voice was weak. "Why not?"

"I *am* back."

The sky got dark, first on the East Side, then on the West Side. Weaver watched Harris dig holes. She sat in the pines experiencing a new sensation—fighting fear and anticipating more.


Dix participated in a press-conference in the late afternoon. The DCPI handled most of the questions, but a few were left to Dix, and when he answered, his responses were perfunctory. He felt as if everything he said was on the borderline between mendacity and evasion. He was covering for the Department, and he was covering for himself. The only man with the answers was in Central Park, and Dix was asked nothing and said nothing about his conversations with this man. Instead, the reporters concentrated on criticism of the Department and the Mayor. The press was losing its patience faster than the public.

When Dix left the press conference, he knew that his presence there had been redundant. He suspected that someone wanted him out of the way. The Commissioner had been unavailable in the aftermath of the rooftop shooting, and Dix suspected that another full-scale operation was in the final planning stages. The Mayor was in Albany, discussing fiscal problems with members of the state legislature, but he'd called Dix and asked him to attend the press conference. The Mayor did not give a

**261**

shit about the press conference. Dix could take a hint. He spent the rest of the afternoon in his office, repeating the same profane disinterest he'd expressed to Maitland: Fuck the Department.

In the early evening Dix was summoned to the mobile command post. Now that all the decisions had been made, he would be briefed on Department strategy. Dix knew also that his presence was required only so that he could perform the narrowest function of his job: report to the Mayor.

The command post was no longer on Central Park West. It had been moved to a location on East 63rd Street, not far from the Central Park Zoo. When Dix arrived, he was immediately aware of the increased activity. The apartments and hotel rooms facing the Park, north and south for several blocks, were being evacuated for the second time. East 63rd Street was barricaded and officers were preparing to divert Fifth Avenue traffic, from 66th Street downtown to 59th. Emergency Service personnel and vehicles lined the block.

Dix went into the command post and found Keller, Curran and Charlie Meyers in conference with a young man in thick glasses and a wrinkled black suit. They were studying a set of complex diagrams pinned to a wall board. Dix interrupted and Keller introduced him to the young man.

"David, this is Kaplan, Department of Water Resources."

Dix shook hands and noticed that Kaplan didn't focus; he had a look of perpetual distraction. Dix acknowledged the other men. "I'm sorry I'm late, gentlemen."

Keller directed everyone's attention back to the diagrams. Meyers used a pointer to indicate a detail and asked Kaplan, "Explain about these water mains under the north section of the park."

Kaplan pushed his glasses up on his nose. "Maybe they're there and maybe they aren't."

Curran: "What the hell does that mean?"

"Well, when those mains were taken out of service, maybe forty years ago, they were filled in with sand to prevent gas buildup. Then again, maybe not. Some of the contractors were dishonest, and they filled only the opening with sand and bricked them up to cut costs. We run into that now and then." Kaplan drew a circle around an area near the center of the park. "Another example here. These old masonry aqueducts, probably six to eight feet high, were abandoned in place when the old receiving reservoir was removed from service in 1929. It's possible that anyone who studied these same plans could dig down into one of these aqueducts, or the water mains, and hide. They could gain access to other tunnels from there. But like I said, maybe the tunnels are there, and maybe they aren't."

Kaplan shoved his glasses up on his nose again and smiled.

Curran said, "Jesus Christ."

Keller studied the diagrams. "All right, Kaplan, but our men could move to a position in this area behind the zoo, via these tunnels off Fifth Avenue."

"Like I said this morning, I think so. The only way to find out is to go down there and try."

The Commissioner asked Kaplan to keep himself available. When he was gone, Keller handed Dix a folder.

"This will apprise the Mayor of the current operation. Everything's set. We're waiting for the equipment to arrive and for SOD to tell us they're ready."

Dix took sixty seconds to look through the contents of the folder. That was all he needed. He closed his eyes for a moment. He heard a voice in a bar—a young voice whose stridency had been softened by alcohol. It was a voice drained of emotion, tired of warnings, resigned to formalities. Dix felt lives slip through his fingers. He opened his eyes. He closed the folder and resorted to form.

"It is your opinion, Commissioner, that we have exhausted all other possibilities?"

Keller glanced at Curran. "Taking into consideration what we've learned and what our investigations have told us, we feel this will give us our best shot at luring the perps out where we can get a crack at them."

Dix didn't blink. "The perps?"

Curran repressed a sneer and said, "Dix, one other thing you'll want to take to the Mayor; our marksmen have confirmed that more than one suspect was in the vicinity of the phone booth when it was fired on."

Dix could feel his mouth hanging open. He sat down in a chair. He didn't know what to say: whether to dispute their claim, to reiterate the essence of his conversations with the man in the Park, or to apologize for distracting the Department with an unreasonable theory.

Curran knew what he wanted to say. "Listen, Dix, we don't know if they voted for the Mayor last time out, or not. We'll let you know."

Keller spoke with absolute neutrality. "Will you excuse us, David?"

Dix left the command post. On East 63rd Street, a man with an automatic rifle said hello to him. Dix knew the man, knew him well, but he could not remember the man's name.

By three in the afternoon, J.T. was worried. He did not want to blow Weaver's exclusive and he did not want to notify the police. J.T. did not like cops. It was not a vague opinion; it was experience. As he'd once told Weaver, the first time you get arrested is the first time you are sure you don't like cops. By six o'clock, though, when there had still been no word from Weaver, J.T. was seriously considering a call to the police. He'd been listening to the radios in Weaver's apartment and had heard several unusual transmissions on the SOD frequencies. These were followed by calls for Emergency Service units and traffic department vehicles, all of them responding to the East Side near Central Park. J.T. knew something was happening.

He held off calling the Police Department and watched the regularly scheduled local news, just in case a story was breaking. He saw a press conference and listened to a song and dance by city officials.

It gave him an idea. He called the office of the Deputy Mayor for Criminal Justice and insisted on speaking with him. The Deputy Mayor was not there, but J.T. told the operator that NonstopNews had information regarding the situation in Central Park and would the Deputy Mayor please return his call as soon as possible. At 7:30, an operator called and J.T. arranged to meet the Deputy Mayor in his office in City Hall. J.T. did not have press credentials, so he called Richie and together they went downtown and met with David Dix.

Dix listened to their story. His first response was human and private. He felt vindicated; he went from demoralized depression to supercilious confidence in one second. He felt like riding the Department's ass in front of the whole world—but he did the right thing. He immediately phoned Keller at the command post and passed on the information that a possible hostage was being held. The Commissioner responded angrily.

"Are you sure?"

"Positive. Her colleagues are sitting in my office right now. She entered the park on the evening prior to your sighting."

"That's the most half-assed thing I've ever heard."

"I know, Commissioner. Completely half-assed. But this changes our situation.

"Hold on a minute."

Dix was put on hold. He looked across his desk at J.T. and Richie. He wondered if they were the newsmen of the future; if this woman, Weaver, a crazy kid wired to the teeth with advanced electronics, was the ultimate end for a belligerent press. He couldn't blame them. The press had been lied to so many times; all that remained was the pursuit of hard, visual information. The reporter's function was no longer to document and analyze; it was merely to record.

Keller came back on the line. "David. It's too late to pull back the operation now. This woman could be dead for all we know. If anything happens to her, I'll take the responsibility."

Dix squeezed the phone. "Yes, sir. I'll make a note of that." Dix restrained himself from pounding the desk. Keller wasn't through.

"One more thing, David. Whoever these kids are that brought you this information, freeze them until this is over. That's your responsibility."

Keller hung up. He could play hardball, too.

Dix held the phone to his ear and listened to static. Finally he put the receiver down. He imagined a letter of resignation; he thought about calling his ex-wife to get drunk and celebrate. Instead he told J.T. and Richie that their colleague's situation was being weighed by the Police Department; he told them not to worry, that they should wait in his outer office and that he would keep them informed; he told them a pile of bullshit.

When he was alone at his desk, Dix reached the deepest point of his anger—with himself, but especially with Keller. The Commissioner had maneuvered him into another untenable position, another set of actions based on expediency. Dix's threshold for honesty, even though it had been shaped and tested by the stresses of public service, was eroding fast. He reminded himself of Maitland, of a possible ace in the hole, of the power over the whole mess that might eventually be his. Let the Department play it out, he thought. Let them make the big mistake.

Dix got up from his desk. As he looked out his window, at the lights below City Hall, he suffered one final confusion of ego and intellect. For one instant, he was almost rooting for the man in Central Park. He forced back the thought, sickened by it. No amount of cynicism or self-disgust permitted such a distortion of duty and morality.

He went to his phone and called Maitland to ask him if he was making any progress.

Weaver woke up suddenly and didn't know where she was. A hand was over her mouth. A black face hovered in front of her eyes.

Harris said, "Shhh. They're back." His face was covered with nightfighter cosmetic. His eyes were huge and white. Fragmentation grenades dangled from the front of his flak jacket. His breathing was short and fast; rushes of energy vibrated in his body and traveled down his arm to his hand to Weaver's face. A warm flush erupted in her chest and she sat up, completely awake.

Harris moved away from her to the bunker on the edge of the firebase. He secured an equipment sack and a large canvas bag, and dragged them back to Weaver. She stood and adjusted her fatigues.

She whispered, "Tell me."

"Creepers." He handed her a jar of nightfighter cosmetic and told her to put it on. As he watched her apply it, Harris taped several more banana clips to a long chain around his neck. When Weaver's hands and face were smudged, he took back the jar and gave her the equipment sack. She was surprised by the weight and almost dropped it.

"Put that on your back. You can handle it. I know."

She hesitated. "What's in it?"

"Grenades."

Weaver didn't move. She held the sack in front of her. She looked at herself, at Harris, at the launcher in his holster, at her hands black with cosmetic.

I've painted myself black, she thought. I'm holding a sack of grenades.

She looked again at Harris. Here was a guy the whole world wanted to know, but couldn't. Here was a mystery that might unfold in front of her. Fear created hesitation; thinking turned into paranoia. Don't think.

The weight of the sack tugged at Weaver's arm.

But there was that little thing about participation. With guns and grenades. Grenades . . . Don't think.

Weaver swung the sack around to her shoulders and placed it on her back.

Harris smiled. "Why don't you calm those eyebrows down a little?"

Weaver touched her forehead above her eyes. She made the curled hairs stand up even farther. Harris checked the magazine in the AK-47 and lifted the canvas bag. He turned for the gap in the wire perimeter.

"There's nothing like it," he said. "Nothing. It really clears your head."

"What's that?"

"Contact."

Weaver followed him out of the firebase. Together they crouched low, moving quietly into the trees and bushes, invisible in the dark.

John Hardy and Dewayne Daniels were standing in front of the Arsenal, inside the entrance to the Central Park Zoo. They were leaning over an open manhole, waiting for a command. Behind them, on Fifth Avenue, were patrol cars, Emergency Service vehicles and officers in combat gear. Two men with automatic rifles came down the steps through the Children's Gate entrance and ran past, into the shadows of the building. The officers joined an ESS squad that had set up a security position on the wide brick walk that led to the rear of the Arsenal and the seal court inside the main body of the zoo.

A voice on Hardy's walkie-talkie asked him if everyone was in position. Hardy was affirmative. The voice told him to get moving. He and Daniels peered down into the manhole. It looked like an entrance to hell, and smelled like it, too. They tightened the straps on the M-16s over their sholders and fastened their flak jackets. They heard an odd machine sound, coming from somewhere to their right, behind the trees on the 65th Street transverse. Hardy raised his head and listened to the humming and the creaking of metal on pavement.

Hardy turned to Daniels. "This is going to be a mother-fucker."

Daniels turned on a flashlight and they climbed down into the cold, black hole.

Daniels aimed the light down a long, narrow tunnel. Both men had to bend over for headroom. They moved forward and their boots splashed through a tiny, six-inch stream of water. The sounds of their movements, of their rifles and cameras banging on the conduit wall, echoed in the tunnel and mixed with static coming from Hardy's walkie-talkie. After a hundred yards they stopped, struggling for breath in the fetid, stale air. They could hear boots echoing and a light appeared several yards ahead of their position. Two other Emergency Service officers crossed their path and disappeared into an intersecting tunnel.

Hardy and Daniels continued on past the intersection until they came to a small opening in the conduit wall. A pipe, twelve inches in diameter, emptied a trickle of water into the tunnel. Hardy removed a diagram from his fatigues and held it up to the flashlight.

"That's it."

"What's it?"

Hardy pointed at the small opening. "That's where we're supposed to cut through to the water main."

Daniels stooped down and examined the pipe. "There? A rat couldn't get through there."

Hardy coughed up some dust. "That's what it say on the chart."

Daniels was disgusted. "You know, I asked that guy from the Water Department when these plans was made."

"What he say?"

"Eighteen sixty-four."

Hardy banged his head on the sewer wall and swore. "Well, that's fine, real fine."

Daniels went on, "He say the WPA was supposed to update 'em in nineteen thirty-two. So I asks him, 'Well, did they?' Know what he say?"

"I think I know this guy."

"He say, 'Maybe they did and maybe they didn't.' "

"Same guy."

Hardy and Daniels backtracked. They followed another tunnel that appeared to lead in the right direction. It took a sharp turn and came to a dead end inside a crawl space underneath a manhole cover. Hardy very carefully pushed the metal disk aside and peeked over the opening. He was in the middle of the 65th Street transverse. He raised his walkie-talkie and called the command post. He told them that the diagrams were inaccurate, which was no surprise to anyone. They asked him to estimate his location and gave him an alternate route. He sank back into the hole and replaced the cover.

After thirty more minutes of wrong turns, bumping into fellow officers and crawling through a crumbling fracture in a fifty-year-old water main, Hardy and Daniels arrived at their destination.

Daniels put the light on the old concrete wall and aimed the beam up a set of rusted-out rungs to a sewer grate six feet above their heads. Then he turned the light back and leaned it against the wall. Each man pulled his M-16 from his shoulder and double-checked his flak jacket. They heard a rumbling and crunching sound on the surface of the Park. Metal creaked and the sound rolled by over their heads. Hardy looked up warily at the sewer grate, folded his diagram and put it away.

"This is it."

"No shit."

Hardy picked up the flashlight and motioned up the ladder rungs.

Daniels scoffed at him. "Fuck you."

Hardy held his rifle in the crook of his arm. "Choose you, blood."

Daniels held his hand up. "Okay, whattya got?"

They both threw out their hands and Hardy said, "Odds."

Each hand showed two fingers.

"Damn," Hardy complained, and handed the flashlight to Daniels. He wiped the sweat from his face and reached for the ladder rungs on the tunnel wall. One of them broke off in a cloud of red dust. Hardy started to throw it angrily down the tunnel, but stopped himself and set it quietly at his feet.

Daniels encouraged him. " 'Member, Jay, just maintain a position. Don't get more'n your shoulders above the ground. When you get tired, I'll sit in the hole."

"Okay, bet." Hardy climbed up the rungs and carefully pushed the grate aside. He saw the dark sky and the branches of trees. He stuck his head up and warm, fresh air soothed his face. He raised his arms and balanced himself in the opening, planting his feet on the rungs inside the tunnel. He pointed the rifle at Central Park and put the selector switch on full automatic.

Hardy tried to make out landmarks in the darkness. He knew that he was not far from the rear entrance to the zoo, but nothing was visible except the trees. He assumed that three other officers were sitting in similar openings, in a rough semicircle around the hill north of the Green Gap arch, but he could not see them either. He put the walkie-talkie to his lips and told the command post that he was in position. They confirmed that the other teams were ready and standing by.

"Ten-four." Ten-four, you motherfuckers. Hardy didn't know who was crazier—his superiors, or the suspects for whom he was waiting in an ambush less than two hundred yards from Fifth Avenue.

Hardy shifted his weight and sweat poured down into his crotch. His torso felt safe. His head and arms were absolutely paranoid. He watched the shadows and dark spaces. He tried not to see things in the trees. Crickets chirped; a horn honked somewhere on the avenue. A thousand projectiles homed in on his face. His ears buzzed and he thought he was going deaf. A grenade kept landing at his feet; he died again and again. Finally, Hardy turned off the bad dreams. He leaned quietly over the grass and was swallowed by the darkness. His mind sent every impulse directly to the finger on the trigger of his M-16.

Harris and Weaver crossed the 72nd Street road near the Mall. They moved through Rumsey playground and Harris stood on the edge of the East Drive, studying the rooftops on Fifth Avenue through his binoculars.

"No more snipers on those buildings. No lights in the windows. Definitely got something going."

Weaver caught her breath and used her elbows to shove the pack full of grenades into the center of her back. She stared blankly at the pavement. "You could be listening."

"What?"

"Radios." She looked up at him. "Why don't you have a scanner in here? You could monitor the precinct."

"I blew up the precinct."

"You know what I mean. You could pick up the pertinent transmissions. You could hear what's going on with SOD. And everybody else."

"I considered it at one time. Too confusing. Too noisy. Now be quiet."

Harris scanned the tops of the buildings one more time and put away the binoculars. He told Weaver to move fast, and they ran back to the middle of the Park, to the Mall, and went south, crossing the 65th Street transverse between the Chess and Checkers House and Wollman

Rink. They cut east and followed the Drive, staying close to the perimeter of the rink, and stopped in the bushes that lined a walk leading into the Green Gap arch.

Harris studied the dark tunnel. No lights or park lamps were shining beyond the opposite end of the arch. Lights had always been shining there before. The area at the rear of the zoo, on the east side of the Drive's embankment, was a black wall. Harris smiled. Talk about an invitation. He pulled the clip from his AK and snapped in the first magazine taped to the chain of clips around his neck. Weaver moved behind him, rustling the leaves, and he turned to her. Something about his face must have frightened her, because her eyes became large and white in the dark smears of cosmetic. He moved close and whispered.

"Don't try and lose me. Whoever's in there is going to blast away. They wouldn't be coming if they thought you had a chance."

He heard her breathing become short and fast; the heel of her boot bounced up and down on the grass. He tried to get her attention, but her eyes were locked on the dark terrain. Harris tapped her knee with the butt of the AK and she fell in next to him. They moved silently along the walk and crawled up the embankment to the Drive. They crossed the pavement flat on their stomachs, stopping in the pine trees on the other side. They could see the dark outline of the zoo, and a broad flat of trees and bushes angling off a hill to their left. Harris put down the large canvas bag and squatted against one of the Austrian pines. Weaver took a similar position on the other side of the tree trunk. Harris's voice was almost inaudible.

"This is what's known as doing an LP."

Weaver whispered back. "Explain."

"Listening post. Send a team outside the perimeter at night to listen for enemy movement. Only we don't have any security behind us. Like about five fire teams would be good."

Harris and Weaver sat in their LP and listened. Fifteen

minutes passed. Every buzzing gnat, every crinkling leaf, all the muted sounds of the city, vibrated in their ears like a hammer in an oil drum. Harris took an amphetamine and tweaked his senses up to a fine tolerance, narrowing that electrical gap between thought and action to its most minute distance. The survivor's edge.

Harris heard a sound. At first he thought it was coming from somewhere on the avenue—a dull, motorized hum. No, it was coming from behind the hill—Hill Two-five-zero. There it was again: a motor, a funny kind of machine noise. Harris sat still, fighting impulses. He listened to a branch snap, a big branch being crushed. Weaver's face was in front of his and he spoke into her ear.

"Set up at the bottom of the hill. Stay close. Mines on top—watch it."

They bent over and shuffled to a location at the bottom of the hill. Harris held the canvas bag over his shoulders and pointed the AK from his hip. He guided Weaver next to a rock outcropping in the middle of the flat ground. They knelt down and Harris peered up the hill into the trees. He stopped his breathing and glared at Weaver. She covered her mouth. Leaves and branches crunched and Harris felt a shudder under his feet. Weaver blurted out, "What is that?"

A horrible realization overwhelmed Harris. He heard the machine; he heard treads grabbing the hill. "I know that sound." He said it out loud. "Oh, goddamn no, it's gonna be an ass-kicker!"

Harris whirled around and slammed into Weaver. They hit the ground and he kneed her, prodding her into a dip in the center of the rock mound. In the same instant the area was illuminated by two high-intensity lamps on either side of the broad flat. Harris was blinded by the light, but he had a quick flash of men sticking out of holes in the ground and aiming automatic rifles. He heard the grind of a motor and turned, shielding his eyes, as an M-48 tank rolled out of the trees on the far side of the hill. Harris's whole consciousness shorted out as he watched the tank grind on toward the Green Gap arch, stop, and then turn slowly and inexorably, pointing its huge gun in the direction of the rock mound and Hill Two-five-zero.

There was a burst of loud cracks and automatic rifle fire tore into the rocks and trees. Harris flattened himself next to Weaver, dumping the canvas bag. He found the pack of grenades on Weaver's back, groped for his M-79 launcher, pushed open the locking hatch and popped in a load. He fired; he reloaded and fired, again and again. The air and gas sucked through the tube and the grenades whooshed out toward their targets. Harris heard the bullets flying next to his head, and then a long line of dull, thudding explosions. The grenades boomed, the high-intensity lamps shattered in a hurricane of fragments and the ground returned to toal darkness. The rifle fire stopped. Harris twisted around and saw a huge muzzle flash. The tank fired and the hill exploded, shuddered, a rain of dirt and debris pelting the rock mound.

Harris tried to disappear. He felt Weaver's shaking body beneath him, squirming, screaming for a god, screaming over and over and over. He held up the launcher and fired another round. Boom. Someone yelled and there was another sickening flash. A tree crashed down and a chunk of hill and rock banged over the ground. Harris tried to roll to the other side of the outcropping; Weaver clutched at him and finally they clawed their way into the dirt, covered by a ledge of stone.

Snap. Bright colored lines shot toward them; tracer bullets ricocheted from every surface. Harris struggled with the canvas bag, trying desperately to get into a firing position.

Weaver's face loomed before him, a black, nightmare visage, her eyes bulging, primitive animal noises gurgling in her throat. He forced her down and raised his AK-47, extending his arms over the rock. He held the gun above his head and emptied the clip on full automatic. His own tracers arched down and away toward the police positions. He yanked out the magazine, rammed in another from the chain and fired. The noise was deafening; a thousand bright tracers crisscrossed over the landscape. Trees were torn apart and pieces of stone flew up and stung Harris' face. He lowered the AK and was loading the launcher when all firing stopped. Weaver looked up; her hands squeezed the ground. She heard what Harris heard and her face contorted. A motor roared; metal creaked again and Harris knew that the tank was beginning to move. His dinner tried to come out of his throat, but he forced it back and said in a voice that had the resignation of doom, "We're pinned. He's gonna move that tank around and come over the top. Right down on us. He's going to grind us up."

Harris waited for the tracers to snake out toward them, but the firing did not resume. Why, he thought? A mistake. Harris lived off mistakes. He secured the canvas bag over his shoulder and crept out from the rock mound. Treads rolled over the Park ground, a monster's feet pounding steadily closer. An old horror swept through Harris. He hissed at Weaver, "Come on!"

She did not appear from the darkness. Harris heard the tank move behind the hill. He crawled back to the rock mound and found Weaver. He grabbed her and pulled her into the open. They struggled through the grass, Harris fighting with the canvas bag, with Weaver, with panic. They stopped inside a group of pines. Weaver knocked Harris' arm away and stared at him, gasping for air. She nodded and crouched down. Harris gave her the canvas bag. He stretched out on the grass and aimed the launcher at the rock mound, twenty yards behind them. He turned away, holding the aim, and with his other hand pointed the AK at the terrain directly in front of his position. He fired the launcher. The grenade exploded against the rock, hundreds of tiny sparks dancing into the air. There was

276

the immediate crack of rifle fire and tracers crashing into the stone. Harris was watching the ground. He saw a rifle flash, maybe fifteen yards ahead, and he fired without hesitation. Screams erupted and Harris and Weaver ran for the sound. They found a man lying halfway out of an open sewer grate. Harris kicked him down into the hole. He pulled a fragmentation grenade from his flak jacket and threw it in after the body. Harris and Weaver ducked and the grenade exploded, echoing beneath the ground.

Rifle and submachine-gun fire came from every direction. Harris tried to stand up, but the tracers whizzed around the trees like some wild laser show. He crawled to the sewer opening. Weaver threw the canvas bag inside and they both climbed down, falling the last few feet to the hard concrete curve of the tunnel.

Their breathing was hard and hoarse and echoed in the pipes. Harris stood and leaned against the conduit wall. He put the AK over his shoulder, bent over and felt around at his feet. He dragged something out of the way and found a flashlight. He turned it on, holding the beam close to the floor. Smoke and dust floated in the stale air. Harris' hands were bloody; a dead man was heaped up a few feet down the tunnel. Weaver groaned. She was standing on the corpse of another man. Dark holes oozed on every inch of his body. His face was in a small pool of sewer water and the water was turning red.

Weaver gritted her teeth, jumped off the dead man and stood in front of Harris. They didn't move. Their eyes darted, unable to focus. They listened to the weapons fire above the surface. When it stopped, Harris held the flashlight over the pack on Weaver's back and selected a grenade, which he inserted in the launcher. He set down the light, took the canvas bag from her hands and lugged it under the open sewer grate. He removed a LAW rocket launcher and armed it.

He choked on the haze. "Okay. This is where I piss all over that tank."

Harris climbed up into the opening and achieved a firing position, balancing his arms on the rim of the hole. He fired the M-79 and dropped it down into the tunnel. A phosphorous grenade exploded on the hill, bathing the area in a sudden white glow. Automatic weapons fire cracked into the trees. Harris watched the tank move into the center of the hill, crushing a small pine. He aimed the rocket launcher and fired. The rocket shot free, a tiny, speeding missile, and smashed into the side of the tank. Metal groaned and disintegrated; the tank stopped and, in the fading glow of the white phosphorus, Harris saw two men climb out of the top, tumble to the ground and run wildly into the darkness, dodging the crossfire of tracers. Harris dropped the LAW on the grass and lowered himself into the sewer tunnel. Weaver stood against the wall, holding the flashlight. Her hand shook and the beam flickered over Harris' fatigues. He pulled the light away from her and set it on the tunnel floor, next to one of the bodies.

"Give me that pack."

She handed it to him and he loaded the M-79. Sweat poured from under his helmet; he wiped his face and cosmetic came off on his palm. He pointed at the opening above his head. "Up. Let's go. Keep your head down and when I lob these bloopers, run back to the rocks and head for the arch."

Weaver ascended the ladder rungs in the tunnel wall. She hesitated in the opening. A rifle cracked and a line of tracers poured into the darkness above her head. She felt something poke her in the ass and she climbed out onto the ground, hugging the grass, waiting for her face to rip apart, begging somebody's god with one final prayer for escape.

In the sewer, Harris decided to ditch the canvas bag. He was starting to climb the ladder rungs when he saw a beam of light pass over the tunnel wall. The light grew stronger as someone approached from an intersecting tunnel. Harris stuck his head above the surface of the Park and set the M-79 next to Weaver's prone form. He lowered himself again and dangled from the ladder rungs, slipping the AK from his shoulder and aiming it down the tunnel. He heard the echo of footsteps.

He saw two men enter the tunnel. They were two Black men, with M-16s, and Harris realized that they did not see him as their flashlight beam focused on the bodies of the dead men. He held out the AK-47 in one hand and was ready to trigger a short burst on full automatic, cutting the Black men down, startling them with one last, ugly surprise.

But Harris didn't do it. For an instant he thought that their black faces were darkened with cosmetic; that they were someone he knew; that they were those willing victims of the night, the soldiers on a lonely patrol.

*What were they doing here?*

Harris was confused. He hesitated. A light hit him in the face.

The men saw him. Harris jumped up, lunging for the opening above his head. A ladder rung broke off in his hand and he slipped. He heard someone yell.

"Die, motherfucker!"

Harris gave one final push. The rungs held and he vaulted toward the surface of the Park. From the corner of his eye he saw the men hold out their M-16s, slide back into the intersecting tunnel and open fire. Harris rolled out onto the grass next to Weaver while, beneath him, a hail of bullets ricocheted inside the pipes. Weapons fire began again from beyond the trees, weaker now, maybe two rifles. Harris turned his face in the grass and located the flashes and sounds. He put the AK over his shoulder and used the launcher to fire three grenades into the dark ground near the zoo. Weaver flinched at the booms and he nudged her forward. They ran and crawled for the rock mound, tracers flying above them into the undergrowth. They knelt behind the cover of the rocks and Harris holstered the M-79. He waited and the weapons fire stopped. He heard someone scream in pain; then the movie ended, and the screaming stopped, too.

Harris pulled the AK from his shoulder. He could feel Weaver's manic energy as she pressed against the stone; she jumped, ready to move, and he restrained her. She yelled. Crack. A rifle began firing. It made a steady snap and Harris knew that it was the only rifle left. He crept to his right, away from the rock mound, and opened up in the direction of the fire. He emptied the clip, the long tracer lines curving down into the dark. He reloaded and expended another magazine. When he was through, there was no return fire. He listened and heard only distant shouts, from somewhere inside the zoo.

A shape bumped into him and Weaver stumbled past in the direction of the arch. Harris ran after her and they went under the Drive, careening through the walkways and trees. The landscape twirled and fragmented; a dark geometry assaulted their senses, every blurred form and space concealing some final horror.

Fear became speed and they kept going, faster, unable to stop, over the transverse road, past Willowdell arch, past the Mall. Weaver raced ahead, through a mysterious jungle, confident now, with the oblivious feet of the survivor. She saw a fence and metal shapes, a tenuous outpost of humanity amid the combat zone, and was disoriented, as all soldiers are, by this startling incongruity. She darted through a gap in the fence and stopped among the swings and slides and monkey bars of Rumsey playground. She collapsed over a water fountain and jammed her head under a cool jet of water. Harris came up behind her and watched her splash and drink. Suddenly, she stood straight up and was silent. They both listened. They could hear a distant cacophony of sirens.

Harris raised his fist and shouted, "Destroy!"

Weaver stepped toward him in the light of a lamp. Her eyes were giant, bulging ovals. Her jaw twitched. Her tongue tried and failed to lick her lips. She stood like that for a long time. Her rasping breath rose and fell. Her eyes never blinked. Harris' eyes were like that, too.

Weaver backed away into the shadows. Something shot through her body; she tumbled through a wild, vertiginous ride. She felt every muscle turning and twisting on her bones. She grabbed a pole on a playground swing and jerked it and kicked it and tried to Destroy. She smashed her fist into the chain-link fence. She danced in front of Harris; he watched her, and in the darkness her image became a memory.

Weaver stood in front of him again, vibrating, every single nerve in her body fired.

"I feel funny," she said at last.

Harris' teeth clicked. "King high. Nothing higher."

"Everything's so clear. So very fine. God, the adrenaline fucks you right over."

"The rocket ship of all time."

Weaver clapped her hands, startling Harris. "Contact! I don't believe that."

Harris smiled. "Yeah, take a trip to Psychoville. One way or round, doesn't matter, man, no rules."

Weaver couldn't stop moving. She walked away and came back. "Those tracer bullets. I never saw anything like that. I like the way they disappear."

Harris tensed. "You know what that means?"

Weaver said the wrong thing. "It means you probably hit something."

"It means you probably hit some*one*." Harris' smile went away. He set down his equipment sack. He wiped his face; the AK tapped against his leg.

Weaver's breathing accelerated again. A hundred colored lines slashed through the air around her head, enthralling her. "No rules, right? That's what you want. I know that now."

Harris turned away; his head pounded. "You don't know shit."

Weaver jumped in front of him. "Come on! Don't stop. You don't wanna stop, do you?" Weaver suddenly saw a tiny TV image, and it was infinitesimal, pitiful; her face felt naked, her vision unobstructed, and it wasn't black-and-white. It was all color. There was only one thing to say. "I wanna do another patrol. We'll do it all night long."

Harris backed up; he lost her dirty face in the darkness. He didn't want to see her, but her voice pursued him.

"That must have been like the real thing for you back there. Coming right at you. I saw it. I saw the whole damn thing."

The words were invisible fists, punching Harris. He stumbled against the fence. Two white eyes appeared from the night and her face loomed over him. He raised the AK and tried to hold her away. She pressed closer.

She said, "Oh, it was real, and I saw it."

Voices spoke to Harris: from two black faces, from a plastic bag; distant voices inside a rain, inside a hole. The voices burned in Harris' throat, shaming him for his fantasy. "Real," he said. "You thought that was real? Your buddies dying is real. Turning stiff with their guts hanging out, giving it up in the mud on their knees."

Harris pushed the AK into her chest, forcing her back. She glared at him. "It can't frighten me now," she said.

Harris exploded. He jerked away from the fence and the only voice that spoke was his own. "I'll tell you what's frightening, asshole! It's when you're a nineteen-year-old kid that plays baseball and goes to church on Sunday and participates and is friendly to everybody, and then you take all this away from him and put a gun in his hand and say, 'Here, kill.'" Harris poked the AK in her face. He pulled out the ammo clip and rummaged through a pouch on his belt. He found another magazine and snapped it into place. He shoved Weaver back farther and said, "You don't think you could do that? Kill somebody? Let me show you what it's like."

Weaver banged into the swings and stopped. Harris approached. He held out the rifle and shouted, "Here, kill!" He pressed the rifle into her arms; he forced her to hold it, her hands falling into place on the stock and trigger. She gripped it awkwardly and the barrel pointed at the ground.

Harris sneered. "Oh, you're not ready yet. But it's so fuckin' fabulous. You get to go out and watch people die. 'Course you feel bad when you grease an old mamasan who points a rake at you, but you're so far out, so goddamn far, you haven't got time to worry about it. And you watch guys so totally wild on patrol that they cut down every living thing in some three-hootch *ville* 'cause anything that moves can kill you. Three days later when your mind is working again, you realize you were one of those guys. 'No shit, it was me blew the tits off that mamasan?' Then you can't stand it and you hate yourself, but only until there's contact again. 'Oh yeah, now I'm straight, things are simple.' And it all carries you away so fast. It's so lovely when you empty your clip into a ten-year-old babysan who just set up your best friend: Oh god, why did he do it, he's a baby, who made him *do* that, and then they tell you, 'Good job, soldier,' and give you a medal. Pretty soon you despise anyone who doesn't know the hate and fear, who doesn't know how desperately you love the thing, that all you're afraid of is that it might *end*. Anybody who isn't listening, who's giving orders—you will pull the trigger on *anybody*. It's so free and easy. Watch the motherfucker die, watch him squirm and bleed, because they said to you when you were nineteen years old, 'Here, kill!' "

Harris pushed her away from the swings. He pointed his finger at her, like a gun. "Here, kill."

Weaver backed up. He kept coming. He pulled out his

.45 automatic, and clicked the first round into the chamber.

"Here, kill."

Harris saw that she was shaking and he moved closer.

"Here, kill."

She raised the rifle and pointed it at him. He aimed the .45 at her head and destroyed her with words.

"Here, kill!"

Weaver pulled the trigger on the AK-47. She pulled it again, and her arms trembled violently. She squeezed the trigger with all her strength, again and again, the rifle jerking in her hands, as if her spasms could force out the killer stream of fire. But nothing happened. There was no explosion of bullets. Only silence, and a soft, alien whimper. Suddenly she froze. She felt a warm flow on her legs and, looking down, watched a dark stain of urine cover her fatigues. A puddle formed at her feet. When she looked up, her face was a black, twisted mask.

Harris pried the AK from her hands. He snapped out the clip and returned it to the ammo pouch with the other empty magazines. He stared at Weaver's wet, trembling body; at the horrible face with the eyes rolled back in the head; at the clenched jaw and the muscles protruding from the neck. He'd seen that look a thousand times. He'd seen it in the mirror.

Harris put the AK-47 over his shoulder and said, "Now that you're way out there, maybe you won't come back."

# III

# Dix

They stood on Madison Avenue at 2:00 A.M., as close as the police would let them—the nighthawks, the newspeople. Others sat in their apartments uptown, above Fifth Avenue, on the side streets in the brownstones. A thousand fantasies were fulfilled; a thousand dreams of lying awake in the combat zone, listening to the distant sounds of battle.

It was all over in twenty-five minutes. Three officers killed, two seriously wounded. There were no pictures, this time, of terrified men crawling from holes in the street, of bloody officers and plastic bags being loaded into EMS ambulances. There were no press conferences; no interviews with John Hardy and Dewayne Daniels, two members of an Emergency Service squad, who were hustled away from the scene after dragging out the dead. When Hardy and Daniels calmed down, when the awful residues of fear and adrenaline wore off, each man tried to describe a black face, a man in green, a dangling specter that materialized from some exotic horror show.

Hardy: "He was there, and then he wasn't."

Daniels: "The motherfucker killed us. We're dead. Now don't ask me any more questions."

Their superiors didn't ask them any more questions.

Nobody was talking, except to make a public statement that the operation had failed. The press went home. A small group of tired men held a brief meeting at Gracie Mansion. They decided to find help. Then they went home, too. At least one of the men was hoping like hell that he wouldn't wake up to the front page of the *Daily News*. He had a vision of a headline and a grainy photograph of Central Park; a high-angle shot, partly obscured by trees, of a dead M-48 tank. Nope, he wouldn't want to see that picture. Ever.

J.T. and Richie didn't answer any questions either. When they were released, they were asked not to talk to the press. J.T. told David Dix, a sleepy assistant district attorney and assorted police officials to go fuck themselves, but he and Richie refused to be interviewed anyway, for the simple reason that they didn't feel like talking. They went back to Weaver's apartment and sat around, not saying much, listening to the radio transmissions. At daylight, they went out to the street, garaged the station wagon, went over to Fifth Avenue and stood in front of the zoo.

The barricades were gone, the avenue was open. Morning traffic was beginning to build. Curious joggers, idle taxi drivers, police officers discussed the night's events. J.T. and Richie heard the comments and speculation. A man said that the National Guard was going to take over the Park—that it would be open by tomorrow. There was a rumor that a gang of Arab terrorists were hiding in the sewer system under the Park, waiting for a propitious moment to make their demands known. There was another rumor that somebody was going to be traded to the Texas Rangers. The Yankee won. The Mets did, too. High today, 95 degrees.

Richie got disgusted; he felt helpless. He told J.T. he was going home to his apartment in Queens and walked downtown, past the hotels and the GM building. As he passed the large, broad entrance to the Park at 59th Street, the Grand Army Plaza, he saw a man setting up a tripod under the equestrian statue of General Sherman. The man placed a telescope on the tripod. A sign underneath it said: FIND THE MAN WHO TOOK CENTRAL PARK 25¢ 2 MIN. Richie looked away, across the street, at the limousines parked in front of the Plaza Hotel. He rubbed his eyes. He caught the E train at 53rd Street and fell asleep in the last car.

J.T. stayed on Fifth Avenue for a while. He watched the tires of cabs hit the tops of the manhole covers. He wondered if there were any bloodstains on the pavement. He walked uptown, keeping his eye on Central Park. He walked back downtown and the traffic gave him a headache. It wasn't the fumes that bothered him—J.T. was born in New York; he got high off the fumes—but the roar of the traffic always hurt his ears. It was constant and pervasive. He thought that someday it would drive him crazy.

J.T. crossed Fifth Avenue at 63rd Street and stood as close to the Park as two policemen would let him. He balanced on the curb, staring at the green wall of trees and bushes. He cursed Weaver. Then he crossed himself and said a prayer for her.

The officers turned their backs. Maybe the kid was nuts, they thought. Maybe he was praying for a dead policeman, or for a city. They didn't want to know. When they turned around he was gone.

J.T. went over to the West Side and rode a bus uptown. He wanted to go home, like Richie, and sleep, but he had five sisters and a mama who depended on him. So he got off the bus at West 90th Street and went into the unemployment office and signed up for benefits. After two hours in line, he came out into the heat and stood on upper Broadway, thinking hard about where he could find a job.

Dix thought Keller looked like he wanted to choke somebody. The Commissioner's teeth were bared. He was sitting at the head of a long conference table and behind him was the biggest map of Central Park that Dix had ever seen. The map towered over Keller; his brooding eyes seemed to stare out of a dangerous landscape and give the room an ominous atmosphere.

Dix moved his chair closer and wrote down in a folder the names of the other men seated at the table. Some of them he knew: Chief Curran, Inspector Lawrence of the FBI and Don Eubank. Dix hadn't seen Eubank since the hospital; he looked pale and thin, with a restraining collar around his neck. He'd arrived only moments before the meeting was scheduled to begin, had nodded at Keller and taken a seat away from the others. He'd spoken to no one.

Three other men were present. Keller had introduced Dix to General Bryant of the National Guard and Lieutenant Mueller, the general's assistant. The third man sat at the opposite end of the table from the Commissioner, and Dix already found something disturbing about the man's looks. He wore a dark suit and his thin gray hair was slicked back. Piercing blue eyes observed the room behind wire-rimmed glasses. Before Eubank's arrival, Dix had leaned over and whispered to Curran, asking him about the man. Curran muttered something about a think tank, and Dix immediately ate two Rolaids.

Keller waited for a staff assistant to distribute water glasses, and when the door to the room was closed, he addressed the man at the end of the table.

"Dr. Warburton."

All eyes turned to Dr. Warburton. He cleared his throat. His voice was even and dispassionate. "Perhaps, Commissioner, it would be best if we hear reports from the other gentlemen at the table, before I make my presentation."

Keller agreed. "Fine. Chief Curran."

Dix thought Curran appeared irritated and uncomfortable. At any rate, he was succinct. "My report is simple. Last night we suffered additional casualties. We gained nothing. I don't think there's any way we can walk into Central Park with a few men and take this guy. We could deploy heavily armed patrols, move slowly on the walkways in daylight, but we'd be sitting targets."

Inspector Lawrence interjected, "But you'd want to draw fire. Correct? One mistake and you've got him."

"Tell that to the men." Curran glanced at Eubank. Eubank had no expression. Curran continued. "Look, three-fourths of the park is under heavy trees. We'd be running around in there until January, stepping on God knows what. I'll tell you, I've learned something in the last four days."

Curran made only the slightest acknowledgment in Dix's direction. So far, Dix liked the way things were going, but he knew that some latent frictions would soon be coming to the surface.

Lawrence wasn't through. "It's a matter of manpower. That's all."

"How many casualties do you tolerate?" Curran replied.

Lawrence spoke to Keller. "May I, Commissioner?"

Keller nodded. "Keep talking."

Lawrence tried to sound authoritative. "The Bureau feels that the situation is now beyond the tactical capabilities of the Department." Curran looked at Keller. Keller looked at Eubank. Eubank didn't blink. Lawrence went on. "The Bureau is prepared to lend the assistance of our anti-terrorist personnel."

Curran snorted. "What are they going to do? Enlist Patty Hearst?"

Dix swallowed a smile. He saw General Bryant look out the window.

Lawrence was patient. "We feel that with our more sophisticated training, we will be able to track this guerrilla to an area of the park where police units can apprehend him."

Dix lowered his head and tried not to listen. Curran was at his sarcastic best. "I forgot, Inspector. Your boys are immune to punji sticks."

The nutshell, Dix thought. Good for you, Curran.

Lawrence was not deterred. "There are a variety of air delivered seismic intruder devices that can detect movement," Lawrence said, "and the AN/PPS-5 ground radar that can indicate a target to an accuracy of twenty yards. There are all kinds of infrared people sniffers."

Curran cut him off. "This isn't Hicksville, New York, you know. The Department has all that equipment."

Lawrence turned to Keller. "Perhaps you need assistance in getting the dust off the technology."

"I'd say your tank got pretty well dusted off."

Dix looked up. General Bryant had made the last comment, and it silenced the argument. Another party heard from, thought Dix.

Keller was glaring at the table. He waited a moment before speaking to Lawrence.

"With all due respect to the Bureau, Inspector, that kind of technical operation takes time. Many of those devices don't work as well as they should. The military has discovered that. At any rate, the equipment is impractical on this type of terrain. There's too much room for error. We'd have to reroute subway trains. We'd have to clear the streets a half mile in every direction, and keep them clear. We can't take that kind of time. We cannot depend on the man in the park making a mistake. We have to come up with something that will directly force the situation."

Keller paused to take a drink of water. He was doodling on a paper next to a stack of folders. Dix leaned over a little and saw what Keller had written. It was a word surrounded by circles. It said: CLAYMORE.

Keller put down his glass. "Now, the Governor has

spoken with the Mayor this morning and offered the use of the National Guard."

. General Bryant took his cue. He was a big man, with a big voice. "Gentlemen. There's no way around it. What you have here is a military operation, and one of the oldest military strategies applies. It's been called the tiger sweep, among other things. This is the basic plan: with units of the 42nd Infantry Rainbow Division, we can surround the park with a ring of soldiers. Teams of mine-detection personnel will precede the column at various points on the perimeter. The ring will gradually pinch in until contact with the enemy is made, and he is either eliminated or surrenders. In an area of this limited size, it's a one-day operation." Bryant didn't sit back and wait for a response; he merely concluded and expected agreement.

Dix studied the table. He saw Keller and Curran look again at Eubank, but still he was quiet, as if the effort to speak would be too taxing. Curran finally responded.

"General, what about barbed wire and booby traps? That will slow you down. Suppose you have to bivouac in there overnight? Believe me, you could receive some pretty heavy fire."

Bryant didn't bother looking at Curran. "Our men are combat-ready and we can come back with a lot more fire than one man or ten could possibly put out, based on what you've told me. We're talking about a very limited enemy."

Keller wasn't so sure anymore. "Suppose he gets down into the sewer system and behind your column, General? It's possible you could be chasing him for weeks. Again, we'd have to have a civilian evacuation on perimeter areas, and the longer any operation takes, the more complicated the situation becomes."

Lawrence could not resist the conversation. "FBI teams can back you up, General."

293

Bryant responded, "The Guard will supply air surveillance."

Lieutenant Mueller was smiling. "Tanks, sir. Remember in Detroit in '67? They brought the tanks in?"

Bryant nodded. "Right. Tanks along the drives and transverse roads."

Lieutenant Mueller: "If it gets hairy, we can lay down mortar fire with the M-2. Range of eighteen-fifty meters, Commissioner, fires HE, illuminating, if we have to move at night, smoke, weighs nineteen kay-gee. Hell of a weapon. Wait till we open up with that."

General Bryant was thinking. "We'll get a line of bunkers dug in."

Curran shook his head. "You'll be shooting at each other."

Lieutenant Mueller didn't hear him. They were talking at the same time. "Right, General, the bunker teams can use those M-60s. Any fortification in there, we go with the 57-mm recoilless."

Curran tried to ask a question. "What's an M-60?"

Lawrence: "A machine gun."

"Gas, sir. Think about it."

"What's the kill radius on those frag mines?"

"Laser beam listening devices, General, field-tested and ready."

Dix felt that he was drowning in the babbling voices. Curran sank back in his chair. Finally Dix raised his voice; he had to shout to gain attention. When everyone turned to him he said, "How much is this going to cost? I'll tell you right now, the Mayor's not going to sit still for the kinds of things you're talking about. Tiger sweep, hell. That will cost the city ten million dollars."

Dix's statement had a sobering effect. Everyone was silent for a moment. Then Curran spoke, as if he were talking to himself.

"It's going to be humiliating if we have to bring in the National Guard to take out one bad guy."

Bryant responded without thinking. "You've already been humiliated."

Keller and Curran flinched, but restrained their tempers. Dix tried to glance inconspicuously at Eubank. There was only a slight narrowing of Eubank's eyes, but Dix caught it, and he thought about the hospital, and how Eubank had been sweating in an air-conditioned room.

There was a commotion at the other end of the conference table. Everyone turned to look. Dr. Warburton was standing in front of his seat.

"May I, Commissioner?"

Dr. Warburton circled the table and stood in front of the huge map of Central Park. Chairs shifted; Keller moved to the side of the map. Dr. Warburton held up a thin metal tube which he extended into a pointer. He began, in his monotone.

"General Bryant is correct in assuming this is a military operation. Matters of pride and expense aside, we will have to respond accordingly. Any further delays will allow this guerrilla fighter to further entrench himself, making any operation that much more difficult." Dr. Warburton turned to the map and touched it with the pointer. "Central Park's approximately nine hundred acres are heavily wooded, essentially flat terrain. It is cut into six roughly rectangular sections by hard-surface transverse roads, here, here, etc., north to One-hundred-tenth Street. This is an important feature, as I will make apparent in a moment. The important thing to remember: in any insurgency operation, the enemy must be killed or captured to reduce the possibility of reinfiltration. Secondly, the insurgent never presents a target. That is why marksmen and patrols are so ineffective. Saturation patrolling requires heavy troop concentration for support and a long-term commitment of ground forces. Therefore, we must reduce the area which the guerrilla can occupy for cover and focre him to reveal his position."

Dr. Warburton removed a sheet of paper from inside

his suit coat and studied it momentarily. Watching him, Dix began to feel very uneasy. He wasn't sure why; maybe it was the wire-rimmed glasses.

Dr. Warburton continued. "Now then. Taking the six rectangular sections of the park, we begin with the area bound by the 72nd Street road on the south and the 79th Street transverse on the north." He outlined it with the pointer, drawing an imaginary line across the park and down the avenues on the east and west borders of the section. "This area is the center of the park and the most heavily wooded, including the Lake and the Ramble. If this section can be effectively controlled, it will cut the park in half with a kind of demilitarized zone that will provide a staging area and reduce enemy movement. The other sections contain less cover, for example, here, the Great Lawn, the reservoir, and here, the Sheep Meadow. The timetable I now describe will be repeated in each rectangle until the insurgent has been either eliminated or driven to the final section." Dr. Warburton cleared his throat.

"0100: a C-123 Provider on loan to the Army Air Guard 42nd Aviation drops fast-acting, limited-range defoliants on a perimeter extending in one hundred yards from the Lake, on heavily wooded areas only. 0600: gas teams enter the sewer system at designated points outside the park and maintain positions at selected intersections of the major arteries, cutting underground movement. 0700: defoliant effective. Armored personnel carriers with ground troops from the Guard's 42nd Infantry enter the park here at 72nd and 79th, east and west, and encircle the perimeter of the section. 0800: if no target is presented, helicopter gunships from the Army Air Guard begin strafing with napalm. 0830–0900: minesweep teams precede ground troops into the section and secure the area by 0930." Dr. Warburton lowered his pointer and turned away from the map. "This process is repeated in each of the sections unless, of course, we get lucky. Advantages:

limited manpower, minimum risk to personnel, high kill factor, and speed. Nine hundred acres can be effectively secured in ten hours." Dr. Warburton faced the table and smiled. "It will also discourage anyone from trying it again."

Dix wasn't breathing. He looked around at the other men. Five mouths were hanging open. Only Eubank was without expression. A weak voice broke the silence. It was Curran.

"Defoliate?"

Dix was thinking of Charlie Meyers; poor Charlie.

Curran stared at the floor. "You . . . we can't burn away half the park."

Dr. Warburton was cheerful. "We can rebuild it. Safer. Better."

"I like it," said General Bryant.

"It's solid," added Lieutenant Mueller.

"It's insane," said Dix, and it was out of his mouth before he could stop himself.

All eyes fell on Dix. Even Eubank's. Dr. Warburton gave Dix a menacing glance and collapsed his pointer with a snap. Keller stood up and walked to the map. Dix could see that even the Commissioner was slightly shaken. Keller extended his hand to Dr. Warburton.

"Thank you, Dr. Warburton. It's remarkable. Really. It would spare lives. Dix will present it to the Mayor with the other proposals." Keller turned to the table and addressed the group. "Thank you, General Bryant; Lieutenant; Inspector Lawrence. General, have you spoken with the Governor?"

"Yes, sir. I'll be standing by, here in the city, until there's a decision on the operation. We can deploy troops from the base at Westchester, as we discussed earlier, and from the armory on 66th Street. There are support units in Roslyn, but that's a non-flying base. If we do call in the Air Guard, we'll have to work that out with our task forces at the other bases."

Keller dismissed the meeting. Dix, by prior arrangement, had asked the Commissioner to remain in the conference room after the presentations were completed, and he'd asked Keller to instruct Eubank and Curran to be present also. The four of them waited until the room was clear. Keller sipped from a glass of water. Curran took a pill. Eubank stayed in his seat at the far end of the table. Dix let everyone relax for a minute while he set up a slide projector. He placed a screen in front of the map of Central Park. He left the room, went to a private outer office and returned with Roy Maitland and a man he introduced as Dr. Hartman.

Dix went through the formalities quickly; Maitland and Dr. Hartman shook hands with Keller, acknowledged Curran and Eubank without speaking. Dix explained who Maitland was, that he was a colonel in the Special Forces, that there was a need for confidentiality. He gave a brief, not too revelatory, description of Maitland's background, and outlined his purpose for attending the meeting.

Dix turned out the lights. Maitland found the projector control. Dr. Hartman lit a cigarette and trails of smoke floated into the beam of light that hit the white screen. Maitland watched the thin wisps rise and dissipate. He hesitated. Voices in a jungle cemetery urged him on with howls of ironic laughter. Maitland pressed the control button and a black-and-white slide appeared. It was a picture of a well-dressed oriental man, about fifty years old, sitting at an outdoor café table. The man was smoking a cigarette and looking into the camera. He wasn't smiling.

Maitland spoke over the hum of the projector. "Tran Chau Dinh. Vietnamese. Sapper. A celebrity. Some say he wrote the book on modern guerrilla warfare. He fought for the Viet Minh in the Fifties. Later the Viet Cong. He switched sides in the early Sixties and worked for us training Special Forces in the south. After that, it's just rumors. CIA says he switched back to Hanoi when Diem was killed. Then he came back to our side after Tet. After that, Cambodia. Tran is an outlaw in Vietnam. They don't trust him. He lives in Paris."

Dix wasn't looking at the slide. He'd seen the presentation earlier in the morning. Instead, his eyes were frozen on Maitland. In the dark room, Maitland's face was lit from below by the projector's light; his head hovered in white smoke, a detached, spectral presence. The face became younger, harder, and Dix saw an agony of fear and death. He saw a man at midnight in a bar, drinking calmly, alone, because even the soldiers, even the marines, wanted to avoid looking in the man's eyes. And when Dix, drunk, careless, talked to the man, he made a discovery that damaged the heart, that left ideals and rules lost and vitiated. Dix discovered that the man did not belong in a bar; that the man had forsaken the world of rules and ideals. The man's only desire was to return to the agony and simplicity of a deep, malevolent jungle.

Dix became a cynic in that bar and in subsequent bars. He fought with himself and others. He sought out Maitland from time to time and forced conversations. It made him feel like he was flirting with danger, until he'd finally found the real danger on his little month in the bush. That had only worsened his cynicism, his confusion—and, on top of that, it had frightened him.

As he sat now, in a conference room long years away, listening to Maitland's disembodied voice, Dix was frightened all over again. He looked at the picture of Tran Chau Dinh. He felt a schoolboy's urge. He wanted to jump up and turn on the lights and say, "Sorry, it was all a mistake, this is too terrible, too insidious," but he didn't, because Maitland was his idea. Suddenly the responsibility paralyzed him; he sat there and watched another slide appear on the screen.

It was a black-and-white photo of Tran, flanked by two shorter, younger Vietnamese. All three men wore dirty jungle fatigues. They were standing in a clearing surrounded by thick undergrowth. The ground around them was littered with debris and corpses. One of the men was holding an object in his hand, pointing it at the camera. Maitland focused the slide. The man was holding a severed human arm. He was shaking hands with it and smiling.

Maitland said, "The man on Tran's right, Vo Phan Huong. On his left, Cao Van Thi. They have been with Tran since 1961. They, too, are exiles from Vietnam. None of these men have any politics. They have skills and they're available for a price."

No one spoke. They sat and studied the slide. Dix waited for a moment and turned on the light. Maitland switched off the projector and Dix returned to his seat. The silence lingered. Dix studied the men at the table. Keller and Curran were still looking at the blank screen. Eubank was looking at Maitland, looking at him with intensity.

Dix turned to Dr. Hartman and nodded. Dix said, "Commissioner, I've asked Dr. Hartman to make a few remarks. He's worked with us before on psychological profiles. In his private practice he's treated several Vietnam veterans."

Keller and Curran returned their attention to the table. Dr. Hartman put out his cigarette and said, "Vietnam soldiers had a phrase, which I'm sure you've heard, Colonel. When a man was through with his tour and processing out, going back home to the 'World'—and of course the guy was happy as hell to be on his way home—his buddies would say to him, 'You're going to be looking for Charlie.' By that they meant the guy was going to miss the awful ecstasy of combat, the sense of purpose. As ugly as it was, it had a certain nobility. It was plain thrilling, too."

Dix glanced at Maitland. He was staring out the window; maybe he wasn't listening. Dr. Hartman went on.

"We call the resulting psychiatric problem the delayed-

300

stress syndrome. Most troubles begin eight to ten years after discharge. The veteran begins to be plagued by sensations and feelings remarkably similar to those suffered in combat. In many cases, hallucinations result—replays of actual war situations. They are more than hallucinations, though. The veteran snaps back to a former reality and exists and lives in this reality for long periods of time. This can result in a repetition-compulsion: an overwhelming need to repeat the experience, to resolve it. This is aggravated by the fact that most of these men were very young at the time of service. They had no time for a normal adolescence, to discover intimacy or to form relationships. Instead, they were confronted with a terrible stress. Their reception back in the United States didn't help. It's true that only in the rarest of circumstances does this compulsion result in violence; certainly, nothing like the situation here. Most vets have handled their problems. But if this man in Central Park is 'looking for Charlie,' by putting three ex-Viet Cong in there, you will be giving him his nightmare and his dream. Then you've got him."

Dix waited for a response from someone, but there wasn't any. Maitland turned in his chair. He appeared satisfied. Dix went ahead and completed his pitch.

"I've spoken with the Chief of Detectives and he told me they've gone through ten thousand service records trying to I.D. this guy. The Chief told me it was impossible. If this guy gets out of the park and escapes, we'll really be in the shithole. Also, there's Ms. Weaver, which may be complicating matters. A small force may be able to deal with that problem. I don't know. Everything else considered—cost, risk to our personnel, the embarrassment of tanks and gunships rolling around Central Park—I think these mercenaries are our best shot. We've used consultants before. I don't know which is scarier, Tran Chau Dinh or Dr. Warburton."

Curran and Keller exchanged glances. There was a

long silence. The Commissioner's expression did not make Dix optimistic. Keller started to speak when he was cut off by a terrible liquid sound. It was Eubank.

Everyone turned to him. His dull, brutal eyes did not move. He was looking at no one but Dix. He looked at him for a long time. He cleared his throat again and everyone cringed. He pointed at the screen, at the map of Central Park. His voice was a painful, distorted hiss.

Eubank said, "It's the only way."

That was it. Eubank said nothing else. Then he emitted a short, wet cough. He held a tissue to his mouth and expectorated a thin strand of bloody, yellow mucus. He touched his restraining collar gingerly, stood up and left the conference room.

Two minutes passed. No one moved. Finally Keller spoke to Maitland. "Time, Colonel. That's our problem."

Maitland gathered his slides. "Tran, Vo and Cao are standing by in London. They can be here in five hours, ready for a mission. I didn't discuss numbers with them. I leave the negotiations to you."

"You misunderstood me, Colonel," said Keller. "I was asking you to assure me that if I send these mercenaries into the park they will complete their mission in a reasonable amount of time."

Maitland held Keller's eyes. "Tran Chau Dinh is more than a mercenary, Commissioner. He's a legend."

Keller and Curran thanked Maitland and returned to other duties—duties that had been neglected for five days. Dix and Maitland took an elevator downstairs and stood in front of Police Headquarters on Pearl Street in Lower Manhattan. They could see heavy traffic moving over the Brooklyn Bridge, curving down over the East River and terminating a block west, near City Hall.

"I have to talk with the Mayor, Roy, but it's only a formality now."

They waited quietly for an empty taxi to appear on the

block. Dix wanted to say something. He decided not to, then changed his mind. "I hope they take him alive."

Maitland gave Dix an odd look and shook his head.

Dix said, "I'm tired of covering things up. As my ex-wife would say, 'It stinks.' I hope like hell they take him alive. Maybe we can learn something about the goddamn war. Once and for all."

Maitland turned his back in disgust. Dix wanted to walk away. He felt lousy. Take him alive. What a load. It was his ego doing the talking—some latent guilt, some desire to be a savior. He'd come to view the man in the park as a symbol, an accumulation of all the soldiers, all the violence and horror. Way back in his last vestiges of honesty, though, Dix admitted that he was participating in a vicarious combat, a reenactment of an ugly and obscure conflict.

Maitland knew. As he flagged down a taxi he turned to Dix and said, "Dave, you don't know whether you're a knee-jerk liberal or a general."

Maitland rode uptown to the St. Regis. He made a long-distance call to London. Then he checked out of the hotel, went to LaGuardia and flew back to Texas.

Weaver wanted to ask someone for help. She shook in her dreams. She sat in the dark, in the bunker, watching the barbed wire. She slept again, sitting up, and the tiniest sound—a leaf falling, an animal rustling outside the firebase—jarred her awake. Her legs trembled again. She shivered and talked to herself, rehearsing the next nightmare. She curled into a ball on the floor of the bunker and the cold ground soaked up her sweat.

She woke up in the sun. The smell of dried urine drifted up from the bunker. She crawled up to the grass beyond the sandbags and stood among the crates and concertina. She felt sick and all she wanted was someone to help her. Her only dream was escape.

Then Harris climbed down out of his observation post in the trees. Weapons appeared. Ammunition was stowed. Magazines were snapped into place. Harris did not speak as his eyes darted over the landscape. He gave Weaver a clean pair of camouflage pants. He took an amphetamine and handed the bottle to Weaver. She swallowed one of the pills. She changed her pants and they walked through the gap in the wire, out of the firebase, into Central Park.

They went south. They observed the M-48 tank, immobilized at the rear of the zoo. They circled north, winding around the Sheep Meadow and the Lake. They patrolled without speaking and, everywhere they went, Harris, driven by a vague anticipation, made Weaver the point man. The point man, the naked man, the total paranoid, whose every step was a terminal illness, who went forward with a bull's-eye on his chest that said, "Kill me, so we know you're there." Harris forced Weaver to advance into the dangerous places; down the corridors of wire and booby traps; close to the tank and the mines and the streets. He kept her always within his sight, sending her forward on brief, lonely missions, to search and possibly to destroy.

The day passed—an endless day. The sun dragged itself over to the West Side. Harris and Weaver kept moving, on and off the walks and paths, zigzagging over the drives, past 85th and 97th; past the Pool and the cascades, to the top of the Park. Weaver walked the point, her eyes darting over the landscape. She crouched and crawled and listened without thinking. A junkie's mix of nausea and pleasure overwhelmed her. And no matter how hard she tried, Weaver could not repudiate the surge of fear and excitement.

Weaver stopped in the heavy bushes on the jogging trail that bordered the reservoir. She looked across the huge expanse of water toward the West Side of Manhattan. The sky was turning orange over the apartment houses. A vapor trail stretched across the sun. A long reflection of trees flickered gently on the surface of the reservoir and, along the chain-link fence, pockets of shadow formed in the tall willows.

Weaver squatted in the undergrowth. Her breathing was controlled, coming in short bursts like a feral cat's. She was alone. She waited. Bird and insect sounds surrounded her. Her face dripped in the hazy, humid air. The edge of nausea returned. She closed her eyes, but a dark jungle lingered on her eyelids. She squeezed her head with her hands and tried to think of a street with trees, of her mother, of a bicycle racing through Brooklyn.

Harris was beside her, suddenly, without a sound. Weaver opened her eyes. Harris breathed in her face. She stood up and followed the jogging trail around to the front of the south gate house. She leaned against the building and the surface of huge stone blocks was still warm. A large window was set in the blocks. It was covered with a thick metal screen, but Weaver saw something in the glass. She stepped closer. She saw a face —a horrible, twisted thing. The eyes were bulging and wild. The face twitched with anticipation.

She spun away from the window. Her legs trembled and she started to cry. Harris stood in front of her. There was no one else, and so it was Harris who heard her cry out.

"Help me!"

He held the AK-47 across his body and used it to force her back into the trees. "Let's move," he said. "This is a patrol."

Weaver whirled around. "I won't do it."

"This is what you wanted. You're just getting the hang of it."

She screamed. "I hate it!"

Harris smiled. "Not for long."

Weaver pushed her dirty face so close that she could see flecks of green in Harris' eyes. Then she said the

**305**

most hateful thing she could think of. "You'd have to be crazy to want this!"

Harris backed away and banged against a tree. His face went blank. He started to speak and hesitated. The words came.

"Crazy. Am I crazy? You think I'm crazy?"

He looked at her and sagged down on the tree, squatting against the trunk. He stared at the ground, then up at the branches. The barrel of the AK drifted over, pointing at Weaver. She moved a little, to be out of the line of fire. Harris didn't seem to notice.

"I'm going to tell you something," he said. Then he repeated it. "I'm going to tell you something." But nothing came again. His eyes drooped until they were almost closed. A minute passed and finally he began.

"I was a LURP. That's long-range reconnaissance patrol. Four-man teams. They take you way back in the bush, by chopper, and drop you. You listen to that chopper fly away and it gets quiet and you know nobody's behind you. I mean, the company might as well be in California. No artillery, nothing. Just you and the VC and God. Right? One time me and my team were out for about three days—we'd been scoping out this big NVA battalion. We never actually saw them, but they were there. And then we're on our way back to the lz to get picked up, when we heard something. You just stop, that's all— you melt into a tree and stay there. You're a statue. If you even fart, you're gonna die. We stood like that for three hours. We could hear them moving all around us. It had to be half the fuckin' NVA army. Talk about freaky? I heard conversations, matches light cigarettes. I could smell their shit on the ground, they were that close. Then we didn't hear anything. They moved out. But you can't be sure, never. So we waited another three hours. Try that sometime, standing still for six hours. So we step out and there's this crack over our heads, just a little snap of a twig and we let go with everything we had, fuckin' rounds and rounds until the guns jammed, your arms are just jerking, trying to make the load go. Finally it gets quiet again, except this one guy is kind of whimpering. Nobody's hit, but there's these little chunks of flesh all around and guts dripping out of the trees. Like we have to know, okay? Just for us, the body count doesn't matter. It took us an hour to find all the pieces. I mean we had to go up in the trees and get part of a head, but this is after three days of psycho shit. And we put it on the ground and made a being out of it, close to it as we could. Then this guy who's whimpering starts to laugh, and then we all laugh. I cried, it was so funny. It turned out to be a monkey."

Harris started to laugh. It became uncontrollable laughter and it stopped suddenly. He put the AK on the ground in front of his feet. He tried to lick his lips. He looked at Weaver and his eyes were still half closed. He asked again, "Crazy?"

Harris leaned back and his helmet bumped against the tree. Weaver moved closer to him, keeping her eye on the rifle. She thought his face was wet with perspiration. It wasn't. Tears trickled down his cheeks. He stared at her suddenly.

"I watch you," he said. "I watch you and it's somebody else all over again."

Weaver looked at her dirty, stained hands. She closed her eyes again and tried to imagine herself sitting on a car hood on Union Street. Harris' voice kept penetrating her thoughts.

He said, "At first I thought the whole thing was like an interruption. A few months and I'd be back home. With my friends, same guy. And I'm sitting in this hole, in the jungle, watching the rain, and it doesn't look right. All of a sudden it dawned on me, I'm not going to be that guy anymore. I'm not anything like him. I'm not going to say 'Hi, Mom,' and sound like him. I realized that you can never look outside and watch the rain come down and not remember how ugly things can get. A hell existed somewhere. It's still out there. It's a world that's alive in your head. And I sat in that hole and I gave it up right there. I said fuck it, I've traded in for another life. I'm somebody else."

Weaver felt her throat burn. Tears came again. She saw the reservoir through the trees, and the tall buildings beyond. She turned and looked behind her, in the direction of Fifth Avenue and downtown, at the distant outlines of skyscrapers and cold steel towers. Nothing welcomed her; nothing enclosed her. She knelt down and tried to see Harris through her tears. "I don't want to be like that," Weaver said. "Not here, not anywhere."

Weaver stopped crying. She didn't feel sick anymore.

Harris looked up from the ground. He nodded. "All I can do is keep on going."

Weaver reached down and picked up the AK-47. She held it up in front of Harris' face and set it down behind her. Her voice was steady. "It's not possible. This is not the jungle. It can never be like that, don't you see? You'll never find it."

"I don't know." Something flickered across Harris' face and he remembered the man in the plastic bag. "I don't know—it's not working." And then it hit him. The fantasy. The fantasy was no good because it could never produce the one thing he needed: the one awe-inspiring, terrifying thing that would keep him going, propel him farther and farther into a parallel world, until he burst through every last threshold of fear and hate and ended up back at himself. Hi, Mom.

Harris needed an insidious, indefatigable enemy, not a fantasy that came and went. He knew now that he would never find him.

His hands were shaking. He stood up. Weaver took a step closer. She reached out and Harris tried to squeeze into the tree. "No," he said. "My body, it's what they used to say. It's a killing machine."

Some basic human response made Weaver put her hand on Harris' face. The touch reassured her; it told her that in this green place, inside a dark city, there was a chance to comprehend something human. There might be a world with no rules, where her own inclinations and conditioning had led her, where she had been briefly seduced by the terror and fear. But here, in front of her, was the instrument of horror, a man so stripped of rules and common perceptions that he was left with nothing but a fantastic attempt to regress, to cry for help. To hold this man was to grasp the last human senses as they slipped away and find the great reassurance that she could feel something after all.

Weaver's hands held Harris' face. She removed his helmet and dropped it. She pulled the flack jacket from his shoulders. She unhooked his belt and set down the M-79 launcher and the sidearm. She pulled off his shirt and then unbuttoned her own. She pushed her breasts against his chest.

"It's okay," she said. "It's okay to touch somebody."

Harris felt a warm pressure on his chest; he let his face fall into her hair. He held her and when they were lying on the grass and leaves, he did not tremble and shake. His eyes did not dart. There was a rhythm and smoothness to his movements. He felt her skin and the muscles turning underneath. He felt inside her, and she spoke to him; and when she sighed, the sound was inside him.

Harris smelled a woman's body. It was not the cold smell of weapons and death. The texture of her skin and hair was like something he remembered. The way he wanted to feel her, to hold her, was like a way he used to be. His desire was not a tortured dream, not a desperate wish that seemed shameful and alien inside the mud and machines. It was a real desire, to relinquish his body to feelings that had lingered only in memory.

Harris held Weaver and the touch was familiar. He

pushed his eyes into her hair and saw himself, a girl's arms clinging to his chest, wrapped tightly around him from the back, a soft cheek resting on his shoulder, wind blowing in his face. Harris got off the motorcycle and made love to the girl in the grass.

Weaver slept in his arms. Harris watched the sky above the trees. It got dark, and he could see the lights of passing jets. For a long time he kept his eyes on the only star not hidden by the city's glow. Weaver shifted in her sleep. He touched her face. Harris slept peacefully, with his eyes closed.

At 10:00 P.M., all apartments and hotel rooms facing Central Park were evacuated. At midnight, Central Park West, Fifth Avenue, Central Park South and 110th Street were closed to vehicular and pedestrian traffic, except RMP cars and police surveillance units. At 1:30 A.M., a police van and two limousines turned off Central Park West and stopped in front of the entrance to the Park on Columbus Circle.

Commissioner Keller got out of one limousine; David Dix, the other. A uniformed officer opened the rear of the van and Tran Chau Dinh, Vo Phan Huong and Cao Van Thi climbed down to the street and stood in front of the steps below the *Maine* monument. Each man was dressed in jungle fatigues and helmet, and carried an AK-47 automatic rifle. Two officers unloaded several heavy equipment sacks and canvas bags. They helped Tran, Cao and Vo attach supply packs and equipment to their shoulders and backs. When everything was secure, Keller walked the three men across the short plaza below the statue and stopped in front of barricades blocking the roadway entrance to the Park. Two ESS officers with M-16s were standing in front of the sawhorses and Keller asked them to take a stroll. The officers went over to Central Park West, across the street from the Gulf & Western building, and lit cigarettes.

310

Keller looked down at the three Vietnamese. The Commissioner was about six foot four; none of the three Vietnamese was over five-five. Keller could see Tran clearly in the light from the streetlamps. Even though Tran was bent over with a heavy load, his face was dry and calm. Keller looked over his shoulder. Dix was on the avenue, leaning against one of the limousines, watching a light stream of traffic take detours from the Circle to 58th Street and from Eighth Avenue past Central Park West to Broadway and uptown.

Keller studied Dix. He ran over in his mind what every officer or detective thought about. Motives. The Commissioner turned back to Tran Chau Dinh and spoke in a quiet voice.

"No matter what you might have been told, this operation has one purpose. Search and destroy. Do you understand?"

Tran nodded.

The three Vietnamese turned and walked into Central Park. Keller crossed the service road and stood near the entrance to the IND subway. He peered into the darkness, over the Park wall, and watched the three men head north on a walk paralleling the perimeter. He could hear their boots scraping on the pavement, but a train went by underground. A blast of hot air and noise came up from the entrance stairs and Keller turned his face. When he looked back over the wall, he could no longer see the camouflaged forms.

A face rose from the dark undergrowth; a black mask, smeared with nightfighter cosmetic. It was Tran Chau Dinh. His narrow eyes opened, tiny white slashes in the humid night air. He looked south, across an open area, and watched the blinking number of a time/temperature clock, high in the looming skyline of midtown Manhattan. The time said 2:10. The temperature, 70°. Tran was beginning to wonder if it ever cooled down in New York.

311

He slipped back into the bushes and moved several yards along a chain-link fence. Cao and Vo were waiting for him, squatting below a rock mound. Their faces were covered with cosmetic; like Tran's, their helmets were decorated with leaves and branches. Cao was checking the locking hatch on an M-79 launcher; Vo was adjusting the load on his back, securing a canvas bag and his rifle. Tran looked through the fence, across a small, manicured lawn, at a building under the cover of tall trees. He held a flashlight close to his hand and consulted a map. The lawn was called the Bowling Greens; the building was a concession area. Tran turned out the light and put his AK-47 over his shoulder. He picked up a six-foot-long bamboo pole and waved at Cao and Vo.

They went up over the rock mounds and down to the West Drive. They moved slowly, silently, Tran poking the ground in front of them with the bamboo pole. They crossed the Drive quickly and stopped in a low flat of trees on the other side of a walk that followed the Drive. Tran could see streetlights and the roofs of apartment buildings on Central Park West. He walked north, Vo and Cao behind him, and they zigzagged back and forth until they approached the 72nd Street road. Tran stopped, just short of a walk that went up a hill toward the avenue. He turned and motioned at Cao and Vo; all three men squatted in the grass. Tran edged forward. He leaned over and studied the walk. A thin wire angled across it, six inches above the pavement, and disappeared into the bushes. Tran followed the wire to where it was connected to the leg of a park bench. He very carefully removed the wire from the leg and reversed his direction, following the wire into the grass, down an embankment to the bridle path, thirty feet below the Park wall and the avenue.

Tran found a claymore mine at the end of the wire. He aimed his flashlight at the glass and put his face next to the ground. Cao and Vo came up behind him. Tran studied the mine. Letters on its curved face said: Front

Toward Enemy. The front of the mine pointed toward the 72nd Street road and the Drive.

Tran turned out the light and said, *"Nhu vay khong tot, khoang da!"*

Cao and Vo smiled. Tran snipped the trip wire close to the plastic surface of the claymore and the three men went up the hill and crossed the 72nd Street road.

As they passed the entrance to the Park at 72nd, Tran saw several police vehicles and officers with rifles. Beyond them, in the background, were huge apartment buildings, the Majestic and the Dakota. The windows were dark. Tran veered to his right, just past the center of the roadway, and led Cao and Vo past a line of benches and down a wooded hill, east, back toward the center of the Park. He discovered another claymore, aimed so that it would explode north, across the exit road branching off the West Drive. When they reached the bottom of the hill, the three men were faced with the Drive, an open area and then a long line of heavy trees which prevented a view east.

Tran brought out his flashlight. According to the map, the Lake was beyond the line of trees. The men crossed the Drive and moved slowly to the shore of the Lake. They stopped and looked across the water. A few park lamps reflected on the surface. To their left they could see a tongue of land, called the Hernshead, jutting out into the Lake. Tran studied the map again, memorizing the shape of the Lake. He knew that he was facing the fat part of the water, and that east, toward the lights, the Lake narrowed down at the Bow Bridge, continuing like a wide river to the Terrace and Fountain, and terminating at the boathouse near the East Drive. Tran decided to follow the shoreline north and west, circling the water, in the direction of the Ramble.

They splashed through muck and water for several yards and then angled back to the Drive, avoiding any direct or straight path. When they rounded a tip of water

**313**

and came to the Hernshead, Tran stopped Cao and Vo in heavy trees and brush off a narrow walk extending out on the small peninsula. He pushed through a tangle of bushes to an embankment of rocks and observed the Lake and a viewing stand at the end of the walk. He went back to Cao and Vo, nodded, and they all cut back away from the peninsula to the West Drive. They stayed in the trees, on a line with the roadway, and approached the 77th Street ramp. All three stopped suddenly and crouched in the bushes. A roll of concertina wire stretched across the Drive, disappearing into the undergrowth on either side. A disabled police car was in front of the wire, surrounded by broken glass.

Cao and Vo pulled their AK-47s from their shoulders. Tran removed night field glasses from an equipment sack. He scanned the wire and terrain. He checked his map and saw how a thin finger of the Lake passed under the Drive, just south of the wire. They could go down to the Lake and enter the water, hoping to come out at the source of the concertina. Tran didn't like that idea; he didn't like their position at all.

He told Cao and Vo, *"Chung ta khong the o day duoc."*

Nobody moved. Tran put away the glasses and got on his knees, aiming the flashlight at the ground. He crept forward, foot by foot, staring at the leaves and grass. He smoothed away some of the cover and found a fragmentation mine. He looked further. He found another mine, then another. He didn't need to find any more. He assumed that the devices formed a line that curved through the trees, cutting any approach to the wire or any attempt to circle it. So much for Tran's thoughts of forming a blocking position at any point along the Drive.

Tran put the light on his map. He studied the terrain features; he looked back at the barbed wire. Tran guessed that this was only one component of strategic strong points that could be defended by aggressive patrols. Any infiltrator would be attracted to these strong points and subject to attack. And, of course, the engagement would take place right where the attacker desired.

Tran moved quickly back to Cao and Vo, being extremely cautious in the placement of his feet.

Tran whispered, *"Don dai duc."*

A hint of tension appeared in the men's faces. Tran took his AK off his shoulder. Keeping low, they shuffled across a walk and the curb, onto the Drive. Tran dropped flat, face down, and eyeballed the surface under the police car in the direction of the barbed wire. They ran as quietly as possible up to the concertina and squatted on the pavement, glass crunching under their boots. They edged along the shiny coils to the west side of the road, away from the Lake, where the roll of wire curved down to the bridle path and the Park wall. They lined up single file and Tran stepped up the curb, next to a walk leading to the 77th Street ramp. He tested the ground with his bamboo pole. The grass caved in and a punji stick spring trap snapped shut over the pole.

The men were startled. They sat down on their feet. Cao turned and kept a watch on their rear. Tran twisted his pole. It was impaled between two wide boards studded with bamboo stakes. The boards were closed tight. Tran freed his pole; the tip was chewed and cracked. He looked up and saw how the roll of wire extended down toward the bridle path. He told Cao and Vo what to do and they returned along the wire to the middle of the Drive. Vo removed two heavy mats from the canvas bag and unrolled them. He and Cao flung the mats out like blankets, until they were draped over the top of the roll of concertina. Cao maintained a security position while Tran and Vo used the RMP car as a ladder and slithered up over the mats, tumbling to the Drive on the other side of the wire. Cao followed them. They retrieved the

315

mats and got off the Drive, heading down into the undergrowth at the northern tip of the Lake and the Bank Rock Bridge.

They stopped on the shoreline under the bridge. They listened to their breathing, heavier now, and the sounds of insects. Vo put away the mats. Fireflies were visible, flying in and out of the beams supporting the wooden catwalk. Tran pointed the flashlight at the water; the surface was murky and covered with leaves. Tran couldn't see the bottom. He stuck his pole in the water; it was only about a foot deep. The three men waded in and crossed to the opposite shore, a distance of thirty feet. Tran told Cao and Vo to wait. He went up the embankment and found a walk winding through the heavy trees, but he didn't like the looks of it. He came back and the men stayed in the water, following the shoreline south until they were on a section of land that jutted out into the Lake. Looking straight across from their position, Tran could see the Hernshead peninsula, only thirty yards away. The two points of land formed a narrow channel leading back to the Drive and the Bank Rock Bridge. Tran liked the looks of this location.

Cao and Vo began unpacking supplies; collapsible shovels, bamboo poles, weapons, ammunition. Tran went down to the water and circled the tip of the section of land. He raised his field glasses and looked across the fat part of the Lake. He saw the distant skyline, and an oval of glowing light hovering around the Park. He walked farther east, examining the muck and leaves, and scaled the rock mounds and embankments. After a hundred yards he was confronted with the dark, overgrown Ramble. He found a small stream, identified as the Gill on his map, coming out of the bushes. He entered the marshy, rock-strewn bed. Trees and boulders formed black walls on either side of the Gill. Tran went deeper into the Ramble, perhaps an additional fifty feet, and

316

discovered another roll of concertina crossing his path. He got down and inspected the ground. He worked his way up the rocks, but the foliage was so thick and dark that he was reluctant to go far. The ground flattened out above the rocks, so he switched the light on briefly and scanned the dirt along the concertina. He saw a trip wire running off into the bushes, just as he expected. Tran turned out the light and climbed down into the Gill. He'd seen enough.

Tran made his way back to Cao and Vo. They were digging a bunker on a strip of land between a curving walk and the shoreline. Tran sat in the dirt and smoked a cigarette. There were only about four hours until daylight. His original intention was to get dug in, and then he and Cao would continue reconnaissance patrols. Now that he'd seen the terrain and what he was facing, he had another idea—but it was going to take a lot of work.

He told Cao and Vo to hurry up. He put out his cigarette. He looked across the channel of water at the Hernshead. The treeline and rocks formed a black, isolated clump. Even in the darkness, Tran could see huge graffiti painted on the rock found that formed the shoreline of the Hernshead. The giant white letters said: JANET. Tran sat quietly, hearing the digging sounds, the crickets, the hum of the city. He imagined the white letters chipping away, disintegrating, exploding in a hail of weapons fire.

Harris squinted in the sunlight. He was lying on his back, his arms behind his head, watching Weaver slip on her fatigue shirt. She brushed the leaves from her hair and sat next to him. She didn't button her shirt and he could see her breasts swaying gently against the spotted green fabric. The sun was behind her head, at a low angle in the east, and her hair was shining. A cool breeze blew off the reservoir behind the trees and the gate house.

317

Harris held up his hand to shield the light. Weaver smiled at him.

"We slept a long time."

Harris nodded. He didn't look at his watch, but he knew it was around 9:00 or 9:30. The days without rest had finally exhausted him. He couldn't remember sleeping. Or dreaming.

Weaver leaned over so that her shadow blocked the sun. Harris lowered his hand. Weaver touched a scar on his chest. Harris looked up through the branches at the hazy blue sky.

He said, "In training, they kept telling us never to hang out with the same buddy, never to sleep in the bunkers with the same guys every night. They said it wasn't a good idea to get too attached to anybody."

Weaver stopped touching his chest. Harris sat up. Leaves and grass clung to his skin. He rubbed them off and put on his smelly jungle fatigues. He sat down across from Weaver, gazing past the jogging trail at the reservoir. He held his helmet in his lap and fiddled with it. He never took his eyes off the glassy water and the reflections of the trees.

"But do you know the only good thing that ever happened to me in combat? My buddies. The friendships that got made. So fast. I never had friends like that. They knew me. They *knew*." Harris turned to Weaver. "Only trouble was, they always died."

Harris stood. He extended his hand and helped Weaver to her feet. They faced each other. Harris kicked away the leaves and put his helmet on. He let go of her hand. When he spoke, his tone was matter-of-fact.

"After we were done building the monkey, we headed back for the lz. But see, the choppers come back for the LURPs at a prearranged time. They only come in for a minute, because the lz's out in the bush are always so hot. If you're not there on time, they don't wait. They leave and come back later, after a certain interval. So when we got to the lz, there was no chopper. We waited. Then we got ambushed. Two of the guys in my patrol got killed. The other one died in the hospital."

Weaver stared at Harris; she saw the green parts of his eyes again. She started to say something, then stopped. She pulled a black curl of hair from under his helmet. He nodded. He nodded again.

Harris bent down and retrieved all of his weapons, his field harness and his flak jacket, but he did not put them on. He held them by the straps, in a bundle, carrying them loosely at his side. Weaver fell in behind him and they went over the footbridge in front of the gate house, and down to the 85th Street transverse. They walked west, in the tall elms lining the road, and crossed the pavement in front of the station house. They passed between the rubble and the charred walls. At the back of the parking lot, they scaled the fence and circled the Great Lawn on the west.

The park was very quiet. As they strolled past the empty baseball diamonds, Harris realized that when they'd crossed the transverse, it had appeared that there was no traffic on Fifth Avenue. He shrugged it off. He kept walking, Weaver next to him, and he never once looked over his shoulder or up at the trees.

They went around the Delacorte Theater and up the stairs to the Belvedere. They stood in front of the stone railing, in the shadow of the gray castle, and looked out over the Great Lawn. Harris turned 360 degrees, observing the skyline and the vast green landscape. The sun felt warm, and he wiped a film of sweat from his chest. He set down his weapons and put his helmet on top of the bundle.

"What are you doing?" Weaver asked.

"Well," Harris answered, "let's go out to Central Park West and see what's happening."

Weaver smiled. "All the way out?"

"All the way out." Harris stepped away from his weapons.

Weaver nodded. She nodded again.

They moved off the Belvedere, south, past the vandalized weather station, and over the 79th Street transverse. Weaver led the way, going down a narrow, circular walk, and cut west at the northern tip of the Ramble. She stayed on the walk, running her hand playfully against the border of bushes and shrubs. She saw the West Drive approaching, and the buildings on the avenue. She tripped on something. Harris stumbled over her and they fell. As their bodies approached the ground, Harris saw, from the corner of his eye, a yellow shape swing across the walk. It whooshed over their heads and slammed into the undergrowth. They rolled over, eyes wide, too stunned to breathe.

A large bamboo Malayan gate, covered with a nest of punji sticks, was embedded in a pine tree a foot above their heads. Moist bark curled away from the punctures.

Weaver gulped. She shook her head. "I thought you knew where all the booby traps were."

Harris couldn't take his eyes away from the bamboo gate. "It's not one of mine."

# IV

# Tran Chau Dinh

The cold, damp air inside the aqueduct made Weaver shiver. She got up and paced around a stack of crates covered with a plastic sheet. She could not see clearly in the dark tunnel and banged her shin on an edge. She sat down again. At the other end of the tunnel, Harris sat inside a circle of boxes and crates. Weaver could see only his dark form, in the dull glow of a flashlight. He was hunched over, scraping, pounding, rummaging through equipment. Weaver looked up at the crumbling masonry over Harris' head, at the manhole cover concealing the entrance to the aqueduct. There had been a thin beam of light shining through a hole in the metal disk, down to the floor of the tunnel. Weaver had watched the beam change its angle, go perpendicular to the floor, then angle away. The beam had faded. Now it was gone. Weaver and Harris had been sitting in the aqueduct for ten hours.

Immediately after the discovery of the booby trap, Harris had marched her back through the undergrowth and walkways to the tunnel. They'd climbed down inside and he'd told her to wait, to sit and not speak. During the long, dark day he said nothing, staying at his end of the aqueduct, cleaning weapons, pacing, sometimes disappearing in the shadows for long minutes. Once he turned out the flashlight and they both sat in pitch blackness for an hour. After that, he'd only appeared one more time from his circle of crates and supplies, to give Weaver some water and food rations.

Weaver shivered again. She was worried. She thought about getting up and going down the tunnel and talking. She'd thought about doing it once an hour, all day long, but she didn't get up. She was more than worried; she was afraid. The booby trap had frightened her, but that wasn't the scariest thing. It was the way the booby trap had frightened *him*.

There was noise at the other end of the tunnel. Harris stood up suddenly. Weaver saw him strip to the waist and kneel in front of the light. His back was to her. His hands moved around his face. He stayed in that position for several minutes. Then he got dressed again.

Weaver waited another half hour. She knew it must be dark outside, and she didn't like the nighttime anymore. A light hit her in the face and Harris came toward her. His steps echoed in the tunnel. Her heart pounded and it surprised her. He stood over her, looking down, and Weaver flinched.

Harris' face was painted with colored stripes—a spectacular, primitive mask of red and green and brown. A bandanna was tied around his forehead. He carried his AK-47, and a bayonet was attached to the barrel.

Harris said, "Get up." Weaver didn't move. He said it again and she followed him back to the circle of crates. He set the light down and told her to sit on one of the boxes. Around her on the floor were long belts of ammunition, grenades, and a large gun she'd never seen before.

Weaver sighed. "Please. Don't do this."

Harris held up several jars of cosmetic colors.

Weaver tried again. "Stop this. Please."

Harris smeared his finger with one of the colors. He reached over and applied it to her face. Weaver didn't move. She didn't stop him. Her eyes watered.

324

"Don't do this," she pleaded. "It's stupid. Let's leave—let's walk out together."

Harris continued to paint her face until it was striped with camouflage like his own. She did not resist. When Harris was finished, he stood up and put on his holsters, with the .45 and the M-79 launcher. He attached four fragmentation grenades to his flack packet and stuffed his ammo pouches with magazines. He attached a canteen to his belt and fitted a field harness and pack over his shoulder. He put the AK over his shoulder, too. He removed the bayonet and slipped it into a sheath tied to his thigh. The last thing he did was swallow two amphetamines and put on his helmet.

Harris squatted in front of Weaver. She was looking at the tunnel floor, her eyes blank and dejected. Harris put a harness and a pack over her shoulders, dressing her like a child. Then he pulled her up and slung two long ammo belts around her neck. They dangled below her waist. She moaned and leaned over a little from the weight. She refused to look at him. Harris picked up the big gun, the M-60 machine gun, from the tunnel floor and moved over to the ladder that led up to the manhole.

The heavy ammo belts tugged at Weaver's neck, and the tips of the cartridges dug into her skin. She forced herself to look up. Harris' painted face danced in the darkness. Sweat glistened on his arms and neck; his eyes darted back and forth. Weaver's mouth went dry. A nightmare specter materialized in front of her. An alien, distant, forgotten war ignited and flared in the blackness. It repelled and attracted her. Looking at Harris, at his startling, ominous mask, she understood the curiosity and the endless search: the war and the nightmare were secrets.

Harris kicked the flashlight over and it went out. They climbed the ladder, from the underground to the surface. They crouched low, and Harris replaced the manhole cover. They began to sweat in the humid air. He put the strap attached to the M-60 around his neck, along with an ammo belt that was already loaded into the firing mechanism. The long chain of bullets flopped against his knees. He turned the M-60 so that it hung across his body. He surveyed the dark terrain; small ovals of light from occasional park lamps dotted the landscape. Harris wished he'd blown out all the lamps. He removed a small penlight from his pants pocket and ran the narrow beam over the ground near the manhole cover. He verified that all the trip wires were in place, extending out to the claymores that protected the area around the supply dumps.

Harris put away the penlight. He nudged Weaver and they took off over a short stretch of open ground, followed a row of trees for fifty yards and stopped within sight of the concertina surrounding the firebase. They sat quietly for several minutes. Weaver fought to control her breathing. She stared at the barbed wire and she felt the fear coming. Her emotions were racing, bouncing around in her head, but she didn't have time to think.

Harris pulled the bayonet out of its sheath. He was drenched with sweat; the M-60, the AK and everything else was really too much of a load for one man. He edged forward, very slowly, poking the ground with the tip of the bayonet, staying at angles to a walk circling the barbed wire. Old instructions echoed in his ears. Never walk along trails or parallel to them. Always test the ground in front of you.

Harris paused at the entrance to the firebase. He told Weaver to wait—not to move one foot. He hurried through the barbed wire, careful to avoid his own booby traps, and dropped down on the edge of the bunker. Nothing seemed out of place, but he did not want to stay long inside the perimeter. He crawled to the Yamaha, unlocked it, and rolled the bike through the gap in the concertina.

Harris and Weaver worked their way east, past the New Lake and the Belvedere. It was a slow, arduous trek,

Harris rolling the cycle for several yards, stopping, going ahead, walking the point, returning for Weaver and the cycle. Finally he stashed the bike in heavy bushes directly below the huge rock mound of the Belvedere, only a few feet from the waterline of the New Lake. He found his notebook of charts under the seat and wedged it in his belt. He camouflaged the bike with leaves and branches, but left the keys in the lock for fast starting.

Harris rejoined Weaver off a walk overlooking the 79th Street transverse. She tried to say something, but he put his hand over her mouth and shook his head. They turned down the small stone staircase that came out on the transverse and a glint of metal caught Weaver's eye. It was her camera and broken VTR, lying in the grass. She paused on the steps. Harris went down to the road and waited. He let her stand for a moment and stare at the TV equipment. She turned away and came down to the road. They crossed to the fire alarm station and beat the bushes until they were inside the Ramble.

They were squatting near an embankment of rocks on an incline of the Gill when Harris' bayonet revealed a small forest of punji sticks. He cleared away the grass and twigs. It was so dark that Weaver couldn't see, so she shuffled closer and leaned down for a look at the sharp yellow stakes. She turned her face to Harris. He was staring at her; right through her. He tapped her with the bayonet and they crouched along the edge of the rocks and went down into the muck and water. They moved quietly up another embankment, out of the Gill and into the bushes on the opposite side.

Gnarled trees and prickly things clutched at them as they executed their moves through the Ramble. They zigzagged over the Gill, passing small footbridges and a network of paths and walks, heading south toward the Lake and the Bow Bridge. They came close to the water once, observing the calm surface through the undergrowth, but it was too far west. Harris didn't like the feel of that direction, so they circled back and stopped on the shoreline under the Bow Bridge's sweeping span.

Fish jumped in the water. Every splash commanded Weaver's and Harris' attention. They waited only a moment and then went up on the bridge. Harris pulled Weaver down and they paused in the middle, kneeling in front of the cast-iron railing. Above them was open sky. There was no breeze, no movement of air. Harris' sweat dripped down on the M-60. He looked across the wide western half of the Lake. He knew he had to make a recondo patrol along that shore, but he'd decided to approach it from the south, rather than curve down on it from the Ramble. The whole northwest area appeared dark and overgrown and lousy. Harris was glad he'd made that decision.

Harris and Weaver left the Bow Bridge and followed the shoreline of the Lake as it wound around Cherry Hill, north along the West Drive. They stayed close to the water. It was faster terrain, because only a few yards of land and a treeline separated the Lake from the Drive. When they reached the Hernshead, the terrain became thick with trees and foliage and they were forced to slow down. They poked and tested their way past the Hernshead peninsula and were coming out of dense bushes when Harris stopped suddenly. Weaver stumbled, making loud rustling sounds as she tried to right herself in the branches. A roll of concertina was a foot away from their faces. The sleeve of Harris' shirt was snagged in a curl of wire.

Weaver could hear Harris' short bursts of breath. The sounds made her eye twitch. She grabbed the ammo belts and pulled them away from her crotch. She tried to lick her lips.

Harris whispered, "Shit." He pulled the notebook from his belt and held the penlight close to one of the pages. He spoke, and a first chilling rush of adrenaline hit Weaver in the spine.

Harris said, "The wire's been changed."

He put the notebook back in his belt. He shifted slightly and his shirt tore away from the wire. He aimed the penlight along the ground and put his face close to the dirt. After sliding his hand around lightly on the surface, he found a thin wire trailing away beyond the concertina. He turned off the penlight.

Harris mumbled, "The old one-two."

He started to turn away and Weaver grabbed his arm. Anger and fear choked her voice. It was not the ecstatic fear, not the wild, thrilling ride. It was desperation. Weaver had been betrayed by circumstances.

She hissed at him. "Stop."

Harris looked at her hand on his arm.

She implored him one more time. "Don't do it." She grabbed the front of his shirt with both hands and pounded him and jerked him around. Then she stopped and knew it was hopeless. Her arms went limp with resignation.

Harris watched her hands drop and said, "Whoever did this to the wire is a very slimy motherfucker."

He stared at Weaver's painted face for a moment. He gritted his teeth and edged forward a little, trying to see where the wire went. It appeared to curve toward the Drive in one direction; he wasn't sure. Maybe it didn't go all the way to the Lake. But what about the mines? he thought. Who knows where they are now? His corridors were nullified. He couldn't be sure where he was. No, wait a minute. He was hit by a terrible realization.

He was in somebody else's corridor.

Harris jerked his head around, startling Weaver. He backed up. He wanted to retreat the way they'd come. His knee bumped something and it didn't feel right. He pushed aside a small bush. A foot-long bamboo stake was protruding from the ground. He switched on the penlight. Sharp stakes, planted like little yellow trees, were everywhere, including the way Harris and Weaver had just approached. He smelled the tip of the stake near his leg. It was covered with something; not fecal matter, but something else. Poison, maybe.

Harris put the penlight away. An electric surge shot through him and he flexed his hands. He felt a flicker of pain. He looked at the wire, at the punji sticks. The Hernshead rose up before him like a black wall. Harris contemplated this mystery; his eyes sought out details and suddenly his perceptions came like reflexes. Harris saw a treeline on a hill; he saw a paddy wall, a dike, a black and impenetrable jungle. The mystery dissolved and Harris felt a cold, familiar fear. His mouth went completely dry. He smiled. The terrain waited for him. There was no other way.

Harris told Weaver to follow directly behind him. He crept forward, dodging the bamboo stakes, and moved out through the undergrowth onto the Hernshead.

A small walk with a heavy border of trees went out to the tip of the peninsula and looped back, rejoining itself. In the space between the loop was dense foliage. Harris stayed on the walk, edging ahead an inch at a time. The path was clear and he stopped, Weaver right on his heels, at the tip of the peninsula.

To his left was a high rock mound. He stood up and beyond the mound was a narrow channel of water. Harris could see the dark shoreline west of the Ramble, on the other side of the channel. He crouched down. Directly in front of him was an open-air lakeside shelter or viewing stand called the Ladies' Pavilion. It was a small structure, with enough space for a few people to sit and view the wide part of the Lake.

Harris whispered to Weaver to sit still. He continued on around the loop in the walk and found an intersecting path that led south off the Hernshead to another viewing stand and the Drive.

A way out, Harris thought. But then he saw a tree that had fallen across the path. It looked lousy as hell. He approached it carefully. He switched on the penlight and examined the ground on the other side of the trunk—the area where a person would step, if he were in a hurry and jumping over the tree. He saw some unnatural piles of leaves and twigs. He brushed away one of the piles and found a fragmentation mine.

Oh, shit.

Harris killed the tiny beam of light and went back to Weaver. Fuck it, he thought. He and Weaver could jump in the water off the pavilion and swim a distance of about twenty yards to the other viewing stand.

"Come on," he whispered.

They crawled out to the pavilion and squatted under the roof. Weaver leaned against the waist-high railing. It was an ornate pattern in cast iron, and the metal dug into her back. She could see the water right in front of the railing and, in the distance, the lights of midtown Manhattan.

Harris said, "We're going in the water." He raised the M-60 and balanced it on his shoulder like a small roll of carpet. Just before he stepped into the water, he had a flash of paranoia. He told Weaver to wait. He waded in; the cool water spilled into his combat boots. He went farther out into the Lake, several feet from the pavilion. He dragged his feet in the mud, feeling around. He stopped and bent over, putting his hand in the water, sliding it back and forth. He touched something. He gripped it carefully, pulling it up a few inches above the surface. It was a rope. He pulled it up higher. It rippled the water and broke the surface, extending from the pavilion several yards in the direction of the other viewing stand.

Nice place for a swim, Harris thought. He muttered out loud, "Slimy. Incredibly slimy."

There was a whistling sound, then a snap and a small burst, like fireworks. Harris looked up at the sky in amazement. An illumination flare ignited, casting a brilliant light over the entire Hernshead. Harris was frozen for one long second as the flare floated down. He dropped the rope, splashed through the water and flung himself to the floor of the pavilion.

Rifle fire tore into the cast iron, bullets dinging and ricocheting. Weaver pressed herself flat, by now a reflex. Harris rolled over and held the M-60 at his side. The rifle fire kept coming and increased. Harris listened and knew it was coming from across the channel. The only thing he could think to do was to get the hell behind that rock mound.

He had started to crawl back into the trees when a horrible whooshing projectile exploded in the Lake. The blast was tremendous, showering the pavilion with water, muck and twirling fragments. Harris didn't wait for another. He wiped mud from his face and slithered off the floor into the undergrowth. Rifle fire strafed over the bushes. He was pinned down, unable to move, unable to operate his weapons.

The illumination flare faded and expired. The Hernshead was dark again. Another whoosh, and a thundering explosion erupted against the rock mound. Chunks of metal and stone slashed through the trees, ripping away branches and leaves.

A nerve snapped in Harris' brain and he screamed, "Incoming!"

He rolled tight against the huge outcropping, trembling uncontrollably. Rifle fire continued and then there was a dull boom, away from the Hernshead, back somewhere near the barbed wire. More booms came toward him; a rain of fragments danced through the foliage and bounced off the rock. Grenades.

Harris saw someone crawling toward him. Weaver. She fell on him and he shoved her away. Two grenades exploded in the water. Harris and Weaver tried to disappear as a storm of water and metal raked across the pavilion. They felt each other's quivering shapes. Through a desperate telepathy, they heard a stream of obscenities and prayers.

The weapons fire stopped. Harris' ears buzzed. This was it. He didn't hesitate. He rolled away from the mound and across the walk. Weaver followed him and he saw the giant white ovals of her eyes as she careened past him. They raced into the water off the peninsula and began a wild struggle for the shoreline in front of the viewing stand near the Drive.

Harris held the M-60 over his head. Water splashed up in his face and over the ammo belt. Weaver was ahead of him in the waist-deep water, pummeling the surface with her fists, trying desperately to make her legs move faster. Harris heard another projectile cut the air; he looked over his shoulder and saw the pavilion explode. The blast deafened him. A spinning hunk of cast iron knifed into the water just behind Weaver. There were big splashes all over the Lake. Rifle fire began again.

Harris and Weaver charged out of the Lake and collapsed onto the viewing stand. Pools of water formed under their legs, soaking the wood floor. Harris was muttering out loud, an inch from Weaver's ear.

"Keep firing, you motherfuckers. Go ahead."

Letting the M-60 dangle from his neck, he removed the launcher from its holster. Weaver was twisting and sliding on the floor, so he put his knee in her back to steady her. He managed to get her equipment pack open and find the 40-mm grenades.

Harris was babbling now. "Frag 'em. Frag the bastards into oblivion . . ."

He moved to the waterline in front of the viewing stand and knelt in the mud, his body protected by a large wooden beam at the corner of the structure. The Lake and the Hernshead stretched out in front of him. The steady snap of an automatic rifle sent rounds whistling through the peninsula and out over the Lake. Harris gauged his target, over the Hernshead, across the channel.

He fired the launcher, reloaded, fired again and again. The grenades spun away, sailing high over the trees. He heard the booms and the impact of fragments and dirt. Harris fired every grenade he had, fumbling hysterically in Weaver's pack for the last rounds. When he was finished, there was no more rifle fire; no more missiles rocketed across the landscape.

Harris jammed the launcher into its holster. Weaver was shaking quietly, watching him. She was wedged under the bench that connected the two corner beams. Harris reached under, grabbed her collar and dragged her out. They bolted off the viewing stand. After crawling their way through a short line of trees, they were on the West Drive.

Because Harris was unsure of the mines and booby traps, he stayed right in the middle of the road and ran north. Weaver trailed behind. She fell; she got up and kept coming. Harris' boots made loud clicks on the pavement. He veered to his left as he passed a dark treeline on the Lake side of the Drive. The Hernshead was hidden behind that treeline.

Harris and Weaver approached the intersection of the 77th Street ramp and the Drive. Harris stopped and squatted. He could hardly breathe; the heat, the fear, the weight of the weapons drained him. Drops of sweat stung his eyes. Weaver plopped down beside him. She kept nodding her head—a continuous nod, acknowledging a secret voice. Harris tried to see ahead on the Drive. He saw the abandoned patrol car, but he couldn't find the roll of concertina that should have been in position across the road. He moved ahead a little more, staying close to the west curb, and saw the concertina. It was farther north; it had been moved, at an angle across the road, above the finger of the Lake that passed under the Drive.

Harris swore. He crept forward until he was on the section of Drive that was a bridge over the finger of the Lake. He crawled to the railing. It was made from concrete in a latticework pattern. Harris had a view through gaps in the design. He looked east. Below, he could see the water passing under the Drive; ahead was a channel of water and, beyond, a very dark section of terrain. There appeared to be a high embankment under dense trees, but it was too dark to be certain. Harris moved his gaze south, keeping a straight line, and discovered that directly across the channel from the wooded embankment was a peninsula of land—the Hernshead.

Harris looked back at the embankment. Yes, yes, yes, you lousy cocksuckers.

Harris felt something on his leg. He jumped. It was Weaver. He pulled her down in front of the railing.

"Shh," he whispered. He stared at her. She appeared to be in shock. She rubbed at the stripes of paint on her face.

Crack. Harris ducked instinctively. Lines of colored light shot out of the distant embankment and raced toward the bridge.

"Oh, shit!" Harris yelled. Weaver yelled too. A hail of tracer bullets slammed into the railing. Harris crawled back toward the 77th Street ramp, his elbows and knees scraping raw on the pavement, the M-60 banging up under his body. He found a sewer grate in the grass just off the curb. He curled his fingers through the metal and tried to lift it. Tracers bounced off the road and the RMP car, whistling into the trees. Harris dropped flat. He saw Weaver crawling toward him. The lethal lines of color closed in on her, shattering the concrete railing above her head. Harris tried the sewer grate again and it popped loose. He tilted it up and pushed it over in the grass. Weaver crawled closer. The weapons fire intensified. Harris watched the light show, watched it fly all around them. Finally she was there; he pulled her into the opening. She dropped feet first and landed in a pile of mud and leaves, only five feet below the surface of the park. Harris climbed in after her. They huddled together, twitching, muttering, their sweat-soaked bodies pressed tight against the cold masonry.

The rifle fire subsided, then stopped. Harris listened for several minutes. He made his legs stop bucking. He twisted around, banging Weaver's head off the side of the wall. She moaned. Harris smelled urine.

He raised his head above the top of the opening. He narrowed his eyes and peered across the road. On the other side of the Drive was the corner of the bridge; past that was a large tree, and then open space. Water. And over the water, the embankment.

Harris pulled his head out from under the M-60's strap. He unfolded the small tripod at the end of the barrel and rested the legs on the pavement just over the curb. He took the ammo belt off his shoulders and extended it along the ground.

Harris aimed to the right of the bridge, for the open space. He pushed down on the top of his helmet, making it snug on the bandanna. Hot moisture poured down on his painted face. He muttered again. His voice was a rasp.

"Destroy."

Tran looked out over the top of the bunker. He was watching the water where it flowed past the bunker's high embankment. The channel narrowed down and passed into a tunnel under the Drive, but the bridge above, the roadway and the terrain were indistinguishable in the darkness.

Tran turned around and accepted a cigarette from Vo Phan Huong. He bent over and Vo lit it behind the bunker wall. Cao Van Thi snapped a new magazine into his AK-47 and resumed a firing position at the top of the bunker. Tran took a deep drag on the cigarette and rubbed his ears. He couldn't hear anything; there was a loud ringing in his head. Balanced on his shoulder was an M-67 90-mm recoilless rifle. It was a short tube, about a meter long, that fired a canister round to an effective range of 450 meters. It weighed about 16 kilograms. Ordinarily it was used as an antitank weapon, but it could also be employed in an antipersonnel role. Tran preferred it for that use; the recoilless made his ears numb, but it tore the hell out of anything in its path.

Vo drank from a canteen. He cleared away shell casings and debris from the floor of the bunker. Tran blew smoke rings. He looked across the Lake at the halo of light over midtown buildings. A helicopter flew slowly by over the skyline. Cao saw it too. He looked at Tran. They smiled, sharing a memory.

A terrifying crack broke the silence. Water and mud flew over Tran's head. He dropped down into the bunker, pressing his body into the dirt. Cao and Vo fell back and shuffled to the end of the large hole. The weapons fire was loud. Bullets sprayed everywhere. Tran listened to the unending stream as it flew over his head into the undergrowth. The fire kept coming. It stopped briefly—reloading, Tran thought—then it resumed. The rounds poured in, chewing up the dirt, tearing into the trees, ripping apart the landscape.

Cao tried to raise his AK above the bunker and fire off a burst, but gave up. Tran shook his head. The bullets came for a long time, but Tran knew it was machine-gun fire, probably a U.S. Army M-60, and that sooner or later the barrel would get too hot and the gun would jam.

A minute later the firing stopped. Dust and leaves floated around the bunker. The men heard nothing except the buzzing in their ears. They brushed pebbles and clods of dirt from their fatigues. They sat quietly, looking up at the black starless sky.

Tran lit another cigarette. When he took it from his lips to flick away the ash, a wad of paper and tobacco stayed behind. His tongue tried to clear the mess from his lips. It didn't work. He didn't have any saliva.

*    *    *

Dix's clock radio clicked on at 6:30 A.M. He rolled over in his bed and woke up. He shivered; the air conditioner in his bedroom was blowing directly on his face. He was too tired to move. A voice on the radio said, "This is WINS, all the news all the time. . . . The sounds of automatic weapons and explosions that rocked Central Park last night are quiet at this hour, but the battle for Central Park continues. The Associated Press has filed an unconfirmed report that three ex-Viet Cong mercenaries have been hired by the New York City Police Department to hunt down the so-called guerrilla terrorist. Deputy Mayor David Dix has denied . . ."

Dix turned off the clock radio. He got up and took a shower. While he was shaving, he tried not to see how terrible he looked. He got dressed. The way he felt, breakfast was impossible, so he left his apartment and took the service elevator to the ground floor. He exited via the service entrance. Before he stepped onto the sidewalk, he looked down the block at the front of his building. There were no reporters or press cars. Even they were tired of listening to him.

By prearrangement, Dix met the limousine at 7:00 A.M. on the corner of East 65th and Third Avenue. They drove uptown on Third, then downtown on Second Avenue until Dix spotted an open cocktail lounge at East 78th Street. The driver waited while Dix went inside and had two Bloody Marys.

Dix came out feeling ballsy. He asked the driver to take the car over to Fifth Avenue. At Madison and East 72nd the limo was stopped at a police barricade. Newspeople and policemen lingered in front of the sawhorses. Dix could see that 72nd was closed between Madison and Fifth, but he rolled down the window and identified himself. Several officers with rifles let the car through on the condition that the driver park short of Fifth and that the car come back in two minutes.

The driver parked the limo in front of a tall apartment building in the middle of the block. Dix got out and walked toward Fifth Avenue, staying close to the buildings. He stopped on the corner, facing Central Park.

The Park seemed to droop after several days of accumulated heat. The sun reflected from the leaves and, in the haze, created a glare. Dix squinted and loosened his tie. The air had a smelly, damp texture, the smell it always had at the beginning of a hot day, but there were clouds visible on the West Side, and the limo driver had told Dix that rain and thunderstorms were forecast for the late afternoon.

Dix stuck his head around the corner of a building and peered uptown on the avenue. It was quiet. No one was on the street. It looked like a forgotten zone. There were no cars; small clusters of trash rested against the curb; flies buzzed over old dog piles. Dix stuck his head out farther. Some of the windows on ground-floor apartments and lobbies were boarded up. Dix looked up the face of the building. He saw people on the roof and went out to the curb to get a better view. The people had telescopes on tripods, binoculars and cameras with telephoto lenses.

Dix went back to the limo. He told the driver to take him to the mobile command post on East 53rd near Madison. They went downtown on Lexington Avenue and Dix was surprised at the light traffic, considering that so many streets were closed. It was early in the morning, but still, he thought, there should be the beginnings of tie-ups. Then he remembered that it was Saturday. He checked the date on his watch. He looked out the window at the stores, at the pedestrians walking dogs.

It was Saturday, July 27. Central Park had been•closed for six days.

Harris and Weaver waited out the night in a dark, smelly tunnel under the 77th Street ramp. The tunnel was actually a huge arch, about twenty feet high at its apex, set back against the highest part of the Park wall on Central Park West. The bridle path passed through the arch and the smell of decaying horse manure lingered in the damp air. Another odor had drifted up to Harris' nose during the night as he sat against the cold stone wall. It was the smell of fear and sweat and gunpowder.

Weaver stayed on the ground, next to him. Sometimes she slept. She nodded off and little spasms moved her legs and arms. She woke, sat up and looked around. Each time, Harris stared at her as if he'd never known her. She stared back, confused. Around 3:00 A.M. Weaver woke with a start. She put her face close to Harris and spoke with great urgency.

She asked, "Who is it?"

She stretched out again, almost immediately, not waiting for an answer, and slept without waking.

Harris did not sleep. Sleep was death. He sat in the wet gravel and, when his ears stopped ringing, he listened to gentle night noises. The crickets chirped loudly, with renewed volume; no crashes, no storms of metal competed with their songs. Harris watched fireflies float in and out of the dark trees under the Park wall. He remained motionless for two hours, regaining strength, breathing deep until his lungs stopped aching. Once an hour, all night long, he swallowed an amphetamine.

When he felt rested enough to move his arms, Harris took the AK-47 from his shoulder, removed the clip and made sure the rifle was working properly. After snapping in a fresh magazine, he did a check on the M-79's locking hatch and firing mechanism. He no longer had the M-60. He'd fired it too long, pushed it too far, until the barrel practically melted. He'd abandoned the M-60 in the sewer hole on the edge of the West Drive.

By 4:00 A.M., Harris' senses were wound up to a high level. He left Weaver's prone form in the gravel under the arch and walked out on the bridle path. He stood in a bush along the Park wall. The city pressed against his back. He stayed in that position for an hour, his eyes fixed on the murky landscape beyond the Drive. He held the AK in front of him and talked to himself.

Kill you, and kill your god.

Just before dawn, Harris went back to the arch and woke up Weaver. He made her drink water and take an amphetamine. He stood over her, watching her nerves get stretched. Despite the stimulant, and the fear, her eyes never lost a dull, blank stare. That was all right with Harris; all she had to do was react.

When he thought she was ready, they moved out of the arch and picked their way through the grass and trees, around Harris' claymores, past the concertina and onto the West Drive. They crawled over the pavement to the opposite side and stretched out on a wooded incline leading down to the Bank Rock Bridge. A tongue of the Lake flowed under the bridge. Across the water was a black clump of undergrowth and the curving slope of an embankment.

Harris and Weaver held their position, lying flat under the trees, and watched the gray early light smooth out the shadows. The wooden beams supporting the bridge became visible. The trees and bushes took shape. A terrain materialized: an awful, menacing place that absolutely no one would wander into.

But Harris was going to go in there. Because he was dancing on a very tight string.

Harris slipped the bayonet out of its sheath. He and Weaver squatted and shuffled down the incline to the water, Harris poking the ground as they moved. He stood on the shoreline and inspected the underside of the bridge. Nothing: no bombs, no charges. Harris studied the small stream that flowed under the bridge. To his right, the water widened to the channel and the Lake. To his left, past the bridge, the water terminated under a huge willow tree that drooped over the surface. There was a glimpse of concertina in the background.

Harris leaned against the bridge supports and observed the willow. A horde of imaginary snipers lurked in the branches. He looked down at the water near his feet. Streams could be booby-trapped, with a grenade on one bank and a trip wire fastened to the other. Harris made a decision.

Harris moved up onto the bridge and Weaver followed. The wooden planks creaked under their feet. Harris pushed Weaver quickly into the bushes on the other side. There was no stopping now. He led the way onto a walk that wound along the edge of the water, holding the AK in front of him, pushing the change lever to full automatic. Water appeared through the foliage. Harris dropped flat and Weaver fell beside him. The Hernshead peninsula was visible across the channel; the rock mound glistened in the slanting rays of sunlight. Huge letters were painted on the mound, but Harris could not make out the word. Half the letters were missing, blown away with large chunks of stone.

Harris held his breath and crawled forward on his elbows. Leaves crunched under his body. A short hill appeared—a pile of dirt and debris, under shredded trees and bushes. The ground was dented with several small craters. Harris crawled ahead another foot and saw a bunker.

Bingo. Harris pulled a fragmentation grenade from his flak jacket. He hesitated. He raised his head a little and got a view over the top of the bunker, maybe twenty yards in front of him. There was no one inside.

What else is new? Harris said to himself. He dropped down again on his elbows. Weaver crawled up next to him, making noises in the debris.

Harris glared at her. She didn't blink.

Nothing moved for ten minutes, except an ant that climbed up the grenade in Harris' hand. Perspiration dripped from Weaver's chin; the drops were colored with cosmetic. Finally Harris turned to her and whispered, "I wish I could prep this with some artillery."

Weaver nodded blankly.

Harris perused the area again. He almost got up and advanced, but an instinct stopped him, saved him. A fantastic suspicion gripped his mind; he tried to deny it. It went away and then transformed itself into runaway paranoia. Now, he couldn't think. He let the adrenaline move him.

He glanced at Weaver again and said, "Watch this."

Harris pulled all the fragmentation grenades from his flak jacket—four of them. Without removing the pins that would arm the grenades, he tossed them toward the rim of the bunker, so that they rolled over and stopped on a section of undisturbed leaves and twigs.

Ten seconds went by. Fifteen. Harris aimed the AK. Twenty seconds. The patch of leaves moved. A man bolted right up out of the ground, leaves clinging to his helmet, a grenade rolling harmlessly from his shoulder. The man screamed and spun around with an AK-47, but his scream was cut off. Harris destroyed him.

The body flew back from the bunker, landing face down in the dirt. Harris fired half his clip into it; the legs jerked and danced and the flesh broke open into a red foam.

Harris took his finger away from the trigger. He couldn't breathe. He jumped to his feet and ran past the bunker, scooping up the grenades. Weaver stood up and walked slowly toward the body. She saw the wounds and the blood; it was a car accident, a jumper splattered on the pavement, a homicide. She squatted next to the dead man and, when Harris walked over to her, he saw that her eyes were clear and focused.

Weaver looked out at the Lake. She said softly, "Oh."

Harris attached the grenades to his flak jacket. He turned to the corpse. It was half buried in dirt, the rifle trapped underneath the chest; the fatigues were bunched up behind the neck. Harris wedged his boot under the dead man's waist and turned him over.

It was Vo Phan Huong.

343

Harris' mouth fell open. His face twisted behind the stripes of paint. His eyes clouded over and spittle appeared at the corners of his mouth.

Weaver looked up at him. She felt sick. She'd seen that face once before. In a window on the south gate house.

As Harris stared at the dead man, every gland in his body emptied. A horrendous rush shot from his head to his feet. His skin burned. His balls tingled. The man had the right face.

Harris jerked around and looked at Weaver. He smiled. "Goddamn! It's a gook!"

Harris had found an enemy.

After hearing the crack of rifle fire, Tran and Cao waited in silence at their position inside the Ramble. When Vo did not appear, they expected the worst. They took separate approaches to the bunker, moving cautiously west, until they rendezvoused on the shore of the Lake, fifty yards from the embankment overlooking the channel. Using a rock mound as a protective barrier, they maintained surveillance of the bunker area for fifteen mintues.

Fish snatched insects off the surface of the Lake. Birds and squirrels played in the trees. Tran smoked a cigarette. There was no movement near the bunker, only an innocuous westerly breeze.

Tran and Cao advanced on the embankment. Tran was careful, but he didn't expect any activity. No one would stay in a known assault position after an engagement; they would abandon it, as he had done, just before daylight.

Except for Vo. But that was another matter.

They found Vo's body face down on the far edge of the embankment; it appeared to have been dragged away from the bunker. Cao reached down to turn over the mutilated corpse. Tran grabbed his arm—an instinct.

Tran found a rope in the heavy equipment bags on Cao's back. He tied one end to Vo's belt, being careful not to move the body. He took the other end of the rope into the bunker and jumped in, along with Cao. They stretched out flat in the dirt, pressing their faces against the cold clay wall. Tran pulled hard on the rope, rolling Vo's body over.

Tran and Cao squeezed their arms under their flak jackets and waited expectantly. In about five seconds there was a dull, thumping burst. Pebbles and bloody wads of clothing flew into the bunker. When the dust settled Tran and Cao raised their heads and exchanged glances.

Tran spit dirt from his mouth and said, *"Tin khong!"*

Harris and Weaver were in the old aqueduct supply dump. The manhole cover was open and a wide cylinder of light hit the floor between them. Harris' face sparkled with fresh colors. His lips were drawn and tense. Weaver sagged from exhaustion. She rested against the ladder while the cold tunnel air dried her sweat.

Harris drank from his canteen, swallowing vitamins. He was exultant. "Do you believe it? Real down-home sappers."

Weaver shook her head. A look of resolve came over her. "You're going to keep going?"

"Charlie's here."

Harris picked up a chain of ammo clips from the floor and draped them around his neck. He secured all his weapons, then ran into the dark tunnel and returned with more clips, fragmentation grenades and M-18 colored smoke grenades, which he slipped into ammo pouches. He stood in front of Weaver. His whole body was bulging with ammo and guns.

"Isn't technology wonderful?" he asked sarcastically. "If we had to do this with our bare hands it wouldn't be shit."

Weaver jumped away from the ladder. Her voice reverberated in the tunnel. "Don't you see? You're going to die. You can't win."

Harris grabbed her shirt and slammed her against the

**345**

wall. In a final outburst, not of confused patriotism but of personal defeat and self-loathing, he screamed at her, "I get tired of losing in Vietnam!"

He let go of her. They didn't speak; they didn't look away from each other. After a minute, Harris pointed the AK up the ladder.

"I won't go up there," she said firmly.

Harris poked her with the rifle. "Listen to me. I'll tell you what. If you want to leave the park, go ahead. We're going out by the firebase. Take off from there. I'll cover you. Maybe you'll make it."

He didn't wait for an answer. He prodded her again and she climbed up toward the bright light at the top. Harris followed behind and stopped her just short of the opening.

"When we get out there, be quick. I don't want any slimy dinks to see me fooling around here."

They reached the surface of the Park and stayed low. Harris replaced the manhole cover and they ran across a short section of open ground. They circled a field of claymores, then another, and entered a short treeline about a hundred yards from the firebase. They stopped under the tall trees on the wire perimeter.

Harris tried to see through the concertina. He was nervous. The only reason he wanted to get inside the firebase was to replenish his supply of 40-mm grenades for the launcher. He'd run out; there were no more in the supply dump. In fact, he was running out of everything. He knew he should have kept the 40-mm rounds in the dump. It was either a minor oversight or a big mistake.

Harris scanned the trees above the perimeter. He paid close attention to the branches hiding his observation post. Nothing looked lousy. He told Weaver to wait.

"When I come back, you get a free ride," he said, almost inaudibly.

As he went through the entrance to the firebase, crouch-

346

ing low, Harris decided in his own mind whether the reason for the trip was an oversight or a mistake. It was a mistake. Somebody else confirmed it.

A grenade exploded just inside the wire, at the far end of the perimeter. Harris fell. His hand split open and he dropped the AK. He rolled and grabbed for the rifle. Another boom and he was showered with dirt. He tried to see. There was the box of grenades; there were the crates and the stove. Rifle fire whipped over the concertina. Where was the bunker? Oh, shit. Harris crawled blindly. Blood flew in his face. An explosion went off in the trees and his observation post broke away, falling to the ground along with a huge branch. Bullets tore into the stack of crates, an inch above Harris' head. He found the bunker and rolled inside.

Harris sat in the dirt, trembling. He held up his hand. Red streams poured out behind his fingers. Boom. Fragments sailed over the bunker and thudded into the sandbags. Harris dropped flat. Rifle fire was continuous. He pulled the bandanna from his forehead and wrapped it around his hand. He gripped the AK-47 and waited.

The firing stopped. Someone yelled. Harris stuck his head up for a look. The firebase was a mess. Crates were broken open; his sniper rifle was tangled two feet up in barbed wire.

Harris heard a burst and then a whistling projectile. He collapsed. It was as if a bomb had been dropped. A tree groaned and the ground shook. The pierced-steel planking that protected the bunker wall gave way, a huge hole ripping open in the center. Harris was buried in dirt. He crawled to the end of the bunker, to the opening he'd punched through the side of the manhole.

Another projectile closed in. The blast knocked Harris flat. He was almost unconscious. There was one last chance. He got to his feet and found a long braid of trip wires dangling through the sandbags. He yanked the braid

347

down and heard ten consecutive explosions as his clay-mores detonated around the perimeter, sending a wall of hurtling metal into Central Park.

There's a thousand dollars, Harris thought as he climbed into the manhole and disappeared.

As he moved through total darkness, on his hands and knees, the stench of foul water and dust choking his lungs, the sounds of weapons fading behind him in the narrow tunnel, Harris congratulated himself for remembering an old piece of advice.

Never go in the back door. Always go out.

Weaver was lying on her side in the grass, under maple trees and low shrubs. Her head ached. An automatic rifle kept up a steady pop somewhere beyond the trees. She felt faint. A red stain was forming in her armpit, getting bigger, soaking through the green material on her chest.

Weaver had been crawling along a walk when everything blew up. She'd panicked and tried to run through the undergrowth. Then everything blew up again. A needle had pierced her armpit, but it was only a tiny sensation. A sound like a thousand sickles cutting hay was all around her and she'd been forced to bury herself in the grass. It was then that she saw the red stain and the little blue circles in front of her eyes. There'd been no pain, but now there was.

The rifle ceased firing. Weaver listened, but there was only the loud ring in her ears. She sat up a little. A warm river of blood ran down her sleeve to her left hand. Nausea tickled her throat. She sighed and looked away at the trees. She could see the sky, because half the maple leaves had been blown to the ground, as if it were November.

Dark clouds were moving in on the West Side. It looked like rain. Rain would be nice, Weaver thought. It was so hot.

Something hot touched her face. She jumped. It was the

348

barrel of an AK-47. She turned around. An oriental man in jungle fatigues, wearing a helmet decorated with leaves, was squatting behind her.

Tran Chau Dinh pointed the rifle at Weaver's chest and smiled.

Cao Van Thi stood behind a railing that curved around the Chess and Checkers House. The small, octagonal brick structure was built on a promontory in the southeast section of Central Park. It was surrounded by tall trees and lightly wooded slopes, but the slight elevation gave Cao a good surveillance position. He raised his binoculars.

To the west he could see the Carousel near the 65th Street transverse, and the ball fields on Heckscher playground. The ball fields were, of course, open land, so Cao didn't spend much time observing the area. He looked north and east, where the terrain was complicated by roads, trees, rock mounds and bridges. Cao surveyed this area carefully. He lowered the binoculars and studied the landscape with his naked eye. Cao knew that the unaided eye was sometimes the superior tool for reading a landscape. Once, many years ago in the Central Highlands, his battalion had annihilated a large army of Montagnard tribesmen, simply because Cao saw a change in the shadows on a treeline when a reconnaissance team with scopes, field glasses and infrared scaners had seen nothing.

Cao walked around the Chess and Checkers House, past small stone tables that were inlaid with black and white squares. Short wooden benches were screwed into the concrete on either side of the tables. Two of the benches were occupied.

Tran Chau Dinh sat across from Weaver. A canteen and food rations rested on top of the table, in the middle of the chess surface. Weaver had her back to the railing and, behind her, Tran could see a walk leading down to a high fence, a brick wall, and a stage and bleaches surrounding Wollman Rink. As Cao walked past, Tran pointed at the walk and Cao descended the stairs for a look. Tran sat up higher to see over the top of Weaver's head. Trees blocked his view of the East Drive and the zoo. He shifted his gaze back to Weaver.

A white cloth was jammed up in her armpit. Dried, caking blood covered her arm. She was quite pale and Tran had thought she was going to collapse during the fast retreat south from the engagement at the firebase, but he'd stopped her bleeding and she'd seemed to drift out of a daze. Now her eyes were clear and alert. Tran wondered if she was beautiful, when she was not covered with blood, camouflage paint and foul-smelling jungle fatigues.

Tran removed his helmet and set it on the stone table. He asked her, "Are you feeling better, mademoiselle?"

"No."

Tran waited for more, but she said nothing else. He tapped out a cigarette from a package next to the canteen. Weaver noticed that the cigarettes were a French brand, Gauloise. She watched him inhale; his movements were slow and controlled. When he turned to get a view over the benches, she saw gray hair around his temples. He was small and muscular, and his tiny eyes never stopped moving. Whenever he looked at Weaver, it stimulated the final twinges of fear that her senses still retained.

Tran pushed the canteen to Weaver's side of the table. "Will you drink something?"

"No."

Tran exhaled. "We were not unaware of your presence, mademoiselle. Do you have anything to say?"

Yes, she did. "Are you getting paid for this?"

Tran laughed. "Oh, yes. My soul has been corrupted by money."

Weaver had a lump in her throat. "How many of you are there?"

Tran frowned. He took another drag on his cigarette. He looked up at the sky. The tall hotels on Central Park South were visible above the trees.

"You know," Tran said, "I lived a very simple life as a child. But the constant fighting forced us from our small rice paddy to the city. Many of the people in our village became accustomed to the city. I never felt that I belonged there. It is where I attended university and became involved with the Viet Minh, though I was not particularly attracted to politics." Tran shrugged and looked back at Weaver. "But for a peasant it was exciting."

Cao appeared on the walk and came up the stairs to the tables. He continued past, circling the benches to the other side of the building.

Tran poured a capful of water from the canteen and drank. He rubbed his eyes. "It is strange, mademoiselle. Cao and I, we will never again belong to the rice paddy. It is a simple square of land, an eternal structure, the kind of simplicity that is unfathomable." Tran put out his cigarette. "I am telling you the truth when I say that boredom is the politics of terror."

Cao came quickly from behind the building. He pointed west. *"Ong duoc."*

Tran stood and put away his canteen. He pulled the AK-47 from his shoulder and inserted a banana clip.

Weaver's heart beat faster. "Don't kill him."

Tran ignored her and put on his helmet.

Weaver said, "Let me go. I can reach the street from here in a few minutes."

Tran shook his head. "I'm sorry, but you are being very useful to us. Why do you think we sit here, an easy target? This man will not risk hitting you. Americans have a strange hierarchy in regard to civilians. Some are expendable, some are not." Tran told Weaver to stand up and said, "Besides, after we terminate him, Cao and I will perhaps remain in the park. They would have a hard time removing us, wouldn't you say?"

Tran smiled and turned to Cao. *"Ong co muon o lai cho cong vien khong?"*

Cao and Tran laughed loudly.

A dull pop sounded from somewhere west and a smoke grenade exploded off the side of the Chess and Checkers House. A huge cloud of orange smoke spilled out over the tables and benches. Cao immediately moved down the walk. Tran grabbed Weaver and pushed her down. Two more smoke grenades exploded. Green clouds enveloped the area. Tran shoved Weaver ahead of him and into the stairs. Nothing was visible. Tran lost sight of the ground. Weaver jerked away from his grasp and disappeared into the smoke. Tran rolled onto the hill and fired two rounds after her.

There was a yell. It was Cao's voice, but Tran could not see him. Three more smoke devices went off. Multicolored smoke poured out, creating a dense fog from the ground to the trees. Tran crawled forward, down the incline. There was a thud to his left. Tran curled into a ball. A fragmentation grenade exploded and bright, spinning needles whistled through dark-purple smoke. Tran jumped up and ran. He collided with a tree and fell. An automatic rifle fired in the distance. Tran got to his feet and, very slowly, with an omnipotent calm, walked forward, feeling his way like a blind man, step by step in the fog, until the sounds of weapons fire and bullets flying within inches of his head were behind him and he walked free in the sunlight on the East Drive.

A green-orange shroud was draped over Cao. Every step he took, a puff of smoke rose up from the ground, like a mist floating on a swamp. The only sounds were his boots breaking twigs. He bumped a dark shape and almost screamed. It was a tree. He squatted against the trunk, breathing hard. A sudden noise was behind him. He whirled around with his AK-47 and emptied half a clip into the smoke. The bullets snaked through the undergrowth, bouncing off unseen surfaces, echoing and fading.

Cao made himself smaller, squeezing into the tree, and listened. Nothing. The smoke curled and drifted and another black shape appeared, but this one moved, gliding by with a soft whirring sound. It was gone in an instant and Cao thought he'd imagined it.

Crack. Rifle fire slammed into the tree above his head. He yelled and rolled away, clutching at the leaves and dirt. The burst of fire lasted only seconds, then it was quiet. Cao jumped up and ran through a clearing in the smoke. He stopped and hid in a clump of low bushes. A yellow cloud enclosed him again. He tried to make his ears sensitive to every sound. An odd noise started again, a quiet motor, and then the foliage crunched behind him. He turned his head slowly and a black thing slithered through the haze.

A smoke grenade exploded in the bushes. Cao fell forward, choking on a purple cloud. He fired his AK blindly, anywhere. The clip ran out of ammunition. He sat on his feet and snapped in a new magazine. Bang. A burst of fire to his right. He returned fire; stopped. Bang. Fire to his left shoulder. He shot again.

If only he could see.

Leaves gave way in front of him. A black form materialized in the smoke. It came toward him. He saw wheels. A bolt of adrenaline hammered his body. Cao fired, pouring twenty rounds across the wheels' path. The wheels kept coming and Cao froze as a motorcycle rolled up to his feet and fell over on its side.

No rider was on the cycle. Cao leaned over. His knees were shaking. He saw odd-looking mufflers. The smoke floated away from the seat. Cao saw three fragmentation grenades attached to the handlebars. The grenades didn't have pins.

Cao didn't have time to scream, to pray. The grenades flashed. He felt warm razors trim away his flesh; he felt himself rising. Was it his soul? He fell back in the cool water of a rice paddy and relaxed.

ESS officers Weissman and Walker were nervous. They stood in front of police barricades on Central Park South, where Sixth Avenue entered the Park and became the East Drive. They'd been at that location for two days, listening to the distant sounds of shooting and explosions. In the last half hour, the activity had come closer, sometimes so close that Weissman and Walker had taken cover below the waist-high wall on the Park's perimeter.

After a series of explosions, the shooting had stopped and they'd resumed their position near Sixth Avenue—not because Walker wanted to, but because Weissman was tired of waiting around listening to guns and cowering every time there was a shot.

"Fuck it," Weissman said. He put his M-16 over his shoulder. "Let somebody take a pop at me. Then we'll just blast. Who gives a shit if we take off some slant-head by mistake? I'd like to get this thing over with."

Weissman turned his back to the Park and looked over at the St. Moritz Hotel across the street. An unmarked car was parked in front of the awning that extended over the sidewalk. Two detectives were inside, sleeping. Weissman shook his head. He looked west on the empty street. The sky was very dark above the Gulf & Western tower. A cool breeze blew open his flak jacket.

Weissman said, "It's gonna pour like hell."

Walker wasn't listening. He was doing his job. He'd heard a noise inside the Park, and now a bloody hand was gripping the top of the Park wall.

Walker took his M-16 off safety. Weissman turned and saw the hand too. The officers dropped to one knee and aimed. Another hand appeared. A head peeked out over the wall and a woman stood up. At least it looked like a woman. She wore floppy combat clothes, covered with dark stains, and when she saw Walker and Weissman pointing rifles at her, she sagged against the wall and put her head in her arms.

Walker thought he heard her say, "I give up."

They asked her a hundred questions in five minutes. She didn't answer any of them. They thought she was in shock, but she wasn't. An EMS medic worked on her arm. It was bleeding again. When the medic was finished applying a temporary bandage, he looked up at Keller.

"She should be in the hospital right now, Commissioner."

Keller was standing with Curran, Dix and several plainclothes officers near the radio console inside the mobile command post. Infrequent transmissions came in over the console speakers—reports from Emergency Service personnel stationed on the perimeter of Central Park.

Keller was angry. "I know you're aware, Ms. Weaver, that you can be prosecuted."

Weaver stared at the men. Her face burned from the soap that had been used to clean away the camouflage paint. Her head twitched from exhaustion.

Keller told the medic, "All right, take her to the hospital." The medic tried to help Weaver up, but she wouldn't move. He tried again and she yanked her arm away from his grasp.

Dix closed his eyes and rubbed his forehead. He didn't want to look at her anymore. He didn't want to see the bloodstains on the camouflage material.

But Dix heard her voice. "He was going to come out of the park."

Dix opened his eyes. Keller and Curran did not look at each other. They did not change expression. There was a long silence. Some of the men shifted uneasily.

Weaver stood up. She made a fist. "Whose idea was this?"

Nobody looked at Dix.

Weaver opened her mouth to say something, a two-word suggestion, but the words wouldn't come. Her hand relaxed and the fist unfolded. The medic helped her out the door of the command post.

Keller and Curran moved away, leaving Dix next to the dispatchers and plainclothes officers. He stared at the floor for five minutes and then went out onto East 63rd Street. The driver of the limo held the door open for him, but Dix shook his head and kept walking.

He went past Madison Avenue and Park Avenue and turned onto Lexington. He stopped in front of Bloomingdale's. Crowds of shoppers were going in and out of the store. The avenue was jammed with cars. Dix bought a soda from a hot dog cart. He went to a pay phone on the corner of Lex and 59th and called his ex-wife.

"Hello, Marianne."

An IRT express roared by under his feet and he waited for the noise to pass. When he could hear, he asked her, "Want to go have a couple of drinks?"

"Why?"

"I just quit my job."

In the obscure and opaque jungle, the enemy moved. Harris' skilled eyes observed the movements.

Harris was standing absolutely still in a forest of trees north of the 72nd Street road. He wasn't breathing; his eyes did not blink. Through the trees, he could see the top of the Terrace and, below the brick and granite steps, the rim of the Fountain.

Lightning flashed. A few large raindrops pelted the leaves above Harris' head. A drop bounced off Harris' helmet, but he did not flinch. Thunder sounded. Harris squatted, using the loud rumbles to mask his movements. He edged closer to where the treeline bordered the Terrace. An odor tickled his nose. After a brief search, he found a pile of feces. They were fresh droppings and, when he leaned over to sniff, Harris knew they were human feces.

Charlie boy.

Harris stayed very still again, sitting on his heels, listening to raindrops hit the trees. Five minutes passed, and then he removed the bayonet from its sheath. He no longer wore the holster with the M-79; he had dumped the launcher in Rumsey playground. It was useless without ammunition.

Harris attached the bayonet to the barrel of his AK-47. Thunder cracked again and he started down the wooded incline that led to the Fountain on the shore of the Lake. He worked his way through the undergrowth, stabbing the ground with the bayonet, until he could see the surface of the Lake. The huge angel atop the Fountain was just visible over the top of the bushes. Harris stopped and moved his head back and forth, trying to get a view through the branches. There was water in the Fountain's enormous pool, and its surface was rippling with large raindrops.

Harris backed up a little and stood against a tree. He was motionless for a long time; only his eyes moved over the terrain. Suddenly, his heart beat faster. That thing that happened sometimes, that instinct, that instantaneous assimilation roared through Harris' brain. There, on the border of the Fountain's plaza, was a dark shape, high in a tree. So silent, so unknown. It was a man; a man with a gun, way up there.

Harris smiled. Slimy motherfucker.

Harris waited for another roll of thunder. When it came, he clicked the AK on full automatic. The rain started to fall harder. Harris slipped into the bushes and crawled toward the plaza. Water dripped from the rim of his helmet. He crawled closer. Lightning flashed. He had a silly thought: People got killed in Central Park by lightning.

Harris stopped in the prone firing position. He lined up the man in the tree.

Bye-bye, most ricky-tick.

Harris shot half the clip up into the tree. The man tumbled out of the branches; a rifle blew out away from the tree. Harris heard a loud thump, followed by a clang.

Harris leaped out of the bushes and ran toward the treeline. He saw the body up ahead. Rain soaked his fatigues as he hurried past the Fountain. He nearly slipped on the pavement.

He saw the Lake, a mist rising from its surface. The body was lying on its side. Harris slid to a stop. He poked the bayonet under the flak jacket and the body rolled over. Harris saw a ghost.

It was the badly mutilated corpse of Vo Phan Huong.

I already killed you once.

Water splashed—not the rain; the quality of the splashing was different. Harris choked. He whirled around. There was a beautiful angel: an apparition of death. A man was standing under the angel in the middle of the Fountain. Water poured from his fatigues and helmet. The man was aiming an AK-47.

Tran Chau Dinh fired.

Harris jerked back from the impact. His AK let out a short, involuntary burst and bullets splattered over the rim of the Fountain.

Tran screamed and dropped into the water. A red cloud formed around his leg. He dragged himself to the rim and rolled out onto the pavement. He crawled to the trees and vanished in the dark undergrowth.

Harris tumbled over Vo's body. His side burned underneath his flak jacket. He rolled away from the corpse and struggled into the trees. Blood dripped down under his belt. There wasn't much pain. God bless plastic, Harris thought.

The rain became a downpour. In the bush everything was obscure.

Harris didn't know where he was. He crawled in mud. There were slopping sounds and shapes slithered in the rain. There was breathing and moaning and Harris didn't know if the agony was his own.

There were voices, young voices, voices overwhelmed by the metallic sounds of weapons. Arms grappled for rifles and Harris heard a monkey cry out. Someone yelled.

The jungle grabbed him, and Harris heard the incoming and the outgoing, the mortars and helicopters and rockets and jets. A rifle exploded in his face and it all disappeared in a long, long scream of death.

Weaver was riding in EMS one-one-five. The ambulance was just passing 83rd Street and Madison Avenue when she heard the transmission on the radio. She sat up on the stretcher. The medic sitting across from her asked her to lie down. She ignored him and stuck her head into the front seat, between the driver and the young cop who'd been assigned to escort her to the hospital.

She shouted over the traffic noise. "That was a ten-thirteen on Central Park West!"

The officer and driver nodded. They'd heard. They were listening closely for further transmissions.

Weaver grabbed the driver's sleeve. "Come on! Goddamnit! Let's go over there."

Another call came over the radio. SOD. ESS units were requested for Central Park West and Seven-two Street.

The driver and the cop looked at each other. The ambulance passed 86th Street.

Weaver shouted, begged and cajoled. The cop nodded. The driver turned on the siren and slammed down the accelerator. The cop and the driver were curious, too. They raced up Madison. The traffic was heavy; the rain had stopped, but the streets were wet. Still, the driver cruised expertly through the lights. Not bad, Weaver thought, but she wasn't feeling frivolous. She was worried—so worried that she did not feel the terrible pain in her armpit.

The ambulance cut west on 110th Street and passed without difficulty through the barricades and police officers. It was free sailing on the deserted streets to Central Park West and 72nd. The driver outraced two RMP cars and stopped on the west side of the avenue, in front of the Dakota.

Weaver looked out the windshield of the ambulance. Police vehicles and personnel lined the street. Detectives with revolvers crouched behind their cars. A line of ESS officers was positioned across the intersection of the 72nd Street road and Central Park West. The men were aiming rifles into the Park.

Weaver, the cop and the two medics got out of the ambulance. They worked their way toward 72nd Street, splashing through puddles, until a uniformed sergeant wouldn't let them go any farther. They stopped behind an RMP car parked on the curb, at the corner of the Dakota. A group of news crews and reporters had assembled behind barricades on 72nd.

Several officers were staring at Weaver. She talked to the sergeant. He explained that ESS officers had spotted a man moving around in the trees just over the hill beyond the entrance to the Park, where the road curved down past the bridle path.

"That was about fifteen minutes ago. We ain't seen anything since."

Weaver waited. She felt faint and leaned on one of the medics. She heard cameras clicking. Photographers were leaning around the corner of the building, taking pictures of her.

There was yelling. The ESS officers darted up to the entrance, around the Park wall, and hid behind benches on the roadway. A man was coming slowly out of the Park.

He was pulling something—struggling hard. He was dragging a body. Weaver couldn't see the man clearly. He came closer. He stood in the middle of the roadway and Weaver recognized him.

Harris dumped the body of Tran Chau Dinh on the pavement of the 72nd Street road.

Three ESS officers, keeping M-16s in front of them, carefully approached Harris. He was not holding a rifle. He held his hands out to the side. The officers said something to him and he stretched out on the pavement on his stomach. They removed the .45 automatic from his side and frisked him. Then they lifted him up and handcuffed his hands behind his back.

There was a burst of activity. Everyone moved toward the entrance of the Park. An ESS ambulance, lights flashing, tried to back up onto the roadway, but the crowd of officers and news crews blocked its path. Weaver pushed her way through. The young cop tried to stay with her, but he got lost in the confusion. Flashbulbs popped. Video cameras pressed close for a shot. Medics ran to Tran's corpse. ESS officers attempted to clear a path to the ambulance. Weaver broke free of the crowd. She saw Harris. A plainclothesman grabbed her. The two officers on either side of Harris stopped, waiting for room to move. Weaver wanted to call to him, but she realized that she didn't know his name.

Harris didn't see her. Blood dripped from his waist onto the pavement. A TV cameraman forced his way in and started to get a shot. It was Marty Gold. Weaver lunged at him.

"No."

The officer restrained her. She tried again and threw a punch at the camera. She missed.

Weaver tried her last weapon. She yelled, "Stop tape!"

Marty took his face away from the eyepiece and swore.

Harris turned around and saw Weaver. The officer shoved him toward the ambulance. His helmet fell off and rolled on the roadway. A reporter picked it up. Weaver yanked it out of his hands. She wanted to give it back, but the crowd closed in around her. Then she relaxed. She could give the helmet back later.

The officers maneuvered Harris to the rear of the ambulance. As he paused in the doorway, Harris turned again and found Weaver. He called to her.

"Hey, I'm back in the World." He smiled. "Valerie."

# THE BEST OF BESTSELLERS
# FROM WARNER BOOKS

**THE NEXT**
*by Bob Randall*                                              *(F95-740, $2.75)*
A growing boy! That's what Kate's ten-year-old nephew was. Yet during
the weeks he was left in her care—while his mother recovered from a car
accident—Charles was growing at an astonishing rate. Love can turn a
boy into a man. But evil can do it faster.

**THE FAN**
*by Bob Randall*                                              *(B95-887, $2.75)*
The Fan: warm and admiring, then arrogantly suggestive; then obscene,
and finally, menacing. Plunging a dawdy Broadway actress into a shock-
ing nightmare. "A real nail-biter...works to perfection as it builds to a
surprising climax...the tension is killing."          — *Saturday Review*

**SEE THE KID RUN**
*by Bob Ottum*                                               *(B95-123, $2.75)*
A chilling race through the dark side of New York with a kid you'll never
forget! Wanted: Elvis Presley Reynolds, aged 14½, who dreams of Mark
Cross, Brooks Brothers and the Plaza—where one day soon he'll pass as
"Somebody." He's an urban urchin with bottomless eyes and an incredible ambition to escape to the good life while there's still time.

**THE TUESDAY BLADE**
*by Bob Ottum*                                               *(B95-643, $2.75)*
"We're looking for one guy carrying seven razors or seven guys carrying
one razor each." That's how a cop summed up the case. But the killer they
were tracking was just one girl—big, beautiful and armed with THE
TUESDAY BLADE. "My current reading favorite...makes 'Death Wish'
look like a kindergarten exercise."          — *Liz Smith, New York News*

**THE IMAGE**
*by Charlotte Paul*                                          *(F95-145, $2.75)*
The gift of sight came to Karen Thorndyke as the bequest of an unknown
man. His cornea, willed to the Eye Bank, enabled the beautiful young
artist to see and paint again. But with that bit of transparent tissue came
an insight into horror. With her new view of life came a vision of death.

# MYSTERY...SUSPENSE...ESPIONAGE...

__ **THE GOLD CREW**
*by Thomas N. Scortia
& Frank M. Robinson*          *(B83-522, $2.95)*

The most dangerous test the world has ever known is now taking place aboard the mammoth nuclear sub *Alaska*. Human beings, unpredictable in moments of crisis, are being put under the ultimate stress. On patrol, out of contact with the outside world, the crew is deliberately being led to believe that the U.S.S.R. has attacked the U.S.A. Will the crew follow standing orders and fire the *Alaska*'s missiles in retaliation? Now the fate of the world depends on what's going on in the minds of the men of THE GOLD CREW.

__ **THE FRENCH ATLANTIC AFFAIR**
*by Ernest Lehman*          *(B95-258, $2.75)*

The S.S. Marseille is taken over in mid-ocean. The conspirators are unidentifiable among the 2,000 other passengers aboard. Unless a ransom of 35 million dollars in gold is paid within 48 hours, the ship and the passengers will be blown skyhigh. A first-class ticket to excitement.

__ **YESTERDAY'S SPY**
*by Len Deighton*          *(B31-014, $2.50)*

Two friends who spied together. But that was in another time and another place—now they fight on different sides. A spellbinding tale of deceit and terror in a world where political reality destroys the most hallowed allegiances.

# TO THRILL YOU TO THE BONE!

## __POLTERGEIST
*a novel by James Kahn, based on a story by Steven Spielberg* (B30-222, $2.95)
This is a horrific drama of suburban man beset by supernatural menace. Like "Close Encounters of the Third Kind," it begins in awe and wonder. Like "Jaws," it develops with a mounting sense of dread. And like "Raiders of the Lost Ark," it climaxes in one of the most electrifying scenes ever recorded on film. A horror story that could happen to you!

## __PSYCHO
*by Robert Bloch* (B90-803, $2.95)
(September 1982 publication)
The book that inspired the Hitchcock movie your nightmares won't let you forget. She stepped into the shower stall. The roar of the water gushing over her was deafening. That's why she didn't hear the door opening...or the footsteps. And when the shower curtains parted, the steam at first obscured the face...the butcher's knife...And YOU will not forget!

## __AUDREY ROSE
*by Frank DeFelitta* (B36-380, $3.75)
The Templetons have a near-perfect life and a lovely daughter, until a stranger enters their lives and claims that their daughter, Ivy, possesses the soul of his own daughter, Audrey Rose, who had been killed at the exact moment that Ivy was born. And suddenly their lives are shattered by event after terrifying event.

## __FOR LOVE OF AUDREY ROSE
*by Frank DeFelitta* (B30-206, $3.95)
Audrey Rose Hoover had died in the flames of a car crash. Then she had been reincarnated as Ivy Templeton only to die in a terrible hypnotic reenactment of her death throes. Had this infant been born to end the awful cycle—or begin it again? What new agony, what soul-wrenching confrontation with destiny must be endured now?

# GREAT SUSPENSE BY
# LEONARD SANDERS

## THE HAMLET ULTIMATUM
*by Leonard Sanders*          (B83-461, $2.95)
World takeover is HAMLET's goal! The mysterious terrorist group has already sabotaged all the
computer networks it requires, even that of the
C.I.A. Now the group is ready for its ultimatum to
the U.S. government: Surrender or watch the
entire Northeast burn in a nuclear disaster. Only
ex-agent Loomis can stop them. And only Loomis
and his team have the courage to oppose the
President and fight the world they want to save.

## THE HAMLET WARNING
*by Leonard Sanders*          (B93-620, $2.95)
Time is ticking away! HAMLET, an international
group, is planning to explode a nuclear bomb in
Santo Domingo, warning the U.S. of an even bigger one that will go off inside its borders. Enter
former CIA operative Loomis who, despite the
CIA's assassination attempts, is now chief of
security for Santo Domingo. Teamed with his former CIA partner, he is enlisted to find the bomb
before it's too late while he also tries to contain a
domestic revolution.

# 5 EXCITING ADVENTURE SERIES
# MEN OF ACTION BOOKS

**DIRTY HARRY**
*by Dane Hartman*
The tough, unorthodox plainclothesman of the San Francisco Police Department tackles crimes and violence—nothing can stop him.

| | |
|---|---|
| \_\_#1 DUEL FOR CANNONS | (C90-793, $1 95) |
| \_\_#2 DEATH ON THE DOCKS | (C90-792, $1.95) |
| \_\_#3 THE LONG DEATH | (C90-848, $1 95) |
| \_\_#4 THE MEXICO KILL | (C90-863, $1.95) |

**S-COM**
*by Steve White*
High adventure with the most effective and notorious band of military mercenaries the world has known—four men and one woman with a perfect track record.

| | |
|---|---|
| \_\_#2 STARS AND SWASTIKAS | (C90-993, $1.95) |
| \_\_#3 THE BATTLE IN BOTSWANA | (C30-134, $1.95) |
| \_\_#4 THE FIGHTING IRISH | (C30-141, $1.95) |

**BEN SLAYTON: T-MAN**
*by Buck Sanders*
Based on actual experiences, America's most secret law-enforcement agent—the troubleshooter of the Treasury Department—combats the enemies of national security.

| | |
|---|---|
| \_\_#1 A CLEAR AND PRESENT DANGER | (C30-020, $1.95) |
| \_\_#2 STAR OF EGYPT | (C30-017, $1.95) |
| \_\_#3 THE TRAIL OF THE TWISTED CROSS | (C30-131, $1.95) |

**NINJA MASTER**
*by Wade Barker*
Committed to avenging injustice, Brett Wallace uses the ancient Japanese art of killing as he stalks the evildoers of the world in his mission.

| | |
|---|---|
| \_\_#3 BORDERLAND OF HELL | (C30-127, $1.95) |
| \_\_#4 MILLION-DOLLAR MASSACRE | (C30-177, $1.95) |

**BOXER UNIT—OSS**
*by Ned Cort*
The elite 4-man commando unit of the Office of Strategic Studies whose dare-devil missions during World War II place them in the vanguard of the action.

| | |
|---|---|
| \_\_#2 ALPINE GAMBIT | (C30-019, $1.95) |
| \_\_#3 OPERATION COUNTER-SCORCH | (C30-128, $1.95) |
| \_\_#4 TARGET NORWAY | (C30-121, $1.95) |

# THE BEST OF ADVENTURE
## by RAMSAY THORNE

# MS READ-a-thon— a simple way to start youngsters reading

Boys and girls between 6 and 14 can join the MS READ-a-thon and help find a cure for Multiple Sclerosis by reading books. And they get two rewards — the enjoyment of reading, and the great feeling that comes from helping others.

Parents and educators: For complete information call your local MS chapter. Or mail the coupon below.

## Kids can help, too!